Portia Da Costa is one of the most internationally renowned authors of erotica.

She is the author of *Continuum*, *Entertaining Mr Stone*, *Gemini Heat*, *Gothic Blue*, *Gothic Heat*, *Hotbed*, *In Too Deep*, *Kiss it Better*, *Shadowplay*, *Suite Seventeen*, *The Devil Inside*, *The Stranger* and *The Tutor*; as well as being a contributing author to a number of Black Lace short-story collections.

Also by Portia Da Costa

The Red Collection

PORTIA DA COSTA

BLACK
LACE

1 3 5 7 9 10 8 6 4 2

First published in 2013 by Black Lace, an imprint of Ebury Publishing
A Random House Group Company

The Random House Group Limited Reg. No. 954009

Addresses for companies within the Random House Group can be found at:
www.randomhouse.co.uk

A CIP catalogue record for this book is available from the British Library

The Random House Group Limited supports The Forest Stewardship Council
(FSC®), the leading international forest certification organisation. Our books
carrying the FSC label are printed on FSC® certified paper. FSC is the only forest
certification scheme endorsed by the leading environmental organisations,
including Greenpeace. Our paper procurement policy can be found at:
www.randomhouse.co.uk/environment

MIX
Paper from
responsible sources
FSC® C016897

Printed and bound by CPI Group (UK) Ltd, Croydon, CR0 4YY

ISBN 9780352347343

To buy books by your favourite authors and register for offers visit:
www.randomhouse.co.uk
www.blacklace.co.uk

Contents

Introduction

When I first decided I'd like to try to be a writer, my earliest efforts were short stories. The very first thing I ever committed to paper was a fan-fiction short about a handsome, sexy zombie, inspired by Michael Jackson's 'Thriller' video which I was dotty about at the time. It was a terrible story, of course, but I loved it and I was so pleased with myself – and amazed that I'd actually managed to string a plot, of sorts, together.

One zombie story led to five zombie stories, culminating in a tragic – in many senses of the word – effort called 'Love Death', but eventually, I got the undead out of my system and began writing erotic stories with different themes and characters. I was writing romantic novels at the same time, and while my novels consistently came whizzing back to me with rejection slips, I was lucky with only my second short-story submission and I was published for the very first time in 1991 in the well-known British erotic magazine, *Forum*. The story, 'The Man in Black', was about a handsome, sexy ghost.

Since then, I've written short stories as well as novels, and now in 2013 I think I've probably had about 150 published altogether, although I can't put a precise figure on it as I'm a significantly better fiction writer than I am a record keeper.

This collection contains the stories I've written for Black Lace anthologies over the years as well as a couple of longer paranormal erotic romances that were published in Black Lace novella collections. No zombies in this lot, but there are a couple of vampires ('Buddies Don't Bite' and 'Sometimes They Come Back'), a very macho fairy ('Ill Met by Moonlight') and a phantom detective who manifests himself through the medium of a haunted television ('Watching the Detective'). The remaining stories are fairly kinky contemporary tales, predominantly BDSM themed and some of them are even linked to novels that I've written. 'Are We There Yet', 'Duet for Three' and 'This Very Boutique' feature two of my all-time favourite characters: Maria Lewis and Robert Stone from *Entertaining Mr Stone* and *Suite Seventeen*; and 'A Study in Scarlet' is a further adventure for Joanna Darrell and Kevin Steel from *Continuum*. In other linkage, 'A Lavish Affair' and 'The Distraction' are about the same pair of lovers, and 'Fireworks Inside' takes place at the same wedding reception as 'A Lavish Affair'.

That's it then, and in case you're wondering why it's called *The Red Collection* . . . well, several of the stories have red-themed titles ('A Study in Scarlet', 'Red Haze' and 'Strawberry Shortcake'), the vampire stories naturally involve a certain crimson beverage, and quite a few of my heroines end up with rather rosy bottoms after being spanked by their dominant heroes! I do hope that you find all the offerings to be red-hot entertainment and enjoy reading them as much as I enjoyed writing them!

Portia Da Costa

Screen Dream

The first thing he saw when he entered the room was the Coromandel screen.

It wasn't the best one he'd ever seen, but he could have sold it at a nice profit, no problem. It was the sort of thing the Goths liked and they were always prepared to splash out on something black and symbolic-looking.

But he wasn't here to think about flogging cheap antiques, was he? He wiped his hand across his brow and found he was already sweating. When he looked back at the screen, he seemed to see something else entirely.

There was a woman sitting behind that lacquer-covered surface, and in his mind's eye she was also black and shiny and desirable. She was wearing a vinyl catsuit that gleamed like varnish, and clung to every curve and indentation. She was like the screen in another way too: not young, but well preserved. She had large breasts, a narrow waist, and her thighs looked like ebony in their vinyl carapace – hard enough to crush a man's skull if he put his face between them.

'Take off your clothes.'

Oh God! Oh yes! That voice . . .

It was low, rich and earthy, yet somehow also quite posh. The cut-glass diction seemed to dance along the length of his cock and make his balls vibrate. He felt as if he knew her somehow. Really. He'd heard that incredible voice somewhere else and now he wanted to hear it say the filthiest of things to him. He'd do anything to hear it purring obscenities. Inside his trousers, he was rigid with thwarted longing.

He felt as if he were a boy again. On the day he'd got his first car; the night he'd fucked his first willing girl; at his first big auction and scoring a bargain worth ten times what he'd paid for it. As he slid off his coat, his heart thumped and his cock got harder.

Weirdly enough, she always enjoyed this much more when she couldn't see the man. Concealed behind her beloved black screen, she could make the punter into a much hotter property than he really was. In her mind's eye, he was a gorgeous movie star, a wild, hard rocker, or even somebody she fancied from an advert. Anonymity gave her total control over him. Not seeing his face or his probably deeply inadequate body, she could just remodel him into any man she wanted.

So the little CCTV monitor stayed blank as she listened to the sounds of him taking his clothes off.

'Are you done yet?' She kept her voice light, but with backbone. She knew he hadn't had time to be anywhere near ready yet, but this way he'd have to speed up, get in a panic, and be anxious. She was turning the screw, but that was the whole point of the exercise, wasn't it? She imagined him fighting with his zipper – sweating and shaking – and she immediately wanted to touch herself.

'N-no!' he stammered, 'not yet.' She heard the jingle of a belt, then a bump and a muffled curse. He'd probably stumbled and knocked himself on the heavy mahogany side table where the props lay. She put her hand over her mouth to stop herself laughing, and pictured him rubbing a bruised hip or thigh, bronzed muscles flexing in his shoulder as he did so. That made her less inclined to giggle, and more inclined to do other things. It was a delicious image, and she fixed it in her mind.

'You may call me "mistress",' she said after another long pause. In her experience the cool, measured approach was far more undermining than snarling and shouting at them. He would be thrown even more off balance now, not knowing quite what to expect, and certainly not getting precisely what he'd specified.

Strict dominatrix demands you follow her orders.

It was corny, but always a winner. The punters loved it. It was amazing how much power a cliché had, and how much money desperate men would shell out in pursuit of it. But even so, she couldn't find it in herself to despise them. The tried and true kinks paid for nice things like antique screens and Georgian side tables. Her other employment paid for the basics, not the frills, as celebrity faces earned much more than unknown voices . . .

'I'm ready, mistress.' His quiet voice surprised her. It wasn't usual for 'slaves' to speak up. They were supposed to be tongue-tied and to wait for instructions. This man sounded respectful, yet stoic – which appealed to her.

'Indeed?' She kept the smile out of her voice. 'Well, I'm not. So just keep quiet and stand still until I'm ready.'

Did he sigh? She wasn't sure. If he had sighed, he'd have to pay for it. Unseen by him, she grinned and ran through a few particularly fiendish humiliations. She fancied something out of the usual run. Something a bit 'extra' – which he'd enjoy, if he'd got the bottle for it, just as much as she would. The beauty of it all was that she didn't have to do a thing herself, not really. All she had to do was talk, use her vocal training and her imagination, and let the man do things to himself. There was no surer way to demean a punter than that!

Was he already erect? Unable to resist prising open her own clothes, she reached in to touch her quim. Tonight was just getting better and better. She couldn't work out why it was so much more fun than usual . . . but it was.

'What's your name?' She looked down at her own body as she pictured his again.

Would he be as aroused as she was? Would the tip of his cock be as wet and sticky as her slit was? She imagined a pearl of juice hanging suspended from the end of his penis, and saw it slowly descending towards the polished floorboards beneath his feet.

Should she order him to touch himself yet? Or even taste his own juice? Ooh, that was cruel! Perhaps he was already masturbating? If he was, he was keeping it quiet.

'My name's John.' The words were tight and staccato with controlled tension. He *was* nervous, but he still had some control over himself, and she liked that. She'd been right; things were really getting better.

'Well, John, I shall call you "slave",' she said, touching her fingertip to her clitoris. The tiny little bead felt moist and polished, and the jolt of pleasure was astonishing. She couldn't believe how much this feeling always managed to surprise her, no matter how much and how often she played with herself.

Circling, she rolled her clit like a ball bearing, and bit her lip to stop herself moaning and panting. It was as hard to master her own urges as it was those of the man she was supposed to be mastering.

'Not very imaginative, I know,' she went on when the surge had crested and retreated, 'but it'll have to do.'

'Yes, mistress,' replied John from beyond the black lacquer that divided them.

'Don't speak yet, slave,' she admonished gently, reaching into her clothing again, with her other hand, and adjusting her bottom cheeks so they were spread against the upholstered surface of the chaise longue. There were two layers of fabric between her anus and the moquette, but even so, it felt grubby and perversely voluptuous as she wriggled. 'Not until I tell you to,' she added, pressing her bottom downwards.

'Caress your body, slave,' she said after a moment or two. It was amazing how just a few heartbeats could ramp up the tension. 'Rub your palms and your fingers over your naked skin . . . but whatever you do, don't touch your cock yet. Do you understand me?'

'Yes, mistress,' he said, and near silence followed. Straining her ears, she could just about hear the faint swish of skin against skin.

The picture in her mind was irresistible now. She saw him squatting slightly, long bronzed thighs flexed as he ran loving hands over his chest, his belly and his bottom. His hips swayed, and his erection – huge and angry pink with hyper-stimulation – bobbed and jiggled to the rhythm. His eyes were closed and his strong, handsome face was taut with the effort of *not* touching himself, and the stress of *not* coming.

She breathed heavily but silently. Part of her wanted to say 'sod it!' and then crawl out from behind her shield to kneel before him and take that juicy shaft into her mouth and suck on it hungrily. Either that, or lie on the panelled floor, legs akimbo, inviting him to push his swollen rod inside her . . .

But that wasn't what he wanted of her, was it? And if she

broke the spell by revealing herself, and seeing him in turn, it would be cheating them both.

So instead, she swivelled her wrist and thrust two fingers slowly into her vagina. This was a better way, she thought, beginning to thumb her clitoris.

Touching himself was a test of his self-control. Rarely in his life had John felt as aroused as he did now, staring at the black screen and focusing hard so he wouldn't come.

With his hands on his thighs, fingers itching to stray to his cock, he took a silent step closer and peered at the four lacquered panels. The even number meant that it was of oriental origin. European repros tended to have an odd number. He'd had lacquered screens like this in the shop many a time – and some a lot better than this – but never one with this strange, almost living quality. It was like a third person in the room with them, and now he was closer, he could see more wear and tear . . .

'Are you still stroking yourself?' Her diction was still exquisite, but also huskier now.

Was she as affected by all this as he was? John licked his dry lips and prepared to reply. Behind her screen was she turned on too, her body hot and horny inside its slinky suit of clinging black plastic?

'Yes! Yes, I am,' he managed to murmur at last, stroking the pads of his fingertips up over the hollows of his groin, brushing his wiry pubic hair. Going close, so very close to his rigid penis.

'But not touching your dick, I hope.' Her voice was as clear and golden as honey, yet dark as blasphemy. 'Not fondling your stiff, red, aching dick . . . Your hard-on. Your rod. Your erection.' She seemed to roll the words around on her tongue as if she were swirling the tip of it around the very organ she named. He looked down, saw the head of his cock jerk and weep thick silver goo. His rod looked as hard as a bar of mahogany and it ached as if she had it in a vice. He clenched his hands against his hips so he couldn't grab himself and wank to oblivion.

'Aren't you going to answer me?' she asked, and across the crazed black lacquer, a vivid picture grew sharper.

She was lying on a Victorian, scroll-ended chaise longue, her sleek body upholstered in firm flesh and gleaming black vinyl. Her slim legs were splayed, and between them an ingenious zip lay open. Her gorgeous slit was open too, the pink folds swollen ripe like segments of red fruit.

'No! No, I'm not touching myself, mistress,' he said, as in his mind's eye she did the thing he wasn't allowed to.

A single long slender finger, the nail painted with a polish as black as her suit, slid into the peachy channel and sought out the very heart of her desire. There was no sound, because it was a silent movie, and any noise from within might make him miss any real sounds, but his mistress's mouth formed a rosy, perfect 'O'. The finger flexed, and the 'O' grew rounder than ever.

'Do you want to?' The fantasy fractured and John saw himself reflected in the screen's blackness again.

The surface of the lacquer had seen better days, and the image was fuzzed, but he saw the faint outline of a white-skinned man, of medium height, with lightish, curly hair. At his groin, there was a shadowy smudge – his dark brown pubic tuft – but no clear detail of his pointing, rampant penis.

When he looked downwards, it was a different story.

He was huge. Bigger than he'd ever been. Bigger than it was possible for him to be. His flesh was red, the skin stretched and shiny with an angry inflamed sheen. His swollen glans seemed to yearn towards the screen and for a moment he had the mad thought that if he struck it against the nearest panel it might shatter the ageing lacquer.

Without thinking, he laughed.

'What's so funny?' There was humour in her voice too, but the fact that she didn't shout frightened him more than anger.

'Me, mistress,' he said quietly. 'My hard-on . . . It's sticking up. It's ridiculous.'

'So ridiculous that you don't want to touch it . . . to caress it?'

There was a smile in the beautiful tones. She was toying with him, playing with him subtly, lightly, almost with kindness.

'No, mistress . . . I mean, yes, mistress.' He felt confused, angry with himself for getting confused; yet more and more excited because of it. 'I do want to touch myself . . . I'm aching. It's driving me mad. I've never felt this hard before.'

'Oh, surely you're exaggerating,' she said. 'That's what all men say . . . They're always the hardest or the biggest. The soonest ready, the longest lasting . . . You men are always the best and most of everything.'

She was mocking him. Putting him down. She didn't care about him at all, and why should she? He was just a client to her, a source of revenue.

And yet . . .

He couldn't hear anything. She'd given nothing away. No rustle of clothing, no uneven breathing, nothing. Yet still he sensed she was enjoying herself. And that made his own pleasure greater. His cock felt as if it had grown another inch, and he didn't care what she said; it *was* the hardest ever!

'But it's true, mistress,' he said boldly. 'I've never been harder. Honestly!'

It was her turn to laugh now.

'All right. I believe you. Now describe it to me.' She chuckled softly. 'Tell me all about your prick and why you think it's so wonderful.'

Oh, he'd been good, she thought afterwards, rubbing her blonde hair dry as she sat on the chaise longue wearing men's pyjamas and dressing gown. She'd just had to shower again and that didn't usually happen.

But there had been something about this John, and the way he'd described his cock and what she'd made him do to it, that had got her going. Unknown to him she'd masturbated furiously throughout the whole diatribe!

As he'd wanked, she'd rubbed and worried at her clitoris; as he'd described pushing a butt plug into his own anus, she'd reached around and fondled and played with her own bottom.

As he'd climaxed, gasping and gulping, she'd come too. It'd been bloody hard to keep her own moans in check, but she'd managed it. And she'd also resisted the temptation to call him back, afterwards, so she could take a look at him.

She felt a pang of regret that the only memento she had of John was the nice pile of banknotes he'd left on the Georgian side table, but there was always a chance he might become one of her regulars. Sometimes that happened; sometimes she never 'saw' a customer more than once.

'*C'est la vie*,' she muttered to herself, abandoning her towel and counting the payment again.

Generous John had left a tidy bit extra, and what with that, and her latest cheque for a series of television voice-overs . . .

Well, it was time, she thought with a smile, to hit the antique shops!

It's a top screen, really it is, thought John, as he arranged his latest acquisition to its best advantage. Technically it was far better than the one that had concealed 'mistress' and yet because it hid no mystery, he didn't like it nearly as much.

Three weeks had passed now, and a dozen times a day he'd considered ringing her number again, but something had happened that made him even more in awe of her.

He'd seen her in an advert on the box. Several times. She was beautiful, blonde and sleek, but somehow not quite how he'd pictured her. The voice had been the same though, and he'd almost come on the spot when he'd suddenly heard it one evening while he wasn't really paying any attention to the telly at all. Deep, dark and complex, it had made a banal advertisement into a siren's song that had stiffened him instantaneously. It even worked now, just from hearing her in his mind.

Embarrassed because there were people in the shop, John moved away to his work area, and opened a sale catalogue. A moment later, though, his concentration drifted. A woman was studying the black, lacquered screen.

Not his mistress, alas. This woman was no television blonde, just an average-looking and slightly dumpy brunette. She looked even less remarkable when she put on a pair of glasses to lean up close and inspect the screen's inlaid design.

But when the woman smiled – presumably in appreciation of the screen – the erection that had just subsided twitched into life again. And it jumped even more when the woman looked across and smiled at *him*.

'A very fine Coromandel screen,' he said when he reached her, and then found himself launching into a rushed and rather jumbled sales pitch. She wasn't looking at his crotch, but he had a feeling she was aware that his penis was hard. The woman said nothing, but nodded knowledgeably now and again as he spoke.

'So, are you interested? I think I can make you a very fair price,' he said in an attempt to stop babbling. The woman was looking him in the eye now – and down at his groin from time to time – in a way that made his head light and his cock as heavy as lead.

Then the woman spoke. In those rich, measured, perfectly modulated tones he'd heard in every dream he'd had since he'd visited her apartment.

'No, thank you. I have a screen already.' She licked her lips and gave him a slight, yet powerful smile that transformed her ordinary face into a beautiful icon. Until a few moments ago, he'd never seen that face before yet it was totally familiar. 'Have you anything else that you'd like to show me?'

In the space it took to draw a breath, questions were posed, then answered in John's mind, and he realised that the face you saw on a TV screen and the voice you heard didn't necessarily have to belong to the same person. And what you *thought* you wanted to see wasn't always what you actually wanted.

'John?' she prompted, her voice so resonant and glorious it seemed to make his cock sing.

His own voice was thin and light, yet it also had strength. 'Whatever you want, mistress. I'll show you anything . . .'

She smiled and nodded, and then – his shop and his customers forgotten – John fell to his knees before her and started tugging at his zip.

The Best of Hands

Yes, I understand perfectly,' murmurs Madame Guidetty, escorting us into the room. A silver coffee jug stands on a tray, on her desk, flanked by two fine bone-china cups and the usual paraphernalia of milk jug, sugar bowl and tongs. There are just two cups because I won't be taking coffee.

'Do be seated,' Madame continues, smiling almost flirtatiously at my Master, 'and we'll have our coffee while I outline our range of services.'

'Thank you, that sounds most pleasant,' my Master answers genially, sinking down into a comfortable, deeply upholstered chair set at right angles to Madame's spacious desk. He glances at me and I blush furiously. He has noticed my transgression – the fact that I am staring about the room, and at Madame, and at him, when I am supposed to keep my eyes lowered at all times and I realise that I will suffer for it soon.

It seems that Madame has observed my slip-up too. 'Perhaps Susan could stand in the corner while we chat?' she suggests pleasantly, although there is, I detect, a faint thread of excitement in her barely accented voice. 'In a display position, possibly? I always find that tends to curb a wilful streak quite nicely, don't you, Monsieur?'

'A good idea, madame,' returns my Master, his own voice rather vibrant too. 'Would it offend you if Susan removes her skirt and her slip? I always find a greater degree of exposure more effective . . . Although if that isn't your practice here, perhaps I could trouble you for the loan of a couple of safety pins?'

'No need for that,' says Madame, 'we too recognise the subduing qualities of partial nudity. It is a measure we rely upon heavily.' She pauses, and I hear a slight click, then the sound of a bell ringing somewhere else in the house. 'There, I've summoned a maid to take Susan's slip and skirt.'

My heart begins to lurch around in my chest. Yet another stranger to see me embarrassed. I colour even harder and feel sweat prickle and run beneath my arms.

'Well, Susan?' my Master prompts, and with shaking fingers I unfasten my skirt. Just as I am stepping out of it, there is a knock at the door.

'*Entrez!*' calls out Madame, and a maid enters, a beautiful dark-haired girl, with a sullen, sultry mouth. Her uniform is old-fashioned and immaculate; her apron is snow-white, and her buttoned shoes shine like polished jet.

'Ah, Florenza, Susan here doesn't need her skirt and underslip for a while . . . I wonder if you would take care of them for her?' Madame speaks to her maid in almost an intimate manner. Against my will, I begin to speculate on the type of duties this Latin beauty might perform. She gives me an expressionless look as I hand her my skirt.

Sliding down my lace-trimmed half-slip, I become more and more conscious of my undies. They are chosen by my Master, as always; and, as always, they are costly and luxurious. The slip is heavy satin, pure white, and was bought at an exclusive Knightsbridge boutique. I sense both Madame and

Florenza silently pricing it, and thus estimating how highly my Master values me.

My stockings and suspender belt, which I will retain, are both equally extravagant. The former are fine deniered, smoke-grey – to match the formal suit I wear – and with a thick welt of lace; and the latter is white silk to match my underslip. My panties, however, are very plain, just the simplest of white cotton interlock, bikini-shaped, but not especially brief.

I pass my slip to Florenza and she folds it neatly, placing it upon a chair, on top of my already folded skirt.

'Florenza,' says my Master, his voice appreciative, although I do not know whether this is in regard to the sight of me, skirtless, or due to the dark girl's undeniable loveliness. 'I wonder if you would be good enough to lower Susan's knickers for her? Just as far as mid-thigh, that will be perfect for our needs.'

'Of course, sir,' replies Florenza dutifully, her voice rather more accented than Madame's and clearly indicating quite a different nationality.

I start to shake as her deft hands go about their business. My Master has not exposed me a great deal to the eyes of strangers, so this is relatively new to me. There was of course the time he invited a few male friends around to watch him cane me, but then I was blindfolded, and the resulting darkness calmed my shame.

Nevertheless, I don't resist as Florenza eases my panties down my thighs, revealing my belly, and the silky blondness of my pubic grove. I am tempted to try and cover myself, but I fight the need. As if sensing my discomfiture, my Master says, 'Hands on head, Susan. There's a good girl.'

Florenza is crouched beside me, seemingly intent on adjusting the position of my bunched white panties, but what she is really doing, I guess, is studying the sight her Madame has not yet seen. A phenomenon that will soon embarrass me even more. As the pretty servant finally straightens up, my Master abruptly calls out, 'Turn!'

I obey.

'*Quel cul ravissant!*' cries Madame, as her eyes light upon my mortifying secret. A naked bottom that's already a brilliant pink.

I feel the scrutiny of all in the room fix on me. They study my soreness, the warmed state of my buttocks. The evidence of my intractable behaviour . . . There is silence for a few moments, then Madame dismisses Florenza. That she has allowed the maid to see me at all is a punishment in itself.

'Yes, I have already had to deal with her,' observes my Master as the door quietly closes. 'Susan is often disobedient and disrespectful in public, but I find a smacked bottom tends to settle her somewhat. We never leave the house without making sure she's nice and red.'

How true that is! I think if my Master had his way, I would spend my whole life with a hot, crimson bottom. Dinner parties, the theatre, the ballet; every function I attend, I attend it feeling sore. Every time I sit down, I'm reminded of his preference.

Today is a typical example of my life. My Master came to collect me at my work place, and when he was ushered into my office, and we were alone, he locked the door. Within moments, I was face down across my own desk, skirts up, pants down, whilst he belaboured my bottom-cheeks with my own plastic ruler. The snapping impacts soon raised a glow of stinging pain.

'An excellent regimen,' comments Madame, her voice approving.

'You may move to the corner now, Susan,' says my Master.

Again, I obey, my steps rendered tiny and awkward by the pants that are bundled around my thighs. I hear the tinkle of spoons and china, and smell the delicious aroma of fresh coffee. As Madame and my Master enjoy their refreshment, she outlines the facilities offered by 'Maison Guidetty'.

'As I described on the phone, Monsieur, we provide a service to dominants like yourself, who, for one reason or another, are unable to attend to their charges themselves. Whether it is due to family circumstances, or to foreign travel or work commitments, we administer discipline, in your stead, and to your exact specifications.' She pauses, then goes on with pride, 'Or if you prefer, we will create an appropriate programme for you . . . We – that is my husband, my son, my daughter and myself – are all extremely experienced with all devices, and conversant with all classic scenarios.'

I can well imagine. Madame is very handsome, with her elaborately chignoned hair, and her Parisian clothes, but she exudes an exciting air of hidden strength. Beneath her hand, a hapless bottom will sting and burn furiously, that's evident. And her eyes, beneath her long, dark lashes, are those of a true, impassioned zealot.

'And we offer a variety of arrangements to suit every need,' she continues, warming to her theme. 'For instance, a charge may simply attend once or twice a week for a sound punishment to see them through until the next visit. On the other hand, we also offer boarding facilities, for those submissives who require continuous attention.'

'I think an arrangement somewhere between those two will suit Susan best,' interposes my Master. 'She has commitments . . . Employment of her own. I wouldn't want to interfere with that . . . Perhaps she could come to you each weekend?' he suggests.

Yes, employment of my own. How ironic. What would my colleagues and subordinates think if they knew I was chairing a meeting with a bottom still raw from the lash? That beneath my Ralph Lauren skirt I was pantieless, because my inflamed cheeks could not stand the slightest brush of underwear? That my buttocks were bruised and wealed by the man I love?

'Of course,' says Madame, concurring. 'Many of our clients specify "weekends only". I would say it's our most popular option.'

They go on to discuss the finer details. And money, which seems so meaningless in this strange and special world. My Master specifies Madame herself to be my disciplinarian, and that my 'treatments' be morning, noon, and night. Especially night. It seems that even though night will not occur at the same time for us during the next few months, he wishes to dream of me lying in my bed with my buttocks scarlet.

Madame coughs delicately. 'And is she to be provided with . . .' Her voice lowers. 'With "release"?'

'Oh, yes, I think so,' replies my Master. 'Perhaps Florenza could oblige?' he suggests, his voice playful.

I shiver in dread anticipation. The dark-eyed servant does not look very kind to me. Pleasure with her might be as testing as the pain.

'A splendid suggestion,' agrees Madame. 'And perhaps I might supervise, to ensure it is correctly dispensed?'

'Of course,' concurs my Master suavely. He well knows how it shames me to be watched while I lose control.

'And now, perhaps a brief tour of the facilities? And

a demonstration?' offers Madame, her soft voice full of anticipation. My instincts tell me she can't wait to get her hands on me.

'Yes! Capital!' My Master can't wait for her to get her hands on me either. 'I would like Susan to be fully acquainted with the tests that lie ahead of her.'

With that, Madame escorts us from the room, still describing the many advantages this establishment offers. I follow, at a slower pace, hampered by my underwear around my thighs, my pulses racing at the prospect of further treatment to my already smarting rump. Progress up the stairs is particularly difficult for me, with my hands still on my head, but my Master gently guides my faltering steps.

The first room we enter offers quite a sight. A young woman, completely nude, is draped over a thickly uphol-stered couch. Her bottom is a blazing pink, all over, and she's sobbing. Behind her stands another young woman, a breathtaking beauty; her face is flushed, her arm is high, and in her narrow, patrician hand she grasps a paddle.

'My daughter, Mariette,' announces Madame proudly, and the enchanting disciplinarian bobs a curtsey.

'Charmed, Monsieur,' she answers prettily, her fingers moving on the paddle she still clutches, as if she is anxious to continue with her task. Her fine eyes settle momentarily on my semi-nakedness, and her lips – so like her mother's – quirk with longing.

'Pray do not let us disturb you, *chérie*,' encourages Madame. 'Monsieur here is anxious to see how we deal with our charges . . . He will shortly be putting Susan into our hands.'

'Of course, *Maman*,' says the young woman pleasantly, returning immediately to her task. She lifts her arm and the paddle descends with unexpected force. Mademoiselle Guidetty is far stronger than she looks. The owner of the unfortunate, becrimsoned bottom wails piteously, her hips shifting and weaving against the surface of the couch. She bears a fresh patch of deeper red on her rounded left cheek, and beneath her pelvis the moquette upholstery is visibly damp. I bite my lip to contain my moan of sympathy.

In the next few minutes, the younger Guidetty treats us to a virtuoso display with the paddle, whilst her charge puts on a show of equal vivacity. The round tongue of leather crashes down with almost metronomic regularity, its point of impact constantly circling its chubby target. The punished girl bucks and heaves across the couch, her strident squealing unrestrained and deeply stirring.

'Valerie has much to learn,' observes Madame Guidetty, and just as she speaks, Valerie howls loudly, her torso stiffening.

It is clear what has happened. Remaining rigid for a couple of seconds, the girl then flails her legs and pumps her crotch against the edge of the couch.

'Oh, Valerie,' murmurs Mademoiselle, accusingly, as the body she has been chastising jerks in orgasm. As we leave the room, she is lifting a cane from a selection in a drawer.

'My daughter is quite a stringent disciplinarian,' says Madame fondly as we move along a corridor. 'I believe she inherits her gift from me.'

My Master nods discreetly, in congratulation. I hobble behind them, my bottom bare, my flesh aroused. Other rooms pose other tests to my frazzled nerves . . .

In one, an exquisitely good-looking young man is hand-spanking an older woman whom I seem to know. I start to sweat again and I gasp, recognising her as a formidable adversary across the bargaining table – my opposite number in another prestigious company. Briefly craning her neck she looks up at me, her eyes languorous, her mouth working as the pretty youth pounds her cheeks. If she recognises me, it seems to be of little importance to her. All that matters now is the growing torment of her reddened bottom.

As we leave, Madame names the gorgeous boy as her son, Jean-Louis. I feel a sense of awe that in just one family there could be such fearsome gifts.

We do not see Monsieur Guidetty. Although we hear his work . . .

Before a closed door, we pause, listening to the sounds issuing from the hidden room beyond. I hear a heavy thudding slap, a ponderous doleful sound, then a low, weak groan. The slapping comes again, and the answering cry is ragged, extenuated, redolent with suffering. The slaps repeat. And repeat. The voice of their recipient gurgles. There is no way to tell whether the cries stem from agony or reflect a state of bliss.

'This client has requested a closed room for his charge,' says Madame in hushed tones. 'And the severe attentions of my husband. No observers . . . No manual pleasure to be given.' Although I am not supposed to, I look up and see her roll her expressive eyes. 'Just the strap. Laid on with energy. For extended periods.'

'And this will be Susan's room,' she says a little later, conducting us into a bedroom decorated in a delicate Victorian style. There is a proliferation of chintz, a very beautiful armless nursing chair, an elegant chaise longue. It is warm and cosy, and the air is rich with the essence of quiet, domestic discipline. I already see myself in a long, white nightdress of perfect purity, my buttocks uncovered as I lie across the bed, waiting to receive what is due to me.

The picture is so vivid, so meltingly appealing, that I long for it immediately to be real. Without thinking I gyrate my naked bottom, and my Master – ever watchful – notices the movement.

'Perhaps Susan can be punished here now?' he suggests, striding over to a dressing table cluttered with antique knick-knacks. He lifts a simple wooden hairbrush from amongst the profusion of gilt and crystal, and holds it out towards Madame, whose eyes light up with undisguised glee.

'Of course, Monsieur, I would be happy to accommodate you,' she says gaily, already seating herself on the chaise and arranging her skirts. My Master catches my eye, then nods in Madame's direction.

Silently, obediently, I shuffle towards her, and skilfully she tips me across her lap.

It takes just a few moments to position me correctly. Madame slides my knickers down to my ankles, but leaves them there. 'I find that underwear left around the feet impedes kicking . . . Especially when tangled around high heels.' My arms are forward, but she asks me to cross my hands at the small of my back. When I comply she firmly grips my wrists.

Waiting, I stare at the patterned carpet, aware that my Master has handed the brush to Madame Guidetty. I smell his cologne as he sits down beside us on the chaise, then feel the gentle touch of his caressing hand as he strokes my hair.

When the first hard blow smashes on to my bottom, I start to cry . . .

That was over a week ago, and now my Master is far away, and overseas.

I miss him, of course, but other pains are soothing the

pain of us being apart. These pains are less abstract, and more absorbing; they divert the mind.

And this is why I'm lying face down, my buttocks bare, on my chintz-clad bed.

A little over a quarter of an hour ago, Madame Guidetty finished giving me a rigorous caning. My nightly punishment. I can still feel the savage line of each sharp cut she laid upon me; the grid of fire she worked so cleverly across my flesh. My snorts of distress are still ringing in my ears.

I cried pathetically, of course, but my Master will enjoy that. I can just imagine his secret pleasure when he receives the video.

Maybe he'll find amusement in the interlude which followed too. The sight of my engorgement being resolved by Florenza's tongue.

So, here I am, my dearest Master, I think, mentally composing an intimate letter to accompany the tape. *My bottom's hot, and it's caned bright red, just how you like it. But because it hurts, it reminds me of you, and I don't feel lonely.*

That's true. Reaching behind me, I finger my weals, their fire my solace.

I miss you madly, but I know I'm in the best of hands . . .

This Very Boutique

'Good afternoon, sir, and welcome to The Boutique. How may we help you this afternoon?'

Sir strolls into the showroom, then halts right in the centre and slowly looks around. His sharp gaze flits hither and thither, alighting on the various samples set out for display in a studiedly casual arrangement across the sideboard, the occasional tables and elsewhere. We offer a very personal hands-on service here in this bijou little establishment and we like our shoppers to feel as comfortable and relaxed as they would do in their own homes. So they'll buy more . . .

It's hard to tell what Sir really thinks about the risqué items we have on show. His expression is inscrutable, mutable, and hard to fathom. The only indication of any kind of emotion is the faintest hint of super-cool amusement. But even that could be a trick of the imagination.

'Please, won't you take a seat?' I encourage, gesturing to the most comfy armchair.

His hooded eyes narrow, but he moves towards the seat, and lowers his tall, substantial form into it, setting the pink paper carrier bag he's been holding on a table beside him, and making a big show of fussing with the panels of his voluminous dun-coloured raincoat. It's not a plastic mac, thank

God, or even a crumpled Columbo jobbie. But it's not exactly an example of metrosexual man chic either, and disturbing thoughts of flashers spring to mind. Especially given the way he's eyeballing me. His face is still bland enough, but there are lights dancing in his intelligent brown eyes.

'Sir?' I prompt, but all he seems to want to do is just sit there smiling slightly, as if he's guarding a special, wicked secret. I get the feeling that he's enjoying the retail experience immensely.

'Sir?' I enquire again, as he looks me up and down, those intensely gleaming eyes doing the grand tour from my boobs to my legs to my general groinal area to my face and then back around again. Suddenly my crisp white blouse feels tight and restricting across my frontage, and to my dismay my nipples choose this moment to want to pop out like organ stops. I can almost hear them go 'Ping ping! Ping ping!' They're acting as if it's cold here in the showroom, when in reality it's already far hotter than it should be and getting hotter with every minute that passes.

'Ah, yes,' Sir purrs at last, focusing that sultry look of his like a technician tuning a high-powered laser, 'I've got a slight problem, my dear.' He taps the pink carrier bag at his side, the one that's been subconsciously bugging me since his arrival. His long fingertips flick at the paper in a way that's vaguely suggestive. 'I bought this item a couple of days ago, from this very boutique, and I'm afraid it's very far from satisfactory.'

I bite my lip, feeling uncontrollable silliness suddenly bubble up inside me for a split second, and then immediately I make every effort to keep my mind on the job. I'm not behaving very much like a professional vendeuse, am I?

Right, back to business . . . and, oh dear, it's a return.

I hate returns. They can be really tricky when you sell

the sort of merchandise we do, and half the time people who bring things back are just in here to try it on. I just hope that Sir doesn't turn nasty. Not that he looks nasty. In fact, he looks about as far from nasty as it's possible to be. To my mind, he looks very nice indeed, with his big burly body, and his face that's so boyishly handsome despite the silver grey in his crisp-cut dark hair. My mind goes cantering away from the job in hand like an out-of-control pony, and I imagine what it might be like to kiss Sir and waylay him for a shag.

'Um . . . in what way is the item unsatisfactory, sir?' My voice comes out rather like a cartoon squeak, and I cast around for a look of servile solicitude instead of the rampant lust that I'm sure is written large and obvious on my face. 'We very rarely get complaints about our merchandise here, sir. But if there is a problem, I'll do everything in my power to resolve it.'

There, that sounds suitably crawly, doesn't it?

Unfortunately, Sir clearly thinks it's crawly too, suitable or otherwise, and he gives me a rather stern look that induces my knees to tremble.

'That's as maybe,' he continues, and strangely, he seems to be the one who's biting his lip now, 'but I'm very disappointed. I don't expect to be sold substandard goods at these prices and I'm accustomed to better customer service than this.'

'I'm very sorry about that, sir,' I murmur obsequiously, 'please let me take a look at the goods, and if they're faulty, I assure you we'll replace them for you.'

Sir hands me the bag, and his brown eyes lock on mine as he looks up at me. I can see that he's still trying to appear indignant, but there's a strange tricky gleam about him, a sort of smile that's not a smile, and I get a distinct feeling I'm in for big big trouble with this one.

I open the top of the bag and look inside.

Uh-oh . . .

There's a very popular item peeking out of the nest of shredded tissue paper. A very popular item indeed, at least with me. I wonder what on earth Sir can possibly think is wrong with it.

'Ah, the Spinetingler Deluxe, one of our best-selling lines . . . We don't usually have any complaints about these. They're usually completely reliable and satisfactory.'

The Spinetingler Deluxe is made of sturdy pink silicone, very thoughtfully shaped and very generously sized. It reminds me of another sturdy, thoughtfully shaped and very generously sized item. One that's always completely reliable and so satisfactory that it has a tendency to make me feel as if it's about to blow the top of my head off . . . It's also pinkish, after a fashion, but more of a flesh tone.

'I'd better test it, I suppose.' I glance at Sir, and notice that he looks remarkably keen on this idea. His big brown eyes are as bright as two stars, and his nice, rather reddish mouth has now curved into a smile. It appears that the severe demeanour of a moment ago was just an act, and one he's already as good as forgotten.

'That's an excellent idea,' he concurs roundly. 'It may just be that the young friend I purchased it for isn't using it correctly, so you'd be doing us all a service if you could just show me how it works. Unfortunately it didn't come with a user manual'

I take out the Spinetingler and set the bag aside, conscious of Sir's eyes following my every move with minute attention. He obviously doesn't want to miss a single detail.

I twist the bezel at the end of the Spinetingler.

It buzzes like a box of angry wasps.

I give Sir an encouraging look.

'Well, it seems to work perfectly . . . Did your friend try twisting the knob?'

I give said knob another twist, and the wasps get – angrier.

'Of course,' he replies, a frown pleating his fine broad brow. 'Are you implying that my friend and I are stupid?'

'No! Of course not! But this Spinetingler seems to be in perfect working order, sir.'

'Ah yes, but is that all it's supposed to do?' His glittering eyes narrow all of a sudden. 'As I pointed out, there weren't any instructions in the bag with it, and it's not immediately obvious how one is supposed to use it.'

That's true. Items like the Spinetingler aren't generally supplied with an operating manual. But then again, any red-blooded woman – or man – should know almost by instinct what to do with it. I get the feeling that Sir is just being deliberately obtuse. You get characters like this in the retail trade all the time, and it's usually best for business to try and play along with them.

The customer is always right and all that stuff, don't you know?

'Perhaps a brief demonstration would help?' he suggests, in anticipation. For a moment he purses his lips, and seems to find it difficult to meet my eyes. But then his broad face straightens again, and he gives me a long, almost imperious look.

'Of course, if you think so . . .'

'Oh, I know so,' he confirms with great authority, settling his large form more comfortably in the chair and tweaking at his long unglamorous raincoat again. He seems to be making certain that it fully covers his lap.

'Well, usually a young lady would tend to use this sort

of item at night, in the privacy of her bed, or perhaps in her bath in the case of the waterproof version.' I twist the bezel again, for effect. 'But sometimes, of course, an armchair will do just as well.'

'Do you often use it in an armchair?' Sir enquires.

'Um . . . yes. Sometimes.'

'And what about bed? Do you sometimes use it there too?'

'Er . . . yes, that too.'

'Which is best?'

'I don't have a preference.'

'Well then . . .' He gives me an encouraging nod, then snags his full red lower lip with his snowy white teeth again. He's sitting very still, but somehow he seems as full of dynamic energy as a tensioned spring at the same time.

Setting the Spinetingler down on the chair arm, I take a seat. This is very embarrassing, but – showing immense presence of mind for me – I manage to get a grip on myself. Reaching beneath my neat grey shop-girl's skirt, I fish around and find the elastic of my panties.

Sir's dark eyebrows lift.

I tug at my pants and slide them down my thighs, over my knees and off.

Sir blinks, his rather beautiful eyes widening

I wriggle in my chair to get comfy, just as Sir has, and he nods pointedly at my skirt, which is still covering the aforementioned groinal area.

'Of course, I'm sorry,' I apologise, then hitch up my skirt so he can see my demonstration.

'No problem,' he murmurs, sitting up in his chair all of a sudden, and leaning forwards.

I pick up the Spinetingler from the chair arm. 'Well, some young ladies rather like to . . . er . . . insert the

Spinetingler, but others prefer to use it externally.'

I suppose I'm stalling for time here, but this *is* rather a personal matter, and it's the first time I've ever had to demonstrate an item for a customer in this way. Furthermore, it doesn't help that I keep getting the distinct feeling that Sir actually *does* know everything there is to know about the use of Spinetinglers and other similar devices, and is actually just sitting there, large as life, and silently laughing his head off as he dares me to make an exhibition of myself.

'Which would you recommend?' he asks, grinning.

'I . . . I usually start off using it externally.'

'Perhaps you could you show me that then?' he suggests.

I twist the bezel and the Spinetingler buzzes loudly. Too loudly, in fact, so I back it down a notch.

'Sometimes it's best to start off gently and build up.'

'That seems sensible enough. Please continue.'

I close my eyes, and guide the pink silicon tip of the device to the target zone.

When it touches me I can't help but let out a gasp.

The Spinetingler really is an excellent product, and its vibrations are right on my frequency. The buzzing and thrumming makes me pant for breath and compels me to wriggle, but I try to stay as still as I can so that Sir can see exactly where the stimulation should be applied.

'And how does that feel?' he asks, his voice suddenly low and silky.

'Um . . . v-very nice,' I stammer, aware that I'm not really going to be much good as a demonstrator. I tend to get pretty inarticulate pretty soon in situations like these.

'You know, I can't really see all that well,' he complains suddenly, although it's not so much a complaint as an observation that comes out in the form of a stifled laugh. 'Perhaps you could open your legs a bit wider? Put your thighs over the arms of the chair, maybe? I'm sure that will provide a much better view.'

I'm sure it will, you wicked old pervert, I want to say to him, but he is the customer, after all, and I'm here to serve. So, trying not to lose my place, I hitch and hutch my bottom around in the chair, and tilt my pelvis so I can drape my thighs across the arms.

The resulting position is not unlike being on a gynae-cologist's couch with all my bits on display for Sir's perusal.

'That's so much better. Please proceed,' he remarks cheerfully.

I apply the Spinetingler to my sex again, keeping my eyes closed so I can't see Sir's avid face. With the vibrations on low I play the naughty silicone widget up and down, to and fro, and side to side, expertly goosing my sticky, swollen folds and all my sexy little hot zones.

All except one, that is . . . Because if I go there too soon this entire demo is over and done with before we've barely even started, and I don't want any more complaints from Sir that I'm not doing my job right.

'Is that usually how you use it?' he asks, his voice sounding rather closer than before. My eyes fly open and I find that somehow, moving lightly and silently for such a sizeable man, he's sneaked out of his chair and he's sitting on the carpet right in front of the one I'm in. He's no further than a yard away from the Spinetingler and my cunt, and when I almost fly up out of the chair, he places a large warm hand on the inside of my knee, as if to calm me.

'I do hope you don't mind,' he says blithely, a look of feigned innocence on his stocky face, 'but I really couldn't see all that well from over there.'

'N-no, it's all right. No problem,' I burble, not sure what to do next. The Spinetingler has slipped out of place and is noisily buzzing to itself.

'Do go on,' Sir encourages. 'This is all extremely instructive.'

As I prepare to comply, I notice that his hand stays where it is.

I circle the buzzing tip again, around and around my entrance, up and down the length of my sex, carefully skirting my swollen clit. My eyelids flutter down again because I can't cope with the intensity of his gaze.

'Ah, I see what you're doing now,' says Sir, his voice not quite steady. 'I get it. You don't go for the obvious place straight away in order to prolong the experience . . . That's very clever, my dear. You're clearly a virtuoso with this particular item.'

I nod my head, because I'm not sure I can actually answer lucidly.

His fingertips curve against the inside of my knee, then slide sneakily upwards. His touch is light and almost diffident, but it encourages me. I reach for the bevel, but even before I can make an adjustment, he murmurs, 'Ah yes . . . that's good. Now show me how you execute the coup de grace.'

Coup de grace? What is he on about?

I need to come now, whatever the hell he chooses to call it.

The Spinetingler seems to howl now, at least inside my head, and as I slide its slick reverberating tip towards the knot of nerves that craves it, my thighs flex and my bottom rises from the chair.

'Good girl,' croons Sir, his hand curling around mine to render guidance.

I hit the red zone and I shout and jerk and come.

The next few moments are a blur of moaning and thrashing and pure dumb pleasure. I forget all about The Boutique, and my sales pitch, and my product. I'm just a bundle of feelings and a throbbing, pulsing clit.

Eventually though, I come crashing down from whatever 'up' place I've been to, and rediscover the fact I've been giving a demonstration. With reluctance, I open my eyes, and meet Sir's . . .

They're dark, so dark, and full of wicked mirth and what looks like a genuine sense of wonder.

'That was excellent, my dear.' His voice is arch and full of delight and slightly shaken by that revealing unsteadiness. 'A very clear demonstration.' He takes the extremely fragrant Spinetingler from my trembling, nerveless grasp, and runs his own fingertips slowly up and down it. 'There's obviously nothing whatsoever wrong with this.'

'Um . . . no . . . It seems to be in perfect working order,' I observe gustily, clutching at the scraps of my composure despite the fact that I'm draped across an armchair with my thighs splayed wide open and Sir's face is barely a couple of feet from my sex.

'Here, let me help you,' he offers as I wriggle and struggle and try to sit up. He offers his free hand to assist me with my efforts, while he springs to his feet with an effortless elegance so surprising in a big man. An instant later I'm back on my pins again too, albeit somewhat shakily, and tweaking my skirt back down to cover my naked thighs. A look of disappointment momentarily clouds Sir's wide handsome face as he looms over me, but then it's gone again, and he's clearly thinking, thinking, thinking . . .

'Yes, the Spinetingler is obviously an excellent product for a young lady like you,' he observes, still fondling the stupid thing, 'but what about a gentleman? Could he use it?'

Oh, I can think of a million ways to use it on you, you disgraceful reprobate, I tell him silently, almost hypnotised by the way he continues to examine and as good as caress the silicone cylinder. Beneath my skirt, I get a naughty little renewed tingle in my sex at the thought of some of the things I'd like to do to Sir, and that reminds me that I'm no longer wearing any knickers.

Where the devil are they?

I glance quickly around, and notice a scrap of white lace peeking out of the pocket of Sir's disreputable brown raincoat. I fleetingly consider accusing him of shoplifting, but it's not really stealing, is it, because my panties weren't on sale anyway?

'So?' he prompts, giving the bezel of the Spinetingler a little tweak, then as it buzzes, he casts an almost coy little glance downwards at his crotch.

I glance too. Then feel *really* coy.

There's a prodigious bulge behind the fly of his charcoal-grey trousers.

'Yes, of course, a gentleman could certainly use the Spinetingler,' I say, trying to retrieve my efficient, helpful salesperson mode. Which isn't easy, when I can't stop snatching quick glances at that whopper down below, and speculating what it would look like outside those elegant grey trousers.

Sir fiddles with the bezel a bit more, and the pitch of the buzz oscillates up and down. 'Perhaps another demonstration would be in order?' he suggests. He doesn't seem to be making any attempt to play the serious shopper any more because he has a wide white grin plastered across his big handsome face.

'Of course, sir.' I'm sure my own grin is just as expansive too, and why wouldn't it be? Any girl would smile at the prospect of getting to grips with a sex toy that promises to be far more impressive than the silicone Spinetingler. 'Take a seat, and make yourself comfortable, and I'll see what I can do.'

He sinks back into the chair that he occupied before and sets the Spinetingler down on the arm, but this time there's no hiding of his light behind the bushel of his drab brown raincoat. This time, he carefully folds it back out of the way, and then, with no further ado, he unfastens his fine leather belt.

When his long deft fingers go to the fastenings of his trousers, I forestall him.

'Allow me, sir,' I say politely, trying to mask the fact that my mouth is watering almost as much as my nether regions are, and that I'm dying to get to grips with his monster.

'Why, that's very kind of you, miss,' he murmurs, then snags his lip again. His wickedly long lashes flutter as I dive for his trouser button, and then tease down his smooth-running zip.

Naughty Sir! He's not wearing any underwear!

And boy does what lives in his trousers live up to my expectations!

The flesh and blood spinetingler easily matches its silicone cousin, and is just as stiff and a good deal rosier and more appetising.

'I'm sorry about that,' remarks Sir, obviously not sorry at all, but proud as any typical male exhibiting his pride and joy, 'I'm afraid your demonstrating had a very stimulating effect on me.'

'No need to apologise, sir. It's perfectly natural. I have to deal with this sort of thing all the time.'

'Really?'

Oops! Does he think I'm a slut?

'Given the sort of merchandise we sell here, these sorts of situations tend to arise.'

Sir licks his lips, and even though I wouldn't have thought it possible, the 'situation' seems to arise even further than it has already arisen.

I reach for the Spinetingler, even though I'm almost certain Sir has forgotten all about it.

'Shall we give it a try then, sir?'

For a moment, the hint of what just might be nervousness flits across those gorgeous features of his, but he nods.

I switch on the mechanism, but keep it at the lowest level. Best not to give the poor man a heart attack, eh?

Very lightly, I allow the buzzing toy to drift up the length of the underside of his shaft. I barely touch his flesh, but still those big, graceful, long-fingered hands gouge deeply at the chair arms and he cries out an impassioned, 'Oh dear God!'

'Are you all right, sir?' I enquire, glad that his long, long lashes have fluttered down and he can't see that I'm grinning like the proverbial Cheshire cat.

'Fine,' he gasps as I delicately circle the Spinetingler's buzzing silicone tip around *his* tip. Which is much bigger and dark as wine with tumescent blood. 'Please continue.'

'But you're not looking, sir,' I point out, withdrawing the toy for a moment.

'I don't need to look, you silly girl,' he growls, his hips lifting as if his marvellous dick is blindly seeking its new playmate. 'Now just get on with it.'

Ooh, getting testy are we?

But then again, who can blame him? He's seconds from detonation and I'm messing about and being very unprofessional. I decide to apply myself – and the Spinetingler – to his predicament. The silicone simulacrum, I slide carefully into his trousers, and apply lightly and delicately to his tender perineum.

And myself?

Well, I apply myself to the real thing. The delicious, gleaming, silky, rampant appendage that's rearing up magnificently in my face.

Sir's eyes fly open as I take him between my lips. I can't speak, because my mouth's full – very full – but I silently challenge him to find better customer service anywhere.

And as I work wickedly and tirelessly with tongue and Spinetingler, he utters a stream of the wildest and most midnight-blue profanity.

But I know he only means it in a nice way . . .

A long, shagged-out while later, I stir sleepily amongst the fallout of my sales pitch. The Spinetingler, the Naughty Nipple Clamps, the Pink Furry Love Cuffs, the Magic Vibrating Egg and a colourful selection of even ruder 'samples' lie scattered around us on the sitting-room rug, and Sir's capacious brown raincoat is draped haphazardly across our sticky naked bodies. Over on the telly screen, an adult DVD is playing silently, on repeat.

Sir groans and his large warm hand curves drowsily around my breast. His wine-scented breath plays like a zephyr against the back of my neck.

'What would I do without you, my love,' he mutters, levering himself up and kissing the side of my throat and my jaw. 'What other woman would indulge a disgraceful old perv like me and play his daft games with him?'

'You're not old,' I observe, snuggling back against him and pushing my bottom against a rising erection that attests to a sexual stamina that would put a man half his age to shame.

He laughs, and nudges me rudely with the thing. Neither he nor I deny that he's a perv. Because he *is* one.

And with every day that we're together, I'm rapidly catching him up.

'I'm glad you think so,' he says as he suddenly leans right over me and starts to fish about under the adjacent coffee table, 'because I've *really* been shopping.'

Despite the fact that I find his penis poking against my backside very distracting indeed, I feel a tingle of purely retail-related excitement.

Sir does very, very good shopping, especially online, and parcels tend to arrive with a delightful frequency.

Agent Provocateur. The Erotic Print Society. Hotel Chocolat. All my favourites.

But the carrier bag he pulls out from under the table is unfamiliar. It's made from shiny blue and gold paper, and it's little and dainty. After a moment's hesitation, he puts it gently into my hands.

The retail excitement turns to a different kind of thrill. Even the unflagging erection nudging my bottom becomes temporarily ever so slightly less of a priority.

I lift out a small blue velvet jewellery box with the kind of dimensions that are coded into the genes of almost every heterosexual woman in the western, capitalist world.

'Just a small item for madam's consideration.' His voice is soft and arch, much as it was during our silly sex shop game, but I also detect a hint of genuine nervousness.

I flip up the lid, and breathe, 'Oh Bobby,' loving him more than ever when I see the box's dazzling contents.

'I'll take it,' I declare, then roll to face him and seal the transaction with a kiss.

Duet for Three

What the fuck?

What is this? I wasn't expecting this. When the woman on reception said there was a bit of a 'do' on, and I was welcome to join in, I didn't expect it to be the bastard child of a fetish party, a rave and Northern wedding reception.

Too weird.

It's a biggish room, an old ballroom or something, I suppose, but tonight it's decked out like a rough approximation of clubland. The music's a solid wall of complex, juddering sound, and there's flashing, strobing light bouncing off the walls and the mass of gyrating bodies.

God, it's all completely mad. But I like it. I haven't felt this psyched up in ages. My ears and my toes, and everything else between, are vibrating in time to the hard, thudding base beats, and my groin is suddenly tight with anticipation.

I suddenly feel an intense desire to get laid.

Smiling, I stroll towards the small, paid-for bar. I was expecting *Strictly Come Dancing* in a place like this – a discreet, out-of-the-way country hotel that I stumbled into by mistake when I got fed up of the motorway – but there's no poncy foxtrotting around here, no way. They're all throwing themselves around like maniacs, lost in the music, and the sweaty smell of adrenaline is almost solid.

Yeah, Jason, you could have some fun here . . . My prick kicks again inside my shorts.

At the bar, Mr Jack Daniels calls plaintively to me, but I ignore him. The fact I've been to a health farm – aka celebrity rehab – is the reason I've ended up in this godforsaken place. And I'm not going to undo all the shit from hell I've just gone through to get clean. Which means no booze for me. And no fags. And none of that other stuff either . . .

But I will allow myself a woman, if I get lucky.

I say, *if* . . .

At one time, it would have been a piece of cake. I could have had a dozen bimbettes a night if I could've coped with them . . . and sometimes, high as a kite, I did. But I'm not part of a headlining boy band any more. I'm not even recognisable – I hope – as a washed-up ex-member of a washed-up ex-boy band. I'm just Jason Ripley, an average guy who'd maybe like to start again as a real singer . . .

So, no JD. I order a mineral water and, as the young chap behind the bar hands it me, he gives me a strange, almost knowing look.

Hmmm . . . Well, maybe I'm not as unrecognisable as I thought. I thought I'd be safe now my long, trademark blond locks are gone, along with my shades and/or my bright-green contact lenses. I'm just Mr Man in the Street with short, nondescript brown hair and an unremarkable pair of glasses. And no designer gear any more either, just a plain shirt, off-the-peg jeans and running shoes.

No, I'm pretty sure the barman hasn't recognised J-Boy Jones of the Forever Boys from Adam. He's serving someone else now and has completely lost interest.

As I sip, I turn my attention to the dance floor. There's plenty to see, once my eyes adjust to the light and the movement.

I was right about the fetish party thing. Although there are plenty of folk in ordinary clothes – jeans, smart casual, some quite dressed up – there's also quite a lot of rubber and leather and all the rest of it.

A man in arseless leather trousers. A woman in a rubber catsuit. A full-on gimp. It's all a bit clichéd. But then I think about some of the stupid stage costumes that I wore, which played around with fetish looks. I must have looked a complete berk. Especially as I hadn't the faintest idea in the beginning what it all meant. These people aren't famous, or particularly glamorous, but at least I get the feeling that they understand kinkiness and perversity in a way that I never did. I was just playing. These dancers are for real.

I'm just about dragging my jaw up off the dance floor at the sight of a truly gorgeous drag queen – who, disturbingly, also makes my prick twitch a bit – when a female voice pierces the cocoon of booming sound.

'Do you come here often?'

My heart jerks. It's a voice I recognise, despite the music.

I turn, and it feels like slo-mo. Surely it can't be her? Why would she be here?

But it *is* her. She's here. And I feel kind of sick inside from a mix of shock jumbled up with guilt. . . and regret.

'Do you come here often?' repeats Maria Lewis, a woman I once dated in London. A lovely girl who I really didn't treat well.

'Maria?'

An oblique smile, not unlike that of the barman, curves

her soft pink mouth and, before I can say anything else, she reaches out and places her fingertips over my lips, to shush me.

I'm semi-speechless anyway, so it doesn't really matter. But the warm contact of her skin almost makes my heart stop.

Fucking hell, she looks amazing.

I didn't know her for long, but she was always pretty, and in a far more refined way than a lot of the Z-list slappers that I went through.

But now, oh hell, she's just beautiful. Blue eyes brighter. Hair shorter, but blonder and wilder in a sort of sexy shag cut. Her perfect heart-shaped face has an inner glow of mystery, of life, of supreme confidence. And her body?

Dear God Almighty, her body is just perfection – the stuff of every wet or waking dream I've ever had.

She's become every inch the superstar that I aspired to be and never was.

'Let's dance,' she purrs, the tip of her forefinger pressing heavily on my lower lip for a second, dragging it down.

I feel as if I've just been struck by lightning. And my cock, which was formerly just perky, has turned to iron.

It's a wonder I don't fall arse over tit into the mass of dancing people. I just can't take my eyes off her delicious bottom as she walks ahead of me, parting the swaying, gesticulating throng like a queen on a progress. Like I said, her body is perfect. And her bottom is more than perfect, if that's possible. It moves and sways and lilts as if she's dancing before we've even found our spot. As if she hears the music in her bones and in her heart.

Was she always this gorgeous? I suppose she must have been, but I was either just too wasted or too full of my own self-importance to appreciate her.

But I'm appreciating her now. Bloody hell, am I appreciating her.

Appreciating that marvellous firm arse, those long, long legs in a sleek, short, but elegant little black dress, and her superb breasts, as she turns towards me and gives me that narrow, cryptic little smile again. A smile that seems to combine with the staccato beat of the heavy, Latin-influenced track that's playing and wind itself around my dick like a serpent.

Shit, I'm in trouble.

And then we're dancing and I feel like a terpsichoreally challenged farmhand with seven left feet, instead of the pretty slick mover I once was. Seeing Maria again has rendered me helpless, almost infantile.

But she moves like a goddess. A wild, uninhibited poem of graceful syncopation. I can't remember if we ever danced together when we clubbed in the old days, but if we ever did, I'm sure she never danced like this.

She commands the space we've found ourselves in, carving out more and more with the sheer force of her personality and the energy with which she twists and turns and sways. Her sinuous body seems to interpret subtle rhythms and embedded harmonies that lesser mortals just aren't equipped to hear. I can hear them, because I was a musician of sorts before I pissed most of it away, but I can't do with this music what Maria does.

Fuck, I want her so much.

Maybe that's why my own feet and limbs just won't work properly. Because my hard-on is so ironclad it's almost agony. It's as if I've been disconnected from all rhythm and co-ordination.

She doesn't look at me. Which is probably a good thing.

She seems ensorcelled by the beats, her white arms lifted to heaven and her eyes closed.

And yet, from time to time, when her eyes do open, she does look at somebody.

We're close to the edge of the dance floor, and when – with enormous difficulty – I can shake my eyes away from her for a few seconds, and follow her eye line, I see that I'm not the only one who's watching her swirl and shimmy.

Lounging at a table, alone, is a large, stocky man with darkish, greying hair, a broad, stubble-shadowed face and intense, gleaming eyes. For a fraction of a second his attention strays from Maria and fixes on me . . . and I feel almost the same sense of shock I get from her.

I'm not gay.

Really I'm not.

OK, so maybe once . . . or twice . . . when I was pissed or high, I had a fumble around with Christian, the guy in the band who was bent. But that doesn't mean I'm homosexual or even bi.

Yet there's something about this guy who's watching us that seems to grab me somehow. Makes me want to shudder and look away, and yet look again. I miss yet another beat and stumble in my pathetic attempt to match Maria's moves. Torn between her and him, I get strange flash visions of being in a room somewhere, doing dark and dangerous things. With her, and also with him.

As my dick gets harder, I feel scared, yet infinitely excited. It's like I'm filled with a sense of anticipation of I know not what. I glance at the happy fetish crowd around me, who all seem to know what they want and why – and I envy them.

Maybe I want what they want? I wish I knew . . . I'm

just feeling more and more confused. Like a disenfranchised stranger in a very strange land indeed.

And it's right at that moment – as if she's read my mind – that Maria suddenly halts, mid-gyration, and fixes me with a steady blue stare. 'Come on. Let's get out of here.' With that she walks from the floor, not looking back, just leading me with her lithe, silky stride in her perfect black heels, and the muscular undulation of her gently swaying buttocks.

I couldn't not follow if my next breath depended on it.

Like an eager, panting puppy, I almost trot after her, out of the function room, across the lobby and to the lift. She doesn't check if I'm following, not once, and I have to run and almost fall into the lift carriage behind her in order to avoid it closing in my face.

'Maria. What on earth are you doing here?' I babble, still to her straight, smooth back and shoulders, 'Look, I'm sorry –'

Whirling like a ballet dancer, she cuts me off, mid-grovel, by the simple expedient of pushing hard on my chest, backing me up against the lift wall, and kissing me. Hard.

And as her tongue pushes imperiously into my mouth, her hand unzips my jeans with astonishing deftness, negotiates my underwear, and takes hold of my cock.

I'm so shocked I almost come all over her fingers.

Yet still, inanely, I try to speak and apologise . . . or something. She allows me my mouth for a moment, even while her fingertips do something infernal to the head of my penis, but her eyes utterly quell me. I can't utter a word. Somewhere in those periwinkle blue depths there could well be the answer to the meaning of the universe, but all I see is a blend of amusement and disdain, coupled with a disquieting foreknowledge of something I daren't even think about.

Then she's kissing me again, and almost dispassionately handling my equipment as if it's some mildly amusing curiosity she's passing a minute or two with while listening to the piped lift music.

There's barely time for a couple of bars of 'The Girl From Ipanema' before the lift door slides open and she drops me like the proverbial hot potato and just walks away, leaving me standing there with my erection poking out of my flies.

Thank Christ there's no one on the landing.

Shoving myself ignominiously and uncomfortably back into my jeans, I scuttle after Maria. That beautiful bottom of hers wafts from side to side as if she's still dancing, still hearing the samba rhythm of Astrud Gilberto. I can't take my eyes off it, and nearly trip on the edge of the carpet runner in my haste to catch up.

Which means that I nearly cannon right into her when she stops abruptly in front of one of the room doors.

The brass numerals read '17', and my eyes bug when Maria reaches into the front of her dress and pulls out a key card, which has presumably been tucked cosily inside her bra.

Lucky card.

The polished door swings open, and I follow her inside to a softly lit room, where astonishingly, it isn't Astrud Gilberto singing, but *me*.

Ack, how I hate some of those songs now. And 'You're My Fire, Baby' is a prime example. Poppy, bouncy, over-produced, conveyor-belt chart drivel. I cringe. Even with all the vocal enhancements at the studio engineer's disposal, I'm barely even carrying the tune. I *can* sing, but this wasn't one of my finest moments.

Maria turns to me and gives me a look of almost pitying amusement.

She obviously doesn't think it's much cop either.

What bothers me even more than my former lack of glory is the fact that the loathsome doggerel is playing at all.

How has that happened? Even I'm not stupid or bemused enough to believe that it's a coincidence. I start to ask, but she silences me again with her fingers across my open lips.

The scent of my cock is still on her skin.

A second later she's kissing me again. Dominating me again with her lips and her hands. Her tongue is dainty and mobile but it seems to fill my mouth, and her fingers move efficiently on the fastenings of my jeans. Loosening them so she can slide a hand inside the back of them – and my shorts – and caress my backside.

It feels so sensational that I groan, muffled by her lips, and my dick hardens anew against her belly. I try to caress her in return, but she presses her curved fingers so firmly and so suddenly against my arsehole that I yelp against her mouth, and I can barely remember my, own name.

And then she abandons me again, and whirls away. With a casual, uncaring grace, she throws herself down into a big, deep, chintz-covered armchair, and I'm left standing around like a dolt, my eyes skittering between the overdecorated bed with its elaborate, also chintz-patterned hangings, and the perfection of Maria's relaxed body and long, sleek legs.

'Look, Maria . . . I . . . um . . . I'm sorry I never called you,' I bluster, then dry up when she raises an imperious hand to stop my babble.

'Shut the fuck up, Jason,' she says in a quiet, unperturbed, almost affable voice, 'and take your shirt off.'

What?

I feel confused and excited again, but I obey her. I've started working out again now I've cleaned up my act, but

I'm painfully aware of the fact that I'm not as buff as I once was. Her all-seeing eyes seem to notice it too, and narrow slightly.

Fucking hell, I wish she'd turn off that music. My own trilling voice mocks me as I stand there shivering despite the gentle warmth from the central heating.

I wait, but she doesn't speak again, and I feel nullified, unable to act or move until she does.

Slowly, she licks her pink-painted lips.

She uncrosses and recrosses her peerless legs, careful not to allow me even the slightest glimpse of what lies between her thighs.

Barely seeming to pay the slightest attention to what she's doing, she reaches back into the low neckline of her black dress and slowly and idly begins to play with her nipple. Her fingertips move like some tiny animal burrowing about beneath the dark fabric and, after a moment, she closes her eyes and gives a little gasp of pleasure.

It's the most erotic thing I've ever seen in my entire life.

I'm in agony. My cock is tenting my jeans, and it's aching for me to wank it. But I know I can't touch it until she gives permission.

I've never done the submission and domination thing. And I've seen no more than odd bits of scenes in films and half-watched documentaries. But suddenly I seem to understand . . . or at least begin to.

It's something I never wanted until now.

I watch and watch as she rubs her long, silky thighs together and continues to fondle her breast. I'm still immobilised, like a pillar of burning salt.

Eventually she gives a little gasp, and a little sigh, and relaxes back into her seat.

Has she come? I didn't think women could do that... just orgasm from rubbing their own nipples. Maybe she hasn't... I get the feeling she's just teasing me, and that's strengthened when she opens her limpid blue eyes, and they mock me.

Men are such idiots, she seems to say, without speaking.

I don't speak either, but while my voice burbles on and on from the sound system, a thousand questions jostle behind my lips.

Chief amongst which is ... why did I ever, in my right or addled mind, let this glorious woman go?

I nearly fall over when she springs lightly to her feet and sashays towards me and, as I fight for composure, she looks me up and down as if I'm some kind of stud animal or piece of meat she's assessing.

'Unzip your jeans. Drop them to your ankles. Don't step out of them,' she instructs, her voice strangely neutral. As if she doesn't really care if I obey her or not.

I do though. I really care.

'Pants now. The same.'

I obey again. My mouth is dry. My heart is bashing against my chest. My cock bounces up against my belly as it's released, tip moist and sticky.

She does that stockwoman looking at the beast thing again, and I have a horrible feeling I've been judged lacking. I feel like a complete idiot standing here buck naked, with my jeans and underpants round my ankles, yet in a slightly sick but overpowering way, I like it. I like it a lot.

There's a knock at the door and I sway, nearly toppling over. Our eyes lock.

'If you so much as move a muscle, you can put your clothes on, get out of here and I never want to see you again.'

I've never fainted in my life, but I feel as if I want to now.

But no way on earth am I going to move. Not a millimetre.

'Come!' she calls out and, as the door handle turns, I realise the door was never locked.

I close my eyes for a moment, and I feel sweat trickling from my armpits and from between my thighs. I imagine if I could stand outside myself, and look at my skin, every inch of it would be blushing, especially my rigid, seeping cock.

'Robert,' she breathes, her voice soft, loving and happy. As she walks right past me the air she displaces feels almost blissfully cool, and a moment later I hear the small, feverish sounds of an intensely passionate kiss.

Fight or flight instinct screams at me to grab up my clothing, bolt for the door and run for my room, then check out as soon as is possible. But another force, a greater force, keeps me in place. Rigid in muscle and in cock. Eyes wide open now and wondering what's going on behind my back. I glance at the mirror on the dressing table, but frustratingly, the angle doesn't show them.

The kiss goes on and on, and not only does Maria purr and murmur, but her mysterious companion – Robert – does too. I remember her kiss and I can't blame him.

'So, my dear, aren't you going to introduce me to your friend?' he says at length, when they disengage and, as he walks forwards into the room, I see that the look of wry, mocking amusement on his face matches the tone in his voice.

It's the big man from the 'do', of course. The one who watched us both so assiduously and made me feel so freaked. He's very tall, and a bit heavy set, and has a vague look of a younger Orson Welles before he went to fat. That, and a character I might have seen on the telly recently, but I don't know what in.

I'm fighting the reflex to shake violently, and I don't know what's the most mortifying to me – my nakedness and my erection, or the fact that my own voice is still issuing interminably from the sound system. I'd give anything if one of them would turn the fucking thing off.

I can, I think, take anything sexual that this pair choose to dish out to me, but I wish to God that all trace of J-Boy Jones and the Forever Boys could be wiped off the face of the earth now and forever . . .

'This is Jason, darling,' declares Maria, her voice arch and her face beautiful in quiet triumph. 'The one I told you about. Don't you recognise him from the magazines? He's changed a little, of course, but when it comes down to it, it's easy to see who he is.'

Robert subjects me to a long, considered scrutiny, his dark gaze returning again and again to my cock.

Hell, this guy is most definitely bisexual. There's hunger in that slow, sly look of his. I find myself glancing towards Maria, wondering what her reaction to this is, and I find her grinning with delight and high approval.

Oh God. Oh God. Oh God. I thought I was worldly and experienced, living large on booze and drugs and faux celebrity. But I know nothing. Nothing at all. Not a thing.

Suddenly Robert frowns. 'Do we have to listen to this?' He cocks his large head, grimacing.

'I don't know. Do we?' Maria sidles towards me, touches first my face and then my cock, and I nearly come. Dragging in air, fighting for control, I shake my head.

Her companion moves to a small console beside the bed and depresses a button, once, twice, three times, cycling through a couple of radio stations until a very different kind of music issues from the hidden speakers.

The delicate melody of what sounds like a piano trio fills the room, stately and elegant and a balm to my overheated soul.

'Excellent,' proclaims Robert roundly, smile widening. 'Mozart . . . a well-known fetishist in his day. Couldn't be more appropriate, could it, my love?' He strides across the room, a looming imposing presence, and suddenly they're both deep in my personal space and owning it completely.

I clench every muscle, every sinew, anticipating his touch as well as Maria's.

But it doesn't come. He gently fondles Maria's breast as she pinches the tip of my cock, expertly containing my hair-trigger urge to shoot my load all over her beautiful black dress.

The couple exchange a look while the fondling and handling continues. A glance that's quick, yet deep and full of transferred intelligence. A decision's just been made, I realise, and whatever my wishes are simply doesn't factor into the equation.

I should be horrified. I should be scared. And yet a sense of tightness, almost of calm settles over me. Everything is exactly as it should be, just like the rippling, swooping phrases of the piano and the strings, every note perfect, precise and virtuoso.

'Shall we begin, my love?' says Maria at length, sounding pleased with herself. She's loving this, but there's no malice in her, I realise. Her happiness is purely from the anticipation of pleasure and entertainment.

'Why not?' concurs Robert, and for just a second his hand curves around hers, cradling my cock.

The touch of a man's hand on my flesh makes my head go light, and something inside me soars and lifts like the rising, dancing notes around us.

But just as I'm accepting and enjoying it, the touch is gone and they both whirl away as if dancing a secret tango. Robert crosses to the dressing table and picks up a small remote, and Maria opens a drawer in a tallboy at the other side of the room, and starts removing a selection of objects. My eyes bug at the sight of them, and then bulge even more when Robert presses a button on the remote, and a whirring and a light tinkling and jingling sound overlays Mozart's exquisite precision phrasing.

To my astonishment, when I look up, I see a set of shackles descending from the ceiling. A couple of tiny, concealed panels have slid aside to release them. Robert tilts his large head on one side, as if calculating, and the cuffs and chains halt in their downward progress and swing slowly in the air.

Real fear now overcomes me, but before I've a chance to voice it, he's beside me, lifting my arms one by one, and snapping me into the restraints. They're padded and surprisingly comfortable around my wrists.

That is until he presses the remote again, causing the chains to retract a little, and me to rise on my toes to ameliorate the sudden strain in my arms.

I can't help it. I whimper out loud. I'm so out of my depth. I'm in a different world to the one I've always known until now.

'Hush, baby,' murmurs Maria, instantly at my side. She smoothes my brow with her fingers, then kisses the side of my face while Robert looks on with approval. I start to feel calm again, despite the grinding, agonising ache of frustrated desire that grips my genitals as if they were trapped in a vice.

She peppers my jaw and the side of my neck with little kisses. Her fingers move lightly over me, touching my chest, then my flanks. I hear jingling again, but this time it's tiny, barely audible. I'm not sure what it is, but in a second or two I find out.

With a dexterity that suggests she's done it a score of times before – possibly to her beloved Robert – Maria straps a neat, carefully crafted little leather harness around my equipment, securing my cock and balls so I remain erect but probably can't get the blessed relief of orgasm. The constriction makes me harder than ever, and my rigid flesh flushes a brilliant crimson. Clear fluid trickles copiously from my tip.

I groan again and she swiftly inserts a gag in my mouth. It's a small rubber sphere that presses down on my tongue, and is buckled into place. I start to salivate around it, drooling above as I do below.

How perfect is this subjugation? How much do I realise that I've always wanted it, even though I didn't know it? Maria understands it completely, although I'm sure she never did when we were together in London.

My eyes are wet too, and it dawns on me that there are tears streaming across my cheeks. I gaze at Maria imploringly, begging her silently to take me down and down and further down into a peaceful, if not exactly comfortable, submissive place. I glance too at the man who I now understand is her mentor. The one who gave her all the knowledge she now possesses.

He comes to me too, and also kisses my face, running his tongue around the corners of my lips where they're stretched around the gag.

'Delicious,' he whispers, kissing me one last time, then kissing Maria deeply and voraciously. 'Thank you, my love,' he whispers to her. 'You always know how to give me the nicest presents.'

'Well, it's a bit impromptu, sweetheart,' she murmurs

back to him, her hands dropping to cup his clearly rampant erection through his trousers. 'But I knew you'd enjoy it. Happy birthday.'

Somewhere in the back of my drifting mind, I hear the receptionist saying, 'There's a bit of a do on . . . somebody's birthday . . . but you're welcome to join in.'

'Come on, let's play with our toy, shall we?' she says brightly, her expert fingers administering just the delicious, detailed and delightful handling to Robert's equipment that I'm currently denied.

'You play with him, my dear,' says Robert, clearly appreciating her attentions. His even teeth look very white in his broad face as he smiles a dreamy smile. Giving her one last kiss, he retreats to the large chintz chair, from which he has a perfect view of my dangling, exhibited body.

As he spreads his long, solid legs and gets comfortable, he unzips his flies to reveal a truly enormous tool. Strapped up the way I am, I feel as if I'm more huge than I've ever been in my life, but next to that rosy, gleaming colossus, my own cock seems almost rudimentary.

He gives me that age-old macho smile of 'mine's the biggest' and promptly begins to stroke it to make it bigger.

My own cock feels like lead.

Mozart plays on.

'So, Jason,' breathes Maria, suddenly in my face again, all glorious breasts, long sinuous legs and miraculous, confident femininity. I remember sleeping with her more than once, and enjoying that fabulous body. But right now I'd be in heaven if she'd just let me kiss her shoes.

'So, Jason,' she repeats, tilting her golden head, almost Medusa-like as she prowls around me, 'I guess you're wondering how we find ourselves together again like this?'

I nod. Even though I don't care what's brought me to this place and this strange condition.

'Pure chance, in the beginning. I would never have expected you to turn up here,' she admits, taking one of my nipples between her prettily manicured fingers. She pinches me – hard – and, as I writhe, I watch the blood turn my teat to exactly the same colour as her nail polish. 'But after that . . . design, my dear. Design. And desire.' She tweaks both nipples now and twists them this way and that, dragging them away from the wall of my chest and making me gobble and bubble behind my gag in a suppressed howl of anguish. I toss my head from side to side, and my cock tries to leap in its bonds, to no avail.

She smiles, both beauty and cruelty personified.

'The people who work here at the Waverley are our friends –' she nods towards her lover, who's still cheerfully masturbating '– and they know my history. You were recognised when you checked in, despite your "new look" and that's why you were invited to Robert's party.'

As she speaks her man's name, she releases me, and reaches down to cup her crotch as if just the word 'Robert' induces an *arpeggio* of pleasure.

Maybe it does? As she massages herself, her lips part and she gasps. She must be as excited as I am in her own way.

'I'm not angry with you, Jason. I never was.' She's circling again, moving behind me now. I try to swing round but she gives me a light slap on the bottom, which doesn't hurt, but still makes my shackled cock lurch and jump. 'It didn't matter about you not calling me. I'd already made my mind up to leave London and come home –' she favours Robert – who's now shifting himself around voluptuously in the plump, padded chair – with an angelic smile '– where the heart is . . . although I didn't realise that at the time.'

I should feel disappointed. Broken. Like nothing. But somehow, I'm almost happy. There's a sense of benediction in my diminishment. A correctness that thrills me and induces a high that's far more potent than any stupid thing I've ever ingested or smoked. I realise now that I've always felt bad about the way I treated Maria. It's bugged me and troubled me and screwed me up. But at last, here in this room, swinging in bondage, I have my chance to put things right with her.

I feel as if I'm floating. Borne aloft by adrenaline, a sense of my new-found identity, and the delicate bubbling music that plays around us. As Maria's hands travel skilfully over me, touching, pinching, probing, I almost weep from the intensity of the torment.

And from the scrutiny of her ever-watching lover. . .

Maria works on me. Like the Mistress she most assuredly is . . .

I hang like a cur in chains as she puts clamps on my nipples, weights on my balls and plagues my ever-reddening arse with fierce pinches and a fusillade of slaps.

Eventually, when she can see that I'm half off my head, she kisses me tenderly, then abandons me in favour of her beloved Robert.

Still facing me, and making me look at her despite my pathetic state, she sits in his lap, hitching up her skirt, pulling aside her knickers, and lowering herself slowly and with great deliberation onto his cock. Her big blue eyes nearly start out of her head as she seems to sink and sink and sink onto that massive edifice, then they close as she leans back and his hands slide around her body to caress her. I moan again, behind my gag, at the sight of his long, flexing forefinger working industriously where I'm no longer deemed worthy to touch. Amongst the sweet, silky curls of Maria's pussy.

It doesn't take long. After just a few moments, her spine stiffens, her legs kick, and she arches back against the substantial, supporting form of her lover, then cries, 'Bobby! Oh, my Bobby!' as she contorts and climaxes.

My eyes swim again, but not with sorrow. I'm excluded, but at the same time included. They won't let me come, yet I'm still part of their pleasure . . .

And even more so, a short while later, when a glowing, dishevelled Maria rises like a debauched empress from Robert's lap, and reveals him to be still erect. While she releases me from my bonds – both greater and more intimate – it slowly dawns on me what my next function is to be.

I'm elevated from inert toy to active participant as I crawl on hands and knees towards the big man in the fussy, chintzy chair, crouch before him, and open my mouth as he sinks his hands into my hair and directs my face towards his crotch.

He guides my head. He makes me take him deep and I almost gag. But there's a special sweetness in the taste of her upon him, and an even greater joy as gentle fingers reach beneath me and play a delicate, loving tune upon my own cock.

Somewhere in the background, a lilting, precisely bowed violin is playing too. A stately yet cheerful air, composed by Wolfgang Amadeus Mozart, the well-known fetishist and brilliant musical prodigy.

With a happy, muffled, gulping groan, I both come and am copiously come into.

Public Domain

Breathing deeply, I pause before the door to the Entertainment Chamber. Efficient as ever, Cicero steps forwards to open it for me. Not for the first time, I admire the sight of his deliciously taut buttocks, and the way they roll and tense enticingly beneath the skintight leather of his trousers as he moves. My fingers itch to reach out and give his firm flesh a squeeze, or even a pinch, but I distract myself by flicking out my fan.

Propelled by his strong arm, the door swings smoothly open, and as he steps back to let me pass, I swear he winks at me. A second later, his face is a picture of innocence.

Oh, but my Cicero is a prime specimen!

My tall dark companion is the perfect body servant. He has the face of an angel, he keeps himself in supreme condition and he knows what I want before I know it myself. Hiding a smile, I congratulate myself for having selected him. It helps, of course, when one's mother is the Matriarch of all the Islands, and one always gets first pick of the annual crop up from the farms.

My heavy-figured satin skirts swish around my thighs and bottom as I sweep into the room, and I imagine Cicero, behind me, dreaming of what's beneath them. He's as familiar with my nether regions as he is with his own, even if it's not really his place to lust after them without my permission. His daily duties include washing every part of me, anointing my body with oils and perfumes and then dressing me from the skin outwards. And as he's a man, my sex must be ever in his thoughts even if tradition decrees it's not supposed to be . . .

The Entertainment Room appears small and intimate, the walls hung with rich tapestries, the lighting warm, the air perfumed with aphrodisiac spices. On the ceiling there's a painted fresco of muscular males toiling naked in a field, their sweating flesh so realistic that one can almost feel the heat of it. Several of my fellow mistresses are already here, lounging on their couches, their body servants just inches away and, as ever, I wonder just who it was who originally decreed that entertainments like this are to be part of public domain. I've asked my mother more than once, and she says she doesn't know either. But it's tradition, and the Matriarchy is big on tradition.

Cicero helps me on to my velvet-upholstered couch, and then decorously arranges my many-layered skirts across my knees and ankles. I say decorously, but in the process he manages to touch me several times, his fingers hot but gentle on my bare skin. With each contact a surge of delicious power arrows upwards and sets a light between my thighs.

Carefully schooling my rising excitement, I affect the same mask of boredom and ennui as the other mistresses. And that's another thing. When did it become the fashion, then the custom, to find coupling with a strong and well-set-up male tedious? I know it's a tradition, but to me it seems a delightful one. Is there something wrong with me that I still look forward to a tumble?

But just look at them . . .

Mistress Layla and her Liam.

Mistress Tanya and her Timon.

Mistress Rosa and her Ryan.

They all look weary and as if they were being seriously inconvenienced. Anyone would think this was a council meeting about the trading figures for meat or metals or wheat, and yet for me the sexual tension makes my loins tingle. As I attempt to settle myself more comfortably, Cicero readjusts my skirts. Other mistresses continue to file in and take their places, and all the while he's caressing my skin with slow light touches.

The last of our number to arrive is Mistress Jenna and her body servant James and, leaning towards him, I sigh for Cicero's ears only. He makes a show of fussing with my hem and gives my calf a delicate squeeze of reassurance.

Hopefully their performance today will be better than usual. I don't hold out much hope, but perhaps we'll all be pleasantly surprised by some original thinking.

Jenna is beautiful, tall and blonde and willowy, imperiously dramatic in a royal-blue gown – but of all of us she has the least enthusiasm for these proceedings. Her James has an excellent body and very fine genitalia, but I always feel that his mistress never really shows him off to his best advantage. Their performances lack 'spark' and originality somehow, even though the sight of any kind of sexual congress always stirs me.

'Good evening, Cerise, how are you?' Jenna's voice is brittle as she catches my eye. Have I revealed my low opinion of her in my expression? Or perhaps she detects my wish that either she, or someone else, would show some daring?

'I'm very well, thank you, my friend,' I reply, giving her a bright smile, 'and looking forward to your pleasure. James is looking in particularly fine fettle today.'

'Which he is, as ever.' Her tone is curt and defensive and she gives me a narrow look, her eyes flicking enviously to Cicero at my side. My man is the acknowledged prize amongst the body servants in our assembly. 'Your Cicero is looking well too. Has he put on a little weight?'

Aha, trying to belittle my beloved stallion!

'Why, yes indeed he has. He's been following a new exercise routine, a most rigorous one. Designed to increase muscle mass and stamina.'

She makes a harrumphing noise. Score a point to me.

'Attend me,' she snaps to James, who hurries forwards.

He removes his clothes, which naturally aren't many. First he kicks off his boots, and then he unbuckles his trousers. A second later, he's stepping out of them, nude, but for his collar of servitude.

His penis rears up eagerly, ready to perform, and I eye it critically, ever the connoisseur.

He's big, but not as big as my Cicero. Not one of the body servants around this circle possesses either his length or his girth. But that doesn't prevent me appreciating the charms of other males. Especially when that male takes his meat in his fist and begins to work it to a sturdier, stiffer erection with considerable enthusiasm. Perhaps we're going to see something special after all?

'Hurry up! Don't take all day!' instructs Jenna, leaning back on her couch, making no effort to hide the fact that she wants this to be over quickly. What a spoilsport! Me, I'd much rather see an extended performance. Something that's wild and energetic and sweaty. Something that's intricate, luscious and unusual. For a moment, I take my eyes from the couple before me and glance at the real man who's standing so close to me that his leather-clad thigh is actually pressed tight against my bare ankle where my gown has slid aside. He's dutifully staring at his polished boot toes as decorum decrees, but as if he's sensed my scrutiny, he turns, ever so slightly, and catches my eye.

There's the faintest superior smile upon his sculpted lips. You devil! I think.

The rules of our society say that it's not his place to judge a mistress or even her servant, but Cicero is ever the uncommon one, and not just in the physical perfection of his body. Only he and I know how much he breaks the mould.

His erection brought to full stand, James reaches reverently for his lady's gown and folds it neatly out of the way. Beneath it, her loins are clad in an elaborate undergarment of ruched lace and silk and Jenna tuts and sighs, rolling her eyes in exasperation as her man removes it. His movements are deft enough, but she finds fault all the same. When her underwear is removed and set aside, she appears, to my eyes, completely unaroused – despite the presence of a fully erect male member barely inches away from her niche.

Indolently, Jenna nods, and James moves obediently to help her into position – adjusting her hips, parting her thighs and then slipping his hand between them.

He rubs. He fondles. He fiddles. And yet still she seems disinterested.

'Use the lotion,' she instructs, sighing again and taking a long swig from the glass of wine at her side.

I glance again at Cicero, and there's still that little smirk playing around his generous red lips. He never has to use the lotion on me.

'May I pour you some wine, mistress?' he asks softly, as a

distractionary tactic. It wouldn't do for my fellow mistresses to get wind of his secret insubordination.

Or would it?

A tantalising idea forms in my mind. Something so outrageous that it whips through my imagination like a forest fire, so vivid that I fancy Cicero himself might be able to see it. As he pours a measure of ruby wine into my goblet and hands it to me, his great head cocks on one side a little, and his brown eyes twinkle. Out of sight of the other mistresses, an expression of pure devilment and wonder flashes across his handsome features.

Do we dare, he seems to say, and in answer I nod. The wine suddenly tastes twice as sweet as I sip and scheme.

Meanwhile back at Jenna and James, the blond man is coating his fingers with the rich scented herb-laden lotion, preparing to anoint her diffident flesh with it. Huffing and puffing, she hitches her bottom along the couch, every action exhibiting impatience and boredom.

Oh, poor Jenna, I think suddenly, feeling pity.

To give James credit, he applies himself with unstinting diligence. Gently massaging, circling, flicking. Jenna's lips tighten as if she's actually resisting the sensations he's seeking to induce, but I can barely keep my pelvis still, imagining I'm being fondled in her place.

I lounge back further on my couch, tweaking and fluffing at my skirts as a cover for the fact that I'm pressing my calf against Cicero's magnificent leather-clad haunches. Through narrowed eyes, I study his hands, clasped loosely behind his back, and imagine those fabulous fingers playing my sex.

He's a virtuoso with those divine digits of his, instinctively seeking out the most responsive and fugitive of sensitivity zones. Pressure. Speed. Angle. He employs subtle variations of all, divinely orchestrated. Even while James perseveres with his unresponsive mistress, my own sex quickens and trembles, just at the thought of the same caress at Cicero's hand.

I glance around at the other mistresses. A little interest is beginning to stir in some of them, I can tell. Which makes me wonder whether I'm quite so different after all? Who knows what goes in the secret privacy of all their residences?

Perhaps Jenna is the only one of us who finds coupling a bore?

And even she is beginning to stir now, thanks to the industrious James. Her narrow hips are shifting now, hitching to and fro on her couch.

'Mount me, you fool!' she cries suddenly. 'I'm ready now!'

So am I, I murmur in silence, aiming my words at the back of Cicero's strong, dark head.

James obeys. And we all gasp when he takes her firmly by the hips and pulls her into position. Precious little deference now, and only the most cursory mumbled words to ask permission. He almost shoves her on to his penis, and thrusts in hard.

Well done, lad! I want to shout. Well done!

Jenna's eyes fly wide open, staring, but for once she doesn't protest.

As James thrusts, and his pale buttocks clench and tense, all eyes around the circle are on those flexing muscles. I bite my lips as Cicero secretly takes advantage. His warm hand is higher on my leg now, under cover of my many layers of flounced and silken skirts. The tips of his fingers are fire against my skin.

As James labours on, and Jenna slowly and almost painfully rises to meet him, my own sex gathers and moistens, excitement fizzing. I press myself against the slow, hot pressure of Cicero's fingertips, surreptitiously adjusting my position to coax him further.

If only it was our turn. If only we could flee the Chamber, be alone . . . and be ourselves.

Eventually a high, clear and strangely abandoned cry signals Jenna's crisis and, despite my excitement, I feel a sense of relief for James. He has despatched his duties, and is now free to relax and take his own pleasure. Jenna kicks him away from her, and he retreats, his moist and reddened member swinging before him. He snatches a cloth from the adjoining console, retreats behind the couch and ejaculates into it.

Cicero catches my eye. His broad handsome face is troubled, and I understand how he feels for his fellow servant's lack of dignity.

That will never happen to you, I tell him without speaking. I will never demean you that way, no matter what the others think or whatever rules and tradition decree. Anything that happens to you will be your choice. I don't know how, but I know he hears my silent pledge.

If Jenna were not so arrogant, I would say she looked shamefaced now, and she snaps and fusses as James attends to her, cleaning her crotch and straightening her clothing. She glances around, looking for someone else to begin a coupling and take the limelight.

I smile at Cicero, and he smiles back.

Let's play, he seems to say. Let's really show them.

With great deliberation, he nudges my elbow and what's left of my wine spills on my dress.

'Oh, Cicero, what have you done?' I cry. 'It's not like you to be so careless or so clumsy.'

'Forgive me, mistress,' he murmurs, falling to his knees, his dark head bent as he takes one of the cloths on our console to blot my clothing.

In a show of fussing worthy of Jenna herself, I primp and prink at my gown, tutting over the damp fabric. 'This is one of my favourite gowns, Cicero,' I say, mock stern. Well, at least he and I know the sternness is feigned. The others around the circle don't seem to see anything amiss, other than a mistress who has been let down by her man.

'I'm sorry, mistress,' he intones solemnly, head still bent. I wonder if the rest of the mistresses can detect the minute shaking of his shoulders which indicates that he's fighting to suppress his laughter. 'Please let me atone for my clumsiness. Please punish me, if it pleases you. I am at your disposal.'

A gasp goes up around the circle. Nobody admits to corporal punishment, but there are always whispers. Whispers of spankings and beatings – and the dark pleasure that overtakes the mistresses who inflict them.

'I think I may have to take you in hand, Cicero. You've been lax in your attentions, and you've displeased me,' I lie. This man has never ever disappointed or displeased me. I doubt if he could let me down if he tried.

'If it is your will, mistress,' he murmurs, bowing lower, pressing his noble brow against the carpet.

'It is my will,' I reply. 'Get up. Strip off your clothes. And give me your belt.'

Light and elegant, despite his great height and his massive muscles, Cicero rises. Within moments, he's naked . . . and so magnificent it makes my heart ache. His body looks as if it's cast from bronze and polished with silk; the plains of his chest and belly are ridged with sculpted muscle. His penis, though not erect yet, is a heavy swelling promise. Lowering his head reverently again, he hands me his thick leather belt.

My hands shake, though I try not to show it. I suspect I'm not the only mistress in this circle who gets pleasure from games like these, but I know I'm probably the only one who'll ever reveal it.

Without a word from me, Cicero bends over, presenting his perfect buttocks for my perusal, and his punishment.

'Do you presume to anticipate me, Cicero?' I ask imperiously, letting the leather swing and swish, flicking it against the back of his thighs.

'Forgive me, mistress,' he answers gravely, and begins to straighten.

I flick him again, and command him, 'Stay where you are.'

He resumes his pose, maintains it immaculately and with dignity.

I strike him. Hard. And accurately. This is far from the first time I've done this.

My beautiful servant makes not a sound, and across his backside appears a crimson stripe. I step back, stare around, and discover eyes, hot and avid, locked upon the mark.

I strike again, struggling with my control, but not showing it. Between my legs my sex glows – just like Cicero's arse. I feel an almost overwhelming compulsion to throw up my skirts, crush my sex against his pain and massage it.

What would my fellow mistresses think to that? I wonder. In fact what indeed do they think of this performance in itself? I know it's impossible, but I can almost seem to taste their fascinated revulsion in the air. The same sense of horror, but also hot, erotic wonder that I experienced the first time I accidentally happened upon this game.

Cicero remains motionless, twin stripes of crimson shimmering across his perfect flesh. Those broad red lines seem to twist and tighten around the very core of my pleasure and embrace it in a fierce and dark caress.

I swing the belt again and it cracks in the air before crashing down on Cicero. He barely flinches but he lets his breath out harshly. He will never cry out, but he's not immune to the glowing agony.

And I'm not immune to the power of his stoicism. Beneath my gown, my sex swims with silken honey.

I continue. We continue. The mistresses continue to gasp, following every stroke.

At last, though, my beloved servant's bottom is one mass of simmering line-blotched red, and I can see tension and emotion quivering in every line of his bowed yet majestic body.

'You may stand,' I instruct him coolly, even though my heart is as wild and flaming as his flesh.

He straightens, still regal despite his ordeal. His broad back is taut, strong and resilient. His noble head is still bowed as he stands tall, facing the couch, and his arms hang at his sides, the light clench of his hands the only sign of his internal struggles.

'Turn now,' I command, unable to prevent myself from licking my lips in anticipation. Slowly, oh so slowly, he obeys my command.

Oh, my Cicero! I'm not your mistress . . . *I* worship *you*!

He is erect, as I knew he would be, his penis jutting from his dark-furred loins like the unyielding branch of a mighty oak.

I want it in me.

I want it now.

I cannot wait.

His eyes meet mine, arrogant and sultry, and there's no

time now to play games of remonstration and imperious disapproval. I throw myself backwards on to the couch's edge, fling up my skirts and open my legs.

Without instruction of any kind, my lover moves between them, sinks naked to his knees again and presses his face between my thighs. Somewhere in the background I hear a faint ripple of outraged disapproval – probably as much for the fact that I'm wearing no undergarments as for Cicero's presumption – but there's nothing they can do about this and they've never been more distant.

To me now, and to him, they no longer exist, even though we all still operate in the public domain.

His tongue seeks out my pleasure, furling to a point, examining my intimate topography with its sensitive touch. He licks, he laves, he teases, cruising this way and that, and up and down, side to side, visiting every part of my sex from top to bottom and back again.

At first he avoids the most critical nexus, delicately skirting around it, except for tantalising flicks. My hips begin to lift of their own accord, seeking him, almost pleading with him mutely to grant release. He's on his knees before me, and I'm the one begging with my body for his beneficence.

I groan, 'Please,' and for a moment I'm dragged out of our zone of inclusion by the ricocheting gasp of outrage and amazement. Even though they all envy me, they can't break the rigid conditioning they're barely aware of.

But still I plead. I mutter. I groan. I whimper. I implore, inarticulately, to be granted ecstasy.

And because he loves me, Cicero smiles against my flesh . . . and grants my wish. He closes his warm lips around my centre and delicately sucks.

I rear up from the couch. I howl and buck. I grab at

Cicero's crisp dark hair and jam his face closer to my crotch. My feet and ankles pummel his broad bare back, thumping and pounding against his bare skin.

It's too much to bear. I black out. Crying his name . . .

Just moments later, I return to myself again. But not to the ghostly babble of feigned indignation and disapproval that I'd dimly perceived as a soundtrack to my pleasure.

No, as I open my eyes, and reach for Cicero, I see a blank white ceiling, not the fresco of labouring slaves. I turn and see the 'off' light glowing red upon the console.

We're alone now, just the two of us, no longer a part of the public domain of the holosphere.

'I don't think you're going to be very popular after that performance, my love,' murmurs Cicero wryly, settling his long, glorious and still rampant body on the couch beside me. 'I feel there will be reports of your recidivist behaviour winging their way, even now, to your mother.'

'I'm sure there will, but do you know? I really don't care,' I proclaim, reaching for the gleaming red-hot bar of his rigid penis. I'm not sure I really want to talk about my mother the Matriarch whilst handling my lover's genitalia in a way that's far from mistresslike. But even so, I decide to clarify my bravado. 'Who do you think I get my wicked ways from, Cicero? Who do you think recommended a rogue like you to me as my body servant?'

Cicero laughs softly, reaching, with a large strong hand, for the back of my head.

Compelled to bow before him, I smile happily and become servant to his master. Taking him into my mouth, I bestow a very private pleasure . . .

Are We There Yet?

'Where are we going?'

'It's a surprise.'

'Oh, go on. Tell me.'

'Don't be so impatient, wench.'

Wench? What is this? A sexy pirate fantasy? It's Stone's clapped-out Toyota we're about to board, not the fucking *Golden Hind*.

At least I *think* it's the Toyota. He doesn't usually use the Merc for jaunts like this. But I can't be sure because he's got me in a blindfold.

Yeah, I'm wrapped around in a world of pitch-blackness, strung-out nerves and one man's perverse peccadillos. It's so exciting that I think I might faint.

'Oof!'

I stumble on the gravel, and obscene messages streak along those tight-strung nerves. For one churning second, I have a horrific feeling that something totally disgusting is going to happen. But luckily it subsides just as quickly and I'm back to being weak and girlie and clutching at his solid muscular arm as he helps me with all courtesy into the car.

'Are you all right, Miss Lewis?'

His voice is soft and genial as he settles me into my seat and fastens the belt across my chest. He has to do this because he's got me in handcuffs, too, as well as the blindfold. I'm totally vulnerable, but I can't deny that I like it.

'Yes, thank you, Mr Stone,' I answer, keeping it bright and pert and slightly insolent because that's the game we're playing tonight.

He murmurs, 'Hmm . . .' as if he suspects my motives, then softly slams the door and makes his way round to the driver's seat.

I know the blindfold is part of the game, but suddenly I wish with all my heart that I could see him as he settles in beside me and starts the engine. I want to see that dear profile of his. The solid, stubbly jaw. Those unexpectedly lush and overtly sexy lips. Long, long eyelashes that make me jealous as hell that it takes three coats of Maybelline to get the same effect. Taken overall, he's not exactly an oil painting but to me he's just sex on two long legs.

He revs the car and the vibrations of the engine play havoc with my insides because of the thing he inserted into me earlier. I hardly dare put a name to it, because it's not exactly the most refined and sophisticated of sex toys. But Mr Stone likes it – so that makes it fine by me.

OK, it's a butt plug, right?

And it provokes the rudest, most insidious of sensations. It feels like . . . It feels like . . . God, I just can't bring myself to say what it feels like. But at the same time, oh boy, it gets me going!

And Mr Stone knows that. Which is why he put it in me before we set out.

My mind flicks back to the bathroom and I start to sweat as if it were happening all over again. I'm naked, bending over, one foot on the edge of the bath. I'm totally exposed in the lewdest of ways and he's just looking, looking . . .

And then there's that sensation. Intrusion. Pushing. Pressure, pressure, pressure, then the give as it goes in. Oh, God! Then I'm exhibiting myself to my lover, slick and dripping, with that stark black rubber base protruding from my fundament.

It just boggles the mind what a girl will do for love.

As I zone back into the world of here and now, I wonder if he's deliberately searching out bumps and potholes. The old car trundles along, bouncing me around in a way that makes me gasp and gulp. The suspension leaves a lot to be desired, and so does my self-control tonight. But Mr Stone loves pushing my buttons and testing my limits.

One particularly juddering lurch has me biting my lip, and, though I can't see him, I know Mr Stone has noticed.

'Are we there yet?' I ask by way of a distraction. And he laughs.

'Impatient, Miss Lewis?'

'No.'

'Liar.'

'I just want to know when we're going to get there.'

'You might not be so keen if I told you.'

My heart kicks, and so does my sex.

Are we going dogging? We've done it before. And done it enough times for me to know that I'm just as much of an exhibitionist as he is.

I remember the first time, travelling there in this car, and it makes me sort of breathless.

I could see, that time, and Mr Stone gave me plenty to look at. And more. He asked me to take his dick out of his jeans and touch him.

Oh, my God, he might even have his dick out now for all I know!

I edge sideways, and begin to lean towards him. I may be handcuffed, but I can still reach over in search of our pride and joy. It's certainly big enough to find in the dark.

'What are you doing, Miss Lewis?'

'Um . . . nothing. Really . . .' I lie. 'Just trying to get comfortable.'

He says nothing, but I can sense that he's smiling. It's a slow, sly, sideways grin. I know it well and it slays me every time I see it. Even after all our months together.

Time seems to dilate and warp. I've no idea how long we've been travelling. I can measure it only in terms of what my body's telling me. The growing pressure in my belly. The growing wetness in my knickers. The way my clit aches and throbs and throbs and throbs. I want to ask if we're there yet again, but there's a pressure on my tongue too. The awareness of what might happen if I speak.

You might be wondering why I call him 'Mr Stone' when we live together.

Well, I don't a lot of the time. Mostly, he's just 'Stone', or maybe 'Robert'. And sometimes he's 'Bobby' when things are close and sweet and tender. But when we go all formal on each other it's a signal. Let the games commence. I only have to hear him say the words 'Miss Lewis' and I want to come.

'So, are we comfortable yet?'

His words make me jump and that plays havoc with my innards. I have to gasp for breath and gather myself before I can answer.

'Well, I don't know about you, but I'm just fine. Thank you.'

'Really? Is that a fact? I was just thinking that by now you might want to touch yourself.'

I've been wanting to touch myself since the bathroom, but I'm not going to tell him that. Instead I sneakily clench my thighs in an attempt to get some stimulation. It's a huge mistake though, and only makes things worse.

'Why on earth would you think that?' I pause, then add sassily, '*Mr Stone.*'

'Have a care, young lady,' he shoots back. More quickly, I suspect, than he intended. He puts on this act of total self-control. Impassive lack of interest in the sexual tension growing between us. But I know I'd be on a winner if I put good money on the fact that he's rampantly erect.

I get that yearning, burning urge to touch him again, and confirm my suspicions. I fancy that I could come from the simple act of touching his thigh. Which is bullshit, really, and I know it. This isn't some flowery, unrealistic romance here. Like any woman, I need my fair share of purposeful, inter-thigh fumbling to get me off. Fingering. Tonguing. What have you. Or maybe a good hard shag? A bit of old-fashioned, tried and true, pneumatic grinding between the sheets with Mr Stone on top, his big size-eleven feet braced against the footboard so he can really put it to me.

Yum!

'What are you thinking about?'

Oh, shit! I realise that not only have I been quiet for several minutes, I've been jiggling about, trying to get some action by knocking that accursed butt plug against the root of my clit somehow.

'Nothing, Mr Stone. Still wondering where we're going and if we're anywhere near there yet.'

'Bullshit,' he observes roundly. 'You're thinking naughty thoughts, aren't you, Miss Lewis? If you aren't, I'll be surprised –' he pauses for a beat '– and disappointed.'

Oh, no!

'All right, all right, I was thinking about coming. And how much I want to do it. And all the ways I could do it.'

'That's more like it.' He starts to change gear and misses the one he wants. And I laugh out loud.

Touché, Clever Bobby, you're as horny as I am!

He treats me to one of the foulest, most disgusting oaths I've ever heard – all delivered in his most cultured and pleasantly conversational tone. Then, a moment later, he brings the Toyota to a halt.

Before I can ask if we actually are there yet, he's out of the car, round my side, and gently but determinedly hauling me out of my seat. He leads me a few steps away from the car, and simply says, 'Come, then.'

'H-here?' I stammer.

But where is 'here'?

I can hear the roar of traffic in the distance, so we must be near the motorway, but, other than that, we could be anywhere.

With anybody watching.

Not that that would bother me too much. It wouldn't be the first time I've put on a show. But still, not actually *knowing* whether there's an audience is unsettling.

I reach out my hands blindly in the dark, but I can find neither anything to sit on nor anything to lean against. And, goddamn him, he offers no assistance.

With a resigned sigh – and a great deal of difficulty, due to being cuffed – I yank up the hem of my skirt and fish about in my knickers.

'Tuck it up,' he instructs, 'and then pull down your pants to your knees.'

I feel faint again, and it's not from disorientation. My head goes light and I feel as if I'm floating on a cloud. Scrabbling and fumbling, and trying not to dislocate my shackled wrists in the process, I obey him. And display my crotch to the chilly night and its thousand eyes.

Remembering certain preferences of his, I spread my legs as much as I can with my knickers at half-mast. I know Mr Stone likes it when I lose my elegance. He likes it a lot. His dark side gets off on seeing me graceless.

I half crouch, half squat, and reach for my sex. It's like a swamp down there, and I'm so sensitised that I moan aloud. The erotic tension, the plug, the darkness. It's all brought me to fever pitch far too quickly. I touch my clit and feel a deep throb that seems to grab at the thing inside my bottom. The temptation to go for orgasm immediately is breathtaking, but I know that Mr Stone wants a performance. So I withdraw from the most critical area and start to wiggle.

I must look a bit of a sight. Half crouched and waving my bum about. I drift into a strangely detached state, while inwardly watching both myself and the man who's watching me.

I suspect that he'll be masturbating too. That is if we're not in a public car park or a lay-by or somewhere with dozens of folk around us. Maybe even if we are? I imagine those big hands on that big dick and I wish I knew exactly where he is in relation to my position. The ground beneath my shoes is soft, and, as Mr Stone is light on his feet, it's impossible to hear his tread. He hasn't spoken for a few minutes either.

But I *should* be able to locate him. After all, he's six foot four and broad with it, and he displaces a lot of air. Yet I've no idea whether he's close by, or many yards away. If it weren't for the fact that I would've heard the engine start, he could have got back in the car and driven away.

And then I nearly faint when I feel his warm breath on the back of my neck.

'You're not trying very hard, are you, Miss Lewis?' he murmurs, so close he could be touching me. And in fact, a second later, he *is* touching me.

I feel his towering form against my back, his erection rampant as his arms come around me. One huge paw cups my breast, and the other swoops low to direct my masturbation.

His middle finger presses mine against my clit and I come like a runaway train!

My mind goes blank for a bit, but as I get myself together again, and realise I'm sagging against a still very insistent prick, I struggle with my cuffs and try to twist around to fondle him.

'Tut, tut! That's enough of that,' he says sternly, swirling his hips away from me while still holding my body aloft.

Even though my entire pelvis is still softly glowing with satisfaction, I feel disappointed. I so want to touch him. I so want to *see* him. I'd love to snatch off this stupid blindfold, reach for his amazing penis, and watch his broad face contort in pleasure as I caress him.

But it seems I'm not to get my wish, because, almost immediately, I'm being gently but firmly manhandled towards the Toyota with my skirt up and my knickers still at half-mast. I try to right them, but I get that 'tut, tut' again so shuffle along the best I can.

So, I'm to sit here with my bush hanging out, am I?

It seems that way, as Mr Stone restarts the engine.

How long have we been going now? How long have I been sitting here with my pants down and my skirt up? How many astonished fellow motorists have glanced idly to one side at the traffic lights – and got an eyeful?

It seems like an age, and it's not only my wandering mind that's telling me that, either. The cups of coffee I drank before we left the house are beginning to make their presence felt.

God, I need to pee! I really, really, really need to pee!

And it's all made worse by the nasty pressure of the butt plug. There just isn't room in my innards for a full bladder and a great, honking chunk of black rubber, too.

Around a dozen times, I consider surreptitiously clutching myself in a pathetic attempt to control the ache. But, even though he's driving, I know Mr Stone will be watching my every move. And even if he isn't actually looking he'll be monitoring me with his sixth sense. The one that can reach through the walls and corridors of the rambling, shambling Borough Hall building where we both work and tell at any given time whether I'm thinking or doing something naughty.

'Still comfortable?'

The bastard! He's read my mind – although it doesn't really require telepathic powers to deduce what sort of state I'm in. He was the one who offered me a second Americano.

'Fine. Are we there yet?'

'Not yet. Why, are you thirsty? There's a bottle of water in the glove box. Why not have a drink?'

Screw you!

'Well if you won't, I will. Can you get it for me?' he continues, his voice perfectly normal to the ear, although with *my* sixth sense I can hear him laughing his head off.

I refrain from pointing out that I can neither see nor use my hands all that efficiently, and just fumble around until I find the glove box catch.

The water sloshes as I pull out the plastic bottle and that does terrible things to my beleaguered bladder. This time I can't stop myself from wriggling, and twisting my thighs around, and Mr Stone notes that with a soft, impatient sigh.

I uncap the bottle and hand it to him, then have to sit there in a state of delicious agonising discomfort while he drinks deep, audibly relishing the cool water as it slides down his throat. With a grunt of satisfaction he hands me back the bottle.

'Sure you won't have some?'

'Absolutely.' My teeth are gritted but I get the word out.

We drive in silence a little longer, and again he seems to be navigating with the express purpose of seeking out the most dug-up and roughed-up bits of road. With every jounce and bounce of the car, I'm convinced I'm going to either cry out or wet myself or both, and eventually I just can't take it any more.

'I need to pee. Please stop. We've got to find a toilet.'

'But there isn't one near here,' he observes blithely. 'I'm afraid you'll just have to wait.'

'I can't!'

And really I don't think I can much longer, either. Things are getting very serious down there and sweat is pouring off me as I fight to control my water.

He utters another sigh. A big, fake, pantomime sigh this time.

'Very well, then,' he says, as if I were seriously dis-commoding him somehow, and it's all very tedious. Which, again, is total bullshit, because he's loving every minute of this. He has a special fascination with pissing games, because he knows I once played them with someone else . . .

We get out of the car – very gingerly and awkwardly in

my case – and there's the sound of voices somewhere near. And – oh, God! – running water. We must be somewhere near the river, maybe in the vicinity of a country pub or a beauty spot. It's night but there are strollers out and about. People who might see me with my skirt up and my pants down. People who might see me when he makes me do what I've got to do – out here in the open.

I'll just have to take a chance. Not that I've much option. It's either go where he instructs me to or wet myself anyway. If we were in the middle of the Borough Hall car park in broad daylight now, I'd probably have to go. He leads me a little way along what feels like a rough path. Tall stalks of grass brush my legs, and with my knickers around my knees every shuffling uneven step makes me gasp.

'Here,' he says eventually, then, without warning, he swoops down. I feel him pluck at my pants, and I get the message. Feeling as if my eyes are going to pop out beneath my blindfold, I step out of my underwear, moaning with every move or jolt.

I don't know what he does with my knickers, but I suspect that I'm not going to get them back. And I don't care. All I want now is to squat down and let it all go.

But, of course, once I'm down, legs akimbo, I can't. And the multicoloured frustration is so keen I want to wail. Even with the rushing river so close by, I'm all locked up.

'I can't go,' I snivel.

'Oh, poor baby,' he murmurs. 'Poor Miss Lewis. Do you want me to help you?'

Oh, God, yes!

I sense his great presence beside me and, if it wouldn't be so appallingly uncomfortable that I'd probably scream, I'd fall down on my knees and press my lips against his shoes.

He crouches at my side, and once more he slips his hand between my thighs.

And when one long, square-tipped finger works its magic, I do scream. But silently, inside, behind my bitten lip as everything cuts loose and I piss and have an orgasm simultaneously.

This time I don't blank, but seem to experience a moment of total clarity. The sounds around me come into sharp focus. The running water. The echo of my own torrent. The bashing and pounding of my heart. The heavy, broken breathing of the man at my side, who's unable to mask his physical excitement in the execution of one of his own particular perversions. He's wanted to do this ever since I described once being brought off this way by a girlfriend in a transport café.

Silently, as I come down, he hands me tissues to clean myself with, then disposes of them I know not where. I don't feel as if I can speak as we track backwards back to the Toyota. I want to touch him again. Or, more properly, touch him for the first time in the course of this escapade. But somehow I know it's not the time yet.

How long is this bloody road trip going to last?

'Are we there yet?'

We seem to have been driving for hours. Certainly long enough for my inner tension, and my libido, to crank right back up to screaming point again. I clench myself hard around the intrusion in my bottom, imagining that it's Mr Stone's magnificent dick.

'I asked you not to ask that again,' he states, mock coolly.

I pout, hoping the mutinous thrust of my lip will goad him. I know I'm acting bratty, but I also know that's what he wants. This magical mystery tour is turning out to be a pick-and-mix of all his favourite kinks, and there's one more I'd like to add to the selection.

I wait two minutes, then I ask again.

'No. But we soon will be. And you'll regret it, young lady.'

Bingo! He's taken the bait.

Or have I taken his?

The car speeds up, and we twist and turn through the unseen roads and streets. There's passing traffic, so we're probably not in the country or by the river, I guess. I can't see him, and he doesn't speak, but there's a quality to the air that seems to press on my skin. He's as impatient as I am, and, even though he's a past master at disguising his emotions, I know him. And I can read him in the silence and the dark.

We stop, he wrenches on the handbrake, and says, 'We're here. Are you satisfied?'

'No,' I say pertly.

'Well, we'll see about that, then, shall we?'

In far less time than it takes me to grapple clumsily with my seatbelt, he's out of the car, round to the passenger side, and hauling me out on to the pavement, or path, or whatever. He's so much less measured now, so much less in control of himself, and that sense of the balance of power tipping makes my innards flutter dangerously. There's just one more component in our three-for-one special, and, in that, the one who seems to have the least say in the matter is always the one who's really in control.

Together we almost run along a hard surface. I hear the rustle of trees, and sense a boundary of some kind on either side of us. It's a narrow alley. There might be hedges or walls flanking us. There's the snick of a gate, and Mr Stone urges me ahead of him through the opening.

I smile. But I don't let him see it.

'You're an impatient travelling companion, Miss Lewis,' he murmurs, bringing us to a halt. A tree, above and to the side, sighs in agreement. 'Not very restful. Not very soothing.' He pauses, grasps my linked hands, and then presses them against the front of his jeans. 'In fact you could say that your presence on this journey has really wound me up.'

I'll say! He's even more gargantuan than usual.

'What do you think we should do about it?' He does his tango hip swivel when I try to get creative and grope him.

'Discipline me?' I suggest, all innocence, while contemplating another lunge for his equipment.

'Really?' He's holding me at arm's length now. Effortlessly. A man of his size has rather long arms. 'And would you like that?'

Trick question.

'Oh, no . . . Please, no . . .' I try for piteous and just get pitiful. No need to worry about my Oscar acceptance speech just yet.

'Actually, I think "yes".'

And with that he manhandles me into position over the back of what feels like a conveniently placed wooden chair or seat of some kind. How handy that something just like that should be there.

I dangle, face down – head resting against my shackled arms, thighs taut, bum in the air. Perfectly positioned. And, when he carefully adjusts my skirt, a perfect target. The black flange of the butt plug will make it easier to gauge the distance, no doubt . . .

I hear a slow, sliding, insidious sound. And then the snick, snick of a heavy leather belt leaving the loops of his jeans.

Uh-oh! He means business.

I almost shoot out of my skin when he trails it lightly over my naked bottom as if he's allowing me to try the leather on for size. I almost wet myself – again – with longing, when he drapes it in the length of my crease, nudging the plug, the smooth leather dangling against the stickiness of my sex.

'Just three, I think,' he purrs, still teasing me with the object of my correction. 'And I think it would be a good idea if you tried not to cry out.'

Fat chance of that, although I know why he suggests it.

With that he whirls away and I hear his firm tread as he moves into position. I like his purposefulness in these matters. He doesn't waste time with unnecessary taunts and overdramatic Grand Guignol threats. He just gets on with it.

The first blow feels as if I'd been whaled on the right bum cheek by a two-by-four, and my attempt not to make a sound comes out like the squeal of the proverbial stuck pig.

The second feels as if the left side of my arse had been struck by lightning and I make a sound that I don't recognise as human.

The third blow is much lighter, but it catches me right in the crease and knocks the evil-demon butt plug right against the nerves that connect to my clitoris.

I climax violently, shout 'Oh, Bobby!' and pee myself a little.

Afterwards, I turn into a sobbing, blubbering, shuddering, glowing, thankful, soppy mess, and he takes me onto his lap – heedless of my soggy state. I come again, lightly, when he whips out the plug and flings it away into the bushes, and, like a little kitten-girl, I try to kiss his beloved hands, and his dear face, while he unclicks the handcuffs and hurls them away too, after the plug.

Which leaves only the blindfold.

'Are we there yet?' I whisper, managing to get my lips against his as he reaches for the ribbon that holds the mask in place.

'I think so, baby,' he whispers, returning my kiss as he gives me my sight back.

My lips cling to his for a moment, then I ease away, almost blinded by the nearness of his broad, beloved face.

Then I blink like a baby owl and glance around.

At the chestnut tree. The toolshed. The ironic garden gnomes. Then up towards the bedroom window where there's a soft glow from the bedside lamp he turned on before we set out.

We're here. We're back home again, just where we started from. And I'm so happy because this is where the bed is.

And this time, Clever Bobby, *I'll* do the driving!

Fireworks Inside

Fireworks! Bloody fireworks. I hate fireworks.

I throw myself into the walk-in coat cupboard and slam the door behind me. I can't take much more of this! They're supposed to be celebrating Cecilia's lavish society wedding, not blowing up a medium-sized city. What the hell are they using out there? TNT? Surface to air missiles? Semtex?

'They're too close to the house, you silly mare! They'll burn the place down, and fry all your guests, and then where will you be?'

Slithering down, I cower in the corner, in the darkness. It's as pitch black as a witch's coal scuttle in here, and there are layers of old coats hanging on pegs above me, and some rather dubious-feeling carpet beneath my thighs as I tuck my legs beneath me. I can hardly breathe, but it's still better than enduring the noise outside. The dust makes me cough, and something smells distinctly mildewed with a side of mothball, but I'll take this over my pathological fear of fireworks any time. I've been petrified of the things since I was a kid, and someone set a giant firecracker off right next to me. I usually spend Guy Fawkes Night tucked up with a couple of sleeping pills, but I can't really get out of attending one of my best friends' wedding, can I?

If only the bloody things weren't quite so loud.

Bang! Boom! Boom! God, I swear they're nearer and/or even bigger now.

'Please stop. Please stop. Please stop.'

But no amount of hands over ears and cringing in a tiny bolt hole of utter blackness seems to be helping. So much for enjoying a glorious knees-up with champagne and a groaning buffet and dancing and a selection of the groom's tasty friends to cop off with. Even on a good day I couldn't pull a tasty bloke in a coat cupboard.

I'm bordering on snivelling and feeling very sorry for myself, when, during a lull in the shelling, the cupboard door flies open, and a large, generally man-sized shape hurls itself inside with me and slams the door shut again.

'Fucking, bloody fireworks,' growls a gruff voice, and suddenly there's a nice smell of spicy high-end cologne to take the edge off the aroma of fusty coats.

The new firework-phobe is right up against me, but I'm not sure he actually knows I'm in here. Should I announce myself, or keep quiet? It's only a *very* small cupboard and he's bound to knock into me any second.

'Don't you like them either?'

The man-shape leaps. 'Fucking hell! You frightened the life out of me. I didn't know there was anyone in here.'

Nice.

'I was here first.' Almost before the words are out, there's another huge detonation, and I screech in terror . . . and throw myself wildly in the general direction of Man-shape.

Luckily, he opens his arms and wraps them around me tight. I don't know whether he's comforting me, or himself, but there's a part of me that's suddenly miraculously immune to the conflagration outside. And much more interested in the idea of fireworks of another kind.

'Sorry I shouted.' It's momentarily quiet again, but I notice he doesn't let go of me. 'It's just that I *really* hate fireworks. It's embarrassing, but I had a bad experience as a kid, and they do my head in.'

'Me too. Incident with a jumbo firecracker . . . Now I can't bear the bloody things.' I sigh. 'I didn't know Cecilia was having a display.' Mm, his arms feel nice, and quite big and strong for someone who's hiding in a cupboard. 'I'd still have come to the wedding, but I might have got a good deal more booze down my neck if I'd known . . . and maybe a few tranquillisers as a chaser.'

'Ditto.'

There's another boom or two, but – and I might be imagining things – they don't seem quite as loud and threatening now. And I'm starting to feel very interested in my companion. He's smelling, and feeling, better and better to me all the time. When I hitch around a bit and manage to stretch my legs out in the darkness, he adjusts his position beside me with his arm still around my shoulder.

During the course of a bit more rearrangement, our faces accidentally brush against each other and, without stopping to think, I go for it and navigate my mouth towards his.

Another firework goes off, but this time I couldn't care less.

Man-shape's mouth is delicious. He tastes of wine and something as sweet and spicy as he smells. I think it might be wedding cake. And then I'm sure of it when he presses his tongue into my mouth.

My nipples start to tingle and, between my legs, my clitoris throbs. I don't know whether this is fight or flight instinct, or a lingering fear of being blown to bits, but suddenly I really want Man-shape. I really, really, really want to fuck.

And he wants me too, it seems. Half dragging me against him, he acquaints me with his cock, which is as hard as steel inside the fine suiting of his trousers. As I curve my fingers around it, I wonder what he looks like. Is he one of the groomsmen? There was quite a troupe of them, and I must admit they were all pretty fanciable.

'Um, sorry about that.' As he hefts his hips to push his hard-on against my hand, he doesn't seem sorry in the slightest. 'I suppose it's my subconscious trying to take my mind off the fireworks.'

There's nothing subconscious about an erection like that, but I'm not arguing. I need something to take my mind off the fireworks too, don't I?

In an attempt to further distract himself, he starts kissing me again, really hard, but in a good way. He's got a cheeky, mobile tongue and it seems to get everywhere. Well, not everywhere, but if I play my cards right, it might get *there* too.

His hands are as naughty as his tongue and his lips and, while I'm still clinging on to his goodies, he goes after mine. I'm wearing a strapless top, and Man-shape exploits its advantages. All of a sudden, the top's around my waist, along with the saucy strapless bra that used to be beneath it.

Ooh, I'm half naked in a cupboard with an unknown man! The darkness is like a tangible force in itself and the close air stimulates my skin. My nipples are like stones when he starts drifting his fingers across them, delicately teasing.

'You feel nice, love . . . I bet you've got absolutely gorgeous breasts. Your nipples are so hard.'

It's a bizarre sort of conversation from a complete

stranger, but I like it. I'll take any compliment I can get and it's a wonderful distraction.

He cups me with one big, warm hand, rolling my nipple between his fingers and his thumb. And as he rolls, I roll too. I can't help myself. I just have to wiggle about as my pussy tingles and clenches. His cock pulses too, warm against my palm.

We've reached action stations from a standing start in the space of about a minute. I can't believe this is happening, but I'm not arguing with fate. Or a huge delicious erection like the one Man-shape has.

We kiss again, devouring each other as we touch and explore. He's quite rough with my breasts, but the more he mauls me, the more I *want* him to maul me. It's raw animal fun, with no inhibitions, no outside context.

After a few moments, he leans me back against some tumbled coats and then kisses his way down my jaw, my throat and my chest until he's mouthing where his fingers once were. His lips and his tongue are simmering hot, and I can imagine him painting the sweet cake taste over the crinkled skin of my teat. When he sucks hard, I moan out loud, grabbing at his hair. His teeth close ever so slightly, a delicate threat that makes my pussy ripple and my honey surge and flow. My posh panties are swimming and saturated.

'Mm . . .' he purrs against my breast, then sucks again, tweaking at my other teat with his warm, clever fingers.

I'm half off my head now, desire grinding low in my belly. My hips surge, blindly trying to get my crotch in his general direction so I can push it against him and get some sort of ease. He helps by surging back at me, and even though we're an ungainly heap of limbs and torsos, I manage to rock myself against some part of him, rubbing my aching pussy against a bit of his suited body.

After an indeterminate period of this tussling about, he lifts his head. I can't see his face in the blackness, but I know he's smiling. And I know that if I could see his eyes, they'd be as black as our little sanctuary, black with lust. His hand goes up my long skirt, and starts hiking it towards my waist, where the bundle of my top and bra sits. Pretty soon, everything's in a bunch around my midsection, and he's fingering my panties.

First he strokes me through the drenched silk of my gusset. He probes and presses and works at the cloth and my pubic hair until there's just the one thin delicate layer between his big square fingertip and my swollen trembling clit. I grab wildly at him as he starts to masturbate me through it.

'Oh God, oh God,' I chant as sensations gather. My pelvis is lifting, wafting about, but that doesn't put him off. He still manages to keep contact with my clit through the silk. He even gets creative. I could swear he's trying to bring me off in a figure-of-eight pattern.

I grab at him, clutching his shoulder and his hand between my legs. I don't have to direct him, because he's doing fabulously on his own, but I can't seem to control the actions of my own hands.

Of course, it doesn't take long and, before I really know it, I'm coming like a train.

My pussy clenches and lurches and boiling waves of pleasure crest in my belly. If I had a functioning brain cell, I'd take note that this is probably the best orgasm I've ever had, but as I've temporarily lost my mind, I just come and come and come.

And I've still got my pants on.

A few moments later, he says, 'All right, love?'

Sex still glowing and fluttering, I gasp, 'Hell, yes!' And with the words still barely out of my mouth, he starts kissing me again, tantalising my tongue with muscular swirls and stabs and lunges.

What a man, eh? He makes me come, takes nothing for himself yet, and still he's happy to serve up more kisses.

Eventually though, he does start to get a bit proactive. He takes my hand and draws it back to his bulging groin. Which is bulging more than ever now. In fact it feels like he's got an anaconda in there!

Time to have a proper feel, even if I can't actually see the goods. He seems to think that's a good idea and helps.

Between us we unfasten his leather belt and his trousers, and then push them and his boxer briefs down his thighs. His monster of a cock bounds when it's released, and I gasp, 'Crikey!' when I take it in my hand.

He's big and hot and hard and just how I like them. If I wasn't so desperate to get him inside me, I swear I'd get turned on by just the prospect of licking and sucking him.

Before I can stop to think, I offer, 'Would you like a blow job? After all, you brought me off without getting anything yourself.'

'What an incredibly sweet offer,' he says, a laugh in his voice. 'And I can't say I'm not tempted.' His gorgeous organ pulses in my fingers as he speaks. 'But I'd really, really like to fuck you, if that's all right?'

'Are you sure? I really don't mind.'

'Oh, all right then, I can't resist . . . Just give me a bit of a once-over with your lips and tongue first, and then we'll shag. How does that sound?'

'Like a plan.'

Surprisingly, I have no trouble orientating myself towards his penis in the darkness. I swear I could find it via heat-seeking alone. He's so hot, and so delicious, and fine and salty and a little bit sweaty and foxy too in a very good way. I flick him with my tongue and lick around beneath his glans, and then suck his knob into my mouth. He makes very raunchy, animal-like sounds in his throat as I work on him. Delightfully uninhibited, he doesn't hold back, and he growls out some purple profanities of appreciation.

After a while though, he says, 'Time out, babe! I need to fuck you now, or I'll unload into your mouth.'

It sounds incredibly crude, but somehow, in a strange way, almost poetic.

We start to wriggle around again, and in the darkness I feel him fishing in his pocket. Ever the opportunist, eh, Man-shape? Condom to hand? But then again, *I've* got some in my handbag. It is a wedding after all, and a traditional occasion to get lucky.

He rips off the foil then, taking hold of my hands in his, puts the rubber between my fingers and guides me to him. Working as a team, we roll and roll the latex down his length.

'Ready?' he murmurs when he's covered.

'Absolutely. But how are we doing to manage this?'

'Don't worry, you feel like a very flexible girl to me.' He laughs wickedly and starts to manhandle me – in the nicest possible way – into position.

We bump and grapple and tumble and wiggle, but eventually I'm on my back, knickers off, with my knees in the air, and he's between my thighs. His yummy rubber-clad cock butts at my entrance, and he reaches down and precision locates the target area. Then he pushes in, with a lurch of his hips, deep and home.

Oh great God Almighty, he feels amazing. I've never been so stretched, so filled. And the awkwardness of our position and the tension in our limbs only make the way he thrusts feel more dynamic and sweet than ever.

He pushes. He shoves. I push and shove right back at him, every action and reaction tugging and battering at my clit. My legs flail about as much as they can in the confined space and coats collapse onto us, wrapping us in a blanket of heat that only makes things feel even more crazy-sexy and frantically hot.

A tumble as mad and wild as this can't hope to last long, but who cares? Within a few moments, I'm coming again, and moaning and groaning. I sense he would have liked to have lasted longer, but he just laughs and curses madly as he comes too. His powerful hips pound me like a pneumatic drill, and as he shoots his semen inside me, he grabs my bottom and holds me nice and firmly in place.

Afterwards, we lie panting like a pair of beached hippo-potami in a mangrove swamp. We're a messy tangle of bunched clothes, sticky, sweaty limbs and coats, lots of coats. I'm almost suffocating, but gently and considerately, he digs me out of the hot stuffy bundle.

It's several minutes before we come back to earth and realise that outside the fireworks have stopped and all is quiet. I've no idea *when* they stopped, but they could probably have dropped a cruise missile on me in the last ten minutes and I wouldn't have noticed.

Suddenly, I start to feel awkward. Should I introduce myself or what? I do think I want to get out of here, because for the first time since I entered this closet, I feel claustrophobic. I start to wiggle my way back into my clothes, hauling up my bra and top, and then setting my skirt to rights. It's tricky, but by silent agreement, Man-shape helps me. The only thing neither of us can find though is my knickers.

'Look, I don't think it's a good idea for both of us to emerge together, do you? It'll look . . . um . . . suspicious.'

I sense him frowning. Have I offended him? Oh, I hope not.

'Good idea. Shall I leave first? Then rap on the door for you if the coast's clear?'

'OK...'

When the door opens, the light from the corridor dazzles me and I clap my hands over my eyes. But when I peek out from between my fingers again, blackness has descended once more.

For a minute, there's silence, and then comes a solid rap on the door.

I start to open it, then snatch it shut again, hearing laughing female voices approaching. I wait and wait in the darkness, until I can't wait any more, but then when I inch the door open a crack and peer out the corridor is empty.

No Man-shape. I think I want to cry.

Throughout the disco afterwards, I don't see any of the groomsmen. Too busy adorning the going-away car, I suppose. Blowing up the obligatory inflatable sheep and getting busy with the shaving foam. If Man-shape *is* one of them, he might be staying out of the way on purpose, not wanting an embarrassing confrontation with his hasty cupboard shag. I thought he was nicer than that, but maybe he isn't.

When the evening winds to a close, fleets of taxis have been hired to take everybody home that's going home and, feeling deflated, I line up with friends from work, and members of the families of the bride and the groom. I know

I shouldn't feel like this. It was just a bit of wedding fun, a tradition as much as the white veil and the confetti.

But just as it's my turn for a taxi and I'm about to step forwards, a hand on my arm stops me in my tracks.

'Can I give you a lift?' says a wickedly familiar voice, and I turn and there's a tall and exceptionally male figure beside me.

Oh goody, it's *the* most handsome of all the groomsmen, the one I really, really hoped it would be. But still I hesitate.

'Don't worry. I had two glasses of champagne earlier, but that's the lot. I'm safe to ride with.' But the way his eyes twinkle suggests a different kind of danger.

'Ooh, yes, in that case, I'd love one. That'd be great.'

Is it him? His voice sounds the same, but then the acoustics in the cupboard were very different.

I follow Mr Tall, Dark, Handsome and Safe to a parking area around the corner, still not sure whether he's my sex-friend from the cupboard. Even if he isn't, I'm not going to argue. He's really mighty fine.

But then, just as he opens the door of a large, dark and rather swish-looking car, I catch a glimpse of something in his top pocket, tucked in there like a handkerchief . . . and it reminds me keenly of the draught that's teasing my pussy.

He notices me noticing my knickers in his pocket and grins. He's got a rather hawkish face, but it's also dreamy in a kind of secret agent way. I really cannot believe my luck tonight.

'My name's Drew, by the way. Drew Richardson. Pleased to meet you.' As he settles into the seat beside me, he offers his hand and I have to laugh out loud.

'Pleased to meet you too. My name's Susan –'

'Susan Grey, yes, I know . . . I asked.'

His fingers are warm and, at their touch, my clit actually tingles, remembering them.

'So, Susan Grey,' he says, looking at my mouth. I can't help but lick my lips. 'Did you enjoy the fireworks?'

I'm puzzled for a moment, then I laugh again. He's a devil.

'Absolutely, Drew Richardson, absolutely. They were awesome.'

Drew Richardson gives me a wink, then releases my hand and starts the engine.

I wink back at him . . . and plan the next display.

Sometimes They Come Back

What's with the shutters? When the hell did she have those fitted?

It'd been three weeks since Richard Lacey had visited the house that he'd formerly shared with his wife Melinda, but even in that short time he could see there'd been changes. For some reason best known to herself his wife had installed heavy metal shutters on every window. Horrible black things they were, grim and bleak and ugly, making the place look like a fortified bunker in the heart of suburbia.

We'll soon see about this!

Richard frowned as he pulled into the drive. What on earth was going on? Mel had ruined the house's aspect completely – when he still owned half of it. She'd no business making drastic alterations and knocking down the value his property like that.

Staring at the dour, uninviting façade, he took a deep breath.

He wasn't here to argue. In fact quite the reverse. Trying to think positive, loving thoughts, he turned off the engine. He planned his little speech and how the scenario that accompanied it might play out. But still he felt uneasy, and it wasn't just the fucking shutters that were to blame.

Stepping out of the car, he stared around him. More shocks.

The garden, always Mel's pride and joy, was looking terrible.

Her roses were in a pathetic state, with dead blooms hanging forlornly on their stems, and ranks of sly, greasy-looking little weeds had popped up in between them. It was a pleasant evening and the twilight was golden, but a dark, unsettling miasma hung over the entire garden. Clutching his peace offering of an expensive bottle of wine and some Belgian chocolate truffles, he strode to the front door and tried to shake off the sudden heebie-jeebies.

Out of courtesy, he rang the bell. Mel was mostly in. She didn't go out much. In fact her lack of interest in social activities was one of the main reasons they'd split. Well, correction, *he'd* walked out. A grinding pang of guilt tightened his gut as he remembered her pleas for him to stay and her floods of tears. But the prospect of life with a party girl like Susan had seemed so much more exciting. As had the copious and uncomplicated sex, a relief after Mel's intense emotion and her frequent, unexplained melancholy.

No answer. Was she even in? With those hideous blinds it was impossible to tell.

Tucking his bottle and his box under his arm, he fished out his key, already feeling the bright edge wearing off his reconciliation plans. Trust Mel to be out, just when he wanted to spring the great news that he was coming back home for good.

The hall was pitch dark. Which made him realise that there were metal shutters even on the sidelights and the fanlight above the door. What the fuck was that all about? He'd get them removed as soon as he was settled back in again. They were an eyesore, not to mention depressing and unnecessary.

Pausing to switch on a lamp, Richard wrinkled his nose.

Christ, what's that smell?

A heavy, pungent fragrance hit him in the face. It was so powerful he half imagined he could see motes of it drifting in the flat air. It reminded him of the crumbling roses outside, but laced with unfamiliar spices and herbs and with something earthy and disturbing at the back of it.

He'd never smelled it before, and it was nothing like Mel's light floral cologne, or even the many polishes and cleaning products she used.

He quite liked it though. In fact he more than liked it. It had a dark and sexy kick that gave him the horn.

Which was a good thing, really. He was planning to fuck Mel anyway, to seal his return with a reunion shag. She'd be so grateful and, since Susan had turned sour on him, he was missing regular action.

He set down his gifts and walked into the lounge. It was in darkness, just like the hall. Switching on another lamp, he went to the window, but he couldn't find the controls for the blinds anywhere. How the hell did one open the bloody things?

Weaving carefully amongst the furniture, he made his way back to the hall.

What the hell is going on? And why am I so incredibly randy?

It was getting pretty serious now. He was rock hard in his jeans. God, he hoped that Mel came home soon from wherever it was she'd gone.

Upstairs, it got worse. The fragrance was stronger and he was so stiff now it was uncomfortable to walk.

At the end of the landing, the door to the master bedroom

was slightly open, and when he reached in and tried to switch on the light inside, nothing happened. Bulb out?

He padded into the room, negotiating by the glow from the hall. The unsettling floral scent was so thick here that it felt like he was struggling to walk through it, like he was wading through treacle. Flopping onto the bed, he was forced to clutch his aching, throbbing groin.

Oh Mel, oh Mel, he thought, stricken by a sudden gouge of desire for his wife. He'd treated her so badly. He hadn't valued her when he should have done. He'd do better now. He'd do everything she wanted him to.

A heavy lassitude drifted over him, and he leaned back on the bed, kicking off his shoes. Wherever she was, he'd wait for her, and be good to her when she got back. Better than he'd ever been.

Stretching out, his hand connected with something soft and flimsy and, drawing it to him, he discovered it was an item of lingerie. A camisole-type thing, he realised, holding it up in the light from the doorway. It was black, and made of silk, and encrusted with lace. Nothing like the sensible white cotton bras and knickers that Mel usually wore. The soft fabric slid through his fingers like fluid, and his cock leaped as he imagined the silk between Mel's legs. Not the delicate cloth, but the satin feel of her arousal.

Desire gripped him by the balls, sluicing through his body, choking him.

Why had he left her? He struggled to remember. He must have been insane. How could he have forgotten how sexy she was? Her perfume filled his brain. Or was it her perfume? What was happening to him? His head seemed to whirl while his cock pulsed and raged, dragging at his belly with an agonising need to fuck.

A raw pitiful sound echoed in the room and he realised it was him, groaning aloud, like a beast in pain.

He was lying on the bed, still in his coat, but, with fingers that shook as if he had a palsy, he ripped at his belt, his trousers, his zip. Opening his fly, he reached in and rummaged in his shorts. Finding his burning cock, he wrapped the cool silk around it, wishing it were Mel's fingers, or her lips, or the soft, liquid paradise between her legs.

He pumped and pumped himself, almost in tears, crying out her name, 'Mel! Mel!'

How could he have left her? She was a goddess . . . He was unworthy of her, he'd been lucky to have been allowed anywhere near her.

His hand was inept and clumsy, not like her gentle hand, the way she'd always held him. Caressed him. Pleasured him. The exotic perfume that reminded him so perfectly of her seemed to be drenching his brain and creating pictures, memories, longing, longing, longing . . .

Confused and frustrated, he felt orgasm barrelling towards him, but as he reached for it, almost clawed for it, a subtle displacement of air stopped him dead in his tracks. The shock of it held him, kept him still, denied his release.

A figure rose with utter grace from the chair in the corner of the room, strangely visible in the darkness as if he were suddenly granted special senses to see it.

'Mel?'

She was here. Walking towards him. His Mel, of whom he wasn't worthy, so familiar yet strangely, utterly different.

'Ah ha, sometimes they come back, it seems, these errant husbands.' In the strange light he saw the ghost of a wry smile on her familiar face. 'Regardless of whether you want them to or not.'

Richard tried to rise, but he'd lost all his strength. It'd been leached out of him by his lust, his remorse.

'Mel ... oh, Mel ...' he managed to gasp, staring at her as he still held his cock in his fist.

How the hell could he have forgotten she was so beautiful? He frowned, his vision blurring and shifting. For a moment, the notion that she never *had* been quite this beautiful flitted through his brain and nibbled at the edge of his consciousness. But then his perception seemed to phase again, and he acknowledged his beloved wife's supreme loveliness.

Her pale face shone in the gloom, her skin white and pearly. Her lips were like bloody rose petals, her eyes like dark stars. Black, thick and shiny, her hair cascaded lusciously to her shoulders. Had she done something with it? No, it had always been like that, hadn't it? So lustrous and so sensuous, so seductive.

And her body ... Oh, her body.

She was wearing a dark silk and lace robe that seemed to be part of the same set as the camisole with which he was rubbing his aching dick. The sleek fabric was mutable, like black liquid metal, forming to the lush contours of her breasts, her thighs, her delicately curved belly and the little mound of her pussy.

She was close, so close now, and the way she'd moved made him feel giddy as if he'd been on a merry-go-round too long. Had she walked, or had she glided somehow?

No, that was ridiculous. People didn't glide, especially his wife. And yet somehow she was here, sinking gracefully down onto the bed beside him, having traversed the room without any discernible effort.

'Mel, I'm so sorry,' he whispered. He couldn't manage

more because his cock was pounding with blood, and he felt as if there were a great weight pushing down on his chest.

'Indeed you are.'

Her voice was as quiet as his. She'd always been soft spoken. Yet the words seemed to resound against his eardrums as if she'd roared.

Reaching out, she dashed away his fingers from his cock and folded her own around it. They felt cool through the silk of the camisole.

Stark fear washed through him. A terror he didn't understand. Dear God, might she wrench his dick off as a horrific retribution?

The way her red mouth curved, promising yet cruel, seemed to suggest that she'd read his very thought.

She began to pump him, slowly and teasingly, her sultry body rocking and weaving as she did so, as if she were pleasuring herself at the same time, rubbing her sex against the mattress as she moved.

Maybe she was? Her crimson tongue flickered out like a serpent's kiss, moistening her lips as her eyes closed and she undulated her hips.

Then she let out a little gasp, as if, astonishingly, she'd come.

A thought whipped across his mind like a bullet train, yet he managed to grasp an impression of it.

Hadn't Mel always been hard to rouse, slow to climax?

Not now though. Oh, not now. She threw back her head, keening her triumph to heaven. Her perfect white throat rippled as she cried out in pleasure.

How? How?

Confused, he found himself noting, as if through a haze, that her throat wasn't quite as perfect as it had first appeared to be. There was a delicate yet pronounced red scar close to her chin, a few inches beneath her ear. It was faint, like two minute red spiderwebs, but it had the look of a fierce wound long healed.

He'd never seen it before, although they'd been married for seven years.

A moment later, she worked her shoulders, opened her eyes and focused on him.

Richard flinched. Was he imagining things or were there glittering specks of red in her pupils?

She looked down. So did he.

Good God, he'd almost forgotten that she'd got his dick in her hand.

With a little 'humph' of displeasure, she whipped the camisole from around his shaft and flung it away. But when her fingers closed on him again, they were still as cool as the silk had been. They felt delightful, sweet and soothing against his feverish, rigid heat.

He looked into her eyes again, but the red flecks were scary. He closed his own eyes, not able to face her, reluctant to think.

For a few moments, she played with him, manipulated him, flickering her cold fingertips up and down his length as if he were a flute and she was picking out a tune.

He still didn't dare open his eyes, but behind his eyelids her image danced and terrified him, all crimson pupils and wild Medusa hair.

When cold moisture hit his glans, he shouted out loud.

His eyes shot open again, and the sensation of being consumed by something cool and wet and mobile compelled him to look downwards at his dick.

Mel was sucking him, her ruby lips moving up and

down along his shaft, as her tongue plagued and tantalised him. He shouted aloud again as her teeth grazed his hardness.

And she was naked too, her robe flung away across the carpet, and her lush body curved over him, utterly graceful. Her magnificent breasts brushed his thigh, her nipples as hard as two studs of icy metal.

Oh God, she's going to bite it off!

Black fear gnawed his gut, but insanely it made his dick even harder. Her soft laughter around his flesh nearly finished him, but she did something infernal with her fingers that kept him hanging, unable to climax.

Releasing his precious member from immediate danger, she straightened up, smiling.

'It would have served you right if I had done it, darling husband,' she purred, her voice low and terribly thrilling. 'But why bite off your dick to spite my face?'

With a toss of her head, she slithered forwards and crouched over him like some beautiful but deadly spider, moving strangely.

Terror surged in his belly as she climbed on top of him and sank down.

The shock of her around him seemed to fracture his perceptions. For a few precarious moments, he grabbed at consciousness, and clarity, and realised he'd been stupefied.

His wife's slick body was cold, so cold around him. He started to soften, but then she gripped him and massaged him, and he stiffened again.

The room rocked and revolved, circling like a carousel, but he clung to the fragments of his sanity.

'Why the . . . the shutters?' he gasped, his voice rising to a squeal as she rotated her hips and jerked his erection this way and that, clasping him and milking him at the same time. 'What's going on?'

He felt like a worm, a peon, gazing up at her. She was goddess, an icon of sex, deigning to look at him, deigning to fuck him, deigning to touch him.

For a while he thought she wasn't going to answer. For a while he thought he was going to pass out or that the top of his head was going to fly off.

How in hell could he have left a woman who could do this to him? Fucking Susan had been like fucking a log of wood by comparison.

'I had an intruder, my dear. Someone broke in,' she cooed, leaning down over him, her sex never faltering in its grip and squeeze, grip and squeeze. 'And you weren't here, so I decided to take precautions.'

'I'm sorry . . . I'm so sorry,' he gasped, not sure what he felt. It was difficult to think straight with his dick plunged into a cold silky paradise.

'I believe you are, Richard.' Her voice was like honey in his ear, and her cool lips were satin against his neck, as she kissed him there. He felt her tongue pop out like a little dart and work delicately against a patch of skin as if preparing it for something. 'Do you still love me?'

The words should have been a shock, but somehow he'd been half prepared for them. And half prepared to give a fully truthful answer.

'Oh yes, Mel . . . Yes, I do!' Her lips pressed against the moistened patch of skin, right over his pulse vein, as her satiny channel rippled around him, a perfect counterpoint. 'I was stupid and cruel and thoughtless, but I won't be again. I won't be again. Believe me.'

She was licking, licking, licking, but somehow at the same time smiling. He could feel it.

'No, you won't, that's very true,' she confirmed, in a zephyr of breath against him. 'And in spite of everything, *I* still love you, Richard. Which is luckier for you than you could ever possibly know.'

Her hips rose and fell, her body, inclined over him, as supple as a contortionist's. Her mouth was open now, against his neck, her sharp teeth grazing.

Sensing his climax near, Richard tried to grab her, but somehow without even touching him she dashed his hands away. He lay stretched out on the bed like a frozen starfish, unable to move, unable to do anything but feel.

She was nipping him now, nibbling and worrying his neck, moaning at the same time, a deep and feral sound. Her vulva fluttered as she was orgasming almost continually.

Richard screamed as she bit hard into his neck, not from the pain of it but from the intensity of coming. Cold light flooded his head and his pounding loins began to empty.

The next day at work, he felt nervy, out of sorts, lacking in energy. He couldn't concentrate on his job and he could barely remember his own name.

His neck hurt and his dick felt as if it'd been through a mangle. Every time he touched it – and he touched it a lot – it tingled with pleasure as if it could remember details he'd forgotten.

He couldn't do anything without thinking of Mel, and yet he couldn't really remember what had happened with her. His brain was fuzzed apart from the remembrance of pleasure. Acute, intense, painful pleasure, the like of which he'd never realised was possible. He couldn't even recall how he'd got out of the house or whether she'd said he could return to it again.

The hours dragged. His neck throbbed and burned. The day was too hot and muggy and the sun was far too bright. All he could think of was the cool darkness of the bedroom back at home and the cool darkness of plunging his cock into his wife.

When evening fell, he left his hotel room, jumped into his car and drove home at faster than the speed limit. For some reason he wasn't sure of, it'd seemed important to wait for nightfall . . . but now, he was in a hurry. He hungered.

Tearing through the streets like a madman, he felt his spirits rise, and his cock too. Soon he would be with her. Soon they would be alone. And fucking.

But outside the house, in *his* drive, there stood another car. A sleek black beast of a car, a beautiful Aston Martin the like of which he would never be able to afford even if he lived for ever. Confusion whirled in his gut, a nausea of panic. Who was here? *Why* were they here? Why couldn't they leave him alone so he could convince the woman he loved to let him come back home for ever?

He rang the bell. He rattled the door. He rang the bell again. It seemed important to observe the courtesies now, and yet the dark churning bile of fear and jealousy overcame him. He pulled out his key and, scrabbling and scratching furiously, he finally let himself into the house.

Again the darkness. Again the overpowering scents. Rotting roses. Ancient spices. Something not quite right that nevertheless wound itself around his aching cock and seemed to caress it.

Richard dashed through the dark house, barking his shins

on furniture and cursing. He had to get to her. Where was she? Who was she with?

The savageness of his jealousy gnawed on him like a rat on a bone, and yet, dimly, he was aware that it served him right that he was feeling it. How much of this dark acidic emotion had he inflicted on Mel? She must have felt it, knowing he'd been with Susan, living with her and fucking her.

Sounds from upstairs nearly made him faint in an agony of mental pain.

It was voices. Mel's and that of a man. Low with pleasure and ragged, as if deliciously close to orgasm.

He almost flew up the stairs, more sure footed now, his anguish lending him wings.

In the bedroom, as he burst in, exactly the tableau that he'd feared assaulted his eyes.

His Mel, astride another man, her body magnificent in torn black lingerie, her eyes wild with lust and hot dark glee as she gazed down at the pale muscular form of her lover. A lean man, ripped and powerful, with long flaxen hair.

Richard froze, unable to speak or move. He could do nothing but watch in a saturation of horror and grinding despair.

Slowly, slowly, Mel undulated and rocked on the body of her paramour, her slender form hypnotic in its grace and almost glowing, fluorescent with sensuality. Slowly, slowly, she turned her head to the side and looked straight at Richard, her beautiful face a disdainful mask of passion. Her eyes still on him, she reached down, to the apex of her thighs, where she sat on the slim hips of her lover, and languidly, almost insultingly, strummed her clit.

Her lips were red, decadently stained, and her neck was

bleeding, just as Richard's had been, and just as the neck of the man beneath her was doing.

Only her blood, and her companion's, was almost black.

Confusion surged like bile in Richard's throat. What did it mean, the biting? The blood? Absurd concepts tried to present themselves to him, but his mind was so blank with shock he could not get a grip on them. Even though she was fucking another man before his very eyes, Richard wanted to go to her, but when he took a step forwards, she growled out a warning, low and ferocious.

As if turned to stone, Richard could only watch.

Mel lifted herself, and slammed down, lifted herself, and slammed down. The blond man made sounds just as unearthly as she had, his long narrow hands coming up and roving all over her body, sliding beneath the remnants of lace and silk and squeezing and fondling possessively. Richard cringed and ached as he saw those alien fingertips slide into his wife's bottom cleft and toy with her there, inducing fierce groans and shimmies of lewd ecstasy from Mel. Tears filled his eyes and streamed down his face when the lean and hungry lover reared up from the bed and latched his stained mouth onto Mel's nipple and began to suck and bite.

The unholy communion went on and on. How long could they last? How long could they torment him with their writhing and mutual pawing?

Sick with humiliation, Richard unzipped himself and took his cock in his hand. He wanted to die, but he wanted to come too. As Mel and her lover fucked and writhed and humped, he wanked himself furiously, barely even feeling any pleasure in it, just driven by a gnawing, raw compulsion.

As they roared in triumph, he sobbed and spurted on the

carpet. Staggering and falling, he curled up into a ball, unable to face the loss, the shame, the sadness.

Richard lay there for an indeterminate period, frozen, paralysed by the weight of his own shortcomings, the faults that had brought him to this misery. Who could blame Mel for taking a lover? He'd done it, and he had much less reason to than her. His anguish was so intense, he wanted to drown in it. He wanted to die.

Then, before he really realised what was happening, he was lifted up. Bodily. Like a feather's weight, like a child.

Stark terror and a strange sense of being nurtured made him keep his eyes closed. It had to be the strong-looking blond man who carried him to the bed, surely? Only a man had the muscle to lift another man.

So why did he imagine, in his fever, that it was Mel? Why did he feel scraps of lace and her sumptuous breasts pressed against him.

'Richard, open your eyes.'

It was a command, all wrapped around in the perfume of dead roses. Fearfully, he obeyed, looking upwards at two faces looking down at him. Unable to help himself, he scowled and twisted away from the blond man.

'Now, now, now, darling, don't be like that.' Mel pressed a long crimson-tipped fingernail to his brow, then his mouth, smoothing out the displeasure. 'This is Sylvester, and he's our friend . . . You'll grow to love him.'

What?

Richard shook his head, trying to clear it. Him, love a man? That was bullshit.

And yet a moment later, he succumbed, when the handsome blond touched him and began to kiss his heated skin.

Sylvester smelled of roses, and also of blood, sharp and

metallic. His long tongue was pointed like a lizard's, as it flicked his throat and his jaw, and slid momentarily into his ear. In Richard's mind it seemed to coil around his cock. Helplessly lost, he closed his eyes and slumped back against the pillows, all the while aware that Mel was working on his clothing.

Her hand slid beneath the panels of his shirt, peeling them back like wings and baring his chest. As Sylvester tongued his neck and shoulder, she pressed a fingertip to his left nipple and delicately swivelled it around, then went in hard, with an excruciating little pinch. The pain was sharp and sweet and he groaned and wriggled, breathing in the man's fragrance, which smelled identical to Mel's.

Then it was his trousers that were torn off him, and his boxers with them. His sticky cock came bounding up, aroused anew. Struggling to find his thoughts, his will, he tried to fight them, but it was hopeless. He was overwhelmed, he was their toy, just eager flesh to play with.

Eyes tightly closed, he tried to ignore the second presence on the bed, but it was impossible. He sobbed, acknowledging that they'd now changed places and it was Sylvester attending to his cock, while Mel kissed his naked chest and bit at his nipples.

Tears streamed down his face as a cold mouth took him in, and he screamed like a child as he smelled blood, dark and coppery. His consciousness wavered, then he realised it was from his chest, not down below.

Pleasure flooded through him, dark and tainted. Hands and mouths roved over his body, touching fondly, kissing, licking and biting. Tongues and teeth grazed and tasted his naked skin.

Finally, he was enveloped again. Cool, lush liquidity

around his cock, which made him whine and squirm.

Mel? Sylvester? He could no longer tell, they seemed one being, one lover, all devouring.

When sharp teeth plunged into his neck, his cock jerked and jerked again, disgorging semen. His world went white, the pleasure unbearable, his soul extinguished.

He felt odd, strange, not himself.

As Richard struggled to wake, it seemed as if his body wasn't his, but someone else's. It felt weak, empty and feverish, yet still aroused.

He couldn't seem to move, but the smell of roses made his dick leap.

'Open your eyes, Richard. Open your eyes.'

He raised his heavy lids and saw his wife, naked and entwined with her lover. Sylvester's hand was between her thighs, slowly moving. Her smile was silky, her body gleamed.

Her eyes were red.

A curtain of misdirection fell away.

'Wh – What are you?' Richard gasped, trembling in fear and sweating with horror, yet still cruelly turned on.

'Oh, I think you know, Richard, don't you? Surely it's obvious?'

'But they're not real . . . V –'

'Hush!' Her soft hand stopped his mouth, even as she writhed in obvious pleasure.

'But how?'

For several moments, she rocked and swayed, then groaned with pleasure.

A second later, she looked straight at him, cool and level.

'I had an intruder, remember?' Leaning over, watching him from the corner of her eye, she slowly licked her lover's neck, scooping up his unnatural blood with her questing tongue. 'But he came back too, and made an offer that I simply couldn't resist.'

Richard felt like weeping again. He loved Mel. He wanted her. And now this . . .

'But I love you,' he said in a small voice, his body aching.

'And I love you too, Richard. Really, I do. And so does Sylvester.'

As if to prove it, the handsome blond reached across and casually and with fingers of ice, stroked Richard's cock.

Intense pleasure speared through him and, at the same time, familiar visions from a dozen movies filled his mind.

He saw the legendary sinister European aristocrat, a familiar archetype with pointed teeth, crimson eyes and a billowing black cloak.

And beside him, his voluptuous bride, voracious, cold and beautiful.

Mel smiled, as if delighted that he finally comprehended. Her sharp white teeth appeared to sparkle and the wound in Richard's neck began to throb.

'Am I like you?'

A great peal of laughter rang out, like a tumbling bell, filling the room.

'Oh no, my sweet. You left me, remember? You don't deserve the big prize.'

Shivers, both cold and febrile, racked his body. He knew he was different, but if not like them, how had they changed him?

'You're our servant, Richard. Our toy, our food, our plaything . . .' She paused, not looking at Richard's face, but watching Sylvester's slender fingers ply his pulsing, aching flesh. Despite everything, Richard was rigid, stiff, responsive.

Despite everything, he was enthralled by the touch of another man.

'Don't you know the Dracula story, husband? Don't you realise?' Mel purred in Richard's ear while her lover pumped his cock. 'You're our Renfield, my love. Our creature. For all eternity.'

As Richard sobbed and jerked and climaxed, he felt quite happy.

Watching the Detective

Uh-oh, here we go! How many times have I heard this theme tune tonight? How many times have I pressed my hand to my heart as if I could stop it pounding fifteen to the dozen? I always get a little tingle when I hear this heavy plinkety-plunking intro. A fluttery tingle in my mid-section and a big fat horny twinge way down low, because I know I'm going to see *him* any second!

Or at least I'll see him if we don't get struck by lightning in the meantime. There's a classic Hammer Horror thunderstorm raging outside and the power's been fluctuating and even gone out momentarily once or twice. It's not all that long since we moved into this old house that my uncle Edgar left me and, frankly, it's a bit of a death-trap. The electric wiring is rudimentary in places – and the plumbing and the heating aren't much better either.

We're warm and cosy at the moment, though, in spite of the crashing thunder, the pouring rain and temperatures outside that feel more like midwinter than 23 June. Our big old bed is like the warren of some animal tonight, a sweaty sexy burrow of tangled sheets and a moth-eaten duvet, all garnished with a liberal smattering of crumbs and crisp bits from our usual television snacking.

Normally, at midnight, I'd be fast asleep, snuggled up against my honey, breathing in his familiar raunchy man-smell and probably smiling in my slumbers.

But tonight isn't a normal night. It's the Midsummer's Eve twelve-hour marathon of my all-time favourite cop show, and my boyfriend Sam and I have decided to watch the whole thing here in bed.

Well, *I'm* watching.

Sam's not the rabid fan of the show that I am, but he's an easy-going soul – bless his heart – so he indulges me in my televisual obsession. He's been passing most of his time catching up on his newspaper reading, and poring over back issues of his beloved car magazines while I worship at the shrine of The Detective.

Oh, The Detective! He's a bit like the chocolate biscuits I've been scoffing far too many of – irresistibly delicious, but detrimental in unrestrained excess. I ought to feel guilty but I couldn't give a monkey's!

It's terrible of me really.

Here I lie, ogling my god while my real sweet long-suffering bloke lies ignored beside me, making his own amusement. Not many other men would stand for such offhand treatment so amiably, so, in a spirit of fairness, and because I'm *very* turned on, I start feeling Sam up during the adverts. There's a less than brilliant episode on just now, so I decide that I can spare some of my attention in order to rub my pelvis provocatively against the man who's actually in my bed. He deserves a treat for putting up with my foibles, and pretty soon he takes notice. I've surreptitiously slipped off my panties and kicked them away down amongst the mangled covers. And when The Detective makes his big entrance, scoping out the scene of the crime, *I* notice that

Sam starts touching me and naughtily flicking my clit. I've got a sneaking feeling this is something of a sly competitive tactic on his part, to see if he can completely wrest my attention from the screen, but who cares what it is when it feels so wicked and so good. Pretty soon, I'm wriggling and pulling at him, Detective or no Detective, and Sam complies obligingly by climbing on top, slotting himself into me and starting to pump.

Mmm . . . that feels so good . . . so familiar, yet also new . . . because I'm still following the course of the investigation . . . oh, bad me!

From time to time, I grapple with my concentration, and attempt to focus on Sam, who I think the world of, and who is undeniably very cute and lovable. But, as my cunt ripples, he drifts inevitably from my consciousness. All of a sudden it's The Mighty Detective between my legs, shagging me senseless.

My Detective, oh my Detective, how can I describe thee? You're so tall and broad and handsome, with your angelic face, your naughty mouth and your bitter-chocolate eyes full of mischief and wisdom. It might actually be Sam putting his back into it between my legs, but it's *your* passionate lips that I'm kissing and *your* huge delicious dick that's surging inside me. And *your* name I moan deliriously as I come.

Oh my God, what a selfish bitch I am! The instant I've stopped fluttering and glowing and I'm back in my body again, a great weight of lip-gnawing guilt descends upon me. It's one thing to have a crush on a television character and fantasise about him during sex – but it's well out of order to let your partner know you're actually doing it at the time!

How could I do that? Isn't it bad enough that I'm subjecting Sam to twelve hours of the big guy on the television?

But my Sam is a saint and, now that's he's huffed and puffed and shot his load, he's feeling more than mellow. He just chuckles and gives me a sloppy affectionate kiss.

'I knew you were pretending I was him,' he growls, mock fierce, and beneath the covers he slaps me playfully on the thigh 'But don't worry, it was *me* you were fucking, and not Sherlock, so I'm still the winner.' Rolling over, he squeezes my bottom, and gives that a little play tap too. Well, slightly more than a tap . . . It's a second slap that stings in a mild but interesting way. 'And you can always make it up to me by giving me a nice blow job when the next lot of news comes on!'

'Um . . . OK.' I feel strangely shaken by those slaps, especially because all of a sudden they make me want to fuck again. We've never actually played spanking games but it's something I've always thought of suggesting.

A few pretty half-baked scenarios flit through my mind during the next adverts, but, after a few minutes of car insurance, teeth whiteners and Andie MacDowell's hair, it's time to commune with my glorious hero again. There's one of my very favourite episodes coming up next but a part of me *still* can't help thinking about those slaps. Sam was only fooling about, but to me they suddenly seem quite deadly serious. God knows, I deserve to be punished after my faux pas over The Great Detective's name!

As the channel ident flashes, I steal a split-second glance at Sam, but he's fast asleep already, mouth open, mad black curly hair sticking up at all angles and a tea stain down the front of his muscle vest. What a contrast to the sartorial *GQ* treat that lies ahead of me.

The story preamble begins. Some nasty perp up to no good as usual, but I'm not yet paying full attention due to

The Detective not appearing until after the credits. Then the credits begin . . . thunder rolls . . . and the room goes black!

'Fucking, fuckety fuck!' I shout, regardless of Sam's slumbers, and, like an idiot, I start stabbing buttons on the remote still in my hand. As if *that'll* restore the electricity.

And yet, against the odds, it does do something. Thunder cracks again and the lights flicker faintly but only for a second. They go out again, but, astonishingly, the television springs back to life. The screen looks slightly blue tinted, but not too badly. It's still perfectly watchable.

And the credits of my beloved cop show are still rolling.

At least it *seems* to be my cop show. My heart leaps again with bubbling excitement. It must be a special episode or something – maybe recorded just for this marathon – because the sequence of images isn't one I've ever seen before. The frames are sharp, ultra clear, almost 3D, and, as they fade from one to the other, each one of the hairs on the back of my neck seem to prickle and rise individually. And, even though it's the same familiar music, and the same graphic styling, there's only the one character featured in the montage.

It's just The Detective with no sign whatsoever of the rest of the team.

And at the end, he seems to walk towards the camera, my guy, tall and intent, dressed in an immaculate thousand-dollar suit of bluish grey. His long stride eats up the ground and, as he approaches, he just keeps on coming . . . and coming . . . and coming . . .

'Vicky Sheridan?' he enquires imperiously when he reaches me, flipping out his handcuffs from the clip at his belt.

But, before I can answer, he grabs me by the shoulder, hauls me from the bed and snaps the cuffs on me while I'm still wondering what's happening and trying to catch my breath.

What?

'You have the right to remain silent. Anything you say can and will be used against you in a court of law.' He grips my shoulder again, and propels me forwards, parroting out the Miranda as if I'm the lowest of low-life scuzz-buckets he's just apprehended. 'You have the right to speak to an attorney, and to have an attorney present during any questioning. If you cannot afford an attorney, one will be provided for you at government expense. Do you understand the rights I have just read to you? With these rights in mind, do you wish to speak to me?'

By now, he's manhandling me through a familiar door into a familiar room, and I'm so gob-smacked I don't have a breath of resistance in me.

It's the interrogation room. We're in a familiar chilly grey box with the mirror and the metal table and chairs that I've seen in scores of episodes. And it's just as soulless and intimidating in real life as it is on the television.

Real life? What the hell am I talking about 'real life' for? My heart's bouncing around as if it's on a bungee and my skin is a pointillist fresco of painful goose-bumps. This isn't real. How can I *be* here? This place is just a film set, really.

It's all got to be a dream but, despite that, I can touch and I can feel.

Especially The Detective.

He still has me by the arm and his fingers are like points of fire against my bare arm while I just stand like a lemon in the middle of this cold claustrophobic room, letting him loom over me like a dark imposing nemesis. All these months – years even – of adoring him, and now I'm too afraid to even lift my eyes and look up into his face. I just stare in awe at the shiny polished toes of his great size-thirteen shoes.

I shiver violently, but it's not just from the refrigerator cold in this oh-so-impossible room.

'Please, take a seat, Vicky,' he says, sort of all polite business and sharp sardonic mockery at the same time. With feigned courtesy he pulls out a chair and pushes me into it.

Is he playing bad cop? Or good cop? Or a bit of both?

As The Detective releases my arm, I shuffle into place. The floor is some sort of shiny institutional vinyl stuff, and my bare feet adhere to it, but far worse is the cold unforgiving metal of the chair itself. I'm reminded with a shock and a gasp that I dispensed with my knickers to fuck Sam. My post-sex stickiness almost audibly squelches against the slick surface of the seat as I inch towards the edge, trying to accommodate my still-cuffed hands behind me.

Despite the burning urge to look, I simply can't bring myself to lift my face, but I hear The Detective pull up a chair of his own and settle his large magnificent body into it.

'So, Vicky, do you know why I've brought you here?'

Oh that voice! It's like the vocal equivalent of velvet, so seductive, so smooth and so challenging. It's the same voice from the show, but somehow it's never sounded quite like this before. Never so intimate, never so sexy, despite my crush on him.

My eyes are still glued to anything but him, and my attention flits from the stark smudged surface of the functional table to the leather binder stuffed with documents that he has open before him. As I watch, he picks up a pen in his left hand and makes a small notation on a yellow legal pad. I've no idea what he's just written, but I sense it's not a plaudit for my good behaviour. All I can do is ogle those fingers, imagining, imagining . . .

'Nothing to say, Vicky?'

I'm just about to shake my head, when a huge mitt of a hand shoots out across the table and lifts my chin, forcing me to look at him.

Oh, God! Oh, God! Am I drowning? I feel as if I'm spiralling down a time tunnel, yet, at the same time, I catalogue each detail of the heartbreak-handsome face before me.

He's smiling. It's a warm wide white smile, but it's tricky. His broad but subtle face is full of secret teasing. We're playing games, I realise, and that makes me relax. My belly warms as his pink tongue suddenly peeks out and sweeps his sexy lower lip.

'Well, no . . . I don't really know what to say . . . I don't know *why* I'm here and I've no idea *how* I got here either.'

The Detective cocks his head on one side and regards me archly. I notice that, in the blue-toned room, his deep-brown eyes look redder than usual and, as I wait for him to say something, they light from within and seem to dance with ruddy sparks.

'We don't bring people here without a reason, Vicky,' he purrs, his fingertip still lifting up my chin. It's just a minuscule contact but it's as solid and secure as the handcuffs. 'This is an interrogation room, so that makes you a suspect. Are you seriously expecting me to believe that you're totally innocent of any misdemeanour?'

Guilt floods me. Heat floods me. Arousal floods me. Literally. My bare sex oozes anew against the cold cheap chair.

I've perpetrated a heinous crime. One that's deeply

shameful and reprehensible. At least it feels like it. I thought about this man, and imagined him in me, while fucking my Sam. That's just got to be on some statute book somewhere, hasn't it?

The Detective nods, and his hand slides lightly up and down the side of my face, before stilling again. He cradles my jaw, holding it delicately with just the tips of his very large fingers. 'That's better,' he observes, his thick lashes drifting down. They give him a hooded look that's deceptively sleepy-eyed and sultry. 'Now we're getting somewhere . . . Now we can negotiate a just retribution.'

It's like being hypnotised. In fact, it's possible that I *am* being hypnotised. Those beautiful eyes are like two hot coals and I can't avoid them.

'I . . . um . . . er . . . shouldn't you be sending for the DA or something?' I stammer, grasping for shreds of the reality of the show I love so much. I don't know what's happening here, but the show is where it started.

The Detective laughs, and it echoes around the grey box we're in like strange deep music. He moves in closer, rising out of his seat and leaning right over the table to get in my face, and it's as if I'm paralysed yet at the same time also in motion. Violent motion on the deepest level, as every cell in my body furiously vibrates with wild desire.

I'm making a pool of lubrication on the metal of my chair, and my nipples are like stones of lust beneath the thin cotton T-shirt.

'Oh, I don't think there's any need to involve the District Attorney's Department at this stage, is there?' He does the head-tilt thing again, ever so slightly, his eyes still locked on me, swivelling in their sockets as his face moves. 'Better to cut a deal between the two of us for now, don't you think?'

'B– but surely it's not legal or regulation or whatever . . . And where's your partner? And the captain? You can't just – just –'

'Just what?' he demands, releasing me, before spinning away like a dancer. He ends up leaning with his back to the great big mirror that covers almost half of the opposite wall. I know from the show that this is a two-way, allowing observation from another room beyond.

But who's watching us? And, if it's the captain or the DA, why hasn't anyone rushed into the room to put a stop to this completely non-regulation interview? I peer at the mirror. I suppose The Detective, with his preternatural powers, could tell me who's behind it, even if he didn't already know. But, to me, the mirror is impenetrable, reflecting only his magnificent back, his dark crisply cut hair and me, trembling behind the table in my T-shirt.

And then he does something. Something that seems to confirm that this is indeed a dream.

Still staring at me, he makes a strange elegant magician's pass with his fingers against the glass . . . and then it ripples and becomes partially transparent like a sheet of water.

The scene that it reveals makes me gasp.

Lit by the flickering illumination of what must be our own television, I'm staring into a familiar room. It's my own bedroom. The one I share with Sam. And there he is too, my tolerant easy-going boyfriend. He's propped up against the pillows, staring avidly back towards the screen. The light is poor, but I can see the flush high on his cheeks and the hot hunger in his hugely dilated eyes. Not only that, he's kicked back the mountain of covers and exposed the fact that he's touching himself, stroking his penis where it protrudes like a fat red bar beneath the hem of his grungy vest.

He licks his lips as if he's keen to see more of what he's watching.

'So, shall we continue?' The Detective pushes himself away from the mirror and returns to the table.

Prowling round to my side, he sits on the table, just next to me, unashamedly staring down the loose neckline of my T-shirt. With his left hand, he reaches casually to one side and touches a fingertip to my nipple – and I leap two inches into the air as if he's goosed it with an electrode. He laughs softly and shakes his great head, then takes a hold of the little bump of stiffened flesh.

'You're quite something, Vicky, aren't you? A real piece of work . . .' He tightens his grip and twists a little, making me gulp and moan and groan like a total slut. 'Mostly when people come into this room, they're nervous and afraid and on edge.'

He tweaks again, and my hips start moving of their own accord, rubbing my slithery sex against the chair. I find myself trying to spread my legs, and sit down harder to open myself. The Detective notes this immediately, and his moist pink tongue sweeps across his upper lip as if he relishes my helplessness.

'But you, Vicky, you're just horny, aren't you?' He grins, his teeth glinting and predatory. 'You're in the biggest trouble, but all you want – all you *really* want – is to get laid.'

Ah ha, Mr Clever Detective! You've slipped up . . . you've got it wrong . . . I don't want to get laid, as such, I realise in a sudden blinding flash. I want something else, sort of similar, but different.

His sparkling demonic eyes widen as if he's read my thoughts. Maybe he has. This is a dream, isn't it? Anything can happen . . . and he's me, isn't he, really? He's from my mind . . .

'So that's the way it is.' He pulls at my nipple. Quite hard. I wrench against the cuffs as sensation streaks from my breast to my pussy, but I can't for the life of me tell whether it's really pain or just a twisted form of pleasure. 'I *knew* I was right about you.'

Inclining sideways, he surprises me with a kiss. He presses his firm lips against mine, and then tickles them with his tongue as if asking for entrance. As I open my mouth, my glance flicks to the glass again, but the surface seems to swim, and I can't see any image but the incriminating one of us.

Is Sam still watching? Was he ever watching? To my shame, sucking on The Detective's warm mobile peppermint-scented tongue, I can't seem to care or worry about Sam's feelings for the moment.

And, for that alone, I know I must invite my fate.

I duel with The Detective's tongue. I press my body against his hand. I part my thighs, press my cunt against the chair and rock and wriggle lewdly.

The Detective laughs joyfully into my mouth as he grips the back of my head with one hand and lets the other slide from my breast down to my belly. His mighty form seems to weigh down on me as he thrusts hard and ruthlessly with his tongue and slips two fingers down between my legs – and then in between my sex lips.

A cry bubbles up from my chest, but he suppresses with his mouth and his sheer force of will. Down at my core, he rubs ferociously, working my clit. My body jerks like a fish on a line, thrashing against his caress and his presence, making the flimsy metal chair clatter and shake. I can't break free of him, but I can't see why I'd want to. All my struggling and writhing is a pure reflex action, more incitement than any kind of escape attempt.

When I come, I feel as if I'm going to choke for a moment, but still he won't free me. He subjects me to more and more tongue, and more and more fingering, without an instant of respite. My head starts to swim and I smell my sweat and my foxy juices – and his cologne, sublime and expensive.

'Naughty, naughty,' he whispers when he finally releases me. He takes out a large monogrammed handkerchief, wipes his fingers, then refolds the white square meticulously and pushes it back into his pocket. 'You just failed your endurance test, and now you really need a lesson.'

Suddenly on his feet again, he drags me to mine, then kicks away the chair. I sway precariously, my head like cotton wool from all the onslaughts on my senses. He holds me by my shoulders, his grip firm and unyielding, and I almost imagine that my feet have left the floor.

'Over you go,' he instructs me, manipulating me in space as if I were a doll made of papier-mâché or some other super-light material.

Before I can protest, I'm face down across the grimy metal table, its hard edge pressing sharply against my crotch. The room's chilly air wafts like a breeze across my labia.

It's very uncomfortable, pressed face down across the table like this, with my hands fastened so I can't adjust my position. My warm cheek is squished sideways against the unfriendly grey surface and my breasts ache where they're flattened by own weight.

I'm vulnerable. Exposed. Hugely excited. Silky fluid slides down the inside of my thigh.

I imagine The Detective's eagle eyes watching its progress. I wait for a sardonic comment but he remains tantalisingly silent. The only sound is a slight rustle from his clothing.

What the hell is he doing? I twist and strain to see him, unconsciously aware that I must not lift my head. Across the desk, I see him drop his jacket neatly over the back of his chair, and then there are faint noises like fine fabric being folded.

The bastard's rolling up his sleeves, ready for action!

It's a shock when I feel his hand slide beneath my T-shirt and touch my bottom.

'I could have you now, couldn't I?' he whispers, leaning right over me, fingertips skittering and flickering over the nervous surface of my buttocks.

I purse my lips, determined to resist him for the sheer devilment of testing our limits. I want him. I think . . . But it's different now. Lusting from afar isn't dangerous . . . and this is.

His fingers slip into the groove of my bottom, sliding downwards, delicately disturbing my slippery folds. I bite my lip, trying not to whine like a horny bitch.

'I could have you . . . but I don't think I will.'

I wait for my own wail of disappointment but it doesn't materialise. Touch is enough, touch and something more assertive.

'I know what you need, Vicky. I know what you want . . . I know what's best for a naughty girl like you.'

Slowly, with what feels suspiciously like reverence, he raises my grungy T-shirt, tucks it beneath my cuffed hands and exposes the trembling cheeks of my naked backside. He steps to my right side and places the points of his fingers on first one buttock, then the other. The whine gets away from me this time and I lift my hips to meet his touch.

'Patience, little girl, patience,' he says steadily, then begins to slowly pat my cheeks, first one, then the other, as before.

It's so measured, so detailed, so leisurely.

The pats become taps. The taps become more forceful. The forceful taps gain momentum, becoming slaps.

And they hurt!

They hurt like hell! Like fire! Like burning, biting flames!

A little bonfire that seeps and flows into my pussy.

I'm making all sorts of noise now. Grunts, whines, groans and whimpers . . . the sound of my own voice turns me on even more. There's something thrilling about being reduced to a giant hormone. A drooling, needing creature of submissive lust . . .

The Detective laughs with delight.

'Now you know,' he announces exultantly. 'Now you know what you really want and really need.' His hand stills on my right bottom cheek, squeezing lightly and making it hard for me to breathe. 'And now we need to resolve the situation.' His voice is brisk. He's still pleased with himself. And he's smiling as he turns me over, sits me on the edge of the desk and induces another groan as my reddened bottom takes my weight.

But what he does next is a total surprise.

With a grace that belies his towering height and his muscular girth, he sinks to his knees, grabs me by the thighs . . . and gives me head.

I sway, I almost topple over, but I manage to rest myself awkwardly on my elbows and my shackled wrists.

The pleasure is exquisite. His tongue is nimble beyond imagining. I shout out loud, my bare thighs clamping round his head.

Within a few heartbeats, he laps me cleverly to my climax and, as I flail about, I feel myself begin to fall . . .

'Wake up, love! You're missing your favourite episode. It's nearly finished.'

Someone's gently shaking my arm and I lurch back into consciousness. It's a bit like that horrible jolting 'stepping into a lift shaft' sensation that occasionally wakes you from a dream of suddenly falling. Flying bolt upright, I try and catch my breath.

The bedside lamp and the television are back on, and The Detective is just about to pull the old bait and switch on some crafty criminal who thinks he's very clever, but is just a microbe compared to the intellect he's up against.

He's on the case, totally focused and playing out his role, just as normal.

He's a million miles away from the demon sex fiend who just licked my cunt.

There's a funny noise and I suddenly realise that it's my teeth chattering.

A warm familiar arm comes around my shoulder and I turn to Sam, who's looking rather worried with a slight side order of guiltiness.

'Are you OK, sweetheart?' He gives me a squeeze. 'I'm sorry about not waking you up sooner, but I was dozing myself and when I opened my eyes I realised this one is nearly over.' He nods to the screen, where The Detective is leaning against the wall of the interrogation room, his arms folded and an arch slightly pitying expression on his handsome face.

The miserable perp has just this moment realised that he's been tricked.

'Don't worry, love . . . I've seen it before. I know what happens,' I find myself saying.

Sam is so sweet. I never realised that he knew what my favourite episodes were, and it was so thoughtful of him to actually worry that I was missing one.

I make a decision, reach for the remote and snap off the telly.

'What on earth are you doing?' Sam demands, but he's smiling. 'You've been looking forwards to this for weeks. Aren't you going to watch it all?'

'Nah . . . I've seen enough for tonight.' I wriggle out of his arms, touch his dear face and then push on his shoulders to encourage him to lie back on the bed. 'I promised you a blow job, didn't I?' I tug down the covers and find a pleasing erection springing eagerly from his groin.

What on earth has he been dreaming about? It couldn't be as vivid as mine, surely, but something's got him up and at the ready.

'Nice . . .' I murmur, letting my fingers walk up his thigh until they reach the cradle of his groin. He lets out a gasp as I make a circle around his cockhead. 'But what's brought this on?' I punctuate the question, by leaning forwards to give him a nice but naughty licking.

Sam puffs out his lips and starts to wriggle a little. He tosses his curly head on the pillow when I point my tongue and start to probe.

'I had this dream . . . this weird dream . . .' he pants. 'It was about you and him. . .'

When I open my eyes and glance sideways at his face, he's nodding towards the television.

A strange unease stirs in me, but it's not fair to break off from my task now, so I continue.

'You were in the interrogation room with him, and he had you handcuffed, and it all got a bit fruity.'

I pop up.

'What happened?'

'He was touching you . . . and he spanked you . . . and then he gave you head.'

The room starts to revolve a little, and I'm back there . . . cowering, ready and yearning, before my hero.

'God, it was hot,' goes on Sam, still moving uneasily against the pillows, his eyes closed, and licking his lips. 'Really horny. . . we shall have to do that spanking thing one of these days, I think . . . Would you like that?'

'Yeah, it'd be fun,' I whisper, feeling wildly turned on again but, at the same time, slightly terrified.

'Hey, don't leave me high and dry, babe!' Sam protests, reaching out towards me and pulling me back in the direction of his dick again.

I comply, and begin to suck him slowly and industriously in the lamplight, but the hairs on the back of my neck are prickling and crawling.

How can Sam have had the same dream as I did? How can he have seen what I dreamt he was seeing through the glass?

My mouth still full of my boyfriend, I can't help glancing sideways towards the television, and I nearly do him a mischief when I see the screen all aglow again.

And there, bathed in the same blue-toned eldritch radiance as before, is The Detective. He's sitting on the edge of his metal table, his suited arms crossed and a silky smirk on his broad handsome face.

What are you doing? You're not real! You're a dream! Sod off!

I close my eyes and apply myself to my delicious task, but, when I weaken a moment later, I sneak a sideways peek at the screen and find him still there and smirking. . .

And, as he reaches for his zip, his familiar eyes gleam red as coals.

The Distraction

He's back again. Distracting me. He's not doing anything he shouldn't be doing. Not at the moment. But just his presence in the room makes me flaky and unable to concentrate.

Why, oh why, does he have to work in *our* offce? Surely there's a place for him elsewhere?

But it seems not. Apparently there isn't a spare desk in the entire building other than one alongside mine here in Personnel.

So I've got the freelance IT guy who's installing the company's new computer system loitering in my personal space for the next six weeks. And it's going to be a long six weeks if he insists on hanging around, flexing his muscles, and God knows what else, right under my nose.

It's a conservative firm and a conservative office. Suits and ties for the guys, and smart skirts and blouses for us women. A good thing really for a forty-year-old bird like me. I'd look stupid in skimpy tops and jeans with a chunky figure like mine. OK, women my age do wear those kinds of outfits, but I like to preserve a sense of decorum, you know?

Not much decorum in me when I steal a glance at 'him', though. It's hot today, muggy as hell, and he's in a tight black T-shirt that clings to his pecs and abs and the muscles of his arms. I'm not a techie, so I've no idea what he's doing, but whatever it is it looks suspiciously as if he's posing at the same time.

Lounging back in his chair, he flaunts himself at me, sitting in a way that automatically draws attention to his crotch. Or is that just me who's unable *not* to look at it? To add insult to injury, or just an additional, slavering layer to temptation, he's a biker too. Which means tight leather bike jeans and heavy menacing boots with zips and buckles.

Oh, God.

Why am I letting these things get to me? He's just not my type, on top of the fact that he appears to be nearly twenty years younger than me too. I just don't do the cougar thing, but even so, I can't stop imagining him taking off his clothes. Imagining it again.

He's gym-toned and tight and he's got gilded-satin skin. In my mind that extends to every bit of him. With the magnificent exception of his cock. My picture of that is of a ruddy monster, thick and veined and hot, hot, hot.

Pretending to focus on the top of a heap of personnel files – old ones, on paper, that are going to have to be manually inputted into the new system – I picture Edward, my lust object, getting naked.

Slowly, in an insultingly leisurely tease, he stands up, turns towards me, and starts tugging the hem of his dark T-shirt out of his waistband. Tug, tug, tug, he tweaks at it until finally it's loose, and then in a smooth animal action, he peels it off.

Oh, his body is just beautiful. It's a dream but I know it's real too. Like heather honey his torso gleams and my fingers slide over the manila surface of the files, experiencing the mundane stuff as firm flesh and silky skin.

He stares at me, forcing me to look at him. But not just

his body, his handsome face too. And handsome he is, with dark-blue eyes, a tender but masculine mouth and a rakish little goatee beard that matches thick brown hair brushed straight back from his brow.

Very deliberately, he touches his own nipple, drawing attention to the single piercing there, and immediately I wonder if he's pierced anywhere else. His ocean-blue eyes glitter mischievously, as if he's heard me.

'Do you want me to show you it?'

His hands are on his heavy belt buckle, fingers tapping.

'Jane, do you want me to show you it? The new login procedure?'

I blink like a fool. He's actually leaning across in his seat, reaching to twist my keyboard towards him.

'Um . . . yes . . . please. Is it sorted now?'

A waft of some deliciously unctuous male cologne floats my way, tickling my nostrils, filling my head. And that's not all that floats. He's been sweating, but it's not bad. It's raw. It makes my mouth water, and not *just* that. A million hormones fire and it's not just the humidity that makes this place a jungle. We're like beasts responding to ancient primitive signals.

Mate. Mate. Mate.

He gives me a slick little smile, the bastard, because he knows.

For five minutes or so, we do some kind of computer dance. I barely pay any attention. I suppose my subconscious is resisting the information – in order to provide me with reasons to seek him out again.

As he pushes his chair back on his castors, and says, 'Now you do it', he's fingering his belt just the way he did in my daydream.

Oh, God!

That belt conjures all sorts of fantasies. Ones I'm not quite sure I understand. He might as well show me the computer manual. It's all arcane mystery, but I know it makes sense to him, that it's powerful.

I muck it up. I make a mess of the login and the damn thing locks me out again.

'Naughty, naughty, Jane. You weren't paying attention. I ought to smack your bottom for wasting my time.'

He laughs, every bit as naughty as he accuses me of being. But in those blue eyes, there's a deadly serious threat.

I ought to tell him not to be so cheeky. That we don't make jokes like that in this office. But I can't. I'm paralysed. Rapt. Frozen, yet burning in a column of heat, seeing myself across those leather-clad knees, my bum bare.

'Come on, Jane, let's try it again,' he says softly.

Perspiration slides between my breasts as I apply my fingers to the keyboard.

After lunch, it's even hotter.

I managed to get logged in earlier and, satisfied, Edward moved on to another terminal. I felt bereft, abandoned, insulted. Then I remembered that all the sexy stuff was purely in my mind and he probably thinks I'm just a silly old uptight middle-aged bitch.

He's back now, though, working at the desk next to mine. Not looking my way, his face placid and calm and untroubled, while I'm going crazy inside, my body wanting . . . wanting something.

Do I want him to fuck me?

Christ almighty, I shock myself even thinking the word, but I'm not quite sure that's exactly what I want.

Edward does his clever things with his keyboard and mouse. He talks on his mobile to people in other parts of the building. He hooks up a drive of some kind, loads more software.

He has absolutely no interest in me, and I'm just being stupid thinking he might ever have had any.

Boink!

I get an email.

Not so unusual, but the back of my neck prickles for some reason. It has an attachment. Again, not usual. People send me documents and forms all the time, and everything's scanned and safe, thanks to Edward having beefed up the system's security.

Still prickling, I open the mail . . . and nearly knock my bottle of water off the end of the desk.

It's an image. Made of pixels this time, not a pattern created by the deluded neurones of my sex-addled brain.

Just what I've been imagining since this morning though.

In a softly lit room, a nude woman is sprawled across the knee of a man in leather jeans. She's face down and, even though it's all in sepia, you can see that the bare rounded moons of her bottom are reddened. His face is in shadow, and his hand's on her back, fingers curved, as if he's stroking and calming her.

The buckle on his belt is an exact match for the one holding up Edward's jeans.

I glance to one side.

No response. Not a twitch. Not a smirk. Total calm and serenity. His finger curves on the dome of the mouse, as if he's stroking and calming it.

I wish someone would calm me!

I snap the email closed but its contents are seared on my

brain. I have to get out of here, away from him. He's the devil.

There's a small office at the far end of the main room. It's for interviews, privacy. Sometimes, when one of us is doing a detailed job of some kind, we go in there and work alone, in peace and silence.

'I need to go through these,' I announce to the room in general and nobody in particular. 'It's cooler in the little room . . . I think I'll go through them in there.'

After sweeping up my water bottle, my pen and a random selection of files that I've already processed, I stride up to the end of the room, heading for sanctuary.

In the little office, the air conditioning hums loudly, but works a treat. It *is* cool. I switch on the terminal there, one that Edward has already hooked up, but I don't log in. I'm not here to work.

How in God's name did he know what buttons to press with me? I don't even know myself . . .

Who was the woman?

When did he spank her? Where? For how long?

Did they fuck afterwards? Did he touch her? Did she suck him, caress his cock with her lips and tongue?

I wish I could open my email from here. I want to see that image again, assure myself it's him.

But of course I can.

Making no errors this time, I key in my password and finesse on into the system.

I open the file again and the sight that greets my eyes again makes my sex ripple.

God, that's never happened before.

Spontaneous desire.

Physical response with no stimuli but vision and

imagination. I clench the muscles of my pussy and my anus, imagining them exposed to him, across his knee, my bottom cheeks jumping from the spasm.

I slump back in my chair, my fingers tingling with energy. They want to stray to my crotch, but I'm trying to retain some semblance of control. I don't do things like this! I'm a grown-up, in command of myself. Responsible and all that.

Yet here I am, horny as a teenager, desperate to play with myself because a hot young man sent me a picture just as hot.

I spread my legs, but I'm not going to touch myself.

I shuffle down, pressing myself against the chair, but I'm not going to touch myself.

I place my hand on the stretched fabric of my skirt, over my thigh. But I'm not going to touch myself.

Feeling my heart turn over strangely, I cup my crotch . . . and the door to the little room swings slowly open.

Every muscle in my body leaps, including the ones that are connected to my clit, but as Edward slides into the room, through the narrow gap of the partially open door, he presses his fingers to his lips in a 'shush', and I subside back into the chair, completely stilled by him.

The door snicks shut, then snicks again as he turns the lock. There's only one window, but it's obscured by a flipped-down blind.

We're alone, enclosed, locked in, wrapped in silence but for the hum of the air conditioning.

Edward glances at my crotch where, I realise to my astonishment, my hand still rests. I should snatch it away, but I can't. It's as if his eyes have the power to paralyse me . . . or compel movement. Slowly, slowly, he licks his firm, sculpted lips.

'So this is what people do in this little room. I've been wondering about it since I arrived here.'

I open my mouth, but I can't speak. Instead, to my horror, my fingers start to grip, move, clasping my pussy through my skirt.

He laughs, and it's a quiet, sweet, strangely wise sound. I count the years again, those twenty or so between me and him, but he seems ancient in wisdom and experience. Like a young god, tall and strong and beautiful, and imbued with esoteric knowledge and exotic preferences.

'I would say you surprise me, Jane. But somehow, you don't. I knew immediately you were a wicked woman beneath that straight, businesslike surface.'

Glancing at the screen, he raises his dark eyebrows.

'Do you like that? I suspect you do.' In a swift, darting movement, he pulls a straight-backed chair from the corner of the room and sets it opposite to me, with the desk and the computer to one side of us. He sinks onto it, all grace, setting his booted feet four-square on the carpet, his thighs slightly parted, gleaming in their leather.

The question loosens my tongue, gives me permission to speak.

'I don't know. It's like nothing I've ever seen.'

Which is a lie, I now realise. I've seen films with hints of this in them. Documentaries. I've watched them, thinking What's wrong with these people!, and all the while I've been ignoring what's going on in my pussy.

Those beautiful midnight-blue eyes darken.

'I think you're fibbing to me, Jane. Why do you do that? Don't you realise that dishonesty is wicked?' His chin comes up, as if in triumph. He's brought the conversation around to exactly the place he wants it to be. With me cast as the wicked, misbehaving bad girl. Or bad woman, more like.

How can I let this happen?

How can I not?

'Do you want me to help you understand?' His voice is low, mellow as honey. It's as if he's controlling me – completely – with dulcet kindness.

I nod my head, unable to speak again. All of a sudden I want to weep. It's a kind of relief. An acceptance.

'Touch yourself, Jane. Through your skirt. Just squeeze a bit.'

I obey him, burning up, gasping aloud as my clasping fingers knock my clit. It's like a kind of sweet electricity stimulating a naked bundle of pleasure receptors. The tiny organ jumps, almost the way it does when I come. But it's not that yet, not quite. I'm very close though.

Just from his voice, and a squeeze, and a lot of thoughts.

'How does that feel? Are you ready to come?'

'Yes.'

I flex my fingers to grab again, work my clit, force the issue.

'Uh-oh . . . no, not yet. Not until I say so.' He rises from his chair and looms over me. I wish he'd give me permission to grovel at his feet and kiss his boots. Either that or just to keep working myself until I have an orgasm. 'We've a way to go yet, Jane. A long, long way.'

Somewhere in the corner of my mind, I wonder what my colleagues outside must be thinking. Me, in the little room, with the technical whizz-kid who wears leather and has the body of a film star. I'm supposed to have authority, keep people in order, but I'm the one who's being kept in order now.

The air in the room is cool, because of the conditioning,

but it feels as thick as pudding on my skin. It presses down, like a blanket of sex, moist and hot. Or is that just me?

I'm moist and hot between my legs. I'm like a pond. My panties are saturated.

As I shift in my chair, imagining I can hear myself squelch, Edward looks down on me, reaches out and touches my hot cheek. His fingers feel cool, gentle yet unyielding. Just like the rest of him, I suppose, feeling dreamy yet wildly, distractedly excited.

'Are you wet, Jane? Is that why you're wriggling?'

My heart thuds, my knickers get wetter. My face burns hotter, so hot I'm surprised he doesn't flinch, singed. But he just slides his fingertips under my chin, making me face him, forbidding me to hide my embarrassment. My mouth is so dry that my tongue cleaves to the roof of it.

But still those blue eyes command me. And his voice too.

'Jane, don't be stubborn. Are you wet?' His voice is still low and mild. He doesn't need to shout. He just has to *be*.

'Yes,' I admit, wondering how all this can have happened. Not half an hour ago, I was annoyed with him. Wishing him out of our office and my life. Yes, I thought he was attractive in his blatant, aggravating way, but in the grand scheme of things, that didn't seem important.

But now . . . now . . . I adore him.

It doesn't make sense.

'There, was that so hard to admit?'

What, the fact that I'm wet, or the fact that I've gradually, without my really knowing, become obsessed with this confident, beautiful man?

'Not really.'

'So what shall we do about it?' He's still touching me, the tips of his fingers against my face. I lean in to the contact and it's as if it's a signal. His hand slides down my face, my jaw, my throat . . . and dips to cup my breast through the fabric of my blouse.

'Ah!'

I can't contain myself when he strums my nipple as if it's his sovereign property.

'You're a horny, beautiful woman, Jane. You make me want to do things to you, you really do.'

He strokes and strokes, then closes his thumb and finger over the tip of my breasts and squeezes quite hard.

I groan aloud, wriggle again in my seat, pressing on my clit with my clenched hand. When my pussy flutters, I toss my head, almost beside myself on a high wave of mixed sensations. Pleasure, pain, frustration, confusion . . . sweet longing.

But what do I want? The same thing as him? As he twists my nipple lightly in his fingers, I gasp, panting in time to the delicate little tweaks. My face turns from his, and my eyes light upon the image still burning on the computer screen. The woman's naked bottom cheeks seem to pulsate, even though the picture is static. I feel her heart beating with excitement in my own chest.

'Yes, that,' confirms Edward. 'That's what I want. How about you?'

I nod. Because I do want it. Here and now. Even with a dozen folk in the room beyond wondering what the hell we're doing. Even though I scarcely know this man from Adam, and he's not my type, and he's far too young, and I don't like arrogant, domineering males . . . and a score of other reasons.

I think I'll die if I don't show him my bare bottom and he doesn't spank it.

The moment seems frozen. My gaze skitters around his face. That neat little beard of his looks masculine, yet soft. Would it tickle my thighs if he was giving me oral sex? Would I still laugh, even if he was lapping at my clit?

His slight smile widens. His blue eyes dance.

'What are you thinking about, Jane? Something naughty?' His brows are dark, lifted in amusement. I want to bite his lower lip it looks so sinful.

'Er . . . nothing. Not really.'

'Liar. Tell me. Don't keep things from me.'

Roaring blood colours my face even redder. 'I was just . . . just wondering about something.'

He makes a little 'tsk' sort of sound, impatient with me.

'I was wondering if your beard would tickle if you went down on me.'

He laughs, and it sounds so happy. As if he's pleased with me. That makes my heart lift in my chest like a bird, and it's more than sex.

'Maybe you'll find out,' he says, with a smile in his voice. 'But you'll have to earn it. You'll have to please me, in my particular way, before we get around to pleasing you.' He gives another little twist to the tip of my breast and this time it really hurts.

I bite my lip, knowing that, even though this room is partially soundproofed, if I scream with thwarted lust and desire, someone might hear it. My clit flutters again. I'm lost . . . lost.

He releases me.

'Undress, Jane. I want you naked. Just like her.'

I know he's talking about the girl in the picture, and suddenly I'm jealous. Not only because he shared a moment like this with her first, but also because she's slim and young and beautiful, and I'm not particularly any of those.

Don't get me wrong. I like myself. I'm happy with my shape and my face and I can't do anything about my age. But, right now, I'd love to be perfect and young, for him.

His hands fall away from me, and so does mine. I start unbuttoning my blouse, reluctantly aware that I've been sweating and I smell a little less than fresh. In these close quarters, he'll smell that, not to mention the pungent aromas of my sex, when I take my knickers off.

But he's commanded me to strip, and strip I will. As he returns to his seat, and sits down, crossing his long, leather-encased legs, the blouse comes off, and I lay it across the back of my chair. My white bra gleams almost fluorescent in the artificial lighting. My nipples poke through the thin cotton, dark smudges beneath it. Being shy at this stage of our journey is ridiculous, but I can't help myself. Instead of exposing my breasts to him, I reach for the zip of my skirt and whir it down. I'm awkward as I step out of my skirt and I have to hold on to the chair. My heels aren't high, but I'm not used to undressing in front of a man. It's a long, long time since I did it, and then never for a man who disturbs me and distracts me the way Edward does.

But I manage to get the skirt off and toss it on top of my blouse. I'm still dithering. I'm still embarrassed. I'm in my shoes, pants and bra in front of a man I barely know and, the worst of it, I know those pants are damp. They're cotton too, finer weave than my bra, and there's a visible dark stain at the gusset, spreading and revealing, where I've seeped for him. There's even moisture gleaming on my thighs.

I start to kick off my court shoes, and he says 'No!' quite sharply, so I leave them as they were. Lounging back in his chair, he uncrosses his legs and exposes a startling erection pushing at the leather fly of his jeans. It's phenomenal and I feel a sudden huge rush of confidence. All that? For me? I find myself standing straighter, standing prouder, almost flaunting myself. I have everything that younger woman he was with in the picture has. My body is ripe, his for the picking, and mine to enjoy and to exhibit.

Daringly, I touch my breast through my bra, and catch my breath as a dart of pleasure spears my pussy.

'Yes!' hisses Edward, through his teeth.

I stare back at him, both challenging and questioning. What do you want, my beautiful leather-trousered boy? Do your worst . . . command anything. I can take it.

I fucking well relish it!

'Turn round. Show me your arse.'

I relish the crude word too. It makes me melt inside, more juice trickling down inside my panties. I never knew I was like this, but I'm glad I've finally found out.

I turn, managing a passable dancerlike spin. Not quite sure what to do, I extemporise, teasing the elastic of my knickers down, a very little way.

'Good. Very good, Jane . . . but leave them like that. Just rolled down a little bit. Just to the crease.' I comply and he praises, 'That's beautiful!'

I can't see him now, apart from a vague, slanted reflection in the computer screen. But the creak of leather tells me he's not quite as still and calm as before.

Are you adjusting yourself inside those skin-tight jeans? Nudging that monster a bit to one side, to get some ease?

I hope so.

'Bend over. Rest your arms on the seat of the chair. Part your legs a bit. I want to see the crotch of your panties.'

Feeling the heavy stickiness between my thighs squelch,

almost hearing it, in fact, I obey his wishes. I've never felt so rude and exposed and vulnerable, and I've still got my pants mostly on. He can see how saturated I am, though. He can see how much I want him. Or even just want *something* from him, perhaps barely a touch.

Or a spank. Yes, that. Definitely that. I want to prove I can take anything *she* can.

He gets up and moves behind me, and I feel his fingertips on my lower back, drifting down to the elastic of my knickers. They hook beneath it, edging it down until it's stretched tighter across the roundest, plumpest portion of my bottom and the cleft is exposed, almost to my anus.

My breath stills in my throat when a hot fingertip slides down there, finds the little vent, and begins to stroke it. Up and down, up and down. Shame, heartbreakingly delicious, bubbles in my chest like effervescent wine and I make a weird animal noise I've never made before, all the time pushing my bottom against his finger, increasing the contact.

The torment goes on for what seems like an age, and I continue to perform for him, waving my arse around because I can't *not* wave it.

'You're a dirty, sexy woman, Jane. You must be or you wouldn't like me fingering you there so much. Admit it!'

I nod, beside myself.

'No, admit it in words.'

'I like you touching me there.'

'Where?'

'My bottom . . . the . . . the hole.'

I feel as if I'm going to faint right here, right now, but I can't stop wriggling like some kind of horny cat on heat. Lubrication is streaming out of me.

'Good girl, good girl,' he murmurs, doing it more. 'But

also . . .' He pauses, finger stilling, resting, right there.
'. . . naughty, so naughty, liking something so dirty.'

I'm beside myself, dying of shame and at the same time
soaring on a wave of dark exultation. I feel as if I've found
something I've being looking for all my life. And it's taken
this wicked, beautiful man to light the path.

'I shall have to punish you, of course.'

The words are perfect and right. I almost sigh aloud to
hear them at last, and it's so strange. Half an hour ago, I
knew nothing, but now, I have wisdom and power, despite
my temporarily subservient position.

His fingertip withdraws. 'Now then, Jane, undress for me.
Bra and panties off, but leave on the shoes.'

I obey, for once not bothered too much about the minor
imperfections of my body. A little roll of extra padding here,
a hint of a droop there. I sense that he's more than satisfied
with me.

When my sticky knickers and my bra, also damp with
nervous sweat, are dropped to one side, he takes hold of my
forearms and positions me. I'm to pose across the table, arms
among a muddle of files and keyboard and mouse and writing
implements. He pushes down on the middle of my back,
making me dish, making my bare bottom pop up, perfectly
proffered for his hand. With a booted foot he nudges apart my
feet, making my wet thighs separate and provide a lewder view.

My heart leaps in my chest when the door handle rattles.
I tense and hold my breath, waiting for a voice to call out
from beyond the door, but Edward massages my back, and
then my bottom in slow, sure circles with the flat of his warm
hand and I calm again.

After one experimental twist, the handle remains still.
There's no more rattling. God alone knows what they're

thinking out there, knowing we are in here together with the door locked. But I don't care. I don't care. I've never cared about anything less in my life.

In these strange, stolen, out-of-time moments, nothing matters on this earth but him and me.

He continues to massage for about a minute. Then he gives me a hard pat on each cheek.

Then a harder one, and a harder one, gentling me into it.

My bottom starts to sting a little, and the next few pats aren't pats but light, lazy slaps, stirring that sting.

Then he smacks me, good and proper, instigating fire.

Oh, God, it really hurts! Oh, God, it's dreadful!

But also not dreadful at all. I don't quite know what I was expecting, but this isn't it. An almost indescribable amalgam of pain to be cringed and shrunk away from, and pleasure, evanescent pleasure, sinking like hot warm honey, into my sex.

My clit throbs like a tiny star, pulsing with each slap. It's almost as if he's hitting me there, knocking the sensitive nerve bundle, even though he's nowhere near it. The impact of his hand, and of his presence, goes right through my muscle and sinew and bone.

I bite my lip, quashing my cries of pain, my moans of delight. I wiggle and weave, and he pauses in his sequence of strikes, and stills me again.

'Behave!' he purrs, then, to my astonishment, he dips down and kisses the reddened crown of each buttock.

Surely the stern master or whatever he is shouldn't do that?

But it seems he's a rule-breaker in this as everything, as badly behaved – when it comes to conformity – as I've become.

I shiver at the utterly delicious outrageousness of him

when he laves his cool tongue over the heat that he's created.

How can anything so wrong feel so right?

And then he's spanking again and it seems to hurt more because of the little gentling that went before. I rock and hitch about, my pussy dripping, and aching as much as the cheeks of my bottom do, but he never misses the target, or a beat in the relentless punishment.

When my behind feels as if it's been turned into Steak Tartare, he finally halts, his hand stilling on the heat.

'Had enough, Jane?' he whispers, inclining over me, his flanks alongside mine, leather against skin. I hiss through my teeth as the smooth hide rubs my flaming haunch.

'No!'

The catch in his breath shows I've surprised him, even though it's not more spanking I want, but something else entirely. I swivel sideways and cram my burning buttocks against him, rubbing them, hoping he'll get the message.

He does, pressing his big, beautiful, randy young man's bulge into the cleft between my buttocks. He's hard, and rude, and it bloody hurts where he presses against the spanked zones, but all the same I want to sing at feeling him there.

'So, you expect me to fuck you?' he demands archly, pressing harder.

For a moment my world falls away and I feel intense sadness. Doesn't he want me after all? Is he just playing some cruel and capricious game?

But no, even though he might be playing the arrogant bastard just a bit, his body is totally honest. It doesn't lie.

'Yes, I do actually. Is that OK with you?' I nearly add a snarl when he drags his nails across the crown of my bum.

'Completely, my lovely wicked Jane. Completely.'

All business now, he positions me yet again, kicking my

legs really wide now and getting in between them, right behind me.

I hear the chink of his belt, the purr of his zip, then tiny sounds of rummaging.

A second later he presses his cock against what feels like the reddest spot on my sizzling bottom.

'Oh yeah,' he sighs, as if the heat in my flesh is exquisite pleasure to him. Maybe it is? He rubs his cock around the war zone, going 'mm . . . mm . . .' and leaving a trail of silky pre-come on my skin. I look over my shoulder, craning hard to see the size and shape of him and the sticky marker he's leaving on me. Leaning a little to one side, he catches my eye and gives me a wink.

'Ready, babe?'

Babe? That makes me laugh, and he laughs too, chuckling to himself while he whips a suspiciously convenient condom out of his pocket and enrobes himself in it. Twisted to one side, I observe the process, loving the expression on his face as he rolls and rolls.

If I was expecting measured finesse I was sadly mistaken. With no further ado, he positions himself with his fingers and then pushes on in. I go 'Oof!' as he shoves me hard against the table and stirs the fire in my abused and reddened bottom.

But the joining is everything I'd hoped for. He powers into me, hard and hot, and slightly ruthless. Thump, thump, thump he knocks me against the hard surface beneath my belly, every impact juddering my clit and stretching me inside.

Within moments, I'm coming hard, seeing stars as I bite my own knuckle to stop me screaming. He's not far behind me, and he hisses a curse as he pumps into me.

*

Afterwards, there's not much to say.

Well, no, that's wrong. I have a thousand things to say to him but they'll all be stupid when they come out. This was just a game, a one-off, a bit of naughty behaviour to tell in my dotage as one of those mad office stories that nobody really believes. And even if there is a stupid, misguided, lonely middle-aged bit of me that wants it to be more, I know such thoughts are pointless. Edward's a stud, with notches aplenty, I'll be bound, on that leather belt of his.

Probably much better and less pathetic for all concerned if I laugh off what's just happened and chalk it down to wild experience.

When I do risk a peek at Edward his face is unreadable, but at least I'm warmed a little bit by the lack of any gloating, macho smugness. If anything, he looks thoughtful. Slightly puzzled.

As I put my fingers on the door handle, ready to brave the no doubt intensely speculating denizens of the office beyond, he opens his mouth to speak. But I forestall him.

'Look, don't say anything, will you? It was just one of those things . . . Like the song says, you know? I won't say that I'm going to forget it, but it was a one-off. A distraction. That's all.'

It all comes out in a bit of a gabble and with far too much vehemence, and Edward looks at me, his mouth compressed and rather hard.

'OK, Jane. Whatever you want. I'm not a guy to kiss and tell, so you've no need to worry.' He slides into a chair in front of the computer. 'I'll just work on this a bit. It'll look better. Less . . .' His smooth brow puckers a moment, but it's not in irritation or displeasure. I don't quite know what it is. '. . . suspicious.'

Then I can't look at him any more, and I grab the handle and dive outside.

But later, back at home, I can't stop thinking about the odd look on his face.

Did I miss an unmissable chance there? I'll never know. It's too late. I've burnt my boats. All the upgrades will be done in a few weeks, and I think I can manage to do the cordial, civil, it-never-happened dance until he's gone. Our extended sojourn in the little office might never have happened as far as everyone else is concerned. Not a single colleague seemed to have noticed. Or at least, if they did, they weren't letting on or smirking.

And now I'm here, in my robe, looking over my shoulder at my bottom. Which sadly also shows little evidence of this afternoon.

No redness. No soreness even. Just a pair of pristine rounds of slightly too plumply rounded flesh. I press with my fingers, imagining his. I give it a little slap, imagining the impact of his hand. I touch myself between my legs, imagining him touching me, then gracing me with his cock.

At least our little escapade has given me plenty of masturbation material for the months to come. Although maybe not right now. I think I need a glass of wine.

But as I'm reaching into the fridge, the doorbell rings.

And I don't know why, but my heart goes pit-a-pat.

I open the door and my jaw drops and my heart sings, both at the same time.

'Look,' he says without preamble, almost pushing me back into the hall by stepping straight over the threshold, 'I don't kiss and tell . . . but I don't do one-offs either! And if you think that's the kind of man I am, you deserve to be punished again.'

Before I can protest, he kisses me hard, his tongue in my mouth while his hand slides over my bottom, through my robe.

But who am I to argue? I don't do one-offs either, and as for the future, I'm far too distracted to give a damn!

A Lavish Affair

'So this is really quite a lavish affair then?'

Edward glances sideways at me from the driver's seat as we scud along, looking as handsome as the very devil done up in a sexy dark suit. It's quite a shock seeing him in formal wear. I'm used to him in leather, or partially – or completely – naked.

'Yes, ultra posh. Beauchamp Manor belongs to Mandy's rich relations and they've given her the reception there as a wedding gift.'

'Sounds like fun,' he says, eyes back on the road.

Fun? What does that mean? My innards tremble. I know Edward's idea of fun. And even though I like it, it's sometimes scary.

I'm still fizzing with excitement that he's agreed to be my escort. We've been involved for quite some time now, but we've never come out like this in public before. I'm a bit nervous. After all, it's not often a fairly straight woman in her forties nabs a gorgeously hot sexy master nearly half her age. And there'll be lots of people from work who'll remember him as the fit young freelance IT guy who set up our new computer system. The one they always speculated about as they wondered just who he was banging.

It was me, everyone! Average old Jane Mitchell from Human Resources. He was fucking me, and spanking me, and God knows what else . . . and he's still doing it!

I can see he's scheming. He loves to make even the simplest of dates an event.

We go out for a meal and he'll make me give him a blow job in the car park. On a trip to the movies, he'll play with me in the darkness. Out for a walk in the woods, and he'll bend me over a fallen tree trunk and thrash me long and hard with his leather belt.

And when we're at his flat or mine, he's even more imaginative.

We drive on for a few miles. It's countryside now. Wooded copses on either side of the road. I think of that tree trunk, and my pussy gets all wet and my panties sticky. I try not to smile, but my heart races and excitement bubbles even more.

'What are you smiling about?'

Ah, it seems I didn't hide my smile after all. He's noticed, and he's smiling himself in that way I know so well.

'Oh, nothing much . . .'

He gives me the swiftest of glances out of the corner of his blue eyes.

Uh-oh, I know that look too.

'Somehow, I think if this affair is as posh as you say it is, we need to have you on your best behaviour, don't we?' He pauses, scanning the road side, as if looking for something. 'I think I need to give you a little something to settle you down.'

I can't breathe. I feel faint. My heart turns over and my pussy ripples with longing.

Almost immediately, he's signalling, and we pull off the road and turn into a narrow lane. It winds away from the main drag and around a few corners then amongst some trees. When Edward finally stops the car, we're out in the wilds and invisible from the road and civilisation. He steps out and hurries round to my side, opening the door and handing me courteously out on to the rough path. He might be cruel as sin sometimes, but he does have gorgeous old-fashioned manners.

'Raise your skirt, will you?' he says conversationally, as we stand beside the car. To him it's a perfectly normal request, and it's one I've become used to myself. It still has the power to thrill me to my core though.

I'm dressed up to the nines, in high heels and a dark suit with a long, narrow skirt, rather Forties style, and glam. The jacket's tightly fitted, plunges low, and I'm not wearing a blouse. I haven't informed him what I'm wearing underneath, but it's a treat I know he'll appreciate, even if he thrashes my bottom for being so brazen.

'Come on, get a move on, you don't want us to be late, do you?' His voice is mild and amused. He's having fun. So am I.

Teetering on my heels, I put one gloved hand on the car, and with the other I snake up my skirt, not hesitating until it's all in a clump at my waist. My stockings are smoke-grey hold-ups and my panties are rose-pink lace, and a pretty lavish affair too. Deep, scalloped lace at the front, and cleverly scooped up at the back, thong-style, to leave my buttocks virtually bare. Just the way Edward likes them. The way his eyes darken as he appraises them is a dead giveaway – even though he looks as calm and cool as ever on the surface. Automatically, I turn, as I know he wants me to, and show him the plump cheeks of my bum.

'Very nice, but very pale. We need to do something about that, don't we?'

I stand, shaking, as he walks towards me. When he's so close I can feel his breath on the back of my neck, he pushes on my shoulders, making me dip over the bonnet of the car, skirt still up.

'Good. That's just right.'

My heart feels as if it's in my throat and I can barely breathe. I hear the jingle of his belt, and simultaneously think, *oh no*, and *goodie*. I'm still not sure how I can hate pain and love it at the same time. Perhaps, though, I don't? Maybe I just love him?

'OK. As it's a special occasion, you may finger your clit at the same time as I beat you.'

'Thank you, master,' I whisper, resting on my elbows, awkwardly, so I can peel off a glove. Then I reach under myself to find the hot spot, and almost come when I make contact, I'm so ready.

Edward steps away, and with no further warning, I hear the hiss of flying leather and there's an explosion of pain and heat across my bottom.

Oh God! I'm never ready for this. It's always a shock. The feeling of a stripe of agony across my flesh. Without control, I whine loudly, shuddering and shaking. Beneath my fingertip, my clitoris pulsates.

He strikes again – harder – and I bite my lip, trying to keep silent. In the all too brief hiatus before the next blow, I rub my pussy, furiously slicking at my clit.

As he hits again, I collapse against the shiny black paint, coming and crying. The waves of pleasure are so hard and wrenching that I barely notice another wallop, the last one for now.

'We'll be late,' I gasp on regaining the power of speech. I'm still gulping in air, my entire body tingling, my bottom burning. I seem to have lost the ability to move, but energy returns to me when Edward strokes my back, encouraging me like a horse-master coaxing a steady old mare into action. He's gentle, though, almost tender, and it makes my heart twist in a strange, non-sexual way.

He's a BDSM freak, but he can be kind, and very sweet.

'Come on then, love,' he says brightly. 'Let's move it, shall we?' He helps me with my skirt, brushing me down lightly, then straightens my jacket. Licking the corner of his handkerchief, he delicately tidies my eye make-up where it's run a bit from my tears. Finally, he hands me my glove. 'There! You look gorgeous, old girl.' He gives me a light, reassuring kiss on my cheek.

'And you look as if you desperately need a shag,' I answer cheekily, glancing down at his crotch. He's got a massive hard-on that's tenting his elegant trousers.

His blue eyes narrow. Threateningly, but with a twinkle. 'If it didn't mean we'd be late, I'd thrash you again for your insolence.'

My head comes up. I like to challenge him sometimes, and he likes it too. He winks at me as he opens the passenger door for me. I hiss through my teeth when I resume my seat in the car, my stripes stinging, but after that I'm quiet and full of thought as we race towards the wedding venue.

I like him. I like him probably more than I should. He's fabulous. Utterly gorgeous. A real catch, handsome as sin, a beautiful man. Tall and dark and roguish with his neat goatee beard, his brilliant eyes and his wicked, teasing smile.

He's everything I want, but I should have found him twenty years ago.

Now stop that, you silly woman. Just don't go there . . .

*

The wedding itself is charming, and takes place in an old country church, but the pews are very hard and unforgiving to my punished bottom. A fact that clearly delights Edward. His eyes glitter, and his smirk is salacious as we share a battered hymnal.

The way he looks at me makes me want to do things that one shouldn't even *think* about in church. Like kneeling the wrong way round in the pew, while everybody else praises the Lord, to give *my* lord and master an extended blow job.

I drift through the reception on a wave of heightened awareness. This whole affair should be about Mandy and her new husband, but somehow they seem distant, on the periphery of my attention. All I can think about is Edward and his hands, his mouth, his cock. Speculative glances follow us wherever we go. I can see the surprise, imagine the muttered comments. Isn't that the IT guy with Jane Mitchell? The hot one who set up the new system a while back? How come those two are here together?

You don't know that half of it, people. And if you did, you wouldn't believe it.

Edward takes every opportunity to touch me, obviously aware of the interest in us. He guides my arm as we enter the house. He touches my back as we head towards the bridal receiving line. He pats my bottom, making me gasp, as we step forward to meet Mandy and her spouse, and, preoccupied as she must be, she seems to notice what he does.

'So glad you could come, Jane, and nice to see you again, Edward.' She grins widely, accepting our congrats.

Throughout the champagne swigging and canapé nibbling, Edward keeps eyeing me, that wicked, arch look on his face. His glance keeps drifting to my frontage, and the deep V of my suit jacket, as if he's speculating about what lies beneath it.

Wouldn't you like to know, mister.

After I've adjusted my lapels a couple of times, to let him know I've noticed his interest, he suddenly takes my champagne glass from me, knocks back the half-inch in it, and grabs me by the elbow and steers me towards the open French windows that lead to the garden. One or two people watch us, including Susan Grey, who works in my office, and I think, *Yes, it's exactly what you're thinking!*

Always clever at finding a secluded spot to have his way with me, Edward directs me around the side of the house until we happen upon what seems to be an old stable block. There are no horses there now, but we find a stall that's filled with old boxes and clearly used for storage.

'Show me!' he commands.

I don't have to ask what he means, and with shaking fingers I unfasten my jacket.

'Oh, very nice,' he breathes, in genuine admiration.

I've crammed myself into a deliciously naughty and very beautiful bustier. It's all pink satin and lace and it matches my skimpy thong. The cups are next to nothing, just a bit of frothy gauze, almost transparent, and my nipples are dark and hard, poking and pointing. In Edward's direction.

He reaches for me, and them, immediately. Cupping and stroking, he rolls the sensitive crests between his thumbs and fingers, squeezing a little as he manipulates me, but not hurting.

'Just gorgeous . . .' With respect for a garment that cost a fortune, and which I would only ever buy to please him, he scoops my breasts out of the fragile cups so that they rest on top of them, flauntingly offered. Then to my astonishment, he swoops down and kisses each teat, using his tongue, licking and anointing.

When he touches me again, the faint film of saliva adds a new layer of sensitivity. I moan and work my hips as he flicks and tickles me.

In these sorts of situations, I usually have to wait for permission to touch him, but right now, I can't help myself. I grab his head, digging my fingers into his thick, shampoo-fragrant hair. When he sucks a nipple again, I groan out loud, loving the sweet tugging sensation that's echoed in my clit. Caressing his scalp, I throw my head back, almost swooning.

I love this man. It's mad but it's true.

Still sucking and toying around my teat with his tongue, he grips my bottom and stirs the flames that are simmering there. It burns hard, yet in my sex the honey flows. I shift my hips about. I can't keep still. I need him in me.

As if he's heard my plea, Edward straightens, his dark head cocked on one side, that knowing smile framed by his goatee.

'If you have it now, you'll have to pay, you know,' he says all low and serious, even though I know inside he's laughing.

'I know.' My voice is small, affectedly submissive. I'm laughing too, inside.

'OK then.' All business, he glances around, looking, I realise, for somewhere for us to fuck that won't ruin our posh wedding clothes. He nods towards an old wooden door, oaken and solid, that leads into an adjoining room. The surface is smooth and looks passably clean. I totter towards it, feeling shaky but horny as hell. Edward follows, pushing me onwards, a force of nature.

He backs me up against the wood and it's hard against my punished bottom. The stripes from his belt are fading now, but I still let out an 'oof!' of breath when he throws himself up against me and starts to kiss me as if I'm a hunk of prime filet mignon and he's a starving wolf. Worry for my make-up shoots through my mind then evaporates. It can be fixed, anything can be fixed. I've got to have him.

'Skirt!' he orders. Rocking back on his heels, he's already unfastening that devilish belt of his, then attacking his trousers and underwear to expose his cock. As I rumple up my clothing, ready and eager, I stare downwards.

And now I'm the ravening she-wolf, slavering over *his* meat.

He's prime, hard and high and reddened, his glans shining and the veins in his shaft sublimely defined. A work of art. And mine. For the moment. For a split second, I scrabble around for the itsy-bitsy little bag that's still dangling from my shoulder, but he just says, 'Leave it!' and reaches into his pocket.

So, we've both brought condoms to the occasion. I have to smile, and he nods and smiles back at me, his blue eyes suddenly beautifully young and merry.

'Great minds think alike.' I grin at my own cliché as he efficiently enrobes himself.

He gives me a despairing yet indulgent look, and then summarily grabs my thigh, lifting me and opening me while pushing aside my thong and positioning his cock at my entrance with his free hand.

No preliminaries. No niceties. No foreplay. Who needs it?

He shoves in hard, knocking me against the door and making me wince at its impact against my bottom. Throwing his weight against me, he starts to thrust, in and up, in a steady rhythm. I grab his shoulders and grunt in sync as he ploughs me.

Oh God, I'll never be able to get enough of this! The fucking and the spanking and the games – and the quieter moments too. Even as he bangs away at me relentlessly, there's a part of my consciousness hovering above us, marvelling at the sexy sight we make.

A beautiful young man, and an older woman made beautiful by the lust for life he's stirred in her. It might be another old cliché, the one about sex making you bloom, but by hell, it's surely happened to me with Edward. I feel doubly alive, full of juice, full of energy.

He thrusts and thrusts, going deep, slamming my back, my bottom and my head against the oak. I feel dizzy and it isn't only from arousal. Or from the way each plunge of his mighty penis knocks my clitoris. I hold on as if my life depends on this. Maybe it does? Orgasm barrels towards me, huge and breathtaking, and I bite my lip, keeping in a scream as it hits me full on. Everything jerks and wrenches and contracts in a delicious spasm. My heart soars even as pleasure tumbles down through me.

Climaxing, I haven't an ounce of strength left. I'm pinned to the door by Edward, and the way he holds me and powers into me with his cock. He makes a growly noise that's halfway between a laugh and groan of pleasure, and then he's coming too, his hips pounding, pounding, pounding me against the unyielding oak. The soreness in my bottom seems a million miles away.

'God Almighty,' I pant, when my brain eventually re-engages. We're sort of propped in a general tangled heap against the door, and for all his usual sang-froid, Edward seems as shell-shocked as I am.

'I couldn't have put it better myself,' he says with a broken laugh as he levers himself off me, and straightens up, pushing against our support with both hands. Still not quite with it, I watch as he whips off the condom, knots it and flings it away. Wonder what someone coming to search the boxes will think when they find a used rubber johnny in the corner of their old storeroom?

Within seconds, Edward is zipped up and immaculate again, and with a couple of swipes of his hand, his smooth brown hair is tidy too. I suspect it might take rather longer to bring my appearance to order, but when I start to fiddle with my bustier, he dashes my hands away. Before I can draw breath he gives my nipples a squeeze or two.

'What a shame to have to cover these. They're so pinchable.' The squeezes turn to little nips, and even though I've just come like an express train, my body starts to be aroused again. It's always like that with him. I'm virtually always ready. 'Wish we had some clamps with us. I'd love to parade you about in front of all these posh folk with your tits on show and clamps dangling from your nipples.'

The way he's touching me, and what he says, make me feel faint. Because I can imagine it so clearly, almost feel it. All eyes on me and my bare breasts, adorned for his pleasure. It'd be shaming, but at the same time I'd feel proud. Like a prize, a barbarian slave girl . . . well, slave woman . . . all captured and tamed by my hot young warrior.

Still playing around with me, he kisses me again, hard and possessive. Where his pelvis is pressed against me, dear God, he's hard again. What is it with us two today? Is it the wedding, a traditional celebration of fertility and sensuality? Is it getting to us and making us extra horny?

Pulling away again, he laughs and reaches for the buttons of my jacket, fastening them up while my breasts are still uncovered beneath, resting on the flimsy cups of the bustier. The sensation of the jacket's satin lining sliding against my sensitised nipples is breathtaking, and I gasp as I move to try and set my skirt to rights.

As if he's loath to cover up my pussy too, Edward reaches down and gives me a rough fondle there, before unfolding the bundle of my skirt and sliding it down over my thighs and my stockings. With a wicked wink, he licks his fingers, savouring my taste.

'Well, I doubt if there's anything as delicious as that at the buffet, but shall we mosey on back inside and see what's on offer?' He smacks his lips wickedly, and gives my crotch a last quick squeeze through the cloth of my skirt.

'I'm going to have to tidy myself up first.' I try and comb my hair with my fingers, even though I know it'll take more than that, and a better mirror than the tiny one I have in my handbag. 'I must look as if I've been dragged backwards through a bush.'

Cocking his dark head on one side, he gives me a strange complex smile, and brushes his fingers lightly against my face. 'You look fabulous. Bloody amazing. And if I didn't think I was depriving you of all the festivities, love, I'd have your skirt up again and fuck you again right now.' The smile widens, becomes salacious. 'Maybe up the arse this time, for variety. Would you like that?'

Desire grinds in my pussy. Dark, twisted desire. The sort that blooms from pain, and strangeness, and intense sensations that dwell in the confused hinterland of dis-comfort and perverted pleasure.

Oh God, I really want that. I really do.

'Would you like that?' he persists, his blue eyes dark and stormy, vaguely satanic.

'Yes ...'

'Yes, what?'

'Yes, master ...' My voice is tiny. I feel light as air, as if I could fall over. But as if he's more attuned to me than I am to myself, Edward holds me by the arm and keeps me upright.

Leaning in to whisper in my ear, he says, 'Very well then, slave. I'm going to have your arse before we leave here, I promise you that.'

Luscious fear chokes me, and between my legs I feel a new rush of liquid. 'But . . . um . . . won't we need lube?'

'Never you worry, dirty girl. Don't you know by now that I'm always prepared?' He squeezes my bottom, and stirs the fire of my earlier punishment again. 'Now let's go.' He pushes me forward, towards the outside, still cupping my buttocks.

I complain, even though I like it, how I like it.

It's later and we've circulated, we've eaten, and I've drunk some more. Edward is a god over this. After a couple of glasses of champers, he's switched to mineral water with a twist of lime. I don't know whether it's simply his responsible driver ethic, or that he prefers to keep a clear head for our little games. I suspect it's a bit of both, but I'm not complaining. I've had more champagne and I'm feeling frisky and crazy and horny, and generally pretty fabulous.

People look at us. They look at us a lot. I still think they wonder what that old bird is doing with the gorgeous young hunk, but I don't care any more. I pretty much stopped caring altogether very soon after Edward and I started seeing each other. And fucking each other. And doing all the other things we do together. Apart from the fact that his face is smooth and unlined, and his body is like a male supermodel's, he doesn't seem like a younger man to me. He's in charge. He's authority personified. He knows the world.

There's a very impressive and disproportionately loud firework display going on now, and people are filtering outside to watch it. Edward winks at me, takes my glass from my hand and leads me out into the hall.

Oh. Game on. Desire charges through my veins and races to my pussy. He nods towards the stairs and urges me up them, touching my bottom as we go up. Just the simple contact makes me want to clutch myself, I'm so turned on. I can barely believe it.

He scans the landing, and we turn right along a corridor. Ahead of us, we see one of the groomsmen, a tall, fit individual I might have yearned for if I'd never met Edward. What the hell is he up to? All of a sudden, he opens a door that seems to lead to a cupboard of some kind, then slips inside, with a secret smile upon his face.

Edward gives me a secret smile of his own. 'Come on,' he says, 'let's find a cupboard of our own, eh?'

This is a rambling house, and exploring more corridors and a staircase brings us to a door that's slightly ajar. Confidently pushing it open, Edward steps inside then beckons me to follow.

It's an old study, someone's private retreat. Small and cluttered, and a bit dusty, it's still cosy in its own way. There are books around the walls, and a couple of old leather armchairs that nearly fill the space. On a sideboard, there's a candelabra, set with fresh, never-lit candles. As I step forward into the room, Edward crosses behind me to turn the key in the lock. I spin around and his eyes are narrowed yet glinting as he runs his gaze over my body.

If I wasn't already primed, I would be now. The way he looks at me seems to own me, and I love that. His scrutiny lingers over my breasts, and my crotch, and when he tips his head, it's an unspoken indication that I should turn around and show him more.

'That arse of yours, love. I'll never get tired of it, you know. Never ever.' There's such honesty in his voice, real enthusiasm. He loves to play the master, but he doesn't fool about with feigning disinterest and aloofness. He never hides the fact he's really into it. 'Come on, show me the goods, you sexy creature.'

Craning to look at him over my shoulder, I ease up my slim skirt, the glide of the silk lining a subtle caress and also a lick of simmering heat over my bottom. The places where he hit me earlier have settled now, but there's still heightened sensitivity and subtle fire there.

'Lean over. Put your hands on the chair arms, and brace yourself.'

I obey him, my heart fluttering. God, I love to show myself to him in this kind of blatant and faux demeaning way. It doesn't actually demean me – it's really the opposite – but the sense of theatre in it excites me as well as him.

He comes over to stand behind me, and nudges my heels apart with the toe of his polished dress shoe. As my thighs separate, I feel the sticky folds of my sex part as well. My thong is sodden, has been for hours, and the odour of my arousal seems to fill the room.

In an action of ownership, Edward thrusts two fingers into my sex. 'Always ready . . . I love that. I love that you're so horny, sweetheart.'

Only for you . . . only for you . . .

I bear down on the intrusion. I love it that I'm so horny too. I love that this beautiful young man has come into my life and switched everything on to full power that was only ticking over before. Right now, I don't care that it's probably only a temporary situation. Knowing Edward – and yes, loving him too – has given me the gift of being able to live for the day, for the moment.

'Oh, you like that, don't you?' he whispers, leaning over me, the smooth cloth of his jacket sliding over my bottom. With his breath whispering against the back of my neck, he parts his two fingers to stretch me. My pussy ripples around them and my clit swells and pulses.

'Answer me,' he growls softly, flexing his fingers even more and making me gasp and moan in my throat.

'I like it.' I force out the words as he tests me, pushing me and making me rise on my toes.

'And would you like it if I put something else inside you?' Push, push, push . . .

'Yes. Anything,' I answer boldly.

'And how about in your arse? The same?'

'Yes . . . the same . . . in my arse.' With his free hand he slips a finger under the ribbon that bisects my buttocks and flicks lightly at my anus, syncopating the touches with the thrust of his fingers inside me.

I can hardly breathe. I can hardly think. I can only anticipate, and feel intoxicated by luscious sexual anxiety.

'Good girl . . . good girl . . .' He continues to fondle me and plague me. I want to tell him to get on with it, to do his worst. But he'll do things in his time. He's in charge. He always will be.

And yet I can't stop myself from moving, hitching about, tensing and stretching. This pose is killing the backs of my legs, but in my ever-gathering anticipation I barely notice the discomfort. It's like being a mechanism that tightens, tightens, tightens, ready to discharge its energy in a huge, frightening burst.

'Be careful, slave,' he warns softly, still working me. The

words are stern, but there's that softer, more tender note again.

That's what makes me come. It's too much. Too sweet. Too great a pleasure. Unable to contain or control myself, I pitch forward in the chair, face first into the cushions, resting on one elbow while with the other I reach down disobediently and press on my pulsing clit to sweeten the moment. My hand jostles Edward's where it's down between my legs.

He doesn't reprimand me, or go all 'master' on me. He just works with me, through the furore, making things better for me with his clever, loving fingers.

'Well, that didn't work out quite how I planned,' he says at length.

I'm sort of in a heap in the chair, crumpling my posh suit and ruining my make-up yet again by burying my face in the cushions. I feel a bit teary and I'm hiding it from him, although I suspect he can probably tell. He's perched on the chair arm beside me, and he's stroking my dishevelled hair slowly.

'Sorry.'

'Don't be, baby . . .' His hand pauses, and he tucks a few thick wayward strands of hair behind my ears. Lord knows what's happened to the hairdo that cost me a fortune. I must look like a well-dressed bag lady by now. 'I like to see you having fun. I like to feel it.'

I roll over, trying to sit straight and adjust my skirt to make myself halfway decent, but he stops me. Quite gently, but he still prevents me from covering myself up.

'No, don't hide it yet.' His blue eyes gleam. 'When I said things didn't quite turn out how I planned, that doesn't mean I've given up altogether.'

Oh, there's that delicious thread in his voice again.

Command. Confidence. Control. Even though I've come so much already today, I start to want again. Want him. Want ... want whatever. With him. I risk a slight smile, then unfold myself from the chair, and assume the position again. In readiness.

'Good God,' he breathes, 'You are a very special woman.' For a moment, he's quiet and awestruck, and then it's like a cloak of power falls back over him and he's all business again. All sex.

'And you have a very special arse too,' he observes, beginning to fondle me there again. 'A very fine arse. An arse that should have things done to it.' He pats and plays around the little vent between my buttocks for a moment, and then pauses and reaches into the inside pocket of his suit jacket. A second later I feel something cool and slippery being poured between my bottom cheeks, saturating the string of my thong.

'Oh, so that's what you mean by coming prepared,' I snip at him, forgetting my role, but he just laughs and continues to lube me.

Oh, it's exciting. This feeling. The wondering. The waiting. We've played like this often enough before, but somehow my brain seems to forget how it's going to feel, how it's going to go. It's always new. Always a cause for apprehension and longing in equal parts. And it always makes me moan, and gasp and pant.

'Steady,' he whispers, firm yet sensitive to my chaos. He slides his sticky hand up beneath my bunched skirt and rubs the small of my back like a trainer calming a skittish horse, then, still rubbing, he reaches away.

A second later, I realise what he was reaching for. There's firm pressure on my anus, something quite narrow but unforgiving, not a part of Edward.

The absolute devil! He's pushing one of the unused candles into my bottom!

Everything surges inside me. Messages along my nerves, pumping hormones and juice, feelings, sensations. I gasp harder, fight for control as he penetrates my rear with the candle.

I hate it. I love it. I can't bear it. I want more.

And all the time he murmurs, 'Steady, steady . . .' to calm my struggles.

He inserts it just an inch or two, not a long way, and just leaves it there. My crazed innards don't know what they want to do. My pussy is awash, slick and flowing, my own lubrication, rather than the artificial kind, streaming down the insides of my thighs and wetting the tops of my hold-up stockings.

With the candle still inside me, he starts to play. Both with me and with himself. I hear the smooth whir of his zip and I know he's got his cock out, even though my eyes are tight shut to help me cope with the overloading of my senses.

He fingers my clit. He pushes a digit inside my vagina. He gives my bare bottom one or two lazy slaps, stirring the heat there. Quite at his leisure, he alternates these various attentions, although he returns most frequently to my clitoris, fondling and petting it.

I'm sobbing now, at my wit's end, but happy with it. The sob sharpens to a wail as he pinches my clit lightly and compels me to come, setting the candle bobbing in and out as my pussy clenches.

With difficulty, I hold my position. I barely know what I'm doing apart from being rocked on waves of dark sweet pleasure. As if from a great distance, I hear the small distinctive sounds of a condom being unwrapped, and a second or two later, I feel the brush of his latex-covered cock against the under-hang of my bottom.

'Decisions, decisions.' His voice is sweet with humour, deliciously devilish. 'Cunt? Arse? Cunt? Arse?' It's like he's a boy choosing a hand for that hidden marble. And then he ends the debate, makes his choice, and I feel the candle slide out of me. Then I hear it hit the carpet as he flings it away.

More pressure on the tender, resisting hole. And this time the intrusion is bigger. *Much* bigger than a candle. He pushes in and my senses riot again; dangerous, forbidden, transgressive messages fly about inside me. But as he forges on, he's still gentling and soothing me with soft words, soft caresses. He holds me steady and rubs my clit as he starts to thrust.

I'm not soft though. I shout and blaspheme, out of my mind with pleasure. I buck about, collapsing again, grabbing at his hand, holding it between my legs, forcing him to fondle me and pleasure my clitoris, and to go on and on doing it as I come wildly, my entire lower body pulsing and clamping and rippling in furious, kinetic movement.

He holds on. He fights for control. But eventually loses it too. His voice is hoarse and passionate as he pumps and climaxes in my bottom. His words are twisted, but I understand them, and my joy is doubled.

A while later, we stagger out of the little study and manage to find a bathroom that doesn't have a queue of waiting guests. Even though they're all filtering back in from the firework display now, heading for the main ballroom and the disco.

We tidy up. We calm down. We exchange hugs and smiles like an entirely normal couple. Maybe we are a normal couple, for all our quirks and our disparate ages? In the aftermath of stormy passion, all is tranquil, all is easy. It's as if we've been together decades, comfortable yet still adoring.

The music's good and we dance, bopping about with the best of them. People seem to have got used to us as an item. Smiles abound. When the slow tunes come along, we drift into each other's arms, to smooch.

'So, weddings,' whispers Edward in my ear after a song or two. 'Big, lavish affairs . . . or small, intimate registry once jobs with a few folk round the pub afterwards?'

I almost freeze on the dance floor, but he buoys me up, keeping me moving to the rhythm, strong and unwavering.

Am I imagining things? Is he asking what I think he's asking?

'Are you asking what I think you're asking?' I didn't mean the words to come out loud but they have.

'Yep,' he says, his hand on the small of my back, gentling me as he did before when he was doing wicked, naughty things to my bottom. 'I'm asking.'

I should weigh things up, think things through, consider this carefully, but instead I just say, 'Yes!'

'Brilliant!' he answers, then kisses me, long and sweet and hard.

When we break apart he smiles and asks again, 'So, small affair or big and lavish?'

I laugh and kiss his cheek. I don't care which, but I answer, 'Lavish!' in his ear.

'Good girl,' he whispers, and moving closer, we slow-dance on . . .

It's Got to Be Perfect

How to Seduce Yourself! Indulge in a Night of Total Fantasy with your Dream Guy!

Yeah, right. Like that would work.

But then again, what else was there to do? Slob on the settee in her sweats, watching reality TV?

Might as well do the self-indulgence thing, and not let the fact that she'd just been dumped bring her down.

Right. First things first. A good old-fashioned long, luxuriating perfumed bath.

Bit of a cliché, but who cared, it was still sexy.

Lucy tipped her best bottle of bath essence under the hot tap and kept it tipped. So what if she used the whole lot? It was her bath essence and her money she'd spent on it.

Dense white bubbles surged up immediately, and the surface of the tub looked as if a washing-up-liquid tanker had been dumped into a cyclone. The pungent scent of roses and exotic spices surged up too, a wall of fragrance that made her feel light-headed.

Tonight was a private festival of indulgence. Excess was everything. No scrimping. No half measures. No holding back.

In the words of the advertisement, she was worth it.

Shucking off her old dressing gown, she bundled it into the cupboard out of sight, out of mind. No threadbare velour with cocoa stains tonight!

Naked, she padded over to the mirror to check out her bod.

Not perfect, but not bad either. Much better than that slag Linda. Simon had no taste. The man was a moron and Lucy didn't know why she'd ever even bothered with him.

That 'summer tan' body lotion was really working for her now, and – joy of joys – she'd lost a few pounds. None of which had gone from her breasts, thank God. There was still a couple of nice handfuls there, and she was going to fantasise about a worthwhile guy fondling them tonight. Some delicious hunk cupping and squeezing and caressing her, his hands tanned and strong, not pasty and slightly hairy like Simon's.

Mm . . . who to choose?

Not too much of a debate, really. She had a huge crush on the big, gorgeous detective guy from her favourite cop show.

Right, Mr Tall and Yummy Detective . . . it's your lucky night, you're my Dream Guy of Total Perfect Fantasy!

And he did have lovely hands. Large, elegant, and prone to evocative gestures. She could well imagine fingertips like that being accurate and sensitive. Perfect for her needs. Hugging herself, she imagined them gliding all over her body, floating over her belly, into the creases of her groin, and up the insides of her thighs.

Oh yeah . . .

Not yet, idiot. It'll be much better if you save it for later.

Bunching her hands to keep from touching herself, she blew her imaginary suitor a kiss, then looked around, ticking items off her erotic nirvana checklist.

Bath, full of hot, silky water, topped with a thick mat of perfumed suds. Tick.

Tea lights arranged around the room in little porcelain holders, each imparting a sexy flickering radiance. Tick.

Champagne in the glass cooler on the shelf, within easy reach of the bath. The best she could afford, with more in the fridge for later if she wanted to get really wasted but in a classier way than usual. Tick.

A big bottle of her fragrance, silk and buttermilk body lotion, and a very posh moisturiser full of exotic rejuvenators for her face. Tick.

And instead of her hidden dressing gown, a set of La Perla lingerie and a sexy silk wrap. Ivory satin, very tasteful, not red or black like that slapper Linda would wear. Tick.

Soft music played in the background from her little hi-fi. A bit of Mozart. She was partial to Wolfgang Amadeus. She'd dismissed Barry White and Marvin Gaye in favour of the piano, light and floating, also very tasteful.

Time to begin the first stage. Lucy poured herself a glass of champers to get things started, and it fizzed and fluffed in the narrow crystal flute. Her best glassware, of course, not her everyday stuff from Tesco.

Gingerly, because the bath was over-filled, she slid into the water. There was just an inch of clearance between the foam top and the bath rim, so luckily it didn't whoosh over and slop onto the floor. But as she pushed her toes down to the bottom end of the bath, Lucy frowned.

The taps. Bugger. They reminded her . . .

An extraneous, non-perfect, non-romantic, non-erotic, non-self-indulgent thought plopped into her head and sat there like a dollop of mud.

When the hell are you coming to fix the pipe under the sink, you git?

Her landlord had been promising to mend a dripping leak under the kitchen sink for weeks. And weeks. She'd endured several cajoling assurances on the phone that he'd be here 'tomorrow', but so far he and his tools were a no-show.

Bastard! Fuck! Plonker!

And now her mind was filled with that scruffy creep when she should be focusing on her gorgeous detective. Her landlord was a clod, and the most ill-kempt creature she'd ever met. She'd never seen him yet in jeans or T-shirts that weren't streaked with paint or full of holes in dodgy places. He always seemed to be in the midst of some protracted DIY or renovation project or other. And yet he couldn't get his arse up to the flat of a prompt-paying tenant and do a simple plumbing job!

Dickhead!

Reaching for her champagne, she closed her eyes and concentrated on the act of drinking. Anything to banish her grungy landlord from her mind and get back to her fantasies.

It was superb. Creamy, biscuity, redolent with fruit yet fine and sophisticated.

I should drink this all the time.

Rolling the fabulous fluid over her tongue, Lucy promised herself that even when she wasn't planning a fantasy self-seduction evening, she'd drink more champagne, and other good stuff, and less of the sweet, cheap Italian plonk she tended to swig down in front of the telly.

The sort of thing her landlord would probably bring if he was seducing a lady. Or a 'bird', as he'd probably call her.

No, get out, you! Fuck off! I don't want you in my head!

Swigging down more champagne without respect for its

quality, Lucy sneezed as the bubbles went up her nose and the water level rocked dangerously.

But as it settled again, it started to have the desired effect. There was a sensation of golden effervescence as if the champagne were actually in her bloodstream and fizzing around her body, banishing all unwanted thoughts and restoring the integrity of her fantasy. Her lover-detective loomed large, sophisticated and refined in the centre of her dreamscape, making her skin tingle beneath the water and electricity flow to her sex and the tips of her breasts.

She drank more bubbly, rocking beneath the foam, aching with need for him.

Her pussy throbbed, and called like a siren to her fingers. *Not yet. Make yourself wait. Wind up the tension a bit.*

Setting aside her glass, Lucy moaned. It was useless. She was so turned on. Waiting was agony.

With her eyes closed again, she let her imagination soar.

The door would fly back, and her 'lover' would stand there in the doorway, utterly magnificent. His body was an arc of dominance in his thousand-dollar suit and his tanned skin and his white teeth gleamed as he smiled at her. Dark and sultry, his eyes had the power to see straight through the scented lather to her body.

Ooh, he was magnificent. A prince of charisma. Utterly male. And when he came to her, she was a princess, and he'd treat her like one. Lavishing complete attention on her, superb lovemaking . . . and rampant orgasms.

'Oh God, yes . . .' she breathed, clenching her inner muscles, trying to believe she was clenching down on *him*. His cock . . . his fingers . . .

He'd think nothing of reaching into the water and drenching his designer jacket, just to play with her because *she* wanted him to. He'd find her clit without any hint of guidance.

Rolling her head against the folded-up towel she'd placed behind her neck, she submerged. Not into the water, but deep into the fantasy.

Her lover whipped off his jacket, rolled up his sleeves, and immersed his strong right arm beneath the foam. His fingertips settled against her breast, stroking lightly in a circle around her areola, flicking against the puckered little crest then alighting on the very tip of her nipple and rocking it gently. The caress was so slight, so delicate, yet somehow also huge. Raw lust fired her senses, making her gasp.

'Oh please . . . oh please . . .' she chanted, knowing she was his, and that he could do whatever he wanted with her.

Riding the silky water, his fingers slipped to her other breast. Their touch was tantalising, barely perceptible, light and frustrating. She began to thrash again and lather slipped and slopped and surged.

'Please . . .' she breathed.

In her mind's eye she saw his eyes, as dark and compelling as they were on the television, but ten times as fiery.

Tell me what you want, he commanded silently. *Tell me, out loud, no holding back.*

'I want you to touch me . . . I want you to touch my clit. I want to come.'

The ghost of a smile warmed his handsome face, adding humanity to its idealised perfection. His fingertips withdrew from her breast and she thought for a moment he might tease her, deny her the pleasure. But why would he? He was perfect . . .

She frowned, losing her grip.

A cold shudder rushed through her, along with a sense of dislocation and uncertainty. This was all silly. A bit sad and pathetic.

No! No! No!

Centring herself, she sipped more champagne. And caught the thread again.

Easing herself down a little way beneath the water, she opened her legs wider.

Immediately, *his* hand found its clever way to exactly where she needed it to be.

Deft fingertips parted her pubic hair, and far, far back in the reaches of her mind, she made a note to wax next time. She imagined herself bare down there, with a neat, smooth-skinned cleft.

Even more perfect for the perfect seductive man.

But in this fantasy, tonight's fantasy, he played with her curls, neatly dividing them and slipping in to discover her clit. Then he settled upon it, just as delicately and ethereally as he'd stroked her nipples.

'Slowly, slowly, not too soon . . .'

Who was she talking to? To her lover . . . or to herself?

But he was clever and he maintained a perfect pace.

Circling, circling . . . gathering up the wetness within the wetness and anointing her with it. His touch was nurturing, but had authority. He was her master.

Lucy wriggled her bottom against the base of the bath, massaging her own nether cheeks as her lover massaged her clitoris.

Her imagined lover.

But the scented air and the champagne made him real to her, not just a fantasy. Everything was perfect, and idealised, just like him.

She pictured his face, his body, his arm in the water, his hand between her legs.

She felt his finger, rubbing her clit, and she came.

The delicious pulses of pleasure were overwhelming. She surged uncontrollably, rocking the mass of perfumed water and sending it over the edge as she soared on a bright, sweet wave. The bath mat suffered, but she didn't care, she only writhed and gasped and climaxed.

Oh lover, you're incredible. You're the man.

But as the orgasm faded, then came the anti-climax. The anti-orgasm. A sense of deflation and the wrench of loneliness and disappointment.

Lucy sat up in the water. She shook her head, flinging off dark thoughts. Bollocks to all that, the night was young. She could still have more fun.

The water was starting to cool now, but while it was still comfortable, she took another hefty swig from her champagne glass, then started to soap herself with a natural sponge and expensive soap. And while she did so, she imagined again that it was the detective washing her, his hands just as deft as when he'd played with her clit.

She was just getting into it again when her stomach rumbled.

Time to satisfy another appetite. There was a mouth-watering platter of gourmet cheese and biscuits with fruit and olives waiting for her. Everything was the best, from the supermarket's finest range. Primo products to match the perfect primo fantasy.

Pausing every moment or two to take a sip of champers, Lucy worked her way through her beautification routine, primping and creaming and fluffing and teasing. By the time she was done, she was feeling slightly tipsy.

Crikey, I'm going to be pissed at this rate!

But what did it matter if she felt loose and freeform? Losing her inhibitions was good for her fantasies.

Right on the point of stepping into her new pair of beautiful but scandalously expensive panties, Lucy stopped dead.

What the hell was that banging noise? A heavy repeated thumping. She scowled and let fly a fruity oath.

There was someone at the door. Someone who didn't have to buzz up to be let in the building.

Oh no!

There were only four flats in the house. The tenants of two of them were away and the third flat was being renovated. Which only left . . . sigh . . .

Her fucking idiot clod of a landlord!

For a fifth of a second she considered ignoring him, but he'd be able to hear her Mozart playing throughout the flat. Bugger!

Abandoning her posh panties, she dragged her scraggly old dressing gown out of the cupboard and bundled herself into it again, belting it up tight. Too tight. She felt as if the sash were cutting her in two, and all her golden champagne-glow mellowness rapidly dissipated.

She was stone-cold sober again, her fantasy in rags.

Shoving her feet into her equally ratty old mules, she hesitated.

I could still ignore him. For all he knows, I really do *have a man in here.*

But as the rapping on the door came again, it was obvious he wasn't going to go away until he got an answer, the stupid donkey.

She stamped to the door, teeth gritted, and even as she

reached it, the panels rattled under another fusillade of blows.

'All right! All right! Keep your hair on!'

Wildly, she swung the door open, making it bounce on its hinges.

Steve, her landlord, grinned at her across the threshold. He was leaning on the door jamb, looking even more ill-kempt than usual if that were possible, with a battered canvas tool bag swinging from his hand. His shabby Southern Comfort T-shirt appeared to have been washed a thousand times and beaten on rocks by tribeswomen, and his jeans were in holes and worn white in strategic places.

Places Lucy really didn't want to be caught looking at but couldn't quite stop herself. There was obviously quite a good-sized tool in there too.

When she glanced up again, Steve had a wide, smug grin plastered across his cheeky, stubble-clad face.

'Hi, babe . . . Didn't know whether you could hear me over the Mozart.' His blue eyes danced over her, settling on the V of her dressing gown, even though it was very snugly fastened and not revealing anything. 'I wouldn't have disturbed you, but I'm going up to town tomorrow for a few days, and I remembered I still hadn't fixed your pipes . . . Is now a good time? It'll only take a moment.'

Scenarios from cheesy 70s porn films flitted through Lucy's mind. Plumbers and their wrenches. Electricians and their socket sets. It was a million miles away from her dreams of her television lover. The very antithesis of them . . .

Here was Steve the randy landlord, not her perfect and sophisticated dream man. Although to his credit, he did at least recognise Mozart when he heard it, she accepted reluctantly.

Still, she sighed inside.

Why on earth did you have to turn up tonight of all times?

Can't a girl have a bit of peace and quiet to have sex fantasies and masturbate?

'Come in . . . it's all right. I'd rather you fixed it now than wait much longer.' She *was* fed up with all the dripping and the wet towels and constantly replacing a bowl beneath the sink.

Sly dark eyes looked her up and down, as if searching for a chink in the tightly belted-up robe.

'Look, if you're busy, I can come back after I've been away.'

The louche expression on his swarthy face dared her not to refuse him. It was actually rather a nice face too, she realised, taking the time to look more closely for a change. You could even call him handsome in a rough-hewn sort of way.

And his body certainly wasn't bad either . . .

A big man, he seemed to displace quite a lot of air when she stepped back and ushered him past her into the flat.

'No, go right in . . . You might not come back for a month and I'm fed up with soggy towels under the sink.'

Steve laughed softly, as if tacitly and unapologetically acknowledging his erratic stewardship of his own property, while Lucy studied his broad back as he preceded her down the passage.

My God, he *was* big. Strapping, in fact, and seeming more massive than ever in the confines of the flat. Heavy of shoulder, his arms and chest and thighs were powerful in a way that reminded her of the detective, although her fantasy man had a refinement and grace about him that her lumbering oaf of a landlord sadly lacked.

Or did he? He was light enough on his feet as he strode towards the kitchen.

Once in there, he zeroed in straight away on the elegant platter of cheese and fruit that she'd laid out for herself.

'That looks nice . . . Expecting someone?' The lift of his eyebrow seemed to speak volumes about his speculations on her sex life.

Words froze on Lucy's lips.

What could she say? How could she explain her fantasy night for one, with possible masturbation?

Steve's eyes narrowed, as if he'd sussed it out already.

'OK, love . . . none of my business, obviously,' he said cheerily, squatting down before the cupboard under the sink and letting his bag of tools drop on the kitchen floor with a heavy clump. 'I'll get out of your hair as quick as I can.'

Lucy dragged in a deep breath, but kept it quiet, not obvious. She wished he hadn't turned up when he had, but still, somehow, there was a strange comfort in having him in the flat. He was a real man. Solid and living. Scruffy and a bit loutish but, in his own way, peculiarly appealing.

Something twisted in her heart, gouging and aching. She imagined a flickering, fluttering sound. . . the card-house of her fantasies cascading to the carpet in disarray.

She couldn't tear her eyes away from his thighs, and the way they flexed as he crouched. They looked hard and packed with muscle. As did his bottom in his faded work jeans.

Fantasy and reality phased in and out of her imagination, making her giddy. Here was a real, very attractive man. Earthy, but desirable. What the hell was she doing with her life? If she turned her nose up at possibilities like this, she was letting Simon and that harpy Linda win.

What's the point in faffing about with fantasies, when I should be reaching out for the real . . . and the available?

She hadn't seen Steve with a girlfriend lately.

'I'll have to turn the water off at the stop-cock,' he announced, straightening up. 'Just for a couple of minutes, though. I won't spoil your evening.' He snuck another glance at the cheese, and had the effrontery to lick his sexy lower lip.

'No problem.'

'But it isn't under the sink.' He gave her another provocative grin. 'It's a renovation, this flat . . . things were changed around. The stop-cock is actually in the bathroom. OK to go through?'

He nodded in the direction of her sybaritic haven. With its scented water, its solitary champagne glass, its flickering tea lights.

Titillating lingerie laid out for nobody to see. Expensive perfume to seduce a man who didn't know she even existed. Mortified, she wanted to grab Steve by the arm and stop him discovering her pathetic secrets, but he was too fast for her. Or maybe, somehow, she wanted him to find her out?

In the bathroom, she half expected a mocking, laddish reaction, but he remained silent, his dark eyes flickering around, taking it all in, weighing it all up. Then his expression grew thoughtful when he paused to glance at her magazine, on the stool and wide open at the 'seduce yourself' article. But his reaction wasn't at all what she'd anticipated. He looked more wry and sympathetic than anything.

Still not speaking, he strode to the sink and opened the little cupboard underneath it. With swift efficiency, he reached in and turned off the stop-cock.

'Won't be a mo,' he said again, his eyes gentle. The kindness was so tangible that to her horror she felt tears well in her eyes, and she could only thank God that he turned away and left for the kitchen again almost immediately.

He felt sorry for her.

He thought she was a sad, frustrated, bloody spinster who couldn't get a real man and had to resort to fabricating faux dates on the advice of silly magazines, and indulging in solitary masturbation pretending a man off the telly fancied her.

Lucy sat down on the side of the bath and wept. Wept so hard that a few minutes later, she couldn't stop when Steve came back.

'Hey, love, what's the matter?'

In an instant, he was perched on the edge of the bath beside her, his big brawny arms around her shoulder. Pulling her to him, he pressed her face against his crook of his neck, and she smelt a whiff of some cologne he must have applied earlier in the day, all blended with healthy male sweat and something volatile like paint or thinners.

It wasn't Gucci or Dior, but it was still sexy, and it was real, not imagined.

'Come on, pet . . . Don't cry. It may never happen.' It was nonsense talk, comfort talk, but his arms around her made every kind of sense. The blue meanies of despair started to retreat.

'You'll think I'm a totally sad bitch . . . all this, it's just for pretend.' While she dragged in a calming breath, he pulled a handkerchief out of his pocket. It was old and well laundered but it looked reasonably clean and she let him blot her eyes with it. 'Girlie fantasy night in, and all that . . .' She sniffed again. 'I've just been dumped and I felt like some self-indulgence . . . know what I mean?'

The words had whooshed out of her like air, and she felt empty, at a loss. But the warm arm around her imparted a glow. Healing comfort. And more.

'Tell me about it, love,' he said in a strangely weary voice.

'It's a bloody cattle market out there. Sometimes, it's just easier to stay in, isn't it?' His other arm came around her, rubbing her arm, squeezing her as if she'd been out in the cold and needed warming up. Which she did. 'I've been working hard on renovations and stuff . . . building up my business. Sometimes I'm too tired for anything more than a night in with Kylie or Madonna or Beyoncé on the box . . .' He paused. 'A few cans of Stella, a takeout . . . and . . . well . . . a bit of the old hand shandy, know what I mean? And some KY with it if I'm feeling sophisticated.'

What?

A feeling bubbled up. Like she'd drunk several more glasses of champagne, straight down, one after the other. Laughter gurgled up and she just couldn't keep it in. She simply guffawed.

'What? You as well?' she gasped eventually, in between hiccups of laughter. 'I mean, not Stella Artois or Beyoncé . . . but the other thing?'

'I'm afraid so.' She drew back, looked at him, and saw the ruefulness in his expression. His big shoulders lifted in a shrug. 'Now who's a saddo?'

'You're not sad. And neither am I,' Lucy announced. More warmth rushed in, and light, and a feeling of conspiracy and companionship. And more of that other thing. The thing she'd never expected in a million years to feel for Steve. 'We're just busy people . . . who . . . um . . . make a logical choice. Sort of . . .'

She looked at him, suddenly really, really liking his shaggy hair and his solid body. He was disreputable and pirateylooking, but he had beautiful blue eyes, a strong, kind face, and the promise of a truly exceptional physique beneath his tatty, paint-stained work clothes.

It took less than a heartbeat to come to a decision.

'Look, I haven't got any Stella . . . but I do have another bottle of champagne. Would you like some?'

The blue eyes, which were *really* beautiful, flared, hot and interested.

'Yeah, why not? I can go upmarket.'

Lucy stood up. She glanced quickly at her lingerie, and her sexy wrap, but Steve caught the look.

'Hey, you look great in what you've got on . . . It's kind of subtle . . . makes a man speculate . . . and fantasise.' He cast another quick glance at the mag, 'That bloke, the one you split up with . . . he's a bloody idiot letting go of a hot woman like you, I can tell you. Come on, let's go and get some of that fizz.'

Lucy's heart thudded as he followed her into the kitchen. She liked the way he'd said 'you split up with' rather than 'dumped you', and his large presence behind her seemed to vibrate, give her energy. And confidence.

In the kitchen, she pulled the second bottle of champagne from the fridge and it seemed natural and companionable to hand it to Steve, so he could do the man thing and open it while she got the everyday glasses from the cupboard.

With an encouragingly deft hand, he uncorked the bottle and poured it out.

'So what shall we drink to?' He handed her a glass, and waited.

Lucy's heart thumped. She looked him up and down. Bollocks to shitty exes, fantasy figures and elaborate idealised scenarios. This was here and now and real.

'How about . . . seduction?' She caught his eye, then clinked her glass to his, still holding his gaze. 'The real thing, not the imaginary kind.'

He laughed. He smirked. But she didn't mind. The rude twinkle in his eye made her laugh back at him, and she loved the way, when he sipped his drink, he went 'Mmm . . .', and smacked his lips, suggesting he had far more in his mind to taste than just champagne.

They drank in silence for a few moments, then Steve took her glass from her. 'We don't need this, do we, love?' He set both their glasses aside with a determined 'clomp'.

Moving closer, he looked down at her, that naughty glow in his expression even brighter. Lucy swallowed, her heart bashing in her chest, and hot blood careening around her body at a pace a fantasy lover could never have induced.

She was burning up. She wanted Steve. And she was going to get him – and far more than she'd ever get from sad dreams of a man off the telly.

OK, so his jeans and mucky T-shirt weren't a match for Armani and Hugo Boss. But he had a hot body, gorgeous eyes, and an imagination that was more than a match for hers.

She grabbed him by the T-shirt, hauled him close to her, then slid her hand behind his head and drew his mouth down to hers.

His lips were soft and full of potential. He tasted like champagne, and his shaggy hair was far lusher and silkier to the touch than it looked. For a moment she hesitated, confidence wavering, but then he pushed his warm tongue gently but firmly into her mouth, and began to tease hers with little pokes and darts and strokes.

He didn't grab her, he just kissed, standing there, letting her control the seduction. But everything about his presence and the stance of his body said he liked it. And wanted more.

Which she gave him, standing on tiptoe, pressing her body against his, feeling his hard cock jut against her belly through their clothing. His answer was a sort of eloquent grunt, his breath in her mouth.

But still he didn't touch her. Infuriating man! But in a good way . . .

Wrenching open her robe, she tried again, pushing her naked breasts against his chest and her soft bush against the denim of his jeans.

Again, the grunt. Still he teased, making *her* do the running.

Lucy laughed, enjoying the challenge.

'You're really making me work for this, aren't you, you devil!' she gasped, breaking her mouth away from his.

'Seduction, babe,' he purred, his expression warm, teasing but amiable. 'Gimme some of it.'

'All right . . . you asked for it!'

Lucy assessed the situation, quickly and excitedly, her bare nipples tingling, her pussy starting to drip. This was so real, so wonderful, so raw. She didn't feel as if she could do anything wrong here. Hooking a finger into a little hole in his shabby T-shirt – from a burn or something – she ripped down and hard, and the ancient, over-washed cotton tore like tissue paper.

'Baby!' he exclaimed, his eyes surprised but darkening with delight and lust.

Ooh, his body was even better than she'd expected. A match, easily, for any fantasy man's. He was muscular, not deeply cut but just believably firm and tanned and strong-looking, with rough hair on his chest. Unable to stop herself, she leaned over and kissed his nipple, licking and biting it playfully.

'Oh, baby . . .' he gasped again, his control breaking as he buried his fingers in her hair.

Steve's skin was salty, a bit foxy, a bit sweaty. His odour was earthy too, but it made her mouth water around his tiny teat. He was all man, and his hips bucked against her.

She wanted more. All she could get. She started pulling at the belt on his jeans and more by main force than dexterity wrenched it open, still lapping and sucking on his nipple.

Belt negotiated, she as good as ripped open his jeans, cooing in her throat on discovering nakedness within. Hot nakedness. Hot, hard nakedness.

Hot, hard nakedness enrobed in silky, velvety skin and slippery with copious sticky fluid.

She had to see it. So with a last nip at his teat, she drew back, broke free of his grip, and looked down at the monster in her hand.

Now that is what I call a tool! And much more fun than anything you've got in your bag, landlord mine!

His cock was reddened with blood, fierce and hungry-looking. Ready to do the business, ready to fuck her.

Steve groaned as she stroked him lightly, loving the feel of him as much as she loved the sound.

Now this was where dream lovers would always fall short, and what vibrators, dildos and Magic Rabbits would never be able to replicate. Because they didn't come powered by strong backs, muscular buttocks and powerful thighs.

'Oh yeah . . . oh yeah . . .' he chanted, folding his big hand around hers and guiding the way she worked and rode him. 'That's it . . . not too hard, I'll come too soon.'

There was pleasure in just touching him. Joy in handling him and feeling his response, his excitement. Power of her own in tugging him gently forwards and rubbing his tip against her bare belly.

He made sounds now that weren't words, just growls and deep throaty utterances of rough male appreciation. Slick fluid poured from the tip of his cock, wetting her fingers.

Lucy wondered how long he could last before coming. She wondered whether it might just be fun to make him come, to exert control over him in a real physical way that she'd never be able to do in her fantasies. But just as she was about to experiment, Steve stopped her, moving her hand away.

'Hey, sweetheart . . . I'm getting all the good stuff here. We need to see to you too.'

With that he lifted her hand to his lips and kissed it. His wicked tongue shot out and licked up his own pre-come, and when she gasped in surprise, he just waggled his eyebrows and winked at her.

How incredibly horny . . .

And then his hand was upon her, settling on her belly, curving delicately and in exploration at first, then moving more purposefully. Long, thick, workmanlike fingers parted her pubic hair, then the middle one dived in between her sex lips like a missile homing in on just the spot that craved it.

'That's better, isn't it?' He began to rock the pad of his fingertip across her clit.

Yes, it was. It was far, far better than solitary, imaginary fantasies with a man she'd never seduce. Oh, masturbation was fine and good, a treat, an indulgence, but not when done in sadness and a yearning for something mutual.

She wrapped her arms around his neck, riding his finger, loving his touch.

It didn't take long. It didn't take long for hot, golden pleasure to ball in the pit of her belly and roll and tighten to an intolerable pitch. It didn't take long for the ball to burst, in ineffable pleasure, making her howl and latch on to Steve like a limpet while she shuddered and climaxed.

She slumped against him, still clinging, her labia still divided by his finger, her chest heaving like a sprinter's.

'Was that nice?' His voice was an awestruck whisper.

'Fabulous,' she panted. 'I should get you to come up here and do odd jobs a lot more often.'

He laughed in a low rumble, delicately patting her clit, as if making sure it knew that there was plenty more of what it had just had available. As he touched her, he pressed his cock against the side of her hip. It was like an iron bar, streaming with pre-come all over again.

'Have you got a condom, love?'

His voice was soft but rough, as if he were trying hard to control himself and only just succeeding.

Oh no!

But . . . yes. Befuddled by pleasure, she visualised a box with a few in it in the bathroom cabinet. Left over from less lean times, sexually, and tucked away out of sight and mind.

'There're some in the bathroom cabinet . . . I'll get them.'

She made as if to move, but he held on to her.

'No need, babe . . . we'll go to them!'

With that he slid his arms around her, beneath her robe, and, scooping his hands under her buttocks, lifted her up. Lucy's thighs parted around him and her arms hooked round his neck, their movements co-ordinated.

Steve laughed and dropped a kiss on her face, then hoisted her more comfortably before striding off in the direction of the bathroom. Still poking out of his flies, his cock bobbed tantalisingly against her bottom as he walked.

When they reached the softly lit room, with its still-flickering tea lights, he laid her down like a precious treasure on the thick, fluffy bath mat and stroked her hair. Then he stood up again, located the cabinet, and rummaged for the condoms.

'Catch!' he said, tossing the little packet to her, then sat down on the seat of the toilet to pull off his work boots.

Boots first, then socks, then jeans, then tattered T-shirt. All off. Only to reveal a body that was almost the stuff of her fantasies, but somehow more attractive and sexually alluring for *not* being quite perfect.

He was slightly chunkier naked than she imagined her dream guy to be, but she liked his solid, latent power. He was hairier too. The nice pelt on his chest and belly was matched by a rough, dark dusting on his legs. Mmm, primitive . . . and good.

He was all man. Real man. Horny and honest. His cock seemed to yearn towards her, bold and pointing, craving her pussy. His smile was macho, pleased with himself, but his boyish self-confidence made her smile back at him.

This was all so easy. No striving to be perfect, to make everything perfect and idealised. It was OK to be a bit clumsy, and to giggle.

Which she did when he knelt down, pushing her thighs apart and shuffling in between them. The sight of his cock bouncing and swinging induced mirth, as well as lust.

'Well, don't muck about, love queen, stick a condom on me,' he urged cheerfully, jutting his hips forwards.

Lucy complied happily. She didn't care about being bossed about, because she knew it was all in fun. He wanted sex, but somehow he also cared. She ripped open a packet and reached for his delightful rod.

It was a fumble, a sticky fumble, with much groaning and

wriggling and touching and more laughing as they squirmed about into position.

'Do you want a bit more fingering, love? I mean, I will . . . but I'm dying to get into you.'

'You're a prince, landlord mine,' she replied, taking hold of his cock and gently dragging it towards its destination. 'But I think I'll manage . . . I'm dying for *you* to get inside me.'

He pushed. She jerked with her hips. He slid in with a mighty thrust, his big organ stretching her.

She wrapped her arms around his torso, and her legs around his hips.

He leaned over and kissed her, his lips gentle in the moment before the action. The words, 'You feel beautiful, babe,' followed, exquisitely soft and full of meaning.

They rocked and bucked, they heaved and shoved, his pubic bone knocking hard against her clitoris as his delicious cock slid and pumped inside her.

It didn't take long until they achieved their goal together, and Lucy flew, her heart soaring on sweet waves of pulsing pleasure, then lifting again as she felt Steve lose it, and pulse inside her.

Later, after using almost all the condoms, and drinking all the champagne, Steve turned the water back on so they could make tea and use it to wash down enormous bacon sandwiches that they scoffed like famished kids. Replete then, they sat in silence, just smiling at each other across the table.

And Lucy realised something as Steve reached across and gave her hand a companionable squeeze.

There was silence from beneath the sink. No dripping leak. Another job well done.

She placed her other hand over Steve's, then winked, and nodded in the direction of the bedroom.

Grinning again, Steve was on his feet fast, reaching for her hand, his fingers warm and sure around hers.

There was still one condom left, so tonight was turning out to be perfect, after all. As might other nights, Lucy hoped. She really hoped . . .

A Stroll Down Adultery Alley

Running footsteps behind me. 'Katie! Wait! Are you going for a walk? May I join you?'

I turn around and think, Thank you, God, what on earth did I do to deserve this? I've been fancying this guy since almost the first instant he moved in with us and here he is chasing me, not the other way around. 'Of course . . . why not?' With my best smile on my face, I hope to do the best I can to impress my mother's latest lodger, Doctor Peregrine Nash, noted academic and all-round tasty morsel of hot quirky male pulchritude.

I wait for him to catch up with me, still hardly believing my luck. With my mum on guard duty there's not really been a chance to show the good doctor I've had the voracious hots for him.

The desire to ogle him is intense, but I manage to restrain myself to sneaky glances as we fall into step along the path to the common, Kissley Copse, and what the locals all call Adultery Alley.

I'm pretty nervous too. This man is brilliant. A real brainbox as well as a cutie, an eminent mathematician newly arrived at the local university. I'm not exactly thick, in fact I'm fairly sharp in my own way and I have a damn good job.

But I'm not in his league where grey matter is concerned.

'Lovely day, isn't it?' he says.

He's nervous. I can tell. A shy guy, despite his academic eminence. And that *is* sexy. I've always had this thing for tutoring a less-experienced man. It's like a major fantasy of mine. And to tutor a gorgeous bloke like this, who's so used to tutoring other people, will be something of a twist. Of course, I could be imagining things and he's got available women coming out of his ears . . . but somehow, my hottie-sex-radar tells me I'm right on the money. And, with any luck, we'll both learn something down the Alley.

'Smashing . . . fantastic day for a walk. I like to get out of the house, you know . . . I mean, my mum is great, but she watches me like the proverbial hawk. She thinks that, just because I'm not married now, I need to be kept under constant surveillance.'

Why, oh why, am I babbling and telling him all my intimate troubles? If I'm not careful I'll be telling him that I'm dying to get laid next. And also that he's the one I'd like to do the honours.

'Yes, quite,' he says, flashing me another cautious little smile, as if he's not quite sure whether he hasn't stumbled into something he really hadn't bargained for. What if he really does only want a perfectly innocent walk in the fresh air with his landlady's divorced daughter?

We reach the edge of Kissley Copse and I'm still trying to weigh him up. It's a warm evening and he slips off his denim jacket revealing a white T-shirt laundered lovingly by my mum. I must admit that he's not really a classic Adonis. He's short, for one thing. No taller than I am. And he's also ever so, ever so slightly chubby, with a rounded face and a stocky little body. But he has got 'it'. The X factor or whatever. Or, in his case, Pi factor or some other esoteric number. He's sort of dark and swarthy with a slightly hooked nose and the maddest mop of black curls. He looks like a delicious combination of sex animal and innocent naif. I could eat him alive.

We don't say anything, but I catch him sneaking the same sort of glances at me as I'm sneaking at him. Sly, discreetly assessing, but also cautious. I'm convinced he wants me but is calculating the precise theorem of a successful seduction pounce. I wish I could tell him that I'm a dead cert. Disgracefully easy in his case, although not as a rule. Well, at least not since . . .

'What are all those cars doing lined up in the lane?'

We've reached the footpath that runs parallel to the Alley, our track separated from it by a sparse and scrubby hedge that looks as if it's been deliberately pushed through in places. Which, of course, it has. This is a prime spot for both sexual exhibitionists and doggers, and voyeurs who lurk on this side of the shrubbery watching the performers both in their cars and out of them. How to explain this to the good doctor though?

'Well . . . um . . . this is a sort of hang-out for people who are having a bit on the side. They come here to . . . er . . . do it in their cars.'

Beautiful brown eyes widen. Brighten. And also darken at the same time as his pupils dilate. His lush mouth curves into a smile that would grace the image of the wickedest-ever sex pixie. And I like that – 'Sex Pixie' – it sums him up perfectly. My mother would go ballistic if she saw the way his eyes glint, and suddenly he licks his lips. She thinks he's a gentleman and above all that sins of the flesh lark. She thinks he's too good for me. But curiously, and conversely, that no man is actually quite good enough for me. Which means that me finding a bloke at the moment is pretty much a lose-lose situation.

She blames me squarely for my divorce and current lack of grandchild-producing potential. And she's right in some ways. It was an error of judgement on my part. But that's by the by. This is not the time to be worrying about what my old mum is thinking and how she perceives I've let her down. 'Everyone round here calls it "Adultery Alley". Because most of the people in the cars are married, but *not* to the people who are in the car with them.' This ought to bug me and make me uneasy, but it just makes me hornier than ever. I'm so screwed up.

'Indeed.' His eyes twinkle again. He's definitely up for something, I hope. 'A sort of "Liaison Lane", I presume.'

Liaison Lane. I like that too. Although it does rather over-dignify the grubbiness of these gropers and cheaters and adulterers. 'If you say so.'

Is he closer now? I never saw him move. But somehow he's in my personal space, smelling sumptuously of a rather expensive cologne. 'And . . .' He hesitates and a cheeky grin spreads across his impish features. Being so dark and saturnine, he always seems to need a shave. 'Do you come here often, Katie? Do you like to observe the fornicators in their natural habitat?'

I'm gobsmacked. I never realised he was so full-on. I suspected he had a frisky rampant satyr's heart beating in his mathematician's chest, but I didn't expect the switch from polite respectful lodger to total horn-dog to be quite so sudden. Still, in for a penny, in for a pound. I take a deep breath that unconsciously, or perhaps consciously makes my breasts lift and displays them to their best advantage. I'm wearing a white T-shirt too, and my frontage is one of my most attractive features.

'Yes, I do. Is that a crime?' My chin comes up and it's like there's a clash of two sabres as our eyes meet and hold. I match his grin with one of my own. 'I like to watch. I can't deny that. And this lot are fair game if they shag in a public place.' I gesture vaguely towards the scrappy hedge and the vehicles parked beyond.

'No crime. None at all. I find your honesty refreshing and healthy. And I must confess to snatching the opportunity to observe a fuck in progress whenever I can too.'

He chuckles. I snigger. We both simmer and gurgle and boil and then nearly collapse, trying not to howl at our own absurdity and alert the shaggers in the nearest cars to our presence just yards away.

Oh, I love his grin. His sparkling eyes. His aura of total naughtiness. He might not be a Greek god, but he makes up for any deficiencies in this newly revealed and scrumptiously open horniness. Whoever would have guessed? I was quite wrong about him. The demure Doctor Peregrine is a rampant, sexy pervert.

'Perhaps we should partake of the show that's on offer then?'

'Way to go . . . um, Peregrine?' I've never called him by his first name. At home, because my mum had me in her 40s and is in her seventh decade now, we observe the proprieties and he's 'Doctor Nash' at mealtimes.

'Perry,' he says softly. 'I'd love it if you call me Perry. All my close friends do.'

And, boy, do I want to be a close friend. The closest of close kind of friend. The kind of close friend who gets to touch and fuck that cute chunky little body. The one I got a glimpse of the other day when he came rushing down to the door to collect a courier parcel, draped in a bath towel. There's a lovely little mat of dark hair on the chest that's hidden behind the snowy T-shirt.

'Righto, Perry. I'm game if you are.'

The conspiratorial smile he gives me lets me know we are in agreement.

We pad forwards, sneaking right up against the hedge. Again, more by design than accident, I trip on a root and he catches me by the arm to stop me falling. And it feels like he's just goosed me with five thousand volts; all the current goes straight to my pussy. I cling on to him, more wrong-footed by his touch than by anything else.

And he's strong too, far more powerful than his modest stature and slightly soft build suggest. He's like a rock I could hold on to forever. 'Thanks,' I whisper, reluctantly releasing my limpet-grip. He gives me an odd, sweet, complicit little smile as we edge forwards again and take up our position.

Here among this section of the scrubby bushes, tucked up against a drystone wall, we're higher than Liaison Lane, and we have a perfect view into the light-blue Japanese saloon car below. Where a middle-aged couple are already going at it.

And they're really bold. They've stripped off completely. She's sitting astride him in the back seat, her heavy breasts bouncing as she pounds up and down upon him. I can't see as much of his body as hers, but the tangly mat of dark hair on his chest reminds me of Perry's delightful pelt. Unable to stop myself, I glance to the side instead of at the raunchy goings-on in the car.

Perry's looking at me. As if my reaction, and my response to the illicit shaggers, is far more interesting and arousing to him than they are. He gives me that devil–cherub smile of his again and waggles his dark brows before nodding towards the car.

Oh, God, I barely care what they're doing now. I just want to grab him, roll down into the dip behind us, and climb on board him just the way the bouncing woman in the Honda is astride her bloke. But Perry gives me a strangely commanding look and nods again to the cavorting couple in the car.

The woman is really putting on a show, lifting and grinding and shimmying. The man's holding her hips, but she's in charge, and she's all about her own pleasure, not his. She's tweaking one of her nipples as she jogs up and down, and her other hand is down between her body and his, obviously rubbing at her clitoris in the nest of her pubic hair.

I want to touch myself down there. Oh, hell, I really, really do. And I want to do it with delicious Doctor Perry watching me do it. My mind more or less blanks out the Honda adulterers or whatever they are and presents a picture, in high definition, of me and him in the back of that car. We're both naked, as they are, but to me we're a much more attractive proposition, our physical shortcomings notwithstanding.

If it were us, I'd be looking down into his chocolatey brown eyes as I twist and gallop, getting off on the wicked smile in them just as much as his cock in my pussy. And instead of holding my hips and just using me as some kind of masturbation aid, as the guy in the car is, he'd be touching me in lovely ways as I fuck him.

Talking of touching, as the woman ups her pace to a frantic thrash and the man shouts 'Oh fuck' so loud it echoes out into the copse we're lurking in, I feel a warm sure hand settle on my back, urging me forwards to lean against the wall.

The touch is light, but there's a definite sense of command

about it. I comply, spreading my arms out across the uneven surface of the top layer of stones. My breasts press against the hard lumpy blocks and I nearly yelp because they're so tender and sensitised, the nipples like swollen foci of sensation. Perry's fingers slide slowly up and down my back, stroking me gently through the cotton of my T-shirt, in a way that's as reassuring as it is intensely arousing. I shimmy – my appreciation expressing itself automatically – and, before I can bite my lip, a little moan escapes from my mouth.

I'm lost. I'm burning. If a simple, almost-chaste caress through the fabric of my T-shirt can send me soaring, how the hell am I going to be if he *really* touches me?

In the car, the man suddenly seems to take control too. He says something harsh that I can't quite make out, and his fingers gouge the hips of his paramour. He holds her hard and he holds her still. She's obviously rushing towards her climax, but he wants her to go slow so he can hold out a bit longer, make it last.

My ex was a bit that way. It was all 'do that', 'do this', 'slow down', 'speed up' with him. All about his experience, rather than mine – the selfish git.

But, without knowing why, I know it wouldn't be like that with Perry. With him, it would be all about my pleasure. As I acknowledge that, it's like he's heard my thoughts, and the stroking of my back takes on a different quality. His fingers dip lower, and slide beneath the waistband of my jeans. They just probe and flutter, working in the confined space then, a moment later, he reaches around the front, undoes the button and eases down the zip.

Oh, God. Oh, God. Oh, God.

All that fantasising and now something's really going to happen. My pussy flutters wildly, even though he's nowhere actually near it yet. A gush of lubrication oozes out and anoints my panties. I literally sob I'm so turned on, so full of desire. My eyes close but, as they do, Perry whispers in my ear, 'Watch them, Katie. There's a good girl.'

I moan again, my clit throbbing as if his words had actually touched it.

The woman in the car is still now, her face tense where I can see it from this angle. I bet my face is tense too, but it's the tension of yearning and excitement and a sudden inexplicable adoration of the man who's standing behind me.

I watch as the woman submits to being handled, the man's hands roving over her now like those of a greedy boy grabbing at sweet things in a candy store. He snatches at her nipples and twists them this way and that in a way that looks quite cruel, although somehow I sense his partner really gets off on it. I send up a silent prayer that Perry isn't *too* gentle when he gets to mine. Something that might well happen soon as he's plucking at the hem of my T-shirt now.

The feel of his fingers against my bare skin is like a spiritual communion. I wonder if the woman in the car feels like this? I doubt it, but I could be wrong. Why should Perry and I be the only ones who can go transcendental?

But I love the way his hand sneaks up my back, then slides round to cup my breast through my simple cotton bra. He just holds me, as if weighing the flesh, then lightly squeezes. Then he abandons my tit and I somehow sense that he likes playing below the waist much better. Or at least that's what he's in the mood for right now.

While the woman in the car continues to get manhandled, I get some of that too, but with considerably more finesse. Moving his hands inside my jeans, Perry slides them down my thighs and then pushes them right down to my ankles.

Briefly he embraces the rounds of my bottom through my panties, then they follow, sliding right down the whole length of my legs to settle on the denim bunch of my jeans.

I bite my lip. I adjust the position of my arms on the wall so I can cram my fist against my mouth and stop myself groaning out loud at the sheer, raw, weakening vulnerability of being so completely exposed like this. It's a form of shaming, yet at the same time an exaltation. I've never experienced anything quite like it in my life before.

'Let's watch them come,' breathes Perry in my ear as he takes his position against the wall at my side.

I want to moan and sob I'm so excited. And I can barely breathe. My pussy feels swollen with blood and it seems to bloom like a flower. Another thick slithery rush of silky juice pours out of it and starts to slide down the insides of both my thighs. I'm saturated and my intimate flesh screams for contact, while Perry the Perverse quietly ignores it and watches another show.

Or does he? When I sneak another glance to the side, trying not to plead with my eyes, he's looking at me again. He gives me an odd enigmatic little smile and then indicates that I should watch the other show too.

They're bouncing again, going at each other wildly, the woman back in the ascendant, getting her own way. Distracted as I am, I still notice that the man's face looks fiery and red in one particular spot. What's happened? Has she slapped some sense into him to make him toe the line and think of her pleasure?

But as I watch them lurch up and down and slam on and into each other, thinking becomes something that's slightly beyond me. And Perry doesn't need telling or slapping, that's for certain.

I'm staring at the car but, as his hand slithers between my legs, I'm not seeing it. I seem to see the two of us from the outside. Me leaning on the wall with my bottom on show, and him, leaning in, his face intent, his eyes dark as he fondles me.

His fingertips comb their way through my pubic hair and swoop into the swamp of my pussy. He finds my clit unerringly, and starts to run circles round it, brushing it lightly, first to one side, then the other, but not going in for the direct heavy manipulation. Which drives me crazy. Of their own accord my hips too begin to circle and weave; my clit follows his pattern as if magnetised and tries to get more action. Things get worse – or better, depending on how you look at it – when Perry starts to play with my bottom from behind, feathering up and down my anal crease with the fingers of his other hand.

He's working me like some infernal puppeteer, using not strings but the electric zones of my pussy. I moan behind my own fist, my pelvis weaving like that of some kind of exotic dancer. I've never felt like this before. Never known I could be such a wanton lust-crazed trollop. But I'm glad I've found out now, because Perry seems to really, really like it.

He starts murmuring in my ear, using just those words – 'trollop', 'slut', 'horny little raver' – and the words sound doubly, trebly, quadruply arousing in his beautifully enunciated, Oxbridge-educated tones.

As if from a huge distance and through a veil of fuzz, I watch the couple in the car finally climax. It's not a pretty sight. Their faces contort and their movements are jolting and ungainly; the woman's breasts jiggle up and down in a way that's hypnotically ugly. But, who cares? They're getting off, and that's what I want too.

'Please,' I whimper, my hips still following Perry's plague-some fingers. I don't know whether I want him to fuck me or bring me off manually and I don't much care. I just want an orgasm. Right now or I think I'll die.

'Please what?' he purrs in my ear, his mouth close to my skin. In fact, all of him is close. I can feel his heat. I can smell his really nice cologne all mixed up with a touch of foxy male perspiration that's just as much of a turn-on. 'Please what?' he repeats when I'm too far gone in frustration to be able to form the English words to answer him.

I'm a vortex of frustration and confusion. Part of me wants to whine for pleasure at his hand. Part of me thinks, Who the fuck do you think you are, mister? Just give me what I want. Now. Because I want it. I think the woman in the car turning the tables has inspired me. 'You know what I want, Doctor. Just get me off!'

He laughs, but it's a merry sort of sound, and when I look over my shoulder at him he looks pleased, and excited, and even slightly awed. 'Your wish is my command, Madam Katie. Nothing would give me more pleasure . . .' He pauses. 'Well, I know a few things, but first things first.'

He reconfigures his hold on me, adjusting the position of his hands and his digits until they're in exactly the right places to give me pleasure. Then he goes to it, as if it's a science. Maybe it *is* to him? But I don't care. He's just too good!

Swirling, pressing, squeezing and teasing, he assaults my clit, and with his other hand he plays around my entire pussy, stroking and exploring. And as he does this with tender skill, he also kisses me, covering the back of my neck and my shoulder with peppering little pecks, then more elaborate caresses with his lips and tongue.

Pleasure gathers, glowing between my legs like an

expanding sphere of heat, like a science-fiction star globe of energy and intensity. I start to wiggle and wriggle again, but he doesn't miss a beat. He just goes on touching me, and basting me with delightful kisses. And it's that which tips me over. The kissing as much as the touching. Despite the raunchy, naughty nature of what we're doing together, it's the fugitive quality of tenderness that turns just sex into the unforgettable.

I almost scream when I come, but at the last millisecond I remember that, if we can hear the couple in the car, they'll be able to hear me if I howl and shout. So, as I nearly faint, I stifle my cries with my fist.

My pussy clenches, my sex ripples, my knees turn to water and I slump against the wall. Perry persists and drives me through the barrier again and again, still kissing, and also whispering much sweeter nothings into my ear this time. I'm not sure what he says, but I've a feeling that, when I regain the use of my brain, I'll be surprised.

The next thing I do perceive clearly, and completely compos mentis, is him and me sitting in the grass by the wall, cuddling. My pants and jeans are still around my ankles but it doesn't seem to matter.

At least it doesn't at first and then, suddenly, real life kicks in, as opposed to some sort of sexual fantasy state, and I'm thinking, Oh, God, Oh, God, what have I done? And experiencing an overpowering compulsion to cover myself up.

I start dragging at my knickers and jeans and manage to get myself in total twisted muddle with them. To my horror, tears of embarrassment and frustration – the bad kind – spring to my eyes. I can't look at Perry but, before I know what's happening, he's helping me in a gentle, careful manner. Working as a team, we manage to get me decent again.

I still can't look at him. 'God, you must think I'm a nightmarish slut. We barely know each other and not only do I lead you to the most notorious place in Kissley, but I let you get my knickers off me without as much as a murmur of protest.' I fish in my pocket for a tissue, but Perry beats me to it, handing me a white handkerchief perfectly laundered by my mother. That makes me feel even worse. I'm just the worthless, no-good trollop I often fear Mother thinks I am. I know she loves me, but I've also 'let her down'.

'Of course you're not a slut. Far from it.'

I wish I could believe he meant it. 'But you said I was one . . . when you were touching me. You said I was all sorts of dirty things.'

He slides his arm around me in an almost fraternal way and gives my shoulders a squeeze. 'But that was just sex talk, Katie. Just fun. A game. Part of the pleasure. For both of us.'

Speaking of his pleasure, I note that the bulge in his jeans is very much at odds with his current mode of brotherly solicitousness. Which makes me feel even more guilty.

'Never mind that,' he says almost casually, as if his own body and its reactions are of no consequence. He takes me by the shoulders, his grip firm yet compassionate and he makes me look into his eyes not at his groin.

'You shouldn't be ashamed of being sexy, Katie. Why would anyone think any less of you because you're a beautiful desirable woman? I don't. I like you and I respect you.' He leans in and kisses me softly on the lips. I nearly swoon it's so sweet, and as longed for as the caresses and the orgasms. 'I'd like us to be friends. Spend time together. Go out, you know?'

I can't speak.

'What's wrong, Katie? What have I said?'

I give myself a little shake, but still he holds me. I like his strength and, amazingly, I feel desire begin to stir all over again. 'Nothing. Nothing wrong at all. It's just me, I'm a bit screwed up at the moment.'

He takes a deep breath, then reaches to brush my hair out of my eyes. 'Tell me about it. What can I do? How can I help?'

I shimmer on the edge of tears again, and it's all mixed up with that new rush of lust.

'It's all mixed up, and crap. I did something, well, a bit questionable and now my mum's disappointed in me. She's old school, she had me late in life, and she believes in traditional values and stuff.'

Perry's expression is almost serene. He seems like a therapist more than a mathematician. He's waiting, apparently without judgement to listen to my woes. Why the hell does that make me want him more?

'I split from my husband.'

'Is that so bad?'

'Well, I was unhappy, I went with another bloke. I didn't even like him all that much, but it gave my husband grounds for divorce.' I drag in breath, and let it out gustily, trying not to start crying again. 'And now my mum is so disappointed with me. But, while I'm saving for a place of my own, she still offered me a home back with her.'

I lose the fight against tears and collapse even deeper into Perry's comforting arms. I've been holding this in for so long, holding it from myself in a way, and even to let some of it out now is so sweet a relief.

He makes a lot of quiet, soothing sounds and mutterings,

along with pattings and strokings of my back. The voice is the same one that called me a 'naughty slut' and all that and, in its way, just as exciting. I feel a great rush of something more than desire, but also tangled up with it. A sort of momentum towards Perry from my heart. I barely know the man but I feel a glimmering of something special, or maybe just the potential of it. Which is enough for now.

Patting and stroking gently morphs into hugging and rocking against each other, and kisses. Actual kisses this time, our mouths pressing, savouring, opening, so our tongues can explore. It's sexy and still naughty, I suppose, to be snogging and making out with my mother's lodger in the undergrowth down the side of Adultery Alley but, somehow, it also feels clean and healthy and right, even though we're rolling about in the grass and dust in a hedgerow.

When Perry slides his hand beneath my T-shirt again, it feels as if he's sweeping away the bad and replacing it with the good. I respond by rocking against him, smiling in the kiss. When I reach down and cup his groin, he laughs in his throat, the sound raw and happy.

'I haven't got a condom with me, you know,' he mutters against my lips, but he doesn't sound too worried about it.

I am worried, though, and I pull back to look at him. I so dearly want to fuck this sweet imp of a man and this is a serious obstacle.

He touches my cheek. 'Don't worry, sweetheart.' He gives me the quirkiest little smile that sets my pussy fluttering without it even being touched. 'There are plenty of nice things to do without penetration. And I know you like being fondled, don't you?'

Fondle? What a word. Sort of old-fashioned, but I like it.

'But what about you?'

He shrugs. 'Oh, a little spurt into the bushes will do me, as long as you have a hand in it.'

'Or on it.'

'Exactly.'

Perry slides his hand right under my top this time, and flips my bra off my breasts with a suspicious deftness. He's certainly done this plenty of times before, but who cares? Who cares when his fingertip is so light and clever in the way it circles first one nipple then the other, 'fondling' them both to stiffness, to a new sensitivity. He pays them extended attention, stroking and playing, the pressure there a perfect conduit to the even-more-responsive zone between my legs.

After ten minutes of this I'm beside myself, pushing my crotch against his thigh. It feels solid and warm and perfect to rock against. I set up a rhythm and Perry helps, cupping my bottom, adding momentum, increasing the pressure.

I want him to touch my pussy, but he keeps rocking me, sliding against me in a syncopated dance, arousing me through my clothes and his. Heat and wetness and excitement gather and gather and gather until critical mass is reached.

I climax furiously, burying my face in his shoulder, my head full of his cologne and his foxy male sweat as he holds my bottom and my back, clasping him close. I want to cry out, but I just sob against his T-shirt. The car we were watching drove away some time ago, but who knows who else might be around and listening.

Shuddering, I come down again, a bit weepy, but happy with it. I have good feelings about this. Better than I've ever had, even in the first days of my marriage.

With a sigh, Perry kisses me, as if setting a seal on my thoughts and my hopes. 'You're beautiful,' he whispers, still holding me. 'So beautiful . . . I love to see you come.'

I look up into his warm brown eyes, and I know he means it. And I also know, when my hands rove to his crotch, that he needs to come too.

His eyebrows shoot up when I unfasten his jeans and get him out, but then his smile widens and goes sort of smug, and very, very male.

He's a nice size. A very nice size. It's a great shame we can't put Tab A into Slot B on this occasion, but I resolve to rectify that situation sooner rather than later. Next time we come out for a walk, I'll have condoms. Lots of them.

I begin to rub him and he cups his hand around mine, guiding my strokes. I don't mind this. I want to please him. I want to give him exactly the kind of wank that he prefers, because, God knows, he got his fondling of me spot on.

We slip and slide, using the silky fluid that flows from his tip as a lubricant. He mutters and whispers, praising my technique and also letting out some far less cogent utterances. It doesn't take long because he doesn't hold back and, pretty soon, he's arching and snarling silently, his penis jerking and jetting out his cream.

I kiss him as he comes, just as he kissed me while I came. And, as promised, his come *does* end up in the bushes.

On the way home, I don't quite know what to say to him, and I find myself worrying about what lies ahead for us. Or for me, because, despite my hopes, there might not be an 'us'. He'll be getting a flat or a house soon, and he'll move away, and out of my circle. My job and his university are miles and poles apart. Perry's hand slips into mine and gently but firmly jerks me to a stop. 'Why the frown?'

It's hard to explain. I still want him. But I want more. And it's awkward. To him this was probably just a frolic, an illicit 'liaison', nothing more. I bite my lip and, just as I'm about to summon up some kind of explanation, not the real reason, but something acceptable and not too embarrassing for both of us, his impish, stubbly face settles into very firm and professorial lines. 'Katie, what sort of man do you think I am?'

I shrug. 'I don't know. I barely know you at all. That's the problem. You must think I'm awfully cheap and easy and slutty.'

'Please, don't go there again. I don't think that at all. Except only in the nicest, sexiest way.' He pulls me to him, and gives me a very chaste kiss on the tip of the nose. 'Now we've broken the ice, I'd like to go back to the beginning, and do things differently. Properly.'

My heart thuds. 'What do you mean?'

'How would you feel about dinner? A trip to the theatre? A stroll that doesn't involve Adultery Alley?'

I'm speechless.

'In fact, I think it would be nice if we took your mother out somewhere for dinner too some time. So she can get used to us as a couple, if you know what I mean?'

'That'd be lovely.'

He smiles. 'I want her to think that I'm above board, and worthy of her daughter.' He gives me a wink. 'So that when I get my own place and you stay overnight, she won't be too cross with me.'

'I can't wait.' I throw my arms around him and give him a hug, my heart lighter than it's been in a long time. 'But do you think we can still pop down to the Alley now and again as well? I'd still like to be naughty on occasion. And I still like to watch.'

He laughs and shakes his head. 'Oh, don't you worry. We'll

still be naughty too.' He slides his arm around my waist, then lets his hand rest on my bottom. 'We'll be incredibly naughty. Naughtier than you can possibly imagine.' My pussy ripples again in anticipation. 'But I think we'd probably best not tell your mother about that.'

'Yeah, probably not.' I kiss him, and the future suddenly looks incredibly bright.

Red Haze

'Good afternoon,' said the tall, blurred shape at the centre of a fringe of red haze. 'It's a lovely day, isn't it?'

'Er, yes . . . yes, it is,' replied Megan, squinting and peering in its general direction. The surgeon had said her eyes would take their own time to recover from the operation, but she was already having some good days with sharper vision, as the spectre of losing her sight altogether receded.

Today, alas, wasn't one of those sharp days. Today was a blob day, and the figure in front of her remained stubbornly rosy-edged and blurred, no matter how hard she tried to bring it into focus.

It was bloody annoying because the blob's voice was gorgeous. Why couldn't her vision clear up for just a second or two? All she needed was enough time to determine whether he looked as amazing as he sounded. Just a flash would do, really. With a voice that deep and resonant, which was playing havoc with all the bits of her that hadn't had a good workout in ages, the law of averages said he had to be a hunk.

'Would you like some help with that?'

That was the sun parasol she was currently grappling

with. Yesterday she'd managed to put it up in a jiffy, purely by touch, but today it was stubbornly defying her.

'Yes, please, that'd be great.'

Should she really be encouraging him? She had no idea who he was. It was too late though, because with a couple of deft clicks, he had the parasol securely up and in place, and she found herself standing in a patch of pleasant shade.

'Er . . . thanks very much. That's fabulous.' What to say next? Should she invite him to join her? Gah, decisions, decisions.

'Could I possibly trouble you for a glass of water?' the velvet voice went on, pre-empting her, and in spite of her natural caution, Megan felt a distinct desire to swoon. Since her op, she'd been feeling horny for no sane reason she could understand, and even though she could see nothing more than vague shapes, all her hormones were silently screaming 'Phwoar!' at her.

'Yes, of course. I'll get you one.'

Cautiously, she edged her way out from under the big parasol. By rights she should be alarmed; she knew that. This guy had obviously just wandered into the garden uninvited, and she didn't know him from Adam. He could be a serial murderer or a rapist or a crack addict intent on harming a woman who was clearly half blind, completely vulnerable, and easy pickings.

'Oh, please don't worry,' said the delicious voice. 'Let me help. I know this house and the owner. I can get a glass myself. I won't be a moment.'

'Er . . . It's OK, I'll get it,' Megan insisted, thinking, *Why ask me, if you know your way around, you perverse bugger!*

Now this was a worry, actually. She couldn't have him meandering around the house, unsupervised. There were all sorts of easily picked-up treasures, and this guy could be a thief, never mind a murderer or rapist, even if he said he knew Sylvia. She decided to go with him, even though there was probably nothing on earth she could do to stop him just taking what he wanted. Especially as it dawned on her now, peering in his general direction, just how big and lofty a shape he actually was. And he hadn't mentioned Sylvia's name at all.

For an instant, her focus sharpened, the red disappeared, and she got a flash of a tall, tall man with a massive frame. His face was broad, and his hair, what she could make of it, was short and dark. His big body was clad all in khaki, probably a shirt and combats, and just before the brief instant of clarity was gone again, she got the impression of a wide, white smile and a pair of dark, compelling eyes.

Then all the detail fuzzed up again, and he was back to being an assembly of ruddy-fringed vague shapes. And those shapes were moving in the general direction of the back door, which led to the kitchen. Silently cursing her temporary infirmity, Megan padded along behind him, feeling her way and trying to keep the army surplus-coloured mass just in front of her.

Once indoors, he went straight to the sink, and a moment later, Megan heard the gush of water from the tap, then the clink of a glass being taken from the drainer. 'May I pour you a glass, too?' the man enquired. Even though she could barely make out the shape of his features, she sensed he was looking at her curiously, perhaps assessing how he should deal with her.

Despite her doubts, some gut instinct told her she wasn't really in the way of any harm. She didn't know why, but the feeling she got from him was more a kind of empathy and tact. She sensed that he could see she'd got problems, but at the same time understood the way her pride compelled her to fend for herself.

'No . . . er, thanks . . . Actually, I think I might have a glass of white wine instead. There's some cooling in the fridge.' She paused and then took a deep breath. He was a total stranger who'd just wandered in from the lane. She shouldn't be encouraging him to stay, but she couldn't help herself. 'You could have some too, if you prefer it to water?'

'That's very kind, but I think I'll stick to water.' She heard the water in question gurgle into the glass. 'Would you like me to get your wine for you?' He'd obviously decided that she did need a bit of assistance after all. 'I'll bring it out to the garden for you. I won't be a moment.'

'Thanks. That'd be great.'

This is insane! Megan berated herself as she shuffled back to the garden and her blanket under the parasol. *I've never set eyes on this man before . . . and I haven't properly set eyes on him now! I shouldn't be giving him the run of a house that doesn't even belong to me.*

She could quite confidently predict that Sylvia would go nuts if she knew that there was a perfect stranger in her kitchen. Her generous friend had offered Megan the use of her country cottage for as long as she needed to recuperate, but had left express warnings about being careful, especially of a local tramp who was supposed to be in the area, petitioning for hand-outs, sleeping rough in people's garden sheds and even stealing the odd item of washing off the line.

Oh my God, what if red and khaki shape is the tramp?

Megan almost collapsed onto the blanket.

He could well *be* a tramp in that ex-army gear. It was just the sort of thing a travelling person might wear, wasn't it? And as far as she could tell, he had nothing with him, so maybe he'd left his bundle – or whatever tramps carried these days – under the hedge. Or maybe he'd already stowed it in the outhouse?

'Oh bugger, what have I done?' she muttered as a firm, even tread brought the possibly dangerous potential tramp towards her blanket.

The large shape hunkered down beside her, then reached for her hand and carefully put a chilled glass into it. Surprisingly, Megan didn't feel the urge to flinch. In fact, the large hand that gently cradled hers felt decidedly nice. The fingers were big, and they didn't feel soft or namby-pamby, but the skin was warm, and as far as it was possible to tell by touch, it felt clean and well kept. In fact, he smelt clean too, and not the slightest bit tramp-like at all.

The large man who now settled down beside her was accompanied by the scent of some kind of light, tangy, woodsy cologne, and maybe just a hint of fresh sweat. But it was the pleasant sweaty smell that came from healthy perspiration. The sort that filmed a well-showered body on a very hot day.

Not to mention the fact that it was full of male pheromones and intoxicatingly sexy. My God, who needed wine with a smell like that in the wind?

Even so, as she took a large swallow of the crisp, fruity Chardonnay, her wayward libido kicked hard for this man she could barely see. And who just might be an unemployed vagrant – albeit a sweet-smelling one.

I should ask him who he is, and what he's doing here, Megan thought. But it was probably too late. He probably had a couple of Sylvia's father's antique silver snuffboxes in his pocket already.

But the words just wouldn't come. It was as if her entire consciousness had gone primal and turned into one big hormone that was responding to the mysterious presence of the large man at her side. And her sudden desire seemed to be preternaturally intensified because she couldn't really see him.

Oh hell, why, oh why couldn't I be having one of my clear days today?

'Will your vision improve?' her companion asked suddenly, causing the glass to jerk in her hand. Swift as lightning, she felt his fingers enclose hers to steady her grip. Even though she was shaking more than ever now at the strange jolt of sensation his touch induced.

Having his large hand around hers confused her, and, as if reading her mind, he helped the glass to her lips and held it there, like a nursemaid, while she sipped again. The delicious taste of the wine and its coolness on her tongue settled her, and after a moment, she was able to speak again.

'Yes . . . in time. The doctor says I'll get my normal vision back. Or near enough . . . I'll probably still have to wear glasses, or contacts, but I don't mind.'

Suddenly tears welled up in her healing eyes, and the terror she'd experienced in recent months – and tried to put right to the back of her mind – overwhelmed her, and to her great confusion she began to sob like a baby.

A combination of relief and the release of a great swell of emotion barrelled through her like a tidal wave, and she was helpless as the man beside her took the glass from her fingers and then enclosed her in his arms and hugged her against his solid chest. Unbidden, her arms snaked around him, and she relished the rock-like feel of him. He seemed immovable, like a safe refuge after a voyage of insecurity. Like life and health after the fear of permanent deficiency.

'Hey, don't worry,' he said softly, big hands moving slowly over her back. 'You'll see again, you know that. These things just take time. You just need to trust your doctor. It'll happen.'

And for the first time, she completely believed it would. In a way that she hadn't throughout all the time of the infection, the deterioration, the operation and the optimistic prognoses of the various eye doctors.

She believed it, thanks to this strange, unknown and unseen man. And as her fears fell away like leaves, her undamaged senses began to flower and fire extravagantly. The scent of him this close was enough to turn any woman's head, and the feel of his strong, huge body and the warmth of his hands were maddening. It had been so long since she'd been with a man. Craig, her casual boyfriend, had somehow filtered off the scene during her recovery phase. And even though, as an olive branch, she'd invited him to visit her here in the country, he'd made excuses about being too busy and then suggested they split as their relationship 'wasn't really going anywhere'.

Well, sod him! Megan thought, her hands moving on her companion's back, exploring the impressive musculature beneath what seemed to be a long-sleeved heavy cotton shirt. Weren't tramps supposed to be thin and under-nourished, living on hand-outs and drinking rough alcohol, and taking all manner of nasty drugs and what have you? The man in her arms was in magnificent, prime condition.

Oh God, I want you!

The words sprang into her mind, and as they did so, she drew back a little, peering myopically into his face. This close up, the red that fringed objects was less noticeable and she gained a better impression of his features. His dark eyes had a definite glint and the general lines of his nose, mouth and jaw suggested that he could be fierce and uncompromising, but also kind. Unable to stop herself, she slid her hand up to the back of his head, her fingers digging into hair that felt short, but with a crisp suggestion of curl as she pulled his face down towards hers.

Her mysterious new friend followed her lead perfectly, settling his warm lips upon hers with a firm, yet velvety, pressure. After a moment, his tongue probed gently for entrance, and she granted it gladly, opening her mouth to his exploration.

Without really knowing what had happened, Megan almost immediately found herself on her back on the blanket, still being kissed. The big, strong stranger loomed over her, his hands first smoothing back her hair and then sliding down her neck in a measured, yet sensual, caress. For a moment, his thumb lingered on her throat, stroking lightly, and she felt a shaft of intense, primal terror. What if he was a murderer? He could strangle her effortlessly, or snap her spine with hands that huge.

But then his warm fingers moved on, drifting down inevitably to her breast.

She felt another intense sensation when he cupped her, but this time it was the opposite of fear. Her body surged, even though his touch was circumspect, almost diffident, and just the very lightest brush of his thumb against her nipple had her moaning. Her eyes flew open.

He lifted his lips from hers and his face was still indistinct above her. Tanned skin, dark, lustrous eyes, the mouth that had kissed hers full and rosy . . . And smiling . . . She could easily tell that he was smiling, although the subtle nuances of the smile were a mystery. There was no way to tell whether he was smug and macho, or sensitive and tender, although the way he began to gently stroke her breast suggested the latter.

Suddenly, she had to know his name.

'Who are you? What's your name?'

There was a long pause, and despite the deficiencies of her vision, she sensed a certain withdrawal in his face.

'Just call me "Guy",' he said, something in his voice, some primitive element of command, compelling her not to question him further. The way his lips came down on hers, harder this time, compounded the impression.

OK, no questions, she thought, turning off all rationality and surrendering to 'Guy' and the predications of her senses. His kiss became more demanding, almost ferocious, and she found herself answering in kind, her tongue fighting, duelling, twining with his. Her hands clutched at his shoulders, his back and his hard, muscular buttocks through the lightweight cloth of what she was certain now was a pair of combat trousers. As he moved against her, his massive body both dominant and protective, the solid bulge at his groin brushed her thigh.

Oh God! Oh God! I think I'm going to fuck this man and I have absolutely no idea who he is, and I don't even want to ask him. Feeling like a slut, yet not in the slightest ashamed of the fact, she surged against him, twisting beneath him and rubbing herself rudely against his magnificent erection.

'Hell, yes!' he murmured indistinctly against her mouth, rocking her against him with one hand while the other traversed quickly down her flank and her thigh, questing and exploring. He plucked at her light summer skirt, and wafted it quickly upwards. A second later, his fingers were stroking the edge of her panties, and then slipping under the elastic in search of her core.

The first touch induced a high, silvery, singing sensation between her thighs. His fingertip was huge, like the rest of him, but he flicked at her clitoris with a delicate and exquisite precision.

'Oh! Oh God!'

Orgasm was like a shock, a huge surprise, right out of left field. She'd known she was aroused but just not how much. Tears sprang in her eyes again at the sheer relief of it as her flesh pulsed and fluttered against Guy's touch. She kissed him messily and thankfully, her arms tightening around him even as she still climaxed and climaxed and her honey flowed. She felt whole again, complete, no longer damaged.

Guy's mouth captured hers again, and captured the kiss too, his tongue thrusting as if to mimic the penis her empty sex was hungrily clutching for. The way it moved promised and incited, giving her an intimation of even better things ahead.

At last, she fell away from him, gasping and somewhat relieved that she couldn't see the expression on his face as he studied her hot cheeks and the red, orgasmic flush across her neck and chest. She probably looked a mess, but because she couldn't see his response to it, it didn't seem to matter.

The garden was still, the heat of the sun hanging heavy around them in a way that suggested the long, balmy days of her childhood when everything was perfect and golden. She suddenly wanted to thank this strange man, this enigmatic Guy, for returning her so effortlessly to such a happy, carefree time. He was so close that her fingertips had no trouble finding first his hip, then sliding sideways to cup his groin.

Oh, but he was a big boy! Her hand gave her a much

better idea of his imposing dimensions than the brushing of his crotch against her thigh. Her wayward sex clenched again at the thought of having him inside her.

She was just massaging him, in happy anticipation, when the sound of voices quite close by stopped her in her tracks.

Shit!

'Look, Guy,' she said, hurriedly tweaking her skirt down, and then pushing on his big chest to make him let her up, 'I might not be able to see the lane and who's in it, but anyone out there can certainly see us.' As he retreated slightly, a cold hand gripped her heart, and she rushed on, not wanting to lose the pleasure of him. 'Come on, let's go inside,' she went on, fumbling for his hand as if just holding him might compel him to stay with her and not go away.

'Yes, I'd like that.' His fingers tightened around hers in a quick squeeze, and then continued to hold them as he got to his feet like a giant, the spirit of the earth, rising from the soil. A second later, he swooped down again, his capable arms enveloping her and whisking her off her feet.

Like in *An Officer and a Gentleman*, he carried her with no discernible effort into the house then up the stairs. The familiar prints that hung beside the staircase passed by her like ruddy blurs. She'd stayed here before and could remember what they looked like. She only wished she could picture just as clearly the face of the man who held her.

'It's the room on the left,' she said when they reached the landing, but despite this, she felt Guy stride determinedly in the opposite direction, and open up a room that she knew was rarely used. It was a small guest bedroom that overlooked the orchard at the back of the house, its décor – what she could discern of it – quite masculine and spartan. He back-heeled the door closed and let her gently slide to her feet.

Megan blinked around and realised they were standing in front of a mirror – a tall pier glass that reflected back not one, but two amorphous, red-hazed blobs.

It was an image of her with Guy standing, nay, looming, right behind her.

His hands slid around her, and she saw the vague shapes move as he first ran the backs of his fingers against her face, then down across her chest to settle over her breast. His tanned hand looked very distinct, dark against the white material of her top.

'One day soon you'll look in a mirror like this and see what I see,' he said softly and then inclined forward to kiss her neck, his tongue stroking her skin. 'An extraordinarily beautiful woman,' he purred against her throat.

Megan laughed, more nervous than anything. First she'd thought he might be a tramp, but now she was worried he might be either a vampire or as optically challenged as she was.

'Are you sure you haven't had an eye operation, too?'

It was Guy's turn to laugh now.

'Now, now, mystery woman, let's have no false modesty. Surely you know how good-looking you are?'

Mystery woman. She liked that. But suddenly she wanted him to know her name too.

'My name is Megan.'

'That's nice. And you are beautiful, Megan,' he insisted, beginning to fondle her breasts again with that powerful, yet strangely respectful, touch of his. A touch that had the ability to befuddle her mind so much she could almost believe the words he said were true.

She could just see her own features, and her short, easy-to-handle cap of blonde hair, and she watched her own pinkish lips part on a gasp of pleasure as he handled her. Her vision sharpened again, and for a second she saw herself biting her lip as he eased up her skirt and found the place he'd claimed earlier, his big hand sliding into her knickers and stretching them away from her mound as he began to stroke and finger her.

The way he slicked at her seemed to turn on her senses all over again, tune them to an extreme pitch, and even activate new ones. Unable to close her eyes, she continued to watch the blurred shapes of their bodies in the glass. She could see her hips wafting as she pressed herself into Guy's caress. Her pelvis seemed to undulate like a dancer's, beyond her control, moving to invite and encourage.

A sharp cry escaped her lips as pleasure gathered.

'Please, can we go to bed? I want you inside me!'

Did I say that? she thought distantly, astonished at her own brazenness. She, who'd always been so quiet and reserved in bed, was suddenly brave and demanding in this vaguely defined world with this brand new and completely unknown man.

Guy didn't laugh or mock her for her impatience. In fact, he didn't speak at all. He simply whisked her into his arms again, and carried her to the bed. It was just a three quarter size, with plain, no nonsense linen, but she knew she wouldn't have cared if there was no bed at all.

With a strange combination of tenderness and almost militaristic efficiency, he divested her of her clothes. Top, skirt, pants, all off in moments. Her sandals were somewhere out in the garden still, beside the blanket. She knew he was studying her, exploring every inch of her body with his eyes, but because he was indistinct to her, she found she wasn't self-conscious or shy. She spread her limbs. Let him admire her.

And then it was his turn to disrobe, and the army surplus garments came off with the same swift competence. Megan didn't strain to see the process, but she relaxed and enjoyed observing the dim, khaki shapes fall to reveal the tall, broad, tanned shape beneath. She saw a blur of darkish hair on his chest, and more at his groin, but his penis remained stubbornly indistinct. To remedy the situation, she reached out and touched him as soon as he joined her on the bed.

Oh dear God!

He was as impressively large as she'd suspected he'd be, and she could barely fold her fingers around the hot bar of flesh. Staring down at her hand, and the might that she held, she did squint now, trying to summon every last fragment of her unreliable visual acuity to make out his superb shape.

'I wish I could see you!' she cried, examining with her thumb and fingers what she couldn't with her eyes.

'You will,' he assured, a smile in his voice, 'One day soon you will. I promise you that.'

Not pausing to dwell on the ramifications of that statement, Megan hitched herself upright and then pushed Guy back against the pillows. Man that he was, he still complied easily, as if sensing what was coming.

She took the tip of him in her mouth, and was rewarded by a long, heartfelt groan and a joyous profanity. His deft but powerful fingers dove deep into her hair, trapping her in her attentions to his cock.

He tasted rich and salty but clean, and the silky skin of his glans was stretched taut and slick with juiciness. Megan could not imagine anything more delicious or any man's penis that she'd ever wanted to worship more. Wondering if this was the man she'd waited for all her life, she licked and sucked, played him with her tongue, took as much of his bulk between her lips as she could manage. As he grunted and murmured indistinctly, in obvious appreciation, it was almost as if she were pleasuring her own sex as much as she was his. Every shift of his strong hips made her swivel her own.

Furling her tongue to a point she flicked it around the flared head of his penis, exploring its savoury topography, dipping into the under-groove, then probing wickedly at its tiny eye. And as she teased him there, she slid a hand between his legs and cradled his balls.

'Oh, Megan, you're a devil woman! You're amazing,' he growled at her, his fingers gripping her head, marshalling her actions. 'But you're going to have to stop now, or you'll get more than you bargained for.' Gently but firmly, he compelled her to back off.

Not that she was complaining. It had been long, long and utterly dry spell while she'd been through diagnosis, surgery and recovery, and one orgasm down in the garden wasn't enough for her. She wanted to feel this beauty she'd just had in her mouth deep inside her. Her fingers, and her lips and tongue, told her he was amazing, even though to her eyes he was just a vague, but weighty, reddish shape.

With the skill of an accomplished lover accustomed to positioning women for sex, he flipped her neatly onto her back and slid his hand between her thighs. His big fingers paddled in her wetness, testing and fondling.

Suddenly a stark thought sprang into her mind, and for a moment her libido was doused by cold, hard doubt.

'What's the matter, beautiful Megan?' Guy purred, coming up and over her. For a moment, she gained a tiny bit more clarity, and she imagined she could see a frown, an expression of concern on his broad, tanned face.

'I . . . um . . . I don't have any protection . . . any condoms or anything.'

'Don't worry.' He placed a light kiss on her lips, then reached out and pulled open a drawer in the nightstand. 'I told you I'd been here before, didn't I?'

A few moments later, he guided her hand to him, and her fingers encountered the familiar feel of superfine latex.

Who the hell are you? she thought as he moved over her again, the muscular immensity of his body coming down on her like fate. *Are you a burglar? Are you the tramp and you've already broken in now and again to pilfer the place? When I finally see your face will it be in a police line-up, for God's sake?*

But then all doubts, fears and thoughts were expunged as he pressed his cock against her and began to enter.

Oh God! Oh my! Oh hell!

What had felt pretty big in her hand now felt enormous as it slid, slowly, slowly, millimetre by millimetre into the sensitive portal of her sex. And yet, despite the size and the strangeness, she felt a deep, sweet sense that somehow both she and Guy were finally coming home. In intimate juxtaposition their bodies fitted each other and were perfectly matched.

Yet again, tears sprang into her eyes, but this time they were thankful tears of joy. She'd known Guy less than an hour, and she couldn't see the features of his face clearly, but in this simple moment she had a sudden feeling of fate. It was completely crazy, but she knew that in one way or another, she'd been meant to make love with this man.

'Hey,' he said softly, 'I'm not hurting you, am I?' Taking his weight on one elbow, he stroked her face, fingertips delicately searching out the teardrops and smoothing them away. The action was so exquisite, so precise, that it seemed a shocking contrast to his great presence between her legs. She found herself gasping again, and great sobs wracked her body.

She shook her head because she couldn't manage words, and as he began to kiss her again, with reverence, she knew he understood.

And as he began to move, all her fears and doubts were shattered. Only pleasure existed. Only pleasure, sublime pleasure, with a loving stranger. As they rocked and jerked and thrust at each other, limbs entwining and sexes combining and working against each other in glorious syncopation, the gates of joy and light and hope were thrown wide open.

Gorgeous sensations rocketed around Megan's body, colliding with skin and nerves and pumping glands and always returning again and again to her core, and to Guy. She knew she couldn't hold out long against orgasm, and she didn't want to. She cried out his name and came and came and came again, her senses filled with his warmth, his weight and the intoxicating scent of his skin.

As she moaned and thrashed, she knew in her heart he was the best she'd ever had or was likely to have.

He lasted the longest too. Exerting some kind of control she couldn't honestly comprehend, he hung on, and on, while she climbed the hill to climax and plunged back down it time and time again. Eventually, she had to plead with him, or lose her wits.

'Please, love . . . Please come . . . I can't take any more! It's just too lovely!'

With a low, husky rumble of laughter, he generously complied, and then almost deafened her with a downright primal shout of triumph.

A few moments, or possibly hours, later, Megan found herself wondering if this was what it might feel like to survive a tropical cyclone or a hurricane. She felt as if she'd been buffeted by a tidal wave or a thunderstorm, but in a good way. There were going to be bruises in all sorts of unexpected places tomorrow, she suspected, but she was almost looking forward to exploring her nooks and niches to find out where they were.

And Guy, like a typical man, was now fast asleep.

Never more than now had she been impatient for her eyes to right themselves. She prayed for just one second of twenty-twenty vision to see his broad face in repose, but it just didn't happen. He remained a vague shape, hazed with red.

That didn't matter though. Not really. Whatever he looked like, she'd always believe in her heart he was beautiful.

But as she leaned over him, straining to see, the sound of the phone ringing, down in the hall, made her jump in her skin.

'Rats!' She slid from the bed, fumbling and feeling about for her clothes.

'You don't have to answer it,' murmured Guy sleepily, also feeling about, but for her, not for clothing.

Megan managed to locate her top and skirt but not her panties. 'I think I have to. It might be Sylvia, and she'll probably send the police around if I don't answer.'

'Mm . . . come back soon.'

'I will,' said Megan, making her way cautiously to the door, and feeling her way along the passage and down the stairs. It seemed to take an age, and still the phone rang on and on.

'Megan! Are you all right?' demanded her friend, just as she'd expected.

'I . . . um . . . um . . . fine.'

That was a massive understatement, but she didn't know how to begin to explain that to Sylvia.

'Are you sure? You sound a bit weird. Sort of spaced out. Has something happened?'

'No! Nothing. Everything's fine.' *Except for the fact that I've just had sex with a total stranger.* 'All's quiet here.'

Sylvia's suspicion almost seemed to ooze out of the receiver.

'Really. I'm fine. I'm having a lovely, restful time.'

'No sign of that vagrant I told you about?'

'Nope . . .' She crossed her fingers. 'But out of interest, if I could see, what does he look like?'

'Well, he's really old for a start, and he doesn't have any teeth and he has a funny foot. But actually, Bernice heard he'd been taken into a hostel or something.'

'That's good.' So Guy definitely wasn't the tramp then.

'But it's not him I was ringing about,' Sylvia went on briskly. 'I just wanted to warn you that you might be getting a visitor any day now.'

'A visitor?'

'Yes, it's my cousin Guy. Well, he's my second cousin, really. He's back in the country, and he often turns up at the cottage when he's on leave or whatever. He likes the peace and quiet.'

'Leave from what?'

'Oh, well, it's all very hush-hush. He's in some kind of elite Special Forces unit. SAS or something similar. Deep cover, covert ops, you know. He's been in the Gulf or Afghanistan or somewhere ultra-sensitive. He's a bit like a cross between Rambo and James Bond. Fiercely patriotic, but he can be ruthless in the field.'

Yikes, her mysterious stranger was a professional mysterious stranger!

'Anyway, he's a lovely man. I'm sure you'll like him, but he can be a bit . . . well . . . unforthcoming. He's the strong, silent type and all that, and he has to be pretty circumspect in his line of work, so he's sort of cagey generally. Doesn't tend to offer much information about himself, so be warned if this great big hunk of a gorgeous manly chap just turns up on the doorstep without much in the way of an explanation.' Sylvia paused, and sighed regretfully, 'It's an awful shame your eyes aren't A1 yet because Guy's really, really good looking! An absolute hunk!'

'I thought he might be.'

'What do you mean, you thought he might be?' Sylvia's voice was filled with a sort of benign suspicion, 'Have you met him? Has he turned up already?'

'Erm . . . yes, he has.'

'And?'

'And what?'

There was a long pause, but Megan could just imagine Sylvia's triumphant grin. 'You shameless hussy, Meg! You've bonked him already, haven't you?'

'I might have . . .'

'There's no might about it, I can tell from your voice.' Her friend laughed softly, 'Well, good for you! It just shows you're well on the road to recovery . . . Vital juices flowing and all that.'

Megan smiled, happy and feeling mischievous. 'And the

worst of it is, I didn't know who the hell he was and I still went to bed with him!'

Sylvia laughed even harder. 'God, I know I shouldn't ask, because he's my cousin and all that, but I heard from a friend of a friend who used to go out with him before he went overseas, and she said he was dynamite in the sack. Is he?'

'He might be. But I'm not going to divulge the sexual secrets of a member of your family to you, am I?'

Sylvia protested, but eventually, Megan was able to get off the line with the promise of a long, boozy lunch sometime in the near future. Much as she would have loved to have a girlie chat with Sylvia straight away, she had other, more compellingly delicious priorities to attend to. She had to get back to bed and back to the adorable stranger in it.

He was her unforthcoming, secretive, sexy, virile, gorgeous, secret agent soldier man, and he might have to go away again before she really got to know him.

But even so, she smiled.

She knew now that no matter how long it took, she'd wait for him. Because without knowing why, she knew that he'd return to her and when all the red haze and fuzziness had cleared at last, she *would* finally see the face of the man she was falling in love with.

Strawberry Shortcake

'I can't seem to do a thing right for him these days, no matter how hard I try!'

The women were in the kitchen, supposedly putting the final touches to the strawberry shortcake for dessert, while the men talked about the company, and politics and football. It had all begun very light-hearted and girlie, but suddenly it had morphed into 'Caroline's Agony Hour', with over-anxious Maggie the one in the confessional.

'How hard have you tried?' Caroline tried not to shout, but it was difficult over the clatter of her noisy old coffee grinder. By rights, the husbands wouldn't be able to hear what she and the other woman said to each other, because the kitchen was a fair way down the hall from the dining room, but knowing her Jonathan, Caroline really couldn't be sure of that. He was so clever and wily he might well find a way to listen in.

'Very!' protested Maggie, 'I know a lot of it's my own fault. And Allen is really good to me. It's just that his standards are so high. He likes everything just so, and sometimes I just think "Oh, sod it!" and I want to do my own thing.'

'That sounds familiar.' Caroline stared wistfully around the kitchen for a moment, knowing just how Maggie felt.

She'd suffered the same sort angst herself in the old days, wanting to be the perfect wife and a successful career woman all rolled into one, and getting stressed and uptight and not doing very well at either. Until she and Jonathan had found a way to resolve all their tensions.

'Did you have problems too?' Maggie's blue eyes were round and appealing, as if begging for answers, for 'the secret'. She was a sweet-natured woman, and Caroline had been happy to take her under her wing when her husband Allen had come to work in Jonathan's department at the company. 'You and Jonathan are so great together. You're like the perfect couple. I can't imagine you ever being anything else but chilled out and contented.'

Ah, sweetheart, if only you knew how we got here. I wonder if you'll understand if I tell you?

'We did have our ups and downs once.' Caroline busied her hands with the coffee preparation, trying not to look upwards, to where certain slightly unexpected objects hung amongst the pans on the kitchen rack. They were hidden from the casual eye, unless you knew exactly where to look. She was convinced that Maggie and Allen were ripe for the answer, but it was a radical solution, and not for everybody. It could bring a glorious new dimension to what looked to her like basically a very happy marriage, but there was always a risk when trying to initiate someone new, who might not understand. 'But we were lucky enough to find an answer, a way of accommodating both our natures.'

'I don't understand.' Anguished, Maggie fiddled with a strand of her long, dark hair.

Caroline's heart twisted. She'd been there. She had to take the risk.

'It's like this,' she said, beginning to set the tray. Routine, displacement activity always helped her to frame her thoughts in any situation; right now, it also tamed a flare of anticipation. 'Jonathan has a strong personality. He's kind, an absolute sweetie in many ways, but he also needs to be a leader and a manager. A master in his own house.' A cup rattled but she steadied it. 'But I've got a strong nature too. I'm unbelievably stubborn and I like to live my own life and do my own thing.' She caught sight of Maggie nodding in recognition. 'But I want to please Jonathan by showing that I respect his dominance too. I suppose a shrink would call it a form of subconscious submissiveness. But it's only really confined to one specific area. In every other way, I'm a card-carrying feminist and I make my own decisions.'

'What specific area?'

Caroline smiled. There was hope for Maggie. The other woman had immediately picked up on the crux of the matter – and she sounded interested, and just a little bit excited.

'We could demonstrate, Jonathan and I,' Caroline said, turning fully to face Maggie and looking her straight in the eye, 'but it might surprise you . . . and it might not be the right answer for you.'

'I'll try anything,' the younger woman said solemnly, 'and I'm sure Allen will be up for it too. He's really a sweetheart, just like your Jonathan, and he's always prepared to work through a problem.'

'OK, then . . .' Caroline didn't dare say anything else. Her knees almost went weak with the old familiar thrill and her entire body was already tingling. She felt a prickle of sweat break out amongst the roots of her short, blonde hair.

'What are you doing? I was looking forward to that!' demanded Maggie.

Caroline was putting cling film over the top of the dish

that contained the base of the strawberry shortcake she'd been just about to decorate with more cream. Not giving herself time to bottle out, she slid the whole thing back in the fridge.

'You'll see,' she replied, her spirits soaring. It was rare that they got a chance to show off outside of certain very special parties, and the regular, much-anticipated fetish nights at a local hotel. At any other time it was almost impossible to indulge her wayward streak as a sexual exhibitionist. Taking a carton of chocolate truffles, she arranged them quickly on a serving dish.

'What's this?' demanded Jonathan when she and Maggie returned to the dining room with the coffee. His dark eyes sparkled at the sight of the relatively empty tray. 'I thought we were having your famous strawberry shortcake? I've just been telling Allen how it's your signature dessert and now he's really looking forward to it.'

'I'm afraid I ate some of it at lunch time. I couldn't resist it,' said Caroline, flashing the astonished Maggie a quick look. 'I thought we could skip dessert, just this once. Surely we've all had enough to eat.'

'But I would like a dessert course, Caroline,' said Jonathan, and Caroline kept her face straight even though she wanted to grin. Her husband had a very modest appetite. For food, that was. 'And I'd promised Allen something special.' His eyes twinkled as he caught on to his wife's game

'I . . . I'm sorry,' muttered Caroline. She couldn't look at Maggie now, or at Maggie's pleasant young husband, Allen. She had eyes only for her own dark, beloved Jonathan. A dark, beloved and very stern-eyed Jonathan now.

'Are you?' he said softly, 'Are you really? I don't think you are.'

'I am!'

'In that case, how do you propose to show me that you're sorry?'

'I . . . I don't know.' She pretended to hesitate, even though her mind was clear and sharp, full of delicious anticipation, and her body was awash with desire. 'I . . . I could offer an alternative dessert?'

'I think you'd better,' said Jonathan, looking distinctly devilish in his black shirt and trousers and his black silk waistcoat. He always loved to ramp up the drama and dress the part. 'Perhaps you could help clear the table a little,' he said, turning his coal-dark gaze on Maggie.

Caroline stole a glance at the younger woman, and saw a flash of confusion, and then rapid understanding, and a slight smile. *My God, she's quick, a perfect natural.* Allen too looked excited, his hazel eyes bright and his cheeks a little flushed.

Between them, the two women moved aside glasses, cutlery and tableware. Caroline's heart thudded. She hadn't been wrong. This was going to work; the other couple were with them. Jonathan himself removed her chair so there was space to move in, as Maggie went back to her seat, and like her husband, sat in silent rapt attention.

Caroline faced her husband. He was a lean man of average height, but somehow he still seemed to loom over her, like a god, like a nemesis.

'Now, my dear,' he said, his voice low and sultry, 'as you've so selfishly denied Maggie and Allen their strawberry shortcake, I think the very least you can do is provide them with the best in after-dinner entertainment.' He pursed his lips thoughtfully. 'Take off your dress, Caroline. We'd like to see your body.'

Caroline's skin flushed, first with the chill of familiar

nerves, then burning hot. She was proud of her body but part of her still balked at the idea of stripping off to order and being exposed to others like a trophy. It was a pure, atavistic reaction. Jonathan was denying her all protection, not just physically but emotionally. He wanted to display her vulnerability, and all her fears and joys to their companions. But even while she hesitated, the coils of passion were stirring and tightening, making her ready, making her wet.

Unzipping her dress, she experienced a hyper-awareness of every movement. Each step, each shift of weight, seemed to make her more aroused. Her pussy was agitated, quickening with lust, already awash. A part of her psyche silently begged her husband to let her retain her bra and knickers; while the other part, the stronger, truer, raunchier side of her nature, revelled in the chance to reveal every bit of her horny state.

Without being asked, Maggie stepped forward to take the unwanted dress from Caroline. She gave her a nervous smile, but her eyes were brilliant and eager. Caroline saw Allen give his wife a nod of approval, and then the younger man's eyes re-focused on the centre of attention. She could almost feel his hot gaze stripping the delicate lingerie from her body.

'Now, your bra, my dear,' continued Jonathan, in a tone that was both arch and conversational, 'Peel down the straps, then get your tits out of the cups so we can see them.' She knew he was being crude to enhance the drama, for effect. Normally he was the most refined and respectful of men.

Caroline obeyed him, longing to fondle her own nipples in the process, but managing to control herself. There was a special sweetness in denial that made her sex throb.

'Now the tights and knickers . . . Just to the knees, I think.'
Demon!

Fumbling with her undies and hosiery, Caroline wanted

to crawl on her knees and kiss her husband's feet. He knew how her submissive side thrilled when she was hobbled this way; that was why he insisted on tights for her instead of stockings and suspenders, the more obviously sexy choice. This arrangement accentuated her bottom too; her best feature in both her and Jonathan's opinion.

'Now, Allen, would you like to help me choose an implement? Maggie, you can do me a favour and check what's going on between my dear wife's sluttish thighs . . . And you, my dear, turn and face the wall, spread your legs a little so she can reach you, then don't speak a word or move a muscle.' The orders were quiet, but they were still orders. Her Master's dictates.

It was difficult to obey them, though, especially when Maggie's gentle, tentative finger slipped between her sex-lips. Caroline was grateful she couldn't see the others' faces; see the way they would be looking at her bare bottom, and her thighs. Jonathan was right about her being sluttish, and the admiration in their eyes would only make her want to show off even more, wriggling and testing the limits of the pushed-down knickers stretched between her knees, behaving like a trollop. The urge to move, and to moan, was almost irresistible, especially when Maggie whispered 'sorry' and began to rub her. The men were murmuring over Jonathan's collection of punishment implements now – his most prized items that he kept discreetly tucked away in the bottom drawer of the china cabinet – and might not have been able to hear her, but Caroline still kept as quiet as she could. Her Master had spoken and for now his word was her law.

'You might caress her bottom a little too, Maggie,' said Jonathan casually, not interrupting his selection process.

'Test the texture of the skin there. Be gentle . . . She might appreciate the memory of that later.'

Caroline closed her eyes. There was a sensation of the ground giving way beneath her, and she fought to brace her legs and not crumple. Maggie's fingers were sticky against the bare skin of her buttocks, and their touch there was more exciting, in a way, than being masturbated.

'You're enjoying this too much, my dear,' said Jonathan in her ear, and Caroline did sway then. She'd been so out of it, so lost in the waiting, that she hadn't heard him move. 'Don't you worry. We'll soon put a stop to that.' She felt him take Maggie by the wrist and lead her away.

The delay after that seemed interminable. Caroline was anxious to proceed; hungry to begin. She wanted the process to be over too, for the pleasures afterwards, but somehow, also, she didn't. The rewards could be heavenly, but the process had its own perverse charms. She almost fainted when Jonathan spoke again.

'Now then, my sweet little show-off, let's have you over the table. You know the drill.' His voice lowered and became sterner, but paradoxically he also sounded proud. 'And with as much grace as you can, Caroline. I don't want our guests to feel cheated.'

Hardly daring to breathe, hardly daring to think how she might get through this with any kind of equilibrium, Caroline draped her body against the damask of the table cloth. The figured cloth was cool and tickly against her nipples, and the hard wood of the table's edge pressured her crotch.

'Keep still, Caroline,' her husband ordered softly. 'You will be moved by one of us, if necessary.'

Caroline bit her lip, wanting to groan with desire but knowing she mustn't.

'Allen, perhaps you'd like to arrange her?' he added after a moment. 'Legs more open, I think. As much as the elastic allows . . . It'd be nice to have more access to the inside of her thighs.'

Strange hands, wider and warmer than her husband's, settled upon her, and the fact that they were shaking was a comfort. Allen and Maggie were as apprehensive and excited as she was. This was a whole new world to them, a new dimension of experience and opportunity. She felt Allen palpate her slightly, then slyly finger her anus in the course of his adjustments. Ah hah, he was clearly just as precocious, and as much a natural, as his wife.

'Now then, you two, why not take up a position behind me?' suggested Jonathan, and Caroline heard the creak of leather, and a swish, as he tested the implement. 'That way you can see everything. Every stroke. Every wriggle. The way the redness blooms . . . Caroline's skin always marks beautifully.'

There was the sound of shuffling, and an intake of breath. Jonathan had shown Maggie the implement now – that was certain.

'Yes, Maggie, it's a leather strap. I'm going to spank my wife with a leather strap as a chastisement for her shortcomings.'

'Will it hurt m-much?' Maggie stammered, and her soft, fearful voice made Caroline want to leap up and cover her new friend's face with kisses. What a sweetie she was.

'Of course it will hurt!' Jonathan laughed merrily and there was the sound of the strap being hefted – very lightly – against his own hand. 'It'll hurt a great deal. It'll be agonising and humiliating. There wouldn't be much point to the exercise otherwise, would there? I can see that Allen has a huge amount to teach you, my dear.' The sound of steps came now; he was getting into position. 'Now come, let's not waste any more time. Caroline?' His attention had at last focused solely on his purpose. Upon her, his bared and penitent wife. 'Do you understand why I have to do this?'

She nodded, almost choking with anticipation, capsizing with love and lust.

'Are you going to be a good girl? And take your medicine quietly and with modesty? No throwing yourself about. No shrieking. No clasping yourself, no touching and no rubbing?'

She nodded again, the very words, the very reminders, already making the sins themselves more infinitely desirable.

'I mean anywhere.' His voice was controlled, yet silken with his own desire.

Caroline nodded, her mind flooding with the sounds and sensations of last time. Her guttural grunting, so crude and animal; her burning thighs spread; her fingers jerking and jabbing; her red bottom waving like a monkey's; Jonathan's sudden, swift possession, his cock like an iron bar, thrusting inside her.

Would she be allowed such a treat this time, in front of her friends? She didn't think so, but it was too late to debate about it now. Too late to be scared of *any* possibility. Too late to do anything at all as the strap came whistling down.

All she could do was whine and claw the table, her buttocks on their way to crimson fire . . .

'I wasn't a very good example, was I?' Gripping herself just behind her knees, Caroline lifted her bottom a little way up off the mattress. The sheets were soft and cool, but even so, the site of Jonathan's handiwork had far too much in common with the strawberries downstairs to press it against the cotton yet.

'You were stunning, love. Magnificent,' said her husband, rolling over beside her and looking down on her with a smile. 'Utter perfection. Never better.' He rested a finger against her left bottom cheek and made her gasp.

'But, Jonny, I had three spontaneous orgasms while you were spanking me . . . Ah!' She caught her breath again as the finger pressed, then moved. 'And after that I climbed up on the table and brought myself off again, even though it meant taking another twenty strokes. I thought we were supposed to be giving our friends a show of discipline . . . and grace under pressure?'

'But it *did* hurt, didn't it?' Jonathan enquired, his finger still moving now, but not in a place that pained her. 'It still hurts, doesn't it?'

Caroline nodded her head, and then thrashed it from side to side as the finger described a slow, sensual pumping action.

'Well, that's what matters then, isn't it?' he persisted gently, bringing his other hand into play, in a different place. 'And there's more than one way of expressing grace.'

Caroline whimpered and squirmed, and grew incoherent, but a short while later, when she could speak again, she said, 'Yes, love, you're right. As ever . . .'

'Of course I'm right,' said Jonathan a little smugly, subsiding onto his back. 'And if you'd been listening carefully for the last fifteen minutes you'd know how successful our little performance really was.' He fell quite silent for a while to allow her to hear much better.

Still holding her bottom and haunches up off the mattress, Caroline listened to the noises that were coming from their guest bedroom. They were excitingly graphic, and she'd never been more pleased that the walls were thin.

Allen's mock-stern voice. Little sobs and pleas from Maggie. Then the delicious tell-tale slaps of a hand meeting flesh – accompanied by the throaty squeals and gurgles of a happy female being punished. Shortly after came more cries – both male and female – and these were nothing at all to do with suffering.

'Do you think it will really work for them?' Jonathan asked, and Caroline felt him shift slightly beside her, almost as if he were feeling a bit uncomfortable himself . . . in a certain way.

'Yes. I'm convinced of it,' said Caroline firmly, smiling to herself. 'They'll be much happier now. Allen's getting to assert his dominant side . . . and Maggie's getting her just desserts. Exactly how she wants them. We'll have to invite them to a Waverley fetish night next. I think they'll love it!'

Jonathan laughed. 'Absolutely, and speaking of desserts, I could really fancy some "afters" now myself,' he murmured, still moving a little. 'And I don't mean your strawberry shortcake, either.'

Caroline looked down the bed – and caught sight of her own most favourite 'dessert' in the entire world.

'You're a greedy man, Jonny, but I love you,' she said, and the flaming state of her bottom only made things all the sweeter as she swung her body up from the bed, and then straddled her beloved husband for a long, happy ride.

And for tomorrow's breakfast there would be strawberry shortcake to share.

A Study in Scarlet

Uh-oh, I'm going to end up in The Study for this.

Joanna Darrell ran her finger over the carefully prepared report on her Master's pet project, Côte Mystère, his beautiful vineyard in the south-west of France. Most of the data within it was beyond reproach, faultlessly compiled, but someone in her section – Financial Analysis – had transposed a figure, it seemed, and the latest set of profit projections were miles out.

Someone had made a mistake, and that someone was her.

Distracted, she pressed her hand to her chest. Her heart was banging like a drum. In the normal course of events, something like this would have been no big deal. She would have corrected it, redrafted the report, and that would have been that. But this was not the normal course of events. There was no such thing now. Now, the most important part of her life was a tapestry of abnormal events, all stitched together by anticipation. It only took one slip to set the strangeness in motion.

Given the vineyard's significance, both to her and her Master, she couldn't understand how she'd made the error in the first place, other than her subconscious had made it on purpose . . . to initiate a response. They didn't really need a starting point, but sometimes, just for form's sake, she created one. And his terse memo had been alive with a secret glee.

Re the discrepancy in the Côte Mystère figures. Kindly see me at the usual place and time. I think you know what to expect.

The text was unsigned and 'sender undisclosed', but she had no need to ask who the scant message was from or what the usual place was. No one else would dare to send such a message. She was one of the company's senior analysts and a stockholder in her own right. She moved in the highest circles, and only her Master could summon her to The Study.

Considering her assumed obedience, Joanna continued to stare at the glassy screen of her smartphone, and faced the same ambivalence she always did at these times. She was being tugged in two different directions by the two different sides of her nature. Sides so mutually exclusive it almost amounted to being two different women. One part of her was independent, confident, brazen, even; while the other one was pliant, submissive and biddable. Her Master's perfect slave. It always amazed her that she revelled in being both. Especially when she was across her Master's knee. Being spanked, or played with somehow.

And it would be a spanking, at the very least. Either that, or the crop or the lash. It might be a combination of several devices, even; her Master was nothing if not inventive. He was greedy sometimes too. He had human faults, for all she almost worshipped him. He seemed to flourish on her tears and entreaties, and grow ever sterner the more she fought and struggled. She remembered the last time he'd corrected her – for arrogantly interrupting him at a forward planning meeting. The resulting session had begun with a warming up – five minutes of light, whippy strokes with a white plastic ruler – then progressed to a formal six cuts with his favourite rattan cane. She'd been feeling particularly vulnerable that night, a little fractious and inclined to whinge; and when she'd wriggled too much, over the end of his desk, then clasped her buttocks before being given permission to, he'd doubled the amount of cane strokes to a dozen, and turned a cool, indifferent face to her protests.

She studied the memo again. It was impersonal, mechanical, produced by cool, indifferent pixels. But she liked it that way. And she liked him to be the same. The thought of his calm, unyielding manner made her quiver and feel red hot. Her thighs were so tense they were almost twitching, and inside her silk briefs, her slim lace-trimmed slip and her pencil skirt, her bottom seemed sensitised already. It was as if the very skin and musculature of each smooth, rounded lobe was anticipating the kiss of retribution. The pain. Her nerves were running test patterns, making sure that every synapse would fire perfectly when, later, the important messages were being passed.

Imagining herself bared for discipline, she felt her face and throat colour rosy pink, and she looked up, around the open-plan office, wondering if anybody else could possibly imagine what would soon be happening. There were others in the company who shared her predilection, but it was bad form to speak of it openly. The secret nature of a punishment was sacrosanct; it belonged to a higher, more rarefied continuum than that of money and everyday dealings. And yet still her curiosity piqued her. There might be untold others who'd be sobbing and crying tonight.

For instance, that young secretary over there could well have misspelt an important client's name. For that she might have her panties removed, and her no doubt very slim and well-toned bottom paddled severely for her sins. Come to think of it, the girl did look a little edgy; her face was flushed, her eyes excited. How embarrassed she would be to know that Joanna was *au fait* with her plight.

But no matter what happened to her sister in distress, it was Joanna's own near future that bothered her. She shifted in her seat, feeling her sensitivity changing into discomfort as the familiar heaviness began to mass between her legs. The waiting period always found her in this delicious, embarrassing, love-it, loath-it state. Her bra suddenly felt a size too tight, and she bit her lip, knowing her knickers were getting soaked.

'A problem with Côte Mystère, is there?' enquired an amused voice from just beside her, and she looked up, flinching wildly, to see Kevin – who was always there to tease – right in her personal space. He was fond of sneaking up like that, and her embarrassment doubled as she met her colleague's stunning eyes; eyes that were a brilliant, merry sky-blue, and which sparkled from beneath a thick, boyish fringe of smoke-blond hair.

'Nothing I can't handle,' Joanna countered smoothly, closing the memo. Those eyes of his might be full of fun, but they were sharp. She was sure he'd seen the text.

'Sure of that, are you?' he said, challenging her as ever. He licked his lips, as if he could see straight through her clothing to the condition of her body. As if he could see into her mind and see what she was anticipating. As if he could see her stretched and humbled across the desk, her knickers pulled down and her bottom about to be rendered scarlet.

Hiding her discomfiture, Joanna kept her voice crisp, and replied, 'Quite sure, thank you,' then turned her attention studiously to the demands of her laptop. As Kevin moved away, she tried not to hear his mocking laugh.

As her Master would expect the amended report to be presented to him at the same time she presented her body, Joanna spent the rest of the day polishing and perfecting it. Or at least the confident, business-like half of her did, while the submissive dreamer simply longed for her fate. At lunch time, she forewent the usual pub lunch with her fellow analysts and managers, fearing that her ungovernable agitation would give her away – especially to eyes as perceptive as Kevin's.

Instead, she went into a neighbouring shopping mall and wandered around aimlessly, imagining, just as she had in the office, that the people who caught sight of her could see her future in The Study.

On passing a small boutique, though, she became more purposeful. Aware of what her high excitement had done to her lingerie, she entered the shop intending to purchase a simple change of knickers. The selection on sale, however, was extensive, and just looking at them, and running her fingers over silk and satin and lace, Joanna couldn't keep herself from imagining how they would feel against her bottom. This pair of fairly plain white cotton briefs with a thin trim of lace around the legs would certainly please her Master. She pictured him running his hand across them as she lay face down over his lap; testing the resilience of her flesh through the thin fabric; assessing possible targets for his hand, perhaps trying a few practice slaps before drawing the panties down.

The next pair that caught her eye were far more elaborate. A deep yet subtle burgundy red, more lace than substance, these briefs were very brief indeed. The sort of knickers her Master often left on her during chastisement. He would take hold of the back of them, and with a deft twist, draw them up tightly into the furrow between her buttocks, while he belaboured her cheeks with his hand or with a slipper. This particular trick Joanna regarded as truly devilish – because every well-aimed blow caused the taut fabric to jerk against her sex. After a dozen spanks, she was helpless, she was coming.

Another pair of knickers, of fuller cut this time, reminded Joanna of a caning she'd taken early in their relationship. She had presented herself wearing something very similar to these pants – a pair of French drawers made of heavy coral-coloured satin. Scared of what lay ahead of her, she had knelt before her Master and abjectly begged him to let her keep her knickers on. She remembered her Master's thin, sardonic smile as he'd agreed to her request; then she remembered her own yowl of pain when she'd discovered that the satin made no difference whatsoever, and that for her impudence, she'd been awarded extra strokes.

Returning to the present, she made her choices – not without some difficulty, and a great deal of expense – and found herself more wound up and full of anticipation than ever, and in great need of one of the garments she'd just bought.

The afternoon seemed even longer than the morning that had preceded it, and Joanna's thoughts were constantly with her Master . . . in The Study. By the end of the office day, she felt so hot and bothered and in such a stupor of anticipation that she had to retire to the lady's cloakroom, and run cold water over her wrists to calm her nerves. She would also have liked to bathe, and to refresh herself in other ways, but to do so would be to keep her Master waiting, so she simply changed her knickers, combed her hair, and made her way to him. To his secret penthouse in a prestigious building nearby.

As she ascended in the mirror-lined lift, she studied

her reflection – the face and body of a woman heading for punishment. Beneath her soft crop of blonde curls, her face was radiant, her eyes were bright and her cheeks were blushing. Even though she was shaking in her high heels, she stood straight – as her Master always insisted. Her figure was lush and shapely in her tailored pin-stripe power suit, and her legs were long and sleek in charcoal-grey stockings.

By the time she reached the top floor, and the lift doors slid open, her heart was pounding fit to burst inside her chest. She was almost fainting as she crossed the stark white elegance of the lobby, and as she pressed the doorbell, and waited to be admitted, she seemed to float. It was as if she had passed through a discreet barrier of some kind, and was now in the world that lay beyond it. A bright new world where different laws applied.

Her Master, ever mindful of life's small courtesies, met her at the door. His greeting was a narrow smile, and a soft, 'Good evening, Joanna.'

Calming her palpitations, Joanna answered with a quick, 'Good evening. I've brought the corrected report you asked for.' She followed this with a respectful, 'Sir,' when she saw his expressive eyebrows lift. Another mistake, she thought, nerves jittering as he escorted her to his inner sanctum: his handsome, quiet, book-lined study – the richly warm, red-decorated room where her faults and errors were often paid for. She called it his Study in Scarlet, which was apt in more ways than one. His prized first editions of Sherlock Holmes took pride of place on the shelves.

Her Master was tall and his bearing confident as he strode before her along the corridor. He was dressed, as he often was on these occasions, in black: a polo-necked sweater and jeans with a heavy belt. His hair was neatly combed back, and it looked darker, as if he'd just showered and it was wet. His wire-rimmed spectacles gave his features a new and serious cast. Just the sight of him like this made Joanna's knees go weak and wobbly. Which made standing, while he sat down in his huge, throne-like, red-leather-upholstered chair, her first ordeal.

'You may raise your skirt.'

His order was all the more implacable for being delivered in an even, conversational tone. Feeling flustered at having to juggle with her bag and her briefcase as she tottered on her high heels, Joanna made a mess of obeying him. Abandoning her belongings on the plush carpet – as there was no one to take them from her – she squirmed her hips to get her narrow skirt and slip up over them, and the end result was an inelegant bundle of silk and linen wedged around her waist by its own tightness. Her Master eyed her momentarily, then held out his hand. Reaching down and fumbling in her briefcase, Joanna fished out a tablet computer loaded with the revised report.

As her Master sat behind his desk and read, flicking the pages with slow, languid strokes across the screen, Joanna was forced to simply stand, her pants and her stocking tops on show. After much debate, she had selected the white knickers, but looking down now, she discovered that the fabric was far sheerer than she'd realised. The dark blonde shadow of her bushy pubic floss was clearly visible through the thin pale cotton, and she knew that if he should choose to look up and glance her way, her Master would be able to see it.

The longer he read, the more nervy and unstable Joanna became. She felt as if she were teetering on the brink of doing something ridiculous and fool-hardy, and she discovered, to her surprise and horror, that her fingertips were touching the welts of her stockings. And stealing inwards. She gasped in shock when her Master suddenly spoke.

'You'll regret it, Joanna,' he said without looking up.

Her heart thumping, she linked her fingers behind her back.

Mercifully, the Côte Mystère report did not take too much longer to read. Joanna had done her best to make it comprehensive, yet precise. Tapping the file shut, her Master laid aside the tablet and looked up at her, folding his long hands lightly on the desk before him. From behind his glasses, his sharp eyes appraised her.

'Well done,' he remarked, one finger stroking the edge of the tablet. 'A pity though, that you could not have done this well first time around . . .' He paused, a familiar expression coming into his eyes. A look that was both fierce and dreamy. 'You could have saved yourself a great deal of suffering, Joanna.'

'I know that,' Joanna replied, experiencing her exposure and desire acutely. Both seemed to feed off the other, their fires stoked by a real and potent fear. She had a classic love–hate relationship with what was about to happen to her, just as she adored her Master, yet still bristled against his total control of her.

There was a long pause while her Master simply stared at her, his gaze intent on her suspenders and her knickers.

'Lower your panties,' he said suddenly, the light in his eyes, behind his glasses, unchanging. He rose from behind his desk, and as he did so, Joanna nervously hooked her thumbs in the waistband of her knickers, knowing that the deed must be done before he reached her. Quickly, she skinned down the thin white briefs as far as her knees, then left them there, bunched up, as he preferred. She wrinkled her nose as she caught the scent of her own arousal, rising up from her crotch, and from the anointed gusset of her underwear, then blushed hard as her Master reached her, smiling.

He walked around her, passing so close that their bodies briefly touched, then he stood behind her and settled his hands on her bottom. 'Delightful,' he murmured, flexing his cool fingers and caressing each lobe. 'Simply delightful . . . ' he repeated, lifting and parting them.

Joanna moaned and pushed her buttocks toward him.

'Have a care, Joanna,' he whispered, his mouth brushing the back of her neck while his hands oh-so-slowly manipulated her. 'Remember why you're here.'

Joanna hung her head, fighting her weakness, her burgeoning desire. Why wouldn't he start? Begin her punishment? Tan her behind until she cried and begged for mercy?

As if he'd heard her plea, her Master suddenly released her. 'Come along then,' he said briskly, 'Let's have you across my knee . . . Hurry up!' Stepping away, he drew out a tall, straight chair from against the wall where it had been standing, and sank down onto it with an easy, studied grace. Then he tapped his lap.

Joanna needed no further urging. Shuffling forward, hampered by her knickers, she moved towards him, then tipped over his dark-clad knees and struck her pose.

She always liked to savour this moment. It was like standing on a diving board, or in the open hatch of an aircraft wearing a parachute. Her Master understood about hesitation – he never felt it, but he knew she did. He allowed her these few seconds to explore her feelings, to change her mind if she needed to. She never had changed her mind –

because she had never wanted to – but the chance was there, if ever she should need it.

The moments ticked by, and the opportunity to turn back was gone. She felt his hand settle on her bare bottom, testing her again, but more stringently this time, squeezing the flesh with his steely fingers and palpating it. One fingertip slid down along the division between her buttocks, then pressed at her tight rear closure – just for an instant, but so firmly it make her gasp.

Her Master answered the gasp with a sigh. An impatient sigh. Her involuntary exclamation was not a sign of acquiescence, and now she'd passed the point of no return, she was his and she must accept his every whim. Or at least try to.

'Are you ready then?' he enquired, still touching her.

'Yes . . . Yes I am,' she said quietly, suffering the delicious torment of his fingers in her sex-cleft.

'Excellent,' he said crisply, then began the spanking.

It hurt, and as ever Joanna had to concentrate intently to prevent herself crying out. Her Master's hand seemed to have acquired a new and alien texture. It was no longer the gentle, soft-skinned hand that could caress her body so lovingly, but a new extremity that was as hard as stone and could move with blinding speed.

As the smacks built up, and the sensations of pain and heat grew rapidly in her buttocks, Joanna asked herself, as she always did, why she let this happen.

Why? she posed as her Master's skilful hand kissed the crown of her right bottom-cheek, then matched it with a stinging impact to the left. He was creating a pattern now, a design of crimson soreness and susceptibility, a redness to match the aura of his beautiful room. The slaps went up and down, and from side to side over the whole area of her tautly toned backside. Occasionally, he would stray down to the upper area of her thighs – in the zone delineated by her stocking top and the crease where thigh and buttock met – and decorate her there with the same glowing ornament. It was an area where her skin seemed especially tender, and his attentions there made Joanna grit her teeth. Her cries and whimpers she still held back, but only barely.

Just with his hands, she thought, struggling for control, for lucidity as her pulsing, flaming rear consumed her senses. He'd hardly begun yet, and already her resolve was crumbling. And a groan escaped her when a deft spank caught her anus.

The fact that he'd invoked a cry clearly pleased her Master. He struck again at the same site. And again. Then repeatedly. Joanna heard an uncouth choking yelp, and knew it was coming from her own lips, but she was too consumed by the waves of feeling to suppress her noise. It seemed as if she had passed inside herself somehow, her whole consciousness was settled in the area of skin and flesh that lay beneath the volley of impacts. The rest of her body was operating on auto pilot. The mouth that cried and keened. The eyes that watered, and so shamingly wept. The legs that kicked. The sex that grew so puffy and engorged . . . and also wet.

'Oh God,' she moaned, feeling her Master perform a devilish trick. He had grasped one coral-pink buttock in his hand, the pressure of his fingertips a pain in itself, and was stretching open her anal cleft to create a target. Each blow now landed fair and square across the portal of her bottom, a zone where he knew she feared it most.

'Agh!' she yelped, her feet flailing through the air, as a sharper slap made her seething vulva quiver.

'Not so stoic now, my love,' whispered her Master,

inclining his lithe body over hers. His lips moved gently against her ear as his fingers cruised her backside, stirring her anguish with the tips of his dragging nails. He paused again at the vent of her anus, prodding the inflamed little entrance in a vulgar rhythm. 'You can't help yourself at all now, can you?' he quizzed her softly. 'I hurt you . . . Hurt you right there –' he pressed again, making her whimper '– and all it does is arouse you even more.' The finger stopped pushing but remained exactly where it was.

Making a supreme effort, Joanna remained still, although every nerve in her was screaming that she move; that she grind her pelvis against his knee and immediately come. It seemed perverse to resist a climax, he'd made her suffer enough for it. Even with his only hand, he'd turned her buttocks into slabs of fire.

But there was a pride in her that still forced her to defy him. It always did. It was the wild and stubborn heart of her that was as dominant as he was, and which always brought her submissive side to grief. Closing in on herself, she ignored her dripping and swollen crotch. She ignored the agony that smouldered in her bottom cheeks. She ignored the delicate, invasive fingertip that sought to enter her rectum. She gritted her teeth, and raised her bottom, to invite him still more.

Her Master laughed. 'It's like that is it?' he said, and though she couldn't see it, she imagined his glacial eyes warming and dancing with amusement, and a smile spreading across his chiselled, handsome face. He loved her to fight him. He delighted in the defiance that gave him permission to test her limits. He pushed his finger a little way into her bottom, and, though it was just what she didn't want to do, Joanna squealed. She heard him laugh again, but the finger was swiftly removed.

His hand touched her back, almost caressingly, as he spoke again. 'It was such a little slip up, my darling. Just a figure transposed. Nothing really.' He sounded amused, mock-regretful, profoundly happy. And so he should be, he'd got exactly what he wanted. 'A hand spanking would have sufficed . . .' He stroked her back encouragingly, through her jacket, seeming to ignore the crimson lobes that beckoned below. 'But you leave me no choice now.' His voice was jubilant, full of excitement, but strangely tender. 'There's no remorse in you yet, Joanna. No genuine regret over anything.' He paused. For effect. She just knew it. 'It will pain us both, but you clearly need a sterner test.' He gave her a pat – on the bottom this time, which made her yap – then helped her, with some difficulty on her part, to get to her feet.

'Please remove all your clothes, my dear,' he said, leaving her swaying as he walked around to the back of his desk. 'Every stitch.' He opened a drawer, seemed to debate for a moment, then took out a thick leather strap about a foot in length. 'But you may bring me your panties, because I'm sure we can put them to use.' He ran a contemplative finger over the length of supple black hide in his hand, tracing its texture and the way it was divided into three equal tongues. 'You're likely to scream soon . . . and I can't concentrate when the noise gets too loud.'

Oh God, thought Joanna as she undid the buttons of her jacket, her fingers trembling. *Why do I always ask for this?* she demanded of herself, stripping off her blouse and revealing her thin silk bra beneath. When her body was naked, she stood there defenceless, her knickers in her hand.

Because you love it, answered her submissive self as she walked towards the desk and prepared to lay herself over it.

Because you love him, she thought, watching her Master's long fingers caress the menacing black taws.

'I hope there won't be any more problems with Côte Mystère, my darling,' said Joanna's Master later, as she lay panting across his denim-clad knees in the scarlet study. She wasn't face down this time, but the torment she felt now was as bad as a spanking – because his rough-textured jeans were harsh against her hot, punished rump.

The discomfort would have been less, she supposed, if she could have managed to keep still. But the way he was touching her – in the cleft between her legs – kept her well-whipped cheeks in motion.

'I'll do my best,' she gasped, 'but I can't make promises . . . Things . . . Agh! Oh God! Th-things happen . . .'

'I know that,' he said, kissing her throat as she climaxed. 'But I want everything to be perfect next time we go to Côte Mystère. I've bought a new birching trestle. And I've put it in the south cellar. All ready for you.'

Joanna's head felt as light as a feather set adrift on a stream. She was sore, terribly sore, but at the same time sublimely relaxed. Her bottom was in agony, but she was blissfully happy. She was deeply in love.

Her Master was obviously pleased with life too. He'd removed his glasses, and his bright, teasing eyes were now twinkling like stars. They were so blue, as Joanna looked up at them, so sweet and wise. She raised a hand and tousled his thick smoky hair, flicking it forward from its combed-back severity into his usual endearingly floppy fringe. He smiled, his expression indulgent as he let her have her way.

'I love you, Master,' she whispered, brushing her fingers over his brow, his elegant cheekbone, his firm, chiselled chin.

Beneath her touch, he shifted his face, then pressed his lips against her palm before he spoke. 'I love you too, Joanna.' He placed his hand over hers, caressing her gently with the same living weapon that had not long ago turned her bottom-flesh to flame. 'But I'm just Kevin now . . . Just ordinary Kevin. Not your Master anymore.'

Joanna laughed. 'No, not until next time there's a problem with Côte Mystère . . . or any other damned thing you can conjure up out of thin air to get me into this abominable red lair of yours!'

Swirling her bottom on his lap, she felt his erection swell and jerk, then echoed his gasp with her moan of pain and joy.

Ill Met by Moonlight

1

It was a dream. She knew it was a dream. But somehow that didn't seem to matter.

She was in a warm place, and she was deliciously, tropically warm. And, even though she didn't recognise her surroundings, she felt as safe and enclosed as if someone she loved and trusted was holding her tight.

Sniffing the air, she caught the scents of pine and balsam. Woodsy odours that were both clean and earthy at the same time.

She was waiting for a man. She'd been waiting for him quite a while, but somehow that didn't seem to matter either. Just to be here, relaxed and ready, was a pleasure.

Who are you? Do I know you?

Lois wondered if it might be Oliver, her ex. But why would she be waiting for him, even in this floating unreality? They'd parted ages ago, in an easy break, and, when she was awake, she barely ever thought of him . . . so why suddenly dream about him now?

In their heyday, though, the sex had been good. So maybe that was the reason? She was horny, so her body had fixed on its last source of satisfaction – other than her by own efforts. She remembered some of Ollie's finer moments with a twinge of hot nostalgia.

The room was dark and full of deep shadows, lit only by a nightlight and the flickering of a low burning fire. There was a womblike quality to the walls, something natural and organic, and she still couldn't work out where she was. She only knew it was somewhere new to her that felt irrationally like home too.

Maybe I was here in a former life?

Now there was a peculiar notion, if ever there was one . . . but, then, everything about the situation was strange and other-worldly.

Maybe I'm remembering something I dreamed once before? Now that's complicated . . . a dream within a dream. Whatever next?

Whatever it was, she couldn't deny that she felt mellow and loose and sexy.

Touching her hands to her body, she was surprised. What the devil was she wearing?

Instead of her habitual shabby T-shirt and overwashed knickers, she found the voluminous and enveloping folds of an old-fashioned brushed-cotton nightdress. Nestling into it like a small furry animal, she sighed. Who'd have thought that something so prim could also be so sexy? The long full nightgown was both cosy and erotic at the same time, and the contrast between being all chastely covered up on top, and bare and devoid of panties beneath was sinfully naughty. As her naked thighs slid against each other, her nipples stiffened and puckered, their tips chafed by the virginal white fabric in a subtle autonomic caress.

I'd rather have a man do that, but where is he? Where is he?

Someone was coming though, she knew that. He just

wasn't here yet. And, in the meantime, she would make her own amusement.

Picturing a pair of hands that were long and elegant, but full of suppressed strength, she clasped her breasts through the soft cotton of the gown and teased them with light squeezes. The mind image was almost supernaturally clear.

Strong hands, sleek golden skin . . .

Graceful fingers that were gentle but strangely cool . . .

Curiouser and curiouser . . . but also mmm mmm mmm . . .

When she flicked her thumbs across the hardened peaks of her nipples, the slight contact sent streaks of sensation flashing along her nerves. She could almost see that too, like little pathways glittering and silvery beneath the white nightdress and her own skin. She watched them zip and twinkle until they popped tiny starbursts in her clitoris. Of their own accord, her hips lifted and she moaned.

Ohmigod, all I've done is touch my breasts and I'm almost there! What's going happen when I really get down to business? Or he does?

Suddenly, she couldn't wait . . . she could hardly breathe.

Wriggling against the crisply laundered sheets, she hitched up her nightgown. Up and up until it was just a scrunched-up crumpled bunch under her armpits.

She was a goddess of sex. An odalisque exhibiting herself for a hundred watching eyes. She'd kicked off the sheets as she'd pulled up her nightgown and now she was on display from her chest down to her toes, her skin lapped by the warm scented air.

Breasts. Belly. Thighs. Pubis. The Full Monty.

She could smell herself too. A new perfume had blended itself into the pine, the earth and the juniper wood smoke. Her arousal, salty and pungent and also of the earth.

She stared down at her body, pale as alabaster against the luminous white sheets, the curls of her pussy a wild sandy shock between her thighs. She could see a glint of juiciness sparkling through the hair there and, shimmying against the mattress, she clenched herself, tensing up her strong inner muscles, and felt the slow honeyed roll of her arousal.

I'm very wet, secret lover . . . very wet. I'm ready . . . where the hell are you?

Should she touch herself? Or should she save herself for *him*? For a moment, she fantasised that he'd tied her hands to the bed-rails behind her head, punishing her, preventing her from stealing that special privilege.

Then, suddenly, because it was a dream . . . her hands *were* tied!

She was lashed to the brass rails with what looked like the cords from a couple of old-fashioned dressing gowns. How bizarre was that?

Instantly, of course, the need to touch her sex ramped up to an almost agonising pitch. Unable to suppress it or ignore it, she threw herself around on the mattress, hips circling and weaving while she tried desperately *not* to imagine her legs being fastened too.

Uh-oh, too late!

No sooner had she thought it than the deed was done and she was bound hand and foot with more dressing-gown cords. Had she ever had a dressing gown like that? Did she know anyone else who had one? Where the hell was all this stuff coming from? She only knew that her ankles were spread wide apart and there was no longer any way whatsoever to get ease from the ravening itch of desire.

And it was now, when somehow she'd managed to make

herself totally vulnerable, that the unknown dream lover finally put in an appearance.

The door swung back just like in an old Dracula movie and a figure appeared in the doorway.

And she didn't have the slightest idea who he was.

Who the hell are you, Dream Lover? And, boy, do you know how to make a big entrance!

Dream Lover was a cliché as well as a total stranger. Your actual tall, dark and handsome, but with a twist, and dressed all in black – a long coat, close-fitting T-shirt, jeans and boots.

And he had the most amazing hair!

It was almost black, yet also blond. Like ebony frosted with gold, and cut short, but not too short. A touch of wild, natural curl set off its startling pale tipping and made it appear to glow in the dim room like a halo, its brilliance second only to the fire in its owner's gleaming, flashing eyes.

Lois blinked. There was something weird about those eyes, but their very brightness made it impossible to work out what it was. She could only stare into them, like a willing patsy totally hooked by a hypnotist's spinning coin.

Talk about a fantasy man.

This is a dream, you fool! Of course *he's a fantasy man . . .*

But still, why the hair? And the eyes that she wished she could see better.

She must have conjured him up from the very depths of memory, from some long-lost book she'd read, or image she'd once seen. A world of faeries or earth spirits, of beings of supernatural power and alchemical attraction that she'd loved in more innocent times before she'd become a techno-geek.

But, however she'd cooked him up, God, how she wanted

him! Between her thighs, she grew wetter, wetter, wetter . . .

The apparition didn't speak, and Lois couldn't. But still those amazing eyes pinned her to the spot, widening with an unmistakeable hunger. He immediately zeroed in on her cunt, and his fine-cut nostrils flared as if he'd smelt her. Which wasn't surprising, because she could certainly smell herself.

And the more she stared at him, the more she thought he was a dish fit for a queen.

He really was quite something. Face broad and intelligent, and vaguely familiar somehow now. Cheekbones high, jaw firm and a mouth that was strong and manly yet ever so slightly pouty in a way that made her long to nibble his plump lower lip. Even as she hungered for him and his eyes told her he was hungering for her in return, his tongue flicked out and moistened those succulent lips. It was pointed and very pink, darting lasciviously.

Almost expiring with lust, Lois hauled in a deep breath, and began to smell Dream Lover as much as he could smell her, getting yet another surprise into the bargain.

Not for him the smells of leather and sweat. Not for him the cool blue smells of male cologne.

No, as he approached her across the cabin, soft-footed on the wooden floor, he brought with him the sweet smell of flowers.

Violets, wild roses, delicate woodland blooms . . . and, most piercingly and headily, the scent of lavender.

It was like swigging down a triple belt of some perfumed liqueur made by monks in the wilds of rural France.

Lois squirmed around against the mattress, the very quick of her body aching like the devil as if the sweet odour was stimulating it directly. She throbbed and throbbed, her simmering flesh begging for contact. Just the tiniest little touch would do it. The stranger's mouth twisted in a slow knowing smile as he drew nearer. It seemed to light his every feature like a candle.

And still they hadn't exchanged a single word.

While Lois watched like a starving beast eyeing up a prime rib, Dream Lover flung off his long dark coat and then knelt on the bed. Having braced herself for the bounce of a substantially muscled body hitting the mattress, she got a shock that made her gasp. He was big – tall and broad and solid – but the sheet on which she lay barely seemed dented. It was the oddest phenomenon, and Lois knew she should be frightened . . . but in a dream, she supposed, weird stuff like this was normal.

That was, if it *was* a dream? Some of it was far too vivid to be imaginary.

Free of his coat, Dream Lover's body was shown off to perfection. His arms gleamed in the firelight as if they were fashioned from polished wood and strength shone around him like an aura. The golden glitter that dusted his thick dark hair was even more breathtaking in close proximity, and his close-fitting black T-shirt embraced the ripped contours of his torso. Beneath the tough dark fabric of his jeans, his thighs were as sturdy as oak branches, and at his crotch there was a fine chunky bulge.

Lois's fingers itched to explore him, but her bonds were disturbingly real in an imaginary situation. She simply could not move, and Dream Lover's velvety, tantalising lips curved at the sight of her struggles. His hand, so conveniently *un*fettered, reached out towards her body, hovering for several seconds over her breast, before dropping to the full curve and cupping it. Lois hissed through her teeth, as his long thumb settled against her nipple as if it belonged there. His skin was as cool as she'd imagined it to be . . .

Her hiss turned to an outright groan as he flicked and tickled her; her mystery man smiled, his passionate mouth widening in a smile that was impish and knowing. With slow calculation, he strummed her again and again, and the compulsion to thrash about and rub the skin of her bare buttocks against the sheet beneath her grew stronger and stronger by the second. She tried to stay still, because for some bizarre reason it seemed important to show a little decorum, but it was hopeless. Wriggling like a strumpet, she knew she'd never looked sluttier in her life.

Why can't I just ask you who you are?

She opened her mouth to speak, but Dream Lover put paid to all questions by tweaking the nipple quite hard now, rolling it between finger and thumb, plucking at it and pulling at it, making it stiffer and pinker than ever. He cocked his gilded head on one side as she bucked against the mattress, attempting to widen her thighs and entice him with her sticky melting sex. She'd never behaved like this before, even in her wildest moments, and her own wantonness both appalled and excited her, goading her aroused body to even greater heights of shamelessness.

Please . . . please . . . she begged him silently, still unable to speak. *Touch my cunt. Stroke me with your fingers . . . Fuck me! Please, please, fuck me* now!

The golden-frosted head cocked again, and he grinned like the sun.

You heard that, didn't you, you bastard? You read my mind!

Maybe mind-reading was standard operational procedure in dreams? Anything was possible. Watching her face, Dream Lover continued to play idly with her breast for a while, all the time watching her face with the intensity of a scientist.

I can't take much more of this.

Lois watched his face for an acknowledgement, but Dream Lover just regarded her benignly as he went on with his fondling.

But Lois didn't feel benign. She wanted to kill him, or fuck him, or even both. Between her legs tension gathered and gathered and her head seemed to be floating it felt so light. Her brain was emptying of thought. She was about to come.

Just from having her breast touched? Surely not? But anything seemed achievable in this wonderful warm place.

But just when it seemed almost about to happen, Dream Lover withdrew his hand.

'You bastard!'

So near, yet suddenly so far, Lois found her tongue at last, and Dream Lover's brow puckered. What was he thinking? Planning some devilish new sexual torture for her, no doubt. He snagged his sinful lower lip with his Colgate-white teeth, and his brilliant eyes sparkled with mischief.

Lois blinked. Surely not? It had suddenly dawned on her what was peculiar about those eyes – they were two different colours. The right one was a sharp, electrical sky blue and the left one was as warm and brown as Armagnac.

She was just about to remark on this unexpected phenomenon, or just simply beg him to fuck her now she'd finally got her voice back, when, without warning, Dream Lover scooted back to the edge of the bed, and then reached down to unbuckle his heavy boots. After kicking them vigorously away across the room, he plucked at the hem of his T-shirt and pulled it out of his waistband with equal impatience. A second later it flew away on the same trajectory as the boots, and she was gifted with the sight of the most awesome male pulchritude. Muscles rippled across his chest and abdomen as he moved, bunching and relaxing beneath skin the colour of honeyed sandstone, almost too beautiful and magnificently male to be real.

Well, I've never wanted to worship a guy before, but I do now, she thought hazily. *What are you, some kind of magical deity? A prince of the world of dreams . . . a perfect lover?*

Coming to her again, he lay over her, his chest hard and smooth against her nipples, while the coarse workaday cloth of his jeans was equally rough against the bare skin of her belly. Lois blushed furiously as he pressed his hard crotch against her mons. She was soaking wet down there and it would surely seep through his jeans and he'd be able to feel it.

But then she forgot about qualms and wetness and jeans and everything. His mouth came down on hers, and she almost drowned in his sweet floral odour.

The contact of his lips on hers was soft at first, almost ethereal, like chilled velvet. Then, after a few seconds, the kiss grew wild and his tongue pushed inside her mouth, bringing with it a taste that was as heady as his smell. Lois gasped. His lips were candy sweet, and his tongue was cool and wicked, darting like a benevolent serpent inside her mouth, tasting and probing, then powerfully devouring. The pressure of the kiss became so intense that her jaw ached a little from the effort of giving back as good as she was getting.

Big hands settled over her smaller ones where they were fastened to the bedhead. He laced his fingers between hers as he used his entire body to caress and excite her, rubbing her with silky skin and with the denim and with the hardness of his muscles and his cock. His strong hips rocked and rocked, and the bulge of his erection somehow worked its way between her thighs, spreading her sex-lips so it could stimulate her clitoris.

And suddenly it was all too much . . . and yet not enough.

Muffled by his tongue, Lois growled a garbled sound of protest, her pelvis jerking against his, commanding him to give her more, more, more.

In return, Dream Lover laughed, his glee as sweet in her mouth as his taste was. Then he slid one hand down her body, visiting her breasts and her belly. His cool skin was a satin kiss against her heat.

Touch me! Touch me down there! Masturbate my clit and make me come and make me come before I die!

But, even if he'd heard her, he was determined to do what *he* wanted.

Working blind, still kissing, he worked deftly at the button and zip of his jeans and uncovered himself. Lois couldn't see his size, but, hot damn, she could feel it. He was huge and breathtaking against her thighs, hard and determined as he sought his target. With just a little help from his hand, he navigated himself inside her. His sex was as strong and sturdy as the rest of him and just its presence, cool inside her, was a thrill.

Aroused beyond anything she'd ever known before, she was stretched around him, and the bulk of his penis almost made her come without him moving. She lay beneath him, trembling on the brink, gasping and dreaming.

But he was a man – even in the dream – and he wanted action. With barely a stroke or two he had her in rhapsodies. Her body clutched and clutched at him, clenching and contracting, the sensations twice as spicy because she was helpless and couldn't wrap her limbs around him. When he freed her lips, she peaked again, howling and whimpering. When he thrust again, her soul soared, swooping and flying.

Higher, higher, higher she arced, and then descended, barrelling back down into her body like the little shooting star she suddenly and distinctly remembered watching earlier.

And with that, she achieved oblivion.

All went dark.

'Shit!'

Lois Hillyard jerked upright, her heart lurching with the sudden disorientation of waking up far too fast and not quite knowing where she was. She stared around wildly, her eyes skittering from object to object in the unfamiliar room.

What the hell am I doing in a log cabin and why is it so bloody cold?

She scrabbled for the quilt, which was on the floor beside her bed and, as she swaddled it around herself, she started to remember things. Things like why she was here in a log cabin in the wilds of nowhere beside the sea, which she could hear rolling outside instead of traffic noises to which she was more accustomed.

And things like stray hot fragments of the dream from which she'd just woken.

'Shit,' she muttered again, burrowing even deeper into the quilt and puffing out her cheeks, still in shock.

What the hell was all that about?

She'd had sex dreams before, but never one so vivid, so strange . . . or so kinky.

Bondage with an unknown man who had gold in his hair and smelt of lavender . . . Where had that madness come from?

Dreams were weird. You usually forgot most of them within moments of waking. But not this one.

Her Dream Lover sprang into her mind instantaneously, every detail like crystal.

He'd been tall, muscular, and graceful with the most astonishing hair and eyes. What possessed someone's subconscious to cook up details like that? Still in her duvet, gripped by the shakes, she tried to analyse him.

Well, the height might have come from a TV actor she was keen on, and the long black coat and funereal garb in general was *de rigueur* for vaguely threatening men of mystery.

But the hair? The eyes? The strangely cool skin? She hadn't the faintest . . .

Face? Well, funny as it seemed, she could pin that. The basic features were her actor again, but there was a touch, just a touch, of the man sharing the beach with her as well.

But why the hell dream about *him* though? It wasn't as if there was any chance, she'd quickly discovered, of getting off with him. No holiday romance there, no way.

Neighbour Guy, as she called him, seemed to have been going out of his way to avoid her, and when they had run into each other he'd been surly at best. He was worthy of fancying, in a purely physical sense, but, in terms of conversation, he seemed to begrudge every monosyllable.

Well, sod you, she'd thought, catching sight of him once or twice, stalking the beach or the rough gravelled track to the local shop, but, somehow, she couldn't help feeling sorry for him too. Somehow, without knowing why, she'd formed a distinct impression that he was a man with a load of sorrow hanging over him. And for that she could almost forgive his chilly grumpiness.

Yes, her fantasy guy of the gilded hair and other

magnificent accoutrements had resembled her unhappy neighbour ever so slightly, but otherwise they couldn't have been more different.

Dream Lover had been full of the joys of life. And rambunctiously overflowing with the joys of vigorous pervy sex!

Her body was still tingling with the aftermath, and between her legs she was humid and sticky.

Ohmigod, I must have come in my sleep!

Well, all this sea air and the woodland ambience must be good for something. It had put her in touch with her earth goddess self, or something like that. Being out here in the wild beyonds of unconnected nowhere was going to be a blast if she had a dream like that every night, and with any luck she'd not miss the internet at all. With no television, and a mobile connection that kept dropping out every two minutes, all she had for entertainment otherwise were a couple of uninspiring novels.

You knew this, didn't you, Sand!

Sandy, her friend and partner in their small web-development business, had been moaning at her for long enough to take a well-earned holiday and get away from it all for a while, and had more or less strong-armed her into accepting this offer of a seaside-cabin break from one of their grateful clients.

Unbeknown to Sandy, Lois had brought her laptop, and had planned to work anyway . . . until, of course, it had dawned on her that she was miles and miles from the nearest wi-fi hotspot!

'Twit!'

That would teach her to take the digital, technological world so completely for granted. It served her right for trying to wriggle out of the rest that Sandy had so kindly levered upon her.

It was still frustrating though. Especially when the weather was unseasonably grim and icy for the end of May and the best place to be was inside the cabin, tucked up with a steaming-hot laptop. But her mobile connection was too erratic and slow and, even if she did work, she had no way to upload anything to the testing server without tearing her hair out waiting for minute after minute after minute.

Better just concentrate on erotic fantasies then . . . They seem to be downloading just fine!

Either that or do some cleaning.

Why the hell is this stupid place suddenly covered in dust? It wasn't here earlier . . . Where is it all coming from?

The cabin had been impressively spick and span when she'd arrived but now a delicate veil of dust lay over most of the surfaces and drifted across the floor. There were even whorls of dust scattered over the bed and on the pillows, with several strange heaps against the head and the foot rails.

What the f–?

She shivered. She sniffed the air. And then tentatively, almost reluctantly, she slipped a hand down into her knickers and touched her wetness. Of which there was a lot. Far more than there ought to have been from simply playing with herself.

But it wasn't the quantity that bothered her, it was the way it smelt.

As she withdrew her fingers, a familiar odour made her head spin.

Lavender . . . It was lavender . . . Why does my crotch smell of lavender?

Pulling the quilt over her head, she tried hard not to think.

2

In human form, Robin crouched on the woodshed roof and tasted the flutters of fear in Lois's mind.

No, this was not what he wanted. Not at all. He'd wanted to give her pleasure, not scare the living daylights out of her. Savouring the physical sensations of sighing, he sent out his mind, and touched hers again, filling it with soothing waves of peace that granted sleep.

There, that was better. Unable to resist the temptation, he disassociated and floated through the roof of the cabin so he could be close to his new object of curiosity.

Touching down, he reassociated, and stood by the bed, just looking at her. Not that there was much to see with human eyes. She was curled up beneath the thick quilt like a hibernating dormouse, and only a few tufts of her tousled blonde hair were protruding from the top of it.

There was much to be said for being what he was though. If she woke up now, and emerged from her hiding place, she would see a man . . . but what she couldn't perceive were the powers he still retained.

He could see through the quilt to the pretty face, and even prettier body that lay beneath.

She was delightful and complex and Robin liked that. Connecting with her gave him everything that was delicious about assuming human form. Every year in the month of May, when the transformation was possible, he tasted and interacted with humans, feasting indulgently on their complicated and sometimes turbulent feelings. His own kind had emotions, true, but they were mild, bland and somewhat basic. Contentment. Satisfaction. A kind of wistful regret, occasionally. The only emotion that really stirred him while discarnate was curiosity. And, in that, he knew he was unusual among his breed.

And one of the very few to pursue the ancient privileges of merry May.

But look where it had got him!

He was addicted now, perhaps polluted somehow. Even while discarnate, he was gripped by powerful yearnings. Feelings had filtered through by osmosis into the whole of his existence and he only felt truly alive when he was 'human' ... or as near to that condition as he could approximate.

And tonight, with beautiful Lois, he'd almost believed for a moment that he was a man.

Dipping lightly into her mind, he relived the delicious episode, smiling at the way her own subconscious had provided all the elements of the scenario.

You didn't realise you were so kinky, did you? he told her sub-vocally, relishing the words he'd picked up from her vocabulary and from others, over the years.

Binding her to the bed and tormenting her with pleasure had stirred him mightily. And it stiffened his temporary flesh now in a way that made his spirit swirl with emotion and heady pleasure.

Now this, he thought, placing his large hand over his swelling groin and giving it a gentle squeeze, was something his own kind were really missing. Yes, they had a melding of sorts, and it was exceptionally pleasant, but it was a pale shadow in comparison to the hot, wild, sweaty, pumping chaos of human sex with its pungent fluids, its loss of control and ecstatic release.

For that alone, with a special woman like Lois, he might be prepared to lose the many powers humans lacked.

As Lois stirred, probably sensing him, he stepped back

from the bed, ready to disassociate and disappear instantaneously. Her head emerged from under the coverlet, and he was struck again by the sweet appeal of her human face.

It was elegant and oval, but with a soft rounding to the cheeks and a rather snub nose that he knew she sometimes fretted about. He'd modelled his own nose a little on it, to reassure her of the attractiveness of the shape. He'd noted too that, despite her qualms, she'd also found the very same feature subconsciously attractive in the man next door, so he'd taken elements of that face too, when creating the image of his own.

His thoughts balked for a moment, troubled as the consciousness of Lois's neighbour briefly touched his own.

Now there was a human emotion he *didn't* want too much of. Grief. Intense sadness. Inconsolable loss. The man in the next cabin had lost a lover, and lost her here, in this place, to the force of the sea. Robin knew what was in the thoughts of Lois's neighbour and, though he felt he understood them, the course of action that the man was planning was anathema to him. Did he not know how precious a thing the human condition was? Even in its darkest, direst hours . . .

Shaking his head as if that might dispel the received sorrow, Robin returned his attention to the warm sleeping woman who lay before him.

Her hair, he considered, was delightful; the shimmering golden colour of sunlight. He knew, of course, that it had been tampered with to make it look that way, but who was he, an entirely artificial human form, inspired by elements from many sources, to disapprove of a bit of creative enhancement? He'd taken his cue from her in acquiring his own sunlit streaks.

She was deeply asleep again now, without dreams, but the

temptation to intervene once more was vivid. His penis was hard, stiff and aching, although the sensation was deliciously pleasant, despite the discomfort. Her body was smooth and warm beneath her untidy T-shirt and panties, and the odour of her sex teased his senses and reinforced them.

How delightful it would be to ensorcell her again and plunge his borrowed stiffness into her.

He experienced a momentary qualm . . . guilt, he recognised. Guilt at exploiting the slumbering woman, and using her for his own satisfaction – even though he had given her pleasure and her subconscious had gladly welcomed him.

No, next time they joined – fucked, had sex, made love, as the humans so whimsically called it, even when they didn't love each other – next time, exquisite Lois would be an active conscious participant. That was a promise he silently made, and swore to keep.

Yet still his acquired flesh ached and ached.

Of course, the answer was to disassociate again. No body. No arousal. No physical ache. But he didn't want to do that. The month of May was precious and there were only a couple of days remaining. He wanted to remain human for as much time as he could.

Settling into his chair, he unzipped his jeans and drew out his cock.

How fine and delightful it felt to caress himself. To fuck the beautiful girl curled up on the bed was obviously the ideal satisfaction, but handling himself had its own particular charm. Curling his large fist around himself, he pumped greedily at his penis, working and working it. There was no need to take his time. No need to delay in order to increase his partner's sensations. He could rush, snatch his release quickly, come fast and hard.

But, when relief came, her name was noiseless on his lips.

For a while afterwards, he just sat there, letting his consciousness roam around the room, examining her possessions and her clothing, learning about her.

Eventually his attention settled on the device set on the rustic table, the one she called her laptop.

Robin had come to understand what the laptop was, and he applauded it as an excellent mode of communication. Humankind might be sorely limited in the way they interacted with one another, but they were ingenious in creating mechanisms to allow themselves to do the best they could, and this small computer was a prime example of what they could achieve.

He touched it and, energised by *his* energy, it sprang to life. Quickly, he rode its patterns of force and deduced the way to mute its operating noises. He didn't want to wake Lois yet. It would be better to 'meet' her for the first time in more acceptable circumstances. Finding an intruder in her bedroom wouldn't get their relationship off to a very good start!

As he played with the device, he sifted through thoughts and notions that he'd gleaned from Lois. She was vexed with her little computer, and vexed with herself over it. Out here, far from so-called civilisation, there was no way for her to connect it to the great web of energy lines she called 'the internet'. It needed something called 'wi-fi' to become a part of that matrix.

Robin smiled. It was simply a node that was required, a nexus that would focus yet another pattern of force. Swooping down, he caught up a big handful of dust and compressed it tightly in his palm.

A moment later, he looked down at a small gleaming

lozenge shape that pulsed softly in the dim light of the cabin.

His kind weren't called magical for nothing, he thought wryly, as he attached the little 'hotspot' to the underside of the desk, well out of sight.

A gift, my Lois, he thought fondly. In return for the pleasure you gifted to me.

With one last longing glance at her, he disassociated and floated away.

'What the fuck?'

Staring at the screen, Lois forgot the shivering chill of the cabin. She forgot the fact that her feet were blocks of ice and she could only keep marginally warm by wrapping the entire duvet and a couple of extra blankets around her. She even, for the moment, forgot the raving hot erotic dream she'd had, that seemed to have burnt itself into her brain in lurid Technicolor detail.

She had a wi-fi connection where one was impossible.

'This is mad!' She refreshed the list again.

But there it was. She was logged into a connection designated '000000' and the signal strength was excellent and the speed frankly phenomenal!

Absently rubbing her chilled toes together to increase their circulation, she went through all the settings, and everywhere, where there should have been strings of figures, she got '000000'.

'This is mad,' she repeated, and then clicked on the icon for Google, which brought up the search engine instantaneously.

The inexplicable connection bugged her, but after a few fruitless minutes of diagnostics, she gave up.

What the hell, at least the IP address wasn't 666.666.666.6.

By the time she'd checked all her favourite pages, and

even uploaded a bit of work to her testing server, the sun was high in the sky and its soft yellow rays were cascading in through the windows to warm up the cabin.

Thank heavens for an oil-fired heating system!

Lois was grateful for that small mercy as she took a shower in the tiny cubicle. It might be absolute rubbish at warming the rooms of the cabin, but at least it provided plenty of hot water.

She needed to be clean after last night. She'd felt icky and sticky and foxy after that dream. Masturbating in her sleep? Nothing wrong with it, really, nothing at all, but still sort of disturbing that she should be so horny, and not actually all that consciously aware of it.

Touching herself before she stepped beneath the spray, she'd been almost afraid she'd smell the odour of lavender on her fingers, and she'd been relieved – but irrationally disappointed – when all she'd smelt was plain old Lois-smell.

The bay was bright and blue when she stepped out on to the shared porch connecting the two cabins. Despite its convenience, the phantom wi-fi connection troubled her more than she cared to think about and, contrary to her every usual instinct and inclination, she'd turned off her laptop and decided to get out into the fresh air and do some 'nature'.

But why is it so bloody cold?

Despite the late-May sun, she was glad of her fleece and her boots as she trudged down the short packed-earth track and on to the beach. With just the two holiday cabins sharing it, the tiny bay was deserted. Lois had no idea where her neighbour was. She'd thought she'd heard him tramping about on the porch earlier, but now there was no sign of him. It would have been nice to make friends because, when she had managed to encounter him briefly once or twice, she'd rather fancied him. He was good-looking in a slightly heavy-set sort of way. But there was nothing doing. His responses had been barely monosyllabic, and a dark pall of 'touch me not' sadness seemed to envelop him.

'Poor bugger,' Lois observed as she stepped out on to the sand and made for the firmer stuff, closer to the water's edge, 'but you can't be happy if you don't give anyone a chance to cheer you up, can you?'

Yes, it would have been nice to forge a little holiday romance with her bay-mate if he'd been amenable, but maybe she didn't really need one. Not with the hyper-real sex dreams she was having! She was having plenty of erotic kink without any of the effort of the courtship dance. It was perfect. She could be as lazy as she liked, and still get satisfaction. Result!

Away from the pull of her computer, and the puzzle of the mysterious wi-fi connection, her experience of last night rushed in again to claim her.

Boy, had it been hot!

Dream Lover might have been chilly-skinned, but every-thing else about him was nothing short of incendiary. Just thinking about it all warmed her up inside her fleece and jeans, despite the spiteful bite of the nippy wind.

Dream Lover rose up before her in her imagination.

The tall dark powerful man out of nowhere was a classic romantic archetype, but where the hell had the image of odd eyes and gold-frosted hair come from? She had no explanation for those.

Not to mention the funky smell of lavender.

She seemed to smell it now, that rich sweet scent. And her body was growing warmer and warmer and warmer, surging and rousing with a rush of reborn lust.

The mysterious stranger advanced through her mind towards her and she felt so weak at the knees that she was forced to stagger to a scrappy outcrop of sand grass that had created a small dune at the edge of the beach.

Cowering on the little hump, she hugged her arms around her, shaken by the intensity of returned lust.

This is mad! Just mad! I'm going crazy!

For the second time in a morning, it was impossible to focus on reality. She was right back in her sweet, dangerous, nocturnal fantasy even while she scanned the bright clear sky above the bay.

A solitary bird was wheeling in the brisk salty air. It was dark, and appeared tiny so far aloft, but, as she watched it, there suddenly seemed a new purpose to its circling. It swooped, and seemed to be flying right at her, inducing a wild rush of Hitchcock-related panic.

Don't be crazy! How can it have seen you? And, if it has, why would it fly at you?

Yet still the bird, a gull of some kind, was closing, diving on dark wings, but revealing a strange mottling to its plumage as it neared. There were lighter speckles among the feathers around its head and its eyes, possibly white, possibly yellow . . . possibly gold.

Lois wanted to spring to her feet, and run back to her cabin, pack up her gear and just get the hell out of Dodge . . . but all she could do was sit and watch, locked in place as the bird began to circle again, slowly, maintaining its distance in the air over the water.

The leisurely repeated sweeps were hypnotic. Her fear ebbed, and the strange warmth in her body grew almost tropical.

And so, to her astonishment, did the low, deep, sweet

welling of desire. Night and day coexisted somehow; she was in her dream, but also awake, in the sunshine.

Half her mind watched a bird. Half of it was back in the cabin, in the soft lamplight, watching Dream Lover approach, anticipating his touch.

'Oh please,' she whimpered, repeating her plea from last night.

She yearned for him, desire flickering deep in her groin for this vivid, but imaginary man. Her nipples tingled, her sex clenched on emptiness, the hunger to be filled so intense it brought tears to her eyes.

No real man had ever satisfied her like him.

Without thinking, she clasped her hand to her crotch, squeezing, trying to ease the ache. Pressing and massaging, she stared up at the strange dark gull, watching it execute a graceful diving spiral, almost in response to her action. Then she looked down again, observing her own pale hand against the stonewashed cloth of her jeans, and wishing it were another hand. One that was bigger and stronger and totally male.

Imagining him behind her, she moaned, longing for it to be his great body on which she leaned while she took her pleasure, longing for his arms to enfold her and gentle her through the spasms.

'Oh! Oh, God!' Crying out, she came in a sudden rush, out of the blue, dimly hearing the gull shriek too, as if applauding her or even sharing her crisis.

Still clutching herself, she wrapped her other arm around her torso, hugging and rocking.

She didn't hear the heavy trudging footsteps until it was too late, and, when they did penetrate her haze, she looked straight up into the frowning face of her next-door neighbour.

'Are you all right?'

Hot blood flooded her cheeks. Oh, God, it must be obvious what she'd been doing, and his dour frown seemed to confirm her worst suspicions. His grim set expression spoilt what was really a very personable countenance. Any normal man would have been smirking at her, turned on by what she'd been up to . . . but not him. He appeared unutterably depressed and disapproving.

'Yes, I'm fine.' Even though it was a lost cause, Lois snatched her hand from her crotch and stuffed it surreptitiously into her pocket. 'Thanks. Just got a bit of a stitch. It's going now. Thanks.'

'Sure?' His brow was still crumpled.

She had no idea whether he believed her but, if he didn't, her little exhibition obviously left him cold. His eyes were bleak and bitter, as if he were already weary of talking to her.

'Yes, thanks, I'm fine,' she parroted, her face flaming.

'I'll be getting along then. Be seeing you,' he concluded gruffly, and, as he turned and stomped away, Lois didn't know whether to be angry or relieved.

He thinks I'm some kind of sex maniac. He thinks I'm disgusting!

'Well, screw you!' she muttered, hurling the suppressed insult at the broad retreating back that had already reached the path and was rapidly receding from view. 'Any *normal* man would be all over me like a rash.'

Attracted by a flash of movement, she realised that the dark gull-like bird had landed only a couple of yards away from her and was regarding her solemnly, its peculiarly mottled head cocked on one side.

'Yeah, yeah, yeah, birdie! I know the guy's obviously got some serious problems and I should feel sorry for him . . .'

She paused, her throat tight all of a sudden, and her eyes hot with unexpected tears. 'But I'm lonely. I'm used to being around people . . . but Sandy said I needed a break.' Bright avian eyes blinked and Lois blinked too. There was something very odd about this creature, and yet she couldn't stop herself rambling on to it. 'I don't know . . . when I saw him, I was sort of hopeful; it's a while since I, um, was with anybody, and I suppose I was hoping I'd get a bit of holiday nookie.'

The bird hopped sideways and flapped its wings making Lois jump.

'Oh fucking hell, I'm talking to birds now! I've had enough of this . . . I'm off to the shop to get some wine and I'm going to get drunk!'

She leapt to her feet and, as she did so, the bird took flight and seemed to hover for a moment, floating above her, before flapping vigorously and soaring away.

Lois shook her head. *I'm going nuts here . . . just another day or so, to keep Sandy quiet, and then I'm back to town, no messing.*

Wondering what kind of wine the small local shop stocked, and how much of it they had, she stomped off towards the path, her sandy footsteps blending with those of her neighbour.

3

'Why is it so bloody cold in here?'

Lois hugged the quilt around her, and took another swig of her wine. It was supposed to be spring but this accursed place felt like the depths of midwinter despite the underfloor heating. The cabin was far from a wretched hovel, with its electricity and plumbing and whatnot, but at the moment she might as well have been residing in a primitive mud hut for all the benefit the mod cons seemed to be providing.

Not the only thing around here that's primitive, she thought, scowling fiercely at her laptop, which sat on the small wooden table, dead as a doornail. The bloody thing had insisted on repeatedly crashing all day, which was doubly frustrating now she'd mysteriously gained a wireless broadband connection. She could probably fix it, but it would take some troubleshooting, and she didn't feel like tackling it in this perpetual depressing cold.

Casting one last fulminating glance at the recalcitrant computer, she set aside her drink but not her quilt, padded over to the wood-burning stove and, using an old potholder to open the front door panel, she peeped inside.

Goddamnit to hell!

The bloody thing was burning down and there were no more logs chopped. The stove was the only thing that seemed to be keeping the room above Antarctic temperatures.

The logical thing would be to turn in, just throw all her clothes and all the available blankets over the top of herself and sleep. But she was restless. Feverish inside, despite the cold. She wanted to stay awake because she had the strangest idea that she needed to.

Nothing in the log basket. Not a splinter.

Was it worth nipping out the back and chopping some wood? Normally she would have copped out and waited until morning, but that funky sense of expectation – and the glasses of wine she'd drunk – made her grit her teeth and pull on her jeans and fleece over her jersey shorts and top. After stuffing her feet into her slippers, she shuffled outside.

The second thoughts kicked in when she reached the hard standing at the back of the cabin, where the chopping block stood. The high full moon made the night brilliant, almost unearthly, but was it really a good idea to start chopping wood at this hour, especially when you'd been drinking and you were probably the world's worst survivalist to start with?

'Just one or two, Lois.' She opened the woodshed that contained the boiler, the wood . . . and the axe.

Third thoughts halted her once she had a log on the block, but dragging in a deep breath she lifted the axe and aimed as best she could.

And missed, sending the lethal tool sliding erratically sideways across the chopping surface.

Another blow resulted in a quarter-inch sliver of the edge of the log.

The third missed again.

'Oh, bloody fucking hell!'

Her profanity assaulted the beautiful night, and echoed back at her from the surrounding woodlands that backed on to the rear of the cabin.

'Can I be of any help?' enquired a soft amused male voice that seemed to emanate unexpectedly from somewhere above her.

What the hell?

Flinging the axe across the hard standing, safely clear of her feet, Lois looked up towards the moonlight sky.

There was a man crouched on the roof of the woodshed.

Oh, God!

She staggered, not even knowing whether she'd spoken aloud or not, and as she tumbled backwards, then landed hard on her bottom, she observed the most astonishing phenomenon play out in slow motion.

The crouching man was big and clad all in black and, as he launched himself from the woodshed roof and jumped down, his long black coat billowed and flapped like the wings of a great dark bird. His descent seemed to take an age, although she knew it was only in her mind, and, when he touched down, he seemed to land as lightly as if he'd been fashioned from thistledown.

'Are you all right, my dear?' The stranger swooped down in a low crouch again, and reached out to touch her.

Lois scuttled away from him, terrified for any number of reasons.

Do I know you?

To her astonishment, and shivering excitement, she realised that she did.

The descending man was also Dream Lover!

The same broad intelligent face. The same dark clothing. Dear God, the same astonishing gold-tipped hair . . . Dazzled, she hardly dared look too closely at him, but she would have put good money on the fact that his eyes were odd too.

In the flesh, so to speak, and in reality, he was quite, quite beautiful. Big, in the sense of very tall, and built like the proverbial, but glorious with it.

His great head tilted on one side; he was obviously waiting for her answer, but the sheer impossibility of his presence had struck her dumb.

Her mouth opened, but nothing came out.

How the hell can you be *here?*

The words were silent, and she blinked at him, expecting him to disappear and for her to be back in the cottage, huddled beneath the covers and dragging herself out of sleep with her hand in her knickers.

But a second later, his gentle but firm hold on her arm was real. And so was the way he effortlessly helped her to her feet.

'Are you all right?' he repeated softly, and, now that she managed to look into his eyes, her suspicions were confirmed.

One was the colour of fire-lit brandy, the other a brilliant aquamarine blue.

'Um . . . yes, I'm fine,' she lied. 'Thank you.'

He was gorgeous, and seemed benign, but still her terror made her lash out.

'At least I would be if you hadn't given me such a shock. What the hell were you doing up there? And who are you for that matter? Skulking around here at the dead of night on people's roofs.'

His face split with a wide personable smile that exhibited a set of brilliant, immaculately even and possibly quite *sharp* teeth. In the moment before he spoke, notions of vampires and werewolves flitted disquietingly through Lois's mind. She loved a horror fantasy as much as the next person, but, until now, that was all they were . . . just fantasies and stories.

Until now . . .

'I'm sorry, that was rather bad of me, wasn't it?' He nodded in the general direction of the woodshed roof. 'But there's such a good view up there, and I was concerned for your safety. Who knows what might be lurking in the forest at this time of night?'

Did he just wink then?

'Well, it's very kind of you to be concerned, whoever you are, but I think I can manage to look after myself, thank you very much.'

'Well, you weren't doing too well at chopping your own wood, were you?' He cocked his head towards her pathetic splinters and the axe lying at the edge of the woods where she'd flung it. 'Would you like some help?'

With what? her stirring libido suddenly prompted. Dream

Lover was even more of a dish standing in front of her, and she was reminded alarmingly of her confession to the bird that morning. She *was* lonely. And it *was* a long time since she'd had the pleasure of a man.

Dream Lover looked as if he was more than enough man for any woman, and if there were the slightest chance that he performed as well in reality as he had in her fantasy . . . Well, wouldn't it be worth taking a chance?

Even so, putting a sharp and heavy axe into the hand of someone who might be a pervert or a stalker, and who peeped at women from roofs was tantamount to booking a slot on *Crimewatch* in advance, wasn't it?

I should run into the cabin and lock the door. Now.

But, instead, she heard herself saying, 'Well, yes, I suppose so. A few logs would be great, if it's not too much trouble?'

Dream Lover beamed, which did weird things to her knee joints, and even weirder, hotter things between her legs. He really did have the most sumptuous white smile.

'Not at all.' Still smiling, he held out a large capable-looking hand. 'And my name is Robin. What's yours?'

'Er, Lois . . . and I'm – I'm pleased to meet you.'

She put her small hand in his big one and only just managed to keep herself from trembling.

His skin was cool and smooth. Just like in the dream. And his lips were cool too. Deliciously cool and firm and supple as he drew her fingers up to them and pressed a light kiss upon her trembling skin.

'And I'm very pleased to meet you, Lois,' he said crisply, releasing her hand, giving her a little nod, before striding away to retrieve the axe. 'Now how much chopped wood do you need?'

'Oh, just enough for tonight, really. That'd be great.'

He nodded again as if she'd said something very wise and sensible, then, after setting the axe on the block, he shed his voluminous black coat.

And then his T-shirt . . .

Dear heaven, what a bod!

Lois watched entranced as Robin hefted the first log on to the block and began to splice and dice it like an expert woodsman. His torso was like wood too, honeyed gold wood, polished and gleaming in the brilliant moonlight, every bit as ripped as that of his dream counterpart and just as toffee-golden.

His muscles flexed and bunched as he worked, like visual poetry.

This is crazy . . . I just dreamt him up . . . Why is he actually here *?*

But there was no denying that Robin was here. The rate at which he was racking up the firewood proved that. Within a few minutes there was a stack big enough to heat twenty cabins.

'Thanks ever so much. That's fabulous!' That prime body was making her gush like a giddy teenager, and she could feel her face getting hot as he straightened up and smiled at her again, axe still in hand. 'I . . . er . . . would you like to come in for a glass of wine or something?'

His strange eyes twinkled at her, almost as if he'd known she was going to say that. Unease fluttered through her, but faced with his beautiful smile – and his beautiful body – she squashed it, embracing the risks.

'Why that would be splendid, Lois,' he said roundly, setting down the axe and pushing his fingers through his crisp gold-tipped hair, 'Thank you, I would be delighted to share a glass of wine with you.'

Oh, his eyes, his mouth, his whole body, even . . . They were all saying how much more than wine it was he hoped to share.

'Cool.' Muttering, Lois scooted for the cabin door, too dazzled to be able to look at him any more. She heard him scoop up his clothes and an armful of firewood and follow her, yet strangely it was the rustle of his leather coat against the wood that marked his progress, not his footsteps.

What is it with him? He barely seems to touch the ground and yet he's such a great big hunk.

Swinging open the door, she wondered just what kind of madwoman she was being. But it was too late. Robin was right behind her and already inside.

For a log cabin, Sandy's hideaway was spacious, and Lois had been favourably surprised on arrival, having expected a dismal shack. But now, however, it felt as if she were in a rustic doll's house, complete with miniature furniture. The kitchen area, the cosy fireside with two comfy armchairs, and the large bed and chest of drawers at the other end of the long room were all dwarfed by the massive man who strode forwards and flung his dark coat and T-shirt across the back of a chair.

Still stripped to the waist, Robin jammed a couple of decent-sized logs into the stove, and then stacked the rest of them in the wood basket. With the age-old seriousness of 'man who make fire', he plied the poker expertly and coaxed the flames. Within seconds the freezing room became a tropical paradise. In fact, far more so than it had a logical right to be.

Stop standing around like a lemon just staring at him! Say something, woman!

But all she could manage to do was stare . . . at a set of

splendid pecs, a narrow waist and a luscious and suggestively packed crotch.

Robin beamed back at her as if he knew that before the night was out they'd be sleeping together.

'Er, would you like a shower or something . . . with all that chopping and flinging wood about?'

She half expected him to laugh, but he didn't.

'Of course, that's a wonderful idea. Thank you.' Before she could stop him, he'd taken off his boots and kicked them away across the room. The next moment, he was at his belt and the zip of his jeans and then stepped out of them.

Lois's jaw dropped. It was a cliché, but she almost had to pick it up off the floor.

Robin wasn't a wearer of socks or underwear, it seemed. He stood there unperturbed, displaying his majestic male equipment as if it were perfectly normal to fling off his clothes in front of a woman he'd met just minutes ago.

'Through there?' He gestured gracefully towards the door to the cabin's small shower room.

'Um . . . yes.' Lois's tongue froze and she swallowed. Hard. Somehow she was incapable of raising her eyes above his waist level.

He was so big . . . and he was actually getting bigger as she watched.

'Thank you, I won't be but a few moments.' Robin's smile was calm, but there was a cheeky confidence in his odd eyes. He was totally aware of the effect he was having on her and, as he strode fluidly towards the bathroom in long loping strides, he had the gall to lightly frisk himself and look back to make sure that she was watching.

'What am I doing? What am I doing?'

Lois ran for the wine bottle on the table and poured a

large measure into her glass. 'What am I doing?' she repeated, cradling it in both her hands like a magical chalice, hoping that the Merlot would wash away the last of her doubts and her qualms about Robin.

He's just bloody glorious!

She drank a few mouthfuls of the rich red wine, trying to concentrate on the positives of having the best-looking and best-built man she'd met in years tucked away with her in this cabin miles from anywhere. At the same time, she tried to dismiss the fact that there were some things that were undeniably strange about him.

Not bad. Just weird . . . very weird.

As the water sluiced down in the room beyond, Lois had a feeling that her new friend had been neither dirty nor sweaty. She'd noticed no odour of work-induced perspiration as he'd passed her, and there was no hint of it now, as she picked up his clothing and couldn't resist sniffing it.

What she did smell set her trembling and grabbing for her wineglass again.

Flowers again, and predominantly lavender.

Lois looked at her bag, her scattered clothes. There were only a few toilet items in the shower room. She could be out of here, in her car and on the road before he had finished showering.

But, almost before she calculated her chances, the water stopped, and she knew she wouldn't have gone anyway. Instead, she wriggled out of her jeans and fleece, then dived across to the mirror over the chest of drawers and frowned into it. The image disheartened her. Her tufted hair, her grungy old sleep shorts and top, and the make-up-free ordinariness of her staring wide-eyed face were less than alluring. She pushed at a few curls, pinched her cheeks to give them some colour and bit her lips, but it was already too late.

The shower room door swung open and Robin walked into the room. He was still nude and casually towelling at his hair.

Lois gasped, aware that this was becoming a habit in this strange man's presence. His naked body was sublime, gleaming and fresh from the shower, and he had no qualms whatsoever about showing it to her. The only problem was that she was having trouble forming coherent thoughts, much less sophisticated adult conversation, with all that male comeliness on show.

'Perhaps I could have that glass of wine now?' Robin let his towel drop around his shoulders, but made no attempt to cover his mighty nether regions.

'Yes. Yes, of course.' Lois scooted for the wooden kitchen table, poured out a glass of red for Robin and surreptitiously topped up her own.

If I'm going to behave as if I'm too stupid to live, I might as well use the booze as my excuse.

Turning, she discovered that Robin had settled into one of the easy chairs by the fire, and the towel lay abandoned on the floor. Lois smiled and felt strangely reassured. He might be her literal Dream Lover right out of her fantasies, but in term of household sloppiness he was a very normal man. She handed him his glass, swept up the towel and placed it over the little drying rack that stood against the wall.

'Oops! Sorry.' Robin's grin said he wasn't sorry at all, cheeky sod.

Lois let herself down carefully into the other seat, still tongue-tied and increasingly aware that her shorts and her little buttoned top weren't a particularly substantial covering.

Of course, if she'd been in her right mind, she would've put her robe back on, but she was in her entirely wrong mind. All she could do was sit, frozen in place, unable to do anything but gaze and goggle at the man sitting opposite her.

His long limbs were stretched out like those of a classical sculpture, and his superb body appeared entirely too big for the modest chair. He looked comfortable though, leaning back into the upholstery, his peculiar eyes closed as if he were dozing.

Great! Just come in, make yourself at home and flaunt your fabulous tackle at me . . . and then fall asleep.

Robin's eyes flicked open. 'Does my nakedness bother you? Shall I put my clothes back on again?'

Yes, put them on and go, because I'm scared shitless of you!

No, stay and never wear a stitch again . . . because it'll break my heart if you cover all that gorgeousness up!

'No, not all. If you're comfortable, that's fine by me.'

Robin nodded and lifted his glass in salute. 'To you, Lois, I'm glad I found you.'

Lois gulped at her own wine, alarmed. 'What on earth does that mean?' she demanded, a droplet of Merlot sneaking down her chin and requiring a swift swipe of the hand.

Lashes that were far too long and pretty for a man with such a large cock swept down, giving him an almost shame-faced look. 'I'm afraid I've been watching you, Lois.' He toyed with his glass, one moment watching the flames from the little stove through it, the next, looking at her. 'You might say I've become enchanted by you. You're very beautiful and I like beautiful things.'

Lois laughed out loud. Oh great, she'd got a stalker with a nice line in compliments now.

'I think you need your eyes testing, Robin. I look like a

bag lady tonight, and I haven't been looking all that great since I got here. I'm on holiday, and as there's no talent around – or there didn't seem to be at first – I haven't been making an effort.'

'Talent?'

'Men. Crumpet. Male totty . . . you know?'

She wasn't sure at first whether he did know, but then he smiled and looked pleased with himself. Obviously he was supremely confident that *he* was totty.

And the way his penis was growing said the same too.

'But you have a neighbour. What about him? Do you not like the look of him?'

'Well, he's all right, but he seems a bit solitary. He doesn't seem to be interested in company.'

Robin looked serious for a moment, his face very pure and solemn. 'Indeed, he is a very unhappy man. A pall of great sadness hangs over him.'

Lois narrowed her eyes. Had he been watching the neighbour too?

Robin shrugged. 'But you said as much yourself.'

What? What the fuck? Can you read my mind?

Robin simply smiled and lounged even more languidly in his chair, one hand loosely cradling his wineglass, the other spread upon his thigh, close to his cock, almost as if he wanted to draw her attention to its gathering might as a diversion.

His beautiful lashes fluttered down again, and he appeared to be dozing.

What the hell was happening? Could he read her thoughts? Again and again the mantra circled in her head: *Who are you? Who are you? What are you?*

But she got no answer from the silent relaxed man.

'I dreamt about you last night.'

The words were out before she could stop herself, and Robin's peculiar bi-coloured eyes snapped open again, instantly flashing their two brilliant hues.

'Did you know that? I dreamt about you,' she rushed on, panicking. 'How can I have dreamt about you when I just met you not half an hour ago? It doesn't make sense!'

Without warning, Robin set his glass aside and slid out of his chair and on to his knees. His cock bounced from side to side as he shuffled across the patchwork rug until he was kneeling in front of her, his great head tilted to one side a little, his gaze questioning and hypnotic.

Compulsively, Lois drank some wine, almost on auto-pilot, but the second she took the glass from her lips Robin reached for it, gently prised it from her fingers and set it aside. Still kneeling in front of her, he took her small warm hands in his much larger cooler ones.

'The woods and the sea are magical places, Lois, and this cabin is right at the nexus of both their influences.' He squeezed her fingers very lightly, as if they were crystal and he didn't want to damage them. 'It's hardly surprising that unusual things happen here. What you dreamt last night might have been a part of the future seeping back into the present.'

'That's ridiculous!'

But she was shaking. Could she do that? Could she want that? It was all very well to imagine kinky things in fantasies, but for real? That was another story. Especially with a man she barely knew.

'The world is strange, Lois,' he murmured cryptically, his thumbs circling her palms in a light soothing caress that seemed to impact all over her body . . . especially between her legs. She suppressed an intense urge to squirm, experiencing his innocent touch deep in her sex. But then the look in his peculiar eyes said that he knew exactly what she was feeling.

'Your dream . . . was it pleasant?' With a slow smile, he lowered his head, looking up at her from beneath his sumptuous lashes, and then brought first one, then the other of her hands to his lips for a kiss.

'I . . . er, yes, sort of. But it was strange . . . not something that could really happen.'

The touch of his lips was cool fire. She was shaking hard now, and she couldn't tell whether it was fear, confusion or extreme lust. Or a combination of all three.

'Are you sure?'

'I don't know! I don't know!' she almost cried.

He shuffled closer, reached for her, and this time brought her mouth to his in a delicate gentling kiss.

'What happened in your dream?' His words were like a whisper of perfumed air against her cheek and her ear.

Furious blood flushed her face as she remembered the game, and her body bound and open and vulnerable to him, hungering for him as it did now.

She tried to turn away from him, but he held her firm, his mouth against her hair.

'I can't! I can't say . . .'

But *his* lips were moving, and she realised he was murmuring softly, describing the fantasy.

'How do you know these things? How do you know? It's impossible for you to know what I dreamt . . .'

'Hush, my dearest.' He kissed her jaw, and then her throat. 'Just call it instinct, intuition . . . My dream, maybe, just as much as yours.'

'But I'm scared! I don't know if I want to do those things,' she protested, her heart fluttering in her chest like a wild bird, the strange gull maybe, in her chest. 'I don't know if I'd ever really want to do something like that.'

Taking her face between his large smooth hands, he forced her to look at him, straight into the disorientating beauty of his eyes.

'Then we can do other things, Lois, anything you like. Just say the word.'

'I d-don't know what the word is.'

'Why it's "yes", of course, isn't it?'

And then he kissed the whispered answer right from her lips.

4

His mouth was tender and flexible, and his cool tongue naughty and daring as it delicately pressed for entrance. Her face was cradled in his long elegant hands and there was no way to escape the kiss even if she'd wanted to.

And oh, his taste was so sweet! She'd read of kisses being described as delicious, but Robin's really were. The flavour of wildflower honey seemed to fill her mouth along with his tongue, the taste and scent of it as intoxicating as the sensuous exploration. Her hands fluttered wildly, and then she threw her arms around his large muscular body, embracing his magnificent back as she surrendered to his kiss.

Dimly, a far way back in her mind, she recognised that she could probably be accused of being wilfully stupid, encouraging this strangest of strangers to kiss her, touch her and much, much more. But she was too ensorcelled to do anything but silence the voice of dissent and hold on to him.

The kiss went on a long, long time, their tongues flickering around one another, teasing, challenging and tasting. Other delightful sensations impinged on her consciousness too.

The warmth of the fire on her skin was a counterpoint to the strange living chill of Robin's body. The contrast was thrilling. He seemed to be able to sear her with skin and flesh that had the silky hardness of polished marble, and her hands couldn't seem to explore it fast enough. Her fingertips roved feverishly over his shoulders, his back and his torso.

Eventually, he freed her mouth and sat back on his heels, just looking at her. His odd eyes glittered with hunger, with devilment, and the flickering light from the fire danced like magic dust over his fast-drying gold-tipped hair.

'You are beautiful,' he said, stealing the exact words she'd been going to utter away from her.

Rapt as she was, Lois found herself compelled to laugh. 'And you're crazy! Have you really looked at me? I'm a mess. I look like a complete fright. My hair's all over the place, my skin is all pale and pasty, and these are probably the nastiest old clothes in my possession.'

He smiled at her and shrugged his big shoulders and silently mimed the word 'Nonsense'.

'Well, I think you ought to get those weird eyes of yours tested then!'

'You're beautiful,' he repeated, a small mild smile playing around his sensual lips. 'You're beautiful and I want to give you pleasure.'

Oh, God, I want you to give it me too!

But she could no longer speak because he came forwards again, and began kissing her neck, then the crook of her shoulder, then her collarbone and chest where her granddad T-shirt was unbuttoned. His hands rested on her thighs as his lips nibbled and travelled.

She looked down at his magical hair, and the smooth planes of his back. Tentatively she touched his satiny skin. The delicate way he was mouthing her almost made her want to swoon, especially when he touched her with the tip of his tongue.

Immediately, her sex surged, as if imagining the sensation of that determined little serpent flickering against the sensitive bud of her clitoris. Unable to prevent herself, the very thought made her groan.

Robin's gilded head shot up and he grinned at her.

Oh, dear Lord, he can *read my mind!*

Big hands reached for her top, deftly opening it to reveal her breasts. Lois gasped. Her nipples were already puckered and tight. The air wasn't cold, but the contrast between concealment and exposure was a little shock.

Robin swooped in with hands and mouth, his lips settling on one breast, while he cradled his fingers around her curves, flexing them lightly to hold her.

His cool tongue moved as it had in her mouth, darting, swirling, tickle-tasting. Lois kicked with pleasure, her bare feet sliding against his thighs, his shins. Her hips started to weave. She was out of control, grabbing on to the arms of the chair for stability.

He gave her breast a long hard suck and she wailed, shooting almost to the point of orgasm. He'd done that in the dream, she remembered hazily, fondled her breast and brought her to pleasure when it shouldn't have been possible.

But suddenly she wanted more, more. She wanted what she'd had in her dream. His cock inside her as he thrust, his strong hips swinging to get in deeper than deep.

She tried to tell him. She tried to rise. But he quelled her, and kept her in her seat. His fingers plucked at the elastic of her shorts, his eyes locking on hers, as if asking permission to remove them.

Oh yes! Go on! Yes!

Efficiently he pulled off her shorts and flung them away, baring her crotch to his gaze in the firelight. A moment later, his spread fingers settled on her belly, pressing gently, thumb stroking. Making a frame for her navel, he dipped his pointed tongue into it.

A sharp, almost painful jolt of sensation shot through her, right to her core. Again, she moaned, even closer to the edge. Her bare feet scrabbled against him again, and her knuckles went white where she gouged at the chair arm. Her hips wafted upwards as if they were inviting him of their own accord to go further.

He placed a slow precise kiss on her lower belly, just at the edge of her pubic bush.

If only I'd waxed, she thought, even though subliminally she knew he didn't give a hoot whether she was jungle-hairy, trimmed or even shaven. Who was to know she'd literally meet the man of her dreams out here in this remote little hideaway. Even her neighbour had been a surprise when she'd encountered him.

'Oh yes, oh yes . . .' he murmured softly, lifting his face a moment, and flashing her a hot look, before diving down again. As his mouth moved ever closer to its target, his capable hands slid beneath her buttocks to cup and lift her.

Like one cat greeting another, he lightly rubbed his cheeks and his chin and his closed mouth against the soft hair between her legs, his nostrils flaring as he drew in her odour. Frustrated by the lightness of the contact, Lois shuffled and stirred, trying to press herself against his face, all the time wishing that she was the one who'd just taken a shower. And

yet, and even more catlike, Robin seemed to purr with satisfaction at the smell of her sex and his lashes fluttered like fans
as he breathed her in.

'Delicious,' he whispered, just touching his tongue against
the soft flossiness and teasing it. Then his juicy mouth curved
into a devilish grin and, supporting her bottom on one hand,
he positioned her leg over his shoulder. Deftly swapping
hands, he repeated the process with the other, and then took
hold of her bottom again to bring her crotch right to his face.

With his lips just inches from her, he paused again, as if
surveying the landscape of her sex in intimate detail. With
her thighs stretched around his head, she was open to him,
moist and revealed in a way that even surpassed her dream.
The sensation of being studied was like a caress in itself.
Stirring and moaning, she reached back and grasped the
chair back behind her to create a base from which to push
herself against him.

She wanted to writhe. She wanted to buck about. She
didn't dare look down at him, crouched and naked, his face
between her thighs.

But she did.

Robin was staring at her sex. His eyes were intent with
knowing expectancy, and he was smiling like a demon. The
fine gold tipping of his dark hair was almost shooting sparks
and, as she watched, he ran his tongue lightly over his lips as
if preparing them to savour her flesh.

And then he looked up. Right into her eyes. His own were
flashing with a brilliant eldritch light that owed nothing to
reflections from the fire or the lamps. Something moved and
danced in those duo-coloured depths, something not of this
world. Lois gasped, riding high on a silvery strand of terror
that only increased her arousal.

But, before she could process it, he plunged in – and she forgot it.

5

The touch of his tongue brought a sharp cry to her lips. She was so ready for it, yet still he surprised her. With cool, delicate precision, he explored her, he caressed her. Flicking his tongue-tip lightly over her slippery folds, tasting and teasing and pleasuring as he went.

The first contact with her clitoris made her drum her heels on his bare back, and her torso arch, pressing her opened sex closer to his face. The second contact made her howl like a woodland animal as he furled his tongue to a silky point and batted it to and fro over the sensitive little button.

The third contact, a firm assertive press with no hesitation or mercy, made her come, shouting and kicking at once.

She couldn't keep still. She twisted like an electrified eel, her muscles taut and her nails gouging the upholstery of the chair back. But still he held her, feasting and lapping at her sex while she struggled, her bottom a foot off the chair and cradled in his hands.

When he sucked her clit, she came again, and his name, wrought by her lips, filled the cabin in a ringing shout of triumph.

And then, it was like being in the dream again. Well, almost . . . Her consciousness wavered, her mind knocked sideways by the intense pleasure, and she blinked and blinked again, as she peered down the length of her own trembling body.

Robin seemed to be clothed in gold, his skin dazzling, and his outline mutable, misty and shifting. She opened her mouth to exclaim in fear and wonder, but then her perceptions shifted again, dropping back into place, and all she saw was the most handsome piece of flesh-and-blood male gorgeousness she'd ever seen, looking up at her, grinning at her across the humid planes of her abdomen, his red mouth shimmering with the moisture from her sex.

Gently, he let her down into the seat again, and slid her thighs from off his shoulders, setting her feet on the floor again. Lois released her death-grip on the back of the armchair and slumped against the upholstery as if she'd had every molecule of air in her lungs knocked out of her.

Kneeling up, Robin loomed over her. He touched her face, stroking it with utmost tenderness, smoothing her sweaty hair away from her brow. He seemed to be soothing her as if she'd endured some stringent ordeal, or suffered something terrible and gruelling on his behalf, and his beautiful eyes were solicitous.

'All right now?' he whispered, taking her hand and bringing it to his lips.

Lois had to laugh, and Robin beamed at her, laughter in his face too.

'Bloody fantastic, thanks to you!' she exclaimed, sitting up, flinging her arm around his shoulder and pulling him close to her for a proper kiss.

He accepted it, still smiling and looking disgustingly pleased with himself.

'I don't know where you learnt to do that, but, man, you are a genius!'

'Sheer instinct, my dearest,' he murmured, dropping an outrageous wink, then stealing another kiss as he drew her by the arms on to the rug in front of the stove.

The wooden floorboards were hard beneath them, and the old-fashioned rag-rug was bumpy beneath her bottom, but what were minor discomforts like that when you were in the arms of a beautiful magical man who'd just given you the best head you'd had in your entire life? It seemed perfectly natural to coil her arms around Robin and continue the kiss where they'd left off.

Only this time he was lying half over her, his body imposing itself on hers, but not weighing her down. As their tongues duelled, she savoured the sweet taste of his mouth, blended with the salty contrast of her own lingering flavour. His skin was silky smooth as it moved against hers, and the sliding contact set strange thoughts circling and flitting around her mind.

He's not normal. He's so not normal . . .

The fact that he was able to drape himself across her and she barely felt his weight just didn't make sense. His body had great size and substance, but seemed to lack the commensurate pounds and ounces. As he scooped his hands beneath her and held her to him, pressing her hard against a truly mighty erection, she seemed to see and hear him leap down from the woodshed roof again. He'd almost floated to earth. How could that happen? It defied all logic.

And then there was the undoubted mind-reading.

Maybe he's just very empathetic, she thought, sliding her hands over his back and his tight male bottom, loving the feel of his skin and its peculiar lack of heat.

And that's another thing!

How could he feel cool, yet warm her up. It wasn't only the stove that was heating her. Her skin seemed to glow wherever Robin touched her – which was just about everywhere – and yet the temperature of his own skin seemed far lower than that of a normal person.

I should be afraid. I should be very afraid . . . And yet I'm not.

No, the only feelings she experienced as Robin worked his

hips, and rubbed his glorious cock against her were wonder, delight and pure desire.

Oh, how I want you!

The thought echoed in her mind. Really echoed. She'd actually heard it twice, the two versions very closely overlaid, Robin's voice on hers.

Without too much effort, she placed her hand on his chest and compelled him to break the kiss and back up a little, so she could look up at him.

His unusual eyes were dark, yet brilliant with desire, and with unfathomable complexity. She sensed great emotion in him, a turbulent well of confused feelings. His eyes were full of a perplexed affection, and warmth, and a poignant yearning.

Oh baby!

Enormous tenderness roiled inside her. She didn't know how, but she knew he was seeking something. Searching . . . reaching out for more than just sex. He was magnificent. Competent. He knew just how to stir her and to pleasure her, but beneath that skill lay innocence and longing.

Whatever it is . . . take it! Take it from me!

Her thought seemed to galvanise him, and his body surged against her, pushing at her with more force. And this time the hardness of the floor did make an impact.

She placed her hand on his chest, halting him. 'Shall we get into bed for this? It'll be much more comfy. The floor's a bit hard.'

Robin stared down at her, and in his face she saw gratitude and a glow of something ineffably sweet. For a moment, she thought he might speak but, instead, he just kissed her forehead, then slid off her, came up on his knees and scooped her effortlessly up into his arms. She coiled her own arms around his neck as he strode lightly to the bed and set her down on it. A moment later, he'd whisked up the quilt from under her, slid his body next to hers, and then settled the quilt back down over them like a soft cocoon of intimacy.

This wasn't at all like her fantasy. It wasn't exotic or kinky, but in many ways it was much, much better. She felt closer to Robin than to any man, ever, in her life. For a moment he just stared at her again, his head next to hers on the pillow, and she read questions in his eyes. She didn't know what they were, but she sensed she held the answers.

Then they were kissing again, their mouths fused as he passively allowed her hands to travel and fondle.

His body was beautiful to her touch, and that much was still part of her fantasy. No common man could be this perfect, this muscled and smooth. She ran her fingertips over his back, his waist, his bottom – all as splendid and cool as living alabaster. When he adjusted the tilt of his hips, she slid her hand naturally to his cock.

Dear God Almighty, he was big! And he felt bigger now than ever. It was as if his very flesh had read her desires and re-formed to comply with them. She'd always longed to be with a really big man.

He let out a soft huff of encouragement as she handled and explored him, tracing the veins of his shaft and the flared shape of his tip. From what she could tell, he was circumcised, and a thin slippery fluid was seeping silkily from his love-eye.

Why did it not surprise her that the feel of it was cool?

There was a lot of it too and, even if she'd not been running wet between her own legs, Robin's slipperiness would have been more than adequate lubrication for his entry . . .

As if that notion somehow shattered his passivity, Robin rolled towards her, then over her, pinning her effortlessly on her back. Between her thighs, his great penis nestled and then pushed.

Condom!

The word rang in her mind like a bell, and, still poised, Robin came up on his elbows and looked down at her. His gold-frosted hair glinted like a halo in the soft light from the lamps, and his eyes were steady, and almost curious.

'You have nothing to fear from me, dearest Lois,' he said, his voice ringing oddly, almost like a hypnotist's.

The cynical man-suspicious Lois of old would have replied, 'Is that a fact?' but the Lois of now, cuddled in the magic womb of the duvet and the heat that wasn't of Robin, and yet came from him, believed him utterly.

Some ancient, primal, unexplainable knowledge in the pit of her brain told her unequivocally that Robin hailed from somewhere that was outside the fear of disease. He had no connection with the world of pain and infection and, if he could make her pregnant, so be it. She suddenly even wanted that despite the fact she'd never ever wanted it before.

She stared back up at him, and thought, with all her power. *This is a dream again, isn't it?*

Robin's beautiful mouth curved in a teasing smile. 'Does this feel like a dream to you?'

He pressed harder, and she could feel the broad silky tip of his penis nudging its way imperiously between her sex-lips, then sliding with unerring accuracy right to her very entrance.

Lois shook violently, her body almost vibrating with a befuddling concoction of pure fear and a lust and desire to be filled so intense it made her push back against him and tilt her hips to aid his entrance.

He can *read my mind! He really can!*

But then fear, uncertainty and the ability to question were all subsumed in the wild overload of sensation. Robin slid into her, slowly, slowly, stretching her as he went, and the feeling of being full, right to the brim with solid male flesh, drove out all extraneous thoughts from her mind as if by main force.

Sublime penetration eradicated all doubt, and Robin settled in as if her body was his home.

As he rocked his hips, and sealed the fit, his voice was a soft zephyr in her ear. 'Are you all right, my love? Are you comfortable? I don't want to hurt you.'

'Don't worry,' she murmured back at him, hitching her own pelvis, trying to get closer and tighter with him, even though it probably wasn't possible. She smiled too, suddenly touched by his question. He was just trying to ease her mind, she knew that. Given what he could do, and what he could sense, there was no way he didn't know already that his cock felt incredible inside her.

And then he began to kiss her, his mouth like lavender honey as he thrust and thrust smoothly inside her. It was like being part of some divine, reciprocal engine, and each movement, each long, delicious plunge, seemed to make contact with a new pleasure receptor in her depths.

She moaned into his mouth with each smooth, deep shove, sipping at his sweetness as the interior stretching did insane things to her clit. His every movement created a divine tugging sensation in the tiny sensitive organ, and on the profound in-stroke his pubic bone seemed to knock against it. She wriggled to adjust the angle of their bodies for even greater perfection, but still Robin kept up his rhythm and momentum.

How can he do this? she questioned dimly, her entire body

throbbing, pulsating, teetering on the brink of some great star-burst of pleasure. *He barely weighs anything, yet he has this power, this force?*

A heartbeat later, there were no more questions, no more thoughts, no more conscious analysis of any kind.

Just pure sensation as her body sparked and heart and soul flew upwards, borne aloft on a giant wave of loving pleasure.

I love you . . . I love you . . . I love you . . .

She heard the words like bells as she soared among the stars, but for the life of her she couldn't have specified who'd said them.

6

Sitting up, letting the quilt slide from his shoulders, Robin gazed down at the sleeping woman at his side.

His human fingers tingled with the intense need to touch her again, and in his heart, also temporarily human, emotion surged.

How beautiful she was with her sex-tousled hair and her flushed cheeks. Her body was warm against his, radiating heat and life. He ached to be able to stay and sleep with her in his arms but, even during this special and almost finished month, he could only be the Robin she knew for a limited period. He could only touch, and feel, and experience this depth of passion for a couple of hours, or a little more, after which he was compelled to disassociate.

And he didn't want to do that in front of Lois.

But just how much would it faze her though?

She was brave, bold and curious. From her thoughts, he knew she was aware that he wasn't quite what he seemed. Yet still she embraced him and gave herself to him.

And, for that, I love you.

And he loved her even, he sensed, in his discarnate form, where emotions were fainter, rarefied and far less intense. When May was over, he might still feel the ache of loss.

She was compassionate too. His fingertips hovered a centimetre above her lips, her cheek and then her brow. He sensed the sympathy she felt for her surly neighbour, who had not been polite to her. She'd seen through the man's bluffness to the sad state of his heart.

Would you feel sorry for me?

His ersatz heart twisted with anguish, as he glanced towards her watch on the bedside cabinet, and heard its tick, tick, tick like a giant tolling bell. His sharp vision noted again the date function.

Tomorrow was the last day of May. The last day of his approximate humanity. How he wished that she'd arrived here on the first of the month.

As if affected by the proximity of the month's end, his form began to waver, so he rose from the bed and gathered his clothes. Not that they would remain if he disassociated. They were part of his illusion. But it seemed important to be as human as he could for as long as he could.

Dressed, he circled the room, wishing there was more he could do for her. When he touched the dark screen of her small computer, he sensed a fault in it and remembered her frustration with it. With a flick of his wrist, he scattered dust across the keyboard and watched as it glittered and sank into the guts of the device, healing the patterns of force as it went.

Well, at least that would bring her some satisfaction in the days to come, and distract her from the loss of her temporary playmate. He knew he could wipe her entire memory of him, just as he could have wiped the laptop's electronic memory if he'd so wished. But the humanity that gripped him made him selfish.

He didn't want to be forgotten. He wanted her to think of him. And at least remember a little of what they'd shared.

Lifting the curtain at the window, he looked outside. The moon and stars were beginning to fade in the sky across the bay, and already the pink intimations of dawn were slowly gathering. His hand, where it held the cloth, was fading too, and a stir from the bed said that Lois was waking.

With an ache of regret, Robin abandoned his form and drifted upwards and away through the cabin's ceiling.

Lois woke early, and for a moment, before her faculties fully reconstituted themselves, she lay warm and huddled in the quilt, bathing in contentment. Never ever had her body felt so relaxed, so sated, so complete.

But as cold – really cold – reality set in, so did a profound and jumbled whirl of feelings.

You were *real this time! You* were *fucking real!*

Gathering the covers around her shoulders against the chill of the cabin, she ran her fingers over the sheet at her side.

No residual heat. No indentation of a large male body. But he *had* been here in the bed, she knew it. He really had.

There was other evidence.

Lowering her face to the sheet, she drew in a great breath of lavender and, as she sat up again, she studied her hand and saw on it that faint veil of glimmering dust she'd seen in the cabin the previous morning.

It was insubstantial. Not in the least bit gritty, it was smooth as silk and seemed to dissolve against her skin. But it was real, and it wasn't just confined to the bed.

Padding around the cabin, she found it dusted across the rag-rug, on the floor, and even scattered thinly across her laptop.

'Great! Now I've got dust in the works as well as corrupted programs!'

But, when out of habit she fired the thing up, not only did the wi-fi connection spring into life, but also files she seemed to have lost yesterday were restored and full of data she'd believed gone forever.

She began to shake. Hard. So hard she had to sit down on the bed again.

'What the fuck are you, Robin?' she demanded of the empty air.

It was impossible to ignore now, the strangeness of him. He'd sprinkled her bloody computer with fairy dust or whatever . . . and mended it.

'Oh, God, help me, what's going on?'

The temptation to dive under the duvet and just hide again was enormous, but she resisted it. The temptation to pour herself a tot of brandy was enormous too, and that she succumbed to, thinking it was a pretty poor turn of affairs that she was driven to drink, boozing first thing in the morning because she was afraid she just might have fucked a supernatural being last night.

She prowled the cabin, stirring up the Robin-dust with the trailing duvet that swept the floor much in the style of a geisha's formal kimono.

'This is stupid! There are no spirits, ghosties, sprites and fairies and what-have-you! And I'm sure you're not a vampire because you've got such lovely teeth!'

But, if he was a real man, where the hell was he? Surely he would have stayed, especially if there was the prospect of a repeat performance?

'Now this is just fantastic! You're either a supernatural spook and you've turned into a pumpkin or something in the daylight . . . or you're just a normal bloke who also happens to be a fuck 'em and run bastard!' She swigged her brandy, then coughed at the bite of it. 'Bloody hell, I certainly know how to pick men!'

But she couldn't sit round getting drunk.

Still trying not to think too hard about anything, she showered and dressed and picked at some cereal for breakfast. She tidied the cabin and swept up, but that just swung her thoughts back to things incomprehensible.

The fairy dust or whatever it was seemed to disintegrate as fast as she brushed at it, and irrationally, seeing it go, she felt an aching wrench in the place where she knew her heart was.

He was magically beautiful and she was destroying his very essence.

She stopped cleaning up and tried to do some work. But it was hopeless. The code danced before her, and all she seemed to see were a pair of bi-coloured eyes, a glinting smile and gold-tipped hair . . . All that, and the most perfect male body, either fantastic or real.

She could feel him too. Deep in the quick of her, it was like having an echo of his penis still there, displacing the tender flesh that had embraced his as he moved and thrust and loved her. As she clenched her inner muscles, caressing a ghost, a deep pleasure gripped her and made her catch her breath.

Staggering almost, she collapsed into one of the easy chairs, her body trembling finely, her nerves, her heart – yes – her sex on fire as if Robin were with her, touching her, fucking her. Ripples of sensation licked over her skin like flames and she couldn't tell if the feeling was real, in her imagination, or in her memory. The agitation in her flesh made her toss her head and writhe against the upholstery, the turn-on far more intense and visceral almost than those moments of displaced lust on the beach. She cupped her breast and her crotch, her heels kicking against the rug as her hands seemed to become Robin's to stir her.

Where are you? Where are you? I need you!

Opening eyes she didn't realise she'd closed, she looked down and seemed to see his glorious face looking up at her from between her legs, just like last night.

He smiled, he winked, and her body surged, the sudden sharp arousal capsizing in an instant, as she kneaded herself and the rough pressure made her come.

As she fell back into herself, the absurdity of her actions scared her. It was either that, or the fact that she wasn't entirely sure they'd been her actions. Her impetus . . .

Had that just been a visitation? What had happened?

Oh, God, I think I'm going mad!

'I can't go on like this! I've got to get out of here!'

The sound of her own voice snapped Lois mercifully from her fugue, and she grabbed her coat, threw it on and set out for a walk.

The day was grim and cold again, and the skies leaden. A brisk wind was whipping up high seas and making spray lash the beach. Gritting her teeth and huddling into her puffed jacket, Lois took the path into the woods, her walking shoes squishing as she tramped the packed earth that had partly turned to mud. She wasn't quite sure where she was going, but her feet just kept putting themselves one in front of the other.

Are you out here, Robin? Is this where you hang?

The silent trees mocked her, and there was no sign of life other than a few dubious-sounding rustles in the undergrowth. She wondered whether to turn back. What if there were foxes, or some other wild animals that might attack her?

Probably nothing more dangerous than the man-thing I fucked last night, she decided, shaking her head, and then strode on.

The woods were dark and dank, and were frankly starting to scare her. But, just on the point of turning back, she seemed to burst out into a little glade that was chocolate-box pretty and lifted straight from an illustrated Victorian fairytale. It was bright here too and, when she looked up, she was astonished to discover that the sun had finally come out and was peppering the little dell with golden light.

There had been nothing about this on the BBC Weather site, but, with her face still lifted towards the welcome sunshine fragmenting through the higher branches, Lois unzipped her jacket. With the light had come heat. She stepped forwards into the glade, and then laughed out loud. Not only was she in a circle of light and warmth, but she was also standing in a fairy ring of toadstools.

'I don't believe this! It's got to be a joke.'

Although she was half expecting Robin to pop out from behind a tree and answer her, nothing happened. She was still alone. Vaguely disappointed but also slightly relieved, she crossed the ring and sat down on a large fallen log, puffing out her cheeks.

'So where are you, Magic Man?'

Her words echoed strangely, almost as if she were in a church, ringing and rebounding.

Still nothing.

Well, not completely nothing. As she sat motionless on the log, there was a rustling in the low brush, and an animal hopped out into the circle, almost floating over the short cropped turf.

It was a hare, long-shanked and lop-eared, mottled in colour, cream and dark brown.

Laughter burst like a bubble from Lois's lips and she instantly expected the timid animal to bolt back the way it had come. Instead, it cocked its head on one side, studying her with bright intelligent eyes.

Bright intelligent eyes that had something really peculiar about them. Peculiar and familiar . . .

Lois opened her mouth to speak, but suddenly there was a loud crack in the underbrush behind her, like the breaking of a twig, and she almost leapt up from the log, swivelling around.

Nothing behind her this time, but, when she whipped back around to face the clearing and dappled light and the toadstools, she was no longer alone.

Robin, standing tall and dark in his long black coat, his head cocked on one side, was studying her with bright intelligent eyes.

He was on the very same spot the hare had occupied.

She'd heard no sound of the animal's movement or his.

No rustle of grass or undergrowth. No displacement of air.

The hare had simply disappeared and left Robin in its place.

The broken sunlight faded, becoming splodged with black as the dell began to spin violently.

Lois fainted.

*

Struggling back to consciousness, she found herself firmly held and encircled. Fight or flight reflex made her jerk and wriggle and try to get free.

She knew whose strong arms were around her.

Or *what's* arms.

That idea made her fight hard. But to no avail. His hold was unbreakable.

'Let me go! Let me go! Get off me!'

The hold loosened, but bizarrely, now she was free, her limbs felt too heavy and lethargic to allow her to move. She stared at her booted toes and his much bigger ones beside them.

They were sitting on the short firm turf, their backs against the log, their legs stretched out in front of them. She could not, dared not, look at him. But his large cool hand gently stroked her face and, against all the odds, it seemed the simplest and most comfortable thing in the world to rest her head against the strength of his shoulder. The backs of his fingers moved slowly and soothingly against her cheek.

'Hush, don't be afraid,' he whispered. 'Nothing to be scared of.'

Lois huffed out a little breath. Easy for him to say that.

'That hare . . . it was you, wasn't it?'

There seemed to be no way she could get away from him, even if she'd wanted to, so it made best sense to meet the issue head on. She shifted around a little and, adjusting her position, she managed to screw up the courage to face him.

His luminous eyes – both blue and brown – were steady, clear and candid.

'Yes.' He gave a little shrug, and his splendid mouth

quirked. 'And I was also the bird, down on the beach, yesterday.'

The little well of bravery she'd gathered around her faltered, and she dragged in a great breath, utterly shaken.

'H-how can that be? How is it possible?' She shook her head. 'I mean, I've watched *Buffy* and *Doctor Who* and all that . . . but they're just stories. Fiction, made-up stuff . . . You can't seriously be, um, I don't know . . . a shape-shifter or whatever they're called. That's just crazy! It's not possible!'

Robin blinked at her, his glorious face troubled, his brow crumpling. 'I am what I am, Lois, and I can change form, become other creatures . . . and be human sometimes.'

Suddenly, a real sadness glittered in his eyes, and Lois realised to her astonishment that the azure and the brandy brown both were shiny with the gloss of real tears.

Human tears?

Her fear vanished. What was wrong? Why so sad? A great need to comfort and nurture surged up in her. It was kind of maternal, and yet not motherly at all. She was too close to him, and he smelt too wonderful and felt too strong to deny more earthy feelings.

'What's wrong?' she whispered, turning her face into his palm, and kissing it impulsively to offer comfort . . . and more.

'I'd like to stay human longer, but, after tomorrow, when June arrives, I can't.'

She supposed there was some great mythology to explain this, and that it would probably be wiser to understand it if she could, but a sudden urgency compelled her to ignore it for the moment. And forget anything but the here and now of Robin, the most beautiful and extraordinary *man* she'd ever met. She was probably being ten dozen different types of brainless bimbo-fools, but, if he had less than twenty-four hours in the shape he currently wore, she couldn't waste a minute debating parapsychology!

And yet, as she took his soft mobile lips in a tender kiss, and breathed in his sigh of relief and happiness, she couldn't help but see how many things now made sense.

His lack of physical weight and the coolness of his skin had seemed downright bizarre, but she supposed a part of her mind had just not asked questions. Or maybe they had, but those questions had been squelched . . . because Robin could read her thoughts, and probably manipulate them.

Which accounted for the erotic dreams too, she supposed.

I should be angry . . . but I'm not.

Oh, and there'd been other clues too.

His hair and eyes could be explained rationally, but not the sudden uncanny manifestation of wireless broadband and the self-mending computer.

It's all magic! Robin's magic . . .

There was magic, too, in the feel of his mouth, although the delicious contact was far from imaginary. He felt real, completely real, and of the flesh.

He's a . . . a . . . something, and I still want to kiss him. He's not human, and I still want to fuck him. This is insane, but it makes perfect sense.

Of course it made sense! If Robin would be gone soon, she had to have him now.

Sliding her hands inside his coat, she pushed it off his shoulders, and then, impatiently, tugged at the hem of his black T-shirt and snuck her fingers under it to cruise his silky skin.

He was cool, of course, but not cold. The contours of his chest and torso were like marble that was just beginning to feel the kiss of the morning sun. Flawless to the touch, and almost as hard in its muscular perfection. That was what magic did, she supposed, caressing his abs, and then flickering up to circle his taut male nipples. Why settle for second best when you could recreate a girl's ultimate wet dream?

Suddenly, she had to see him. In the arboreal sunlight, and maybe for the last time.

'Coat off, whatever you are,' she commanded, sweetening the order with a pepper of kisses against his throat.

Robin obeyed, and his grin showed that he'd forgotten his momentary distress and was now into the spirit of things. He slid off his heavy coat, then whipped his black T-shirt off over the top of his head, ruffling his golden-tipped hair endearingly in the process.

What the devil are you? Lois demanded silently, admiring the sweetly ripped lines of his chest, arms and shoulders. *In fact*, are *you a devil?*

Robin shook his curly head and Lois felt a great rush of relief.

'What then? An angel? A ghost?'

Again, he shook his head.

'You must be something though . . . just tell me!'

Leaning forwards, he pressed his lips to her ear and whispered a few words into it, all very low and very quiet.

7

'Get away with you!' Lois laughed and reached out to stroke his cool face. 'You're too big and butch and macho. Whatever happened to gauzy wings and pointy hats and perching on bluebells and all that? And, anyway, I thought they were all girls?'

'Oh no.' Robin smiled slyly at her, his eyes naughty. 'I can be whatever I want, if necessary, but my natural inclination is towards the male.' His big hand settled on her cheek, then slid down her throat and her shoulder, before settling on her breast. 'Especially now . . .'

His fingers cradled her flesh with perfect delicacy, and his lips were just as apposite as they pressed against hers. He seemed confident, but also a supplicant.

Be with me, I beg of you, he seemed to say in her mind. *Please be with me, there isn't much time*.

Lois responded, fighting the anguish that threatened to overwhelm her. She'd finally found her ideal man, but he wasn't actually a man. She wanted to be with him forever, but there were only a few hours before she'd lose him and not see him again for a year. If then.

She kissed him back hard, letting her own hands wander again over the firm muscular contours of his body. His need, and her own, made her bold. Pushing him by the shoulders, she urged him downwards, making him lie on the turf so she could surge over him and revel in the male splendour laid out for her pleasure.

And his too, really, she supposed. She couldn't imagine him making himself look ugly if he had the choice.

He tried to reach for her again, but she took him by the hands, and then pressed her lips to his palms, one after the other.

'Relax, Magic Man, let me explore you,' she murmured, pressing his arms back at his side, forcing him to lie inert, waiting, accepting. He seemed to be submitting, but the hot glint in his strange eyes told another tale. The King of the Grove was only *allowing* her to play with him. He looked more like a pasha accepting homage than a boy-toy at her bidding.

She touched her fingertips to his chest, flicking them over his nipples and then smiling when he wriggled and made a little sound of appreciation. She let her hand drift lower and the sound became closer to a growl.

His hips lifted when she traced his zipper with her fingernail.

'I think it's time we took a look at your wand, eh, don't you?'

Robin's strong arms came up, grabbing for her, but she pushed him back down again, tut-tutting and revelling in the way he allowed her to master his strength. For the time being at least.

As if accepting the status quo, he folded his arms behind his head, as a pillow. 'Help yourself,' he purred, a twinkle in his eyes.

Lois attacked his belt with gusto, unfastening the heavy buckle, then the button that lay beneath it. The black clothing, the archetypal garb for the dark predator . . . where did it come from? Were the coat and the boots et al. magic too? A part of him? What would happen if he disappeared while he was out of them?

Toying with his zip, she looked into his face rather than at his crotch, knowing it was quite likely that he was reading her mind.

'All this – the way you look? Where does it come from? I mean, is it from your imagination, or do you have some sort of . . . um . . . template or something?'

'Inspiration comes from many sources, my sweet.' His gaze flicked from her hovering fingers to her face. 'Just as you garner images for your web designs from here and there and everywhere, I gathered them from around me . . . and from your mind.'

Pausing in her explorations, Lois sat back a little, frowning. Peering at him through narrowed eyes. The face, yes, she could see it now . . . Familiar elements . . .

Looking at Robin, she suddenly recognised the likenesses.

One of her favourite actors, yes, there was a bit of him there. And the clothes, she suddenly realised, they came from a different character in a different show that she liked. His nose, faintly snub, she realised with astonishment, was not dissimilar to her own, only bigger of course and innately masculine . . . and, by God, he even had a bit of a look of the neighbour about him too if you looked closely enough!

'Well, I've never seen anyone with hair like yours before or eyes that are different colours. Where the hell did those come from?'

Robin laughed softly and, defying her edict, he half sat up and reached out for her hands again, drawing them towards his groin area.

'Well, those touches are uniquely my own. I have to be allowed a little creativity, don't I?'

'It's pretty bizarre though, isn't it, to have one blue eye and one brown, especially when . . .' She crumpled her brow, and peered more closely. 'Especially when the colours actually seem to swap places from one time I see you to the next!'

'But I *am* bizarre, Lois, aren't I?' His large but deft fingers stroked the back of her hands where they rested against his crotch. 'But a good fellow all the same, don't you think?'

The glint in his eyes shimmered like a spinning Christmas firework, and his words seemed to dance and shimmer just as teasingly. For a moment, just a tiny, tiny fraction of a second, her paramour seemed to ripple and glitter and become all the colours of the rainbow, then just as quickly, he was simply a man again.

A beautiful big, very male man, with an imposing hard-on swelling in his jeans.

Lois shook her head. Enough already! Enough of this fanciful madness. Robin was completely real, for the moment, and he wanted her. He wanted her, he was gorgeous . . . and she wanted him right back.

She resumed her attack on his jeans, undoing the button and whizzing down the zip. His erect cock sprang out in a way that was as comical as it was sudden, and before she could stop herself she'd giggled.

Immediately she felt a wash of remorse. Were super-natural male beings as sensitive about their equipment as their human counterparts? In which case, had she mortally offended his feelings and put him off?

'Whoops!' said Robin cheerfully, an inordinately proud grin on his face.

No insecurity problems there, obviously. Lois grinned back at him, and reached for the member in question. It was hard, as cool as the rest of him, and silkily textured.

'Well, I must say I like your magic wand!'

'So do I, and I . . . I like it even more when you're touching it!'

Robin stirred against the greensward, lifting his hips to meet her caresses as she handled him and traced the beautifully defined veins that adorned his cock.

He was thick and long, and the tip was flared and red and hungry-looking with a stretched and open 'eye' that was already weeping copious pre-come. Taking a little of this satin fluid on her thumb, Lois slowly and meticulously massaged him.

'Mmm, oh, my dear . . . that's wonderful, wonderful,' he burbled, his eyes closing and his hands clenching and relaxing, clenching and relaxing against the turf as she ministered to him.

Lois had never been a great one for giving hand-jobs. Oh, she'd done it often enough, and been praised for her touch sometimes, but mostly she'd always been keen to move on to more mutual pleasures.

But not with Robin.

To touch him was a joy in itself. His skin was so smooth, so fine to the touch, and holding him and stroking him seemed to impart a refined aesthetic experience that was quite unique. She'd also never touched a cock that seemed quite so very clean before. It was as if it was brand new, and expressly fashioned to please her senses.

Which she supposed, in a way, it was.

Of course, it was totally impossible to resist tasting him.

Inclining over his strong, jean-clad hips, Lois settled her mouth over the crown of Robin's penis – which, despite being what she most wanted to do at that moment, she still found to be quite a job.

The head of his cock was as big as a shiny ripe plum and ten times as delicious, and she had a dainty and feminine mouth. Her lips stretched around him as she took him inside, and she was aware that she was probably drooling all over him.

I probably look an awful sight!

But when she snuck a peek at him, up the length of his glorious torso, she discovered that Robin was smiling at her with such tenderness, such wonder and such gratitude that her heart turned over with love and a huge desire to pleasure him.

Washing and lapping at him with her tongue, she folded her fingers lightly and ripplingly around his shaft, co-ordinating the actions of her hands and her mouth. She sipped and tasted him, adoring the sweet perfumed, honeyed flavour of him that reminded her more of the old-fashioned confectionery of her childhood than any other man she'd ever given head to.

You're like the most delicious lollipop I ever tasted!

No sooner had the thought materialised than Robin laughed out loud with joy and cradled her head gently in his hands.

Working with fingers and tongue, and with suction and long sweeping licks, Lois went about her sacred duty with enthusiasm. It suddenly, almost, didn't seem as if she needed pleasure of her own. This attention to Robin was the sole focus of her being. He'd be gone soon, but, before he went, she'd make him come.

Magical fingers tightened around her cheeks and ears, and she felt him trying to encourage her to lift her mouth from him.

'Lois, my love, you must stop now. If you don't, I feel it'll be too late . . . and I'll be selfish.'

Lois held station and, still holding him lightly between her lips, she shook her head infinitesimally. Then went about her fellatial duties with new gusto and as much artistry as she could muster.

She swirled her tongue. She sucked as hard as she could. She flicked and flirted and played, stroking him all the time with fingertips that travelled the length and breadth of his shaft, and even ventured down into his jeans to stroke his balls and his perineum.

When she managed to crook her wrist enough to get a

finger in and press against his anus, he wailed almost like the gull-bird on the beach, and then jerked and filled her mouth with perfumed semen.

Pulse, pulse, pulse . . . it leapt from the tip of his cock, coated her tongue and then trickled down her throat. Lois swallowed eagerly savouring his pleasure as much as his taste, as the creamy fluid overflowed her lips and ran down her chin.

As if from a great distance she seemed to hear her lover sobbing. And then, as she released him, she realised he actually was in tears.

When his glittering, jewel-like eyes met hers, he sat up, reached for her and drew her up along his body and embraced her. Murmuring and muttering almost unintelligible thanks, he kissed her sticky lips and caressed her face with utmost reverence.

'You are a wonder, sweet Lois,' he whispered, his long pink tongue swooping around his own lips for a moment, cleaning his own transferred essence from their surface. 'A true miracle. If there's magic here, it's in you, my love, in you.'

My love? Did he really mean that?

For a moment, Robin put her away from him a little distance, so they could look into each other's eyes.

'Of course I love you,' he said simply. His face was beautiful with emotion, and yet, in the mismatched depths of his eyes, Lois could see pain.

'What's wrong? There's something . . . Is it because you have to – to go tomorrow?'

'Yes.' He bit his lip, hesitating, and Lois screamed silently for the whole truth.

'But it's more than that,' he went on, his expression

serious. 'When I can't be human any more, I stop feeling as a human does . . . I might lose this emotion. I might forget what I feel for you, and that I love you.' He took her hand in his and squeezed it in a way that came closer to hurting than anything he'd done to her before. 'And, though I don't want that to happen now, in a while, it might not matter as much to me.'

'I don't understand.'

'Nor do I, completely, when it happens.' His broad intelligent brow puckered in a frown.

'But don't you feel emotions when you're – you're how you normally are?'

'Yes, sort of, but they're faint. Like tiny ripples on a pond. Whereas now, when I look at you, I feel like the sea out there, surging and crashing and full of wildness. I feel love. And I want to *be* loved.'

She could see it, the turbulence of feeling in his expressive features.

'But I'm afraid that, after tomorrow, in the space of a few weeks, all I might still feel is curiosity, and not much more.'

Lois tried to imagine it. But she couldn't. Her life had always been a tapestry of feelings, richly coloured, not always happy, but mostly. How would it feel not to feel? It was incomprehensible.

'I just can't imagine how that would be,' she said, touching her fingertips to his face. His skin was smooth and cool, and she realised that there was no stubble, as such, on his cheeks. 'I – I mean, what do you remember of other years? Have you, um, interacted with other women?'

'Not in this way.' He turned his face, kissing her palm. 'I remember observing mostly. Observing couples. You're the first woman to come here on her own.' Long, long eyelashes flicked down, as if he were bashful, and a little ashamed of himself. 'I fear I may have taken advantage of you because of that. Forgive me.'

Lois laughed. He looked like a naughty little boy who'd stolen some sweeties. 'If that's being taken advantage of, keep on taking, Magic Man, keep on taking.' She slid her hand down his strong jaw, his neck and across the hard muscular planes of his superbly formed chest.

'I serve your wishes, beautiful Lois –' his eyes darkened – 'for as long as I'm able.'

Silent communication passed between them. It wasn't his mental telepathy. It was deeper even than that somehow. It was as if they were having the same thought.

'Let's not waste any time then.'

8

Assertive in her hunger, Lois pushed hard on Robin's chest, compelling him to lie back so she could enjoy him and savour his astonishing male beauty.

First she pulled off his boots, then his jeans, rendering him naked in the enchanted little glade. Submitting to her, he lay back like some kind of strange amalgam of utterly masculine stud and compliant sex slave. He was like no man Lois had ever encountered . . . in more ways than one.

She touched his skin. She kissed his eyes, his throat and the inside of his elbows. She adored him, with her heart, with her eyes and fingertips. But, before long, just exploring and caressing was not enough.

'Why have I still got all these clothes on?' she demanded, then laughed when Robin gave a 'search me' shrug and it made his gloriously stiff erection dance and sway.

Ripping at her jacket and her shoes, her jeans and the rest of her clothing, Lois got naked faster than she could ever remember doing before. Buttons and zips, hooks and elastic all seemed to give way with supernatural ease. She laughed again as she realised that her things *were* coming off unnaturally fast. Robin might be lying there like a lounging gigolo, but he was helping her disrobe at the same time.

At last, she was as bare and untrammelled as he was . . . and she wasn't even cold. The chill of the coolest May for many years had disappeared completely, and they might have been basking in the gilded sunshine of midsummer.

She threw her leg across Robin's pelvis and hovered over him.

'I . . .' She paused, distracted by the slow slide of his silky tip against the inside of her thigh. 'I mean . . . Do I need protection? Do you know what I mean? Condoms and all that? I don't suppose I do, do I?'

Robin's face grew momentarily solemn. 'This body has never been with another. And it isn't human. There is no danger to you of any kind.'

Only to my heart . . .

Once again, Robin's remarkable face darkened with remorse. She felt his guilt, his regret that he'd made her fall for the most impossible of partners. One who might forget this tryst, and feel no pain of loss in the months to come the way she would.

'I'll *make* you remember, Robin! I swear I will!' she cried, flashing him a brilliant, imperious smile as she positioned him carefully at the snug entrance to her body, then began a slow, slow descent upon his cock.

She seemed to slide down, and down, and down, for what seemed like an eternity, her body flexing and expanding to accommodate his splendid, magical length and his impressive girth. He seemed to be moving not only into the quick of her sex, but also into her heart, her nerves, her cells.

Maybe he was even doing that literally? Somehow managing to infuse her flesh with his enchanted aura, stirring it to pleasure on a molecular level as well as simply entering her as a man?

Sliding, settling, Lois swayed. It was too much. Robin was too much, but somehow she seemed to open to him, accept him and take him all.

'Are you all right, my love?' He came up on his elbow, watching her face closely, his own face twitching a little with strain, as if fighting a huge rush of pleasure. 'I'm not hurting you, am I?'

'No! Not at all! You feel amazing!'

Big hands settled around her hips, holding her, securing her while he bucked upwards, plumbing her even deeper, possessing her utterly.

Lois groaned, overwhelmed, undulating slowly on the fulcrum of Robin's sex, loving the sensation of being stretched and being loved so hugely from within. Her clitoris leapt, and then leapt again when she saw his smile of hot delight when she reached down to touch herself. To stroke her own pleasure centre was to caress her lover's too.

She flicked her finger, and it was Robin's turn to toss his gold-frosted head, subsiding back against the turf, his hips lifting again and again. His long hands tightened, pressing his fingertips into the flesh of her buttocks, and Lois relished the desperation she felt in his grip.

'Lois! Lois!' he cried, writhing as she writhed, rising as she descended, grabbing at her to hold her on him, as she grabbed and caressed him from within.

'Lois! Oh my love, my love,' he exhorted her, his neck arching, his head tossing from side to side.

Then suddenly, his powerful hips came up and he remained still for moments, moments that seemed like frozen time, and then he was pushing again, his pelvis jerking convulsively in the rapid unmistakeable dance of orgasm.

Filled in heart and body, Lois joined him, almost fainting from the exquisite rolling ripples of sensation. But, even as the pleasure threatened to overwhelm her, she exerted a supreme effort – and kept her eyes open when they would normally have fluttered closed.

Remember this! she commanded silently, staring down at Robin's face, still so beautiful despite his tense orgasmic grimace. *Remember it! Remember everything about it!*

But, as she cascaded forwards, wilting over her lover's prone body like a lily whose stem could not bear the weight of its flower, she couldn't work out which of them the unspoken cry had been really aimed at.

They did not speak much as they gathered their clothes, dressed again and returned to the cabin. They did not speak much as they made love there, again and again, sometimes tenderly and sometimes ferocious in their passion.

But, all the while, Lois was acutely aware of Robin's total focus on what they were doing, and his concentration.

He is *trying to remember it all*, she thought in wonder as she looked up into his face when he entered her yet again, his eyes so dark and intense that for that moment they did appear to match each other. *He's trying to imprint it on his mind, his consciousness, or whatever he has . . . so he can retain it.*

Eventually they rested, though, because Lois was exhausted. She suspected that Robin could go on indefinitely, and his body would rouse again and again where a normal man's could not, but she was just human, and prone to fatigue no matter how fabulous the sex was.

Sleep claimed her for a while, and she drifted and skittered through strange dreams of loss where she was running through the woods and along the shore, chasing something intangible. Which, she realised, when she awoke again to find Robin watching her, might be an accurate reflection of the next eleven months without him.

'I'm going to keep coming here, you know.' Sitting up in bed, she grasped his large hand and squeezed it. 'I'm going to be around here, reminding you of all this. I'm not going to bloody well let you forget me because I'm going to be in your face, Magic Man, even when you haven't actually got one!'

For a moment, she thought she might have offended him, but Robin's guffaw of mirth immediately dispelled her worries. 'I'll watch you, beautiful Lois, I'll watch you, and, if there's a way to remember this feeling, I will.' Leaning over her, he kissed her again, at first tenderly and then with increasing purpose.

Again?

'Yes, again, my love, again,' he growled, pressing her back against the pillows.

A long time later, after night had fallen and the moon was in the sky, they tumbled from the bed, showered together and donned their clothes. Neither one of them spoke much, but, time and again, Lois found herself sneaking swift peeks at her little alarm clock.

Midnight was approaching. And with it the end of May.

'Let's go for a walk on the beach,' said Robin suddenly, reaching for his long dark coat.

'Um, yes, OK,' Lois agreed, her heart sinking. Even though they were no longer naked, she'd wanted there to be the option.

He held out her jacket, helped her into it, his fingers settling it on her shoulders almost lovingly, and then turned her around so he could zip it up and dress her like a daddy dressing his little girl.

'When the time comes, Lois, when the time comes, let me walk away as if I were a real man. Let me pretend to be a real man. Your real lover.'

'You *are* a real man to me, Robin.' She grabbed his arm, forcing him to look at her. 'And you're certainly the realest lover *I've* ever had!'

His eyes gleamed and, despite the angst of the moment, she could see he was pleased with himself. Lois grinned up at him.

Men! Even if they were magic imitations, they still liked to hear praise for their sexual prowess!

'Come on then, let's go for that walk.'

As she led the way to the door, though, something caught her eye. Her digital camera, on the table.

'One minute, Robin, let me take your picture! That way, I'll have something to remind me of you while you're . . . well . . . away.' She paused, thinking, thinking. 'And, when you come back, you'll have a template for when you take human form again.'

Robin looked impressed, but then he shrugged. 'We can try it, my love. It's a very good idea . . . But my kind are extra-ordinarily difficult to photograph.'

Lois snatched up the camera and, directing Robin to pose, she reeled off a few shots of him sitting, standing, smiling and looking moody.

She took upwards of twenty fast shots, using a variety of settings, but, frustratingly, they all came out strangely fuzzy and lacking in definition.

'Why are they so blurred?' she railed, flicking through the shots.

'Maybe because I'm becoming blurred, losing my focus.'

Lois's eyes flicked to the clock. Not long to go. With a sigh, she set down the camera, and then reached for Robin's hand – which still felt substantial and wonderful to her touch.

'Shall we walk then?'

They headed for the beach by silent mutual consent. Again, no telepathy. Lois just seemed to know that was the right place to head for.

The full moon was high as they walked, and she found herself stealing glances, again and again, at her companion, and tightening her fingers around his.

He was so real. And that perplexed her utterly.

How could she love a man who didn't really exist? A man she'd known for barely more than a day? A man, but one who was nothing more than a magical construct, made up from fragments and images in her mind, an amalgam of many other men?

And yet she did. Mad as it seemed. She simply did.

The sand was firm beneath their feet and, in the brightness from the moon, they could see it stretching away ahead, along the shore, unnaturally white and scattered with driftwood and skeins of dark seaweed.

'What's that? Over there?'

By the edge of the lapping waves lay a small dark bundle. Clothing, what looked like a pair of boots and the glint of glass.

With Robin padding behind her, Lois ran to the bundle. She recognised her neighbour's warm coat, his beanie hat with a watch laid neatly on top of it, and an empty bottle that had once contained Glenfiddich whisky beside them.

'Where is he?' She scanned the water, and then turned to Robin. 'Surely he's not gone swimming at this time of night? In this cold and full of booze? The water must be freezing.'

Her companion was peering out into the bay, his eyes narrowed. 'He's out there.' He pointed to the waves. 'He's swimming now, but I don't think he will be for long.'

'What do you mean?'

'I believe he's trying to end his life. I sensed it in him before, but I thought that it was just a fleeting notion, not a real intention.'

Oh, God, she'd sensed the neighbour was unhappy, but not this bad.

'But we've got to try and help him! He's been drinking . . . He'll feel different when he's sober.'

She surged forwards, kicking off her shoes as she went, and flinging off her coat, but the water knocked the breath out of her before she reached waist depth it was so cold, so bitterly cold.

'Fucking hell!' she gasped, staggering and almost falling into the waves.

But, before she capsized, strong arms grasped her, and lifted her up on to her feet.

'Go back into the shallows! I'll get him,' Robin commanded her. He'd already flung off his long coat and his boots. His face was hard and determined in the moonlight. 'Go back to safety now.'

'But Robin, I can help . . . Help drag him in.'

The bitter irony of the moment suddenly crashed in on her with more power than the biggest of the waves.

It was almost midnight. These were their last moments before eleven months apart, and yet she knew the man out in the bay stood his best chance of being saved if she let her lover plunge into the water after him.

'Go back, my love, I'll get him.'

For one brief second he crushed his lips against hers, and then he put her from him and threw himself forwards into the dark and bitter water.

9

Robin had never swum in human form before, but like all natural skills it came to him effortlessly and he struck out hard in the direction of where they'd last seen Lois's neighbour, the man known as Edgar.

But was he too late?

Edgar had already slipped beneath the waves and was descending into the depths, his lungs waterlogged and his hold on life ebbing. Plunging down after him, Robin grabbed for his shoulders.

The reaction was predictably violent. Just as a normal man would have struggled for survival with every last fibre of his being, Edgar seemed bent on struggling to achieve his death and he thrashed and struggled, kicked out and punched with what remained of his strength, and even Robin found it difficult to hold on to him.

Let me help you! Please don't do this! It's not the way!

He spoke directly into the man's mind. It was the only way. It was too late now to worry about the niceties of explaining who he was . . . and what.

A life was at stake. A precious life. A *human* life – something he would have cherished, at all costs, if he'd had it himself.

And, in this strange, unnatural hinterland between life and death, Edgar seemed to accept the fact of unspoken communication.

Leave me alone! Let me go! She's here . . . I want to be with her . . .

His thoughts were weak, yet Robin understood. He didn't know what to do, and his grip on the rapidly ebbing Edgar faltered.

The dying man wriggled feebly and slid away.

Robin grabbed for him again.

No! Please! Let me be with her!

Such desperation. Such love.

Robin felt the keen pain of it. He felt it himself. Wouldn't he undertake the most drastic and most extreme act in order to be with Lois? And it could well be true. Edgar's lover might be here in spirit, somewhere close.

Disassociating momentarily, Robin sent out his consciousness.

Yes, indeed, he sensed a hovering presence, watching, waiting.

The weight of human sadness, passion and love descended on him. This was how they lived, and it was terrifying, yet still it seemed worth all the tumult if it meant a life with the one you adored. A woman like Lois.

Robin hesitated.

Life was sacred. He couldn't just let Edgar die.

He attempted to reach for the fading man, and found he couldn't.

No!

Midnight, the perennial witching hour, had just this moment passed.

It was June, and he could no longer assume the form of a human man.

But could he still persuade Edgar to live? He reached out again, this time in intangible form, searching for Edgar's mind.

Too late. He was gone. Robin felt a rising, rushing surge in the ether as the human's spirit swept up, flying to meet the one who waited, and, at the same time, his mortal shell began to descend.

Robin watched the body dropping in the water.

Until moments ago, it had been hale, hearty, strong and alive. A perfect vessel.

Could he? Dare he? Would it work? His people spoke of such things, passed down tales, stories . . . but had such a phenomenon ever really been achieved?

The vision of Lois seemed to shimmer before him, and he sensed her back there on the beach, distraught with worry and fear, readying herself to wade into the water again.

He had to try it. He had to try. Even at the risk of his own extinction in the process.

'Robin! Robin! Are you all right?'

Lois had never shouted louder in her life, and it was making her throat sore and her lungs hurt, bellowing out into the bay again and again. But she couldn't see anything. There was no sign of her lover or her neighbour at all now, just the waves and the glitter of moonlight glancing on their crests. She waded out into the water, thrashing and struggling, then realised it was pointless. Not the strongest of swimmers, she'd never had any lifesaving training, and she wasn't even sure what direction to go in.

'Oh, Robin! Please!' she howled, staggering backwards and falling in a heap on the sand beside her neighbour's abandoned clothes.

What about rescue? Was there a lifeboat she could summon or something? Struggling into a sitting position, she felt in her pocket for her mobile, and discovered she'd left it in the cabin.

'Fuck!'

What about her neighbour? Did he have one? Plunging into the pile of clothing, she rummaged in all his pockets, but found nothing.

'No! No!'

Tears streaming down her face, she sprang to her feet again, staring out into the empty bay and the waves.

The cabin. There was a landline there. She could phone from there.

But, just as she was about to set out, something caught her eye. Or, more correctly, the *lack* of something.

Where was Robin's coat? His boots? They'd been flung out on the sand, next to her neighbour's stuff . . . and now they were gone.

'Oh noooo!' she keened again. 'Robin! Robin!'

He was gone. Turned back, along with his clothes, into whatever he'd been before.

What if it'd happened under water? What if he'd drowned too?

Could he drown? Maybe he was still around here somewhere?

'Robin! Robin! Robin!' she yelled, shouting now to the intangible presence, not the man.

As she stared out over the surface of the waves, shielding her eyes against the almost unnatural brilliance of the moonlight, she suddenly saw a shape breach the surface of the water.

A head!

Someone was coming. Wading towards her.

'Robin!' she screamed, plunging back into the cold sea, floundering towards the human figure that was labouring in her direction, staggering to his feet when he hit the shallows, then falling into the surf again.

'Robin,' she sobbed in a small broken voice when she reached the naked retching figure, who knelt on all fours, coughing up seawater and gasping for breath.

Not Robin, she thought, her heart bereft as she slid her arms around her neighbour's bare shoulders and helped him half crawl and half stagger towards the safety of dry land.

Robin, where are you?

Lois sat in the armchair by the stove, cradling a cup of tea in her hands as she tried to warm up. It had a hefty slug of brandy in it, in an attempt to fire her up from within, but, so far, it wasn't making much in the way of an inroad into her inner chilliness.

It was over an hour since she'd half dragged and half carried her neighbour into her cabin and helped him on to the bed then rubbed him dry with towels and spare blankets. He'd seemed virtually comatose on his feet, and unable to speak, and had lapsed into what could be unconsciousness or maybe just sleep almost as soon as he was horizontal.

When she'd decided it was safe to a leave him for a moment, Lois had run back down to the sand, calling for Robin – in vain, she knew – and scouring the moonlit ocean for any sign of him. She'd even peered up into the sky, hoping to see him in the gull-like form he'd assumed before.

But there was nothing. No trace of him either physically . . . or intangibly.

With a heavy heart, she'd scooped up her neighbour's clothing, and, on returning to the cabin, had discovered from a postcard in his jacket pocket that he was called Edgar.

She stared at Edgar now, sleeping the sleep of a baby, in her bed.

I wish you were Robin!

Immediately, she felt guilty. She wished that *both* of them had come back out of the water, improbable or impossible as that might have been. She padded over to the side of the bed and sat down on the hard chair bedside it, staring down at the slumbering man, something keen twisting painfully inside her as she observed certain aspects of his appearance that reminded her of her supernatural lover.

'Well, he did say he took some "bits" from you,' she muttered, recognising a certain line to the jaw, and perhaps the shape of an eyebrow, the tilt of a cheekbone.

Edgar was older than her beautiful Robin, though, and stockier, and his drying hair was frosted with grey rather than highlights of gold. Under other circumstances, she might have found him attractive, especially now the colour was coming back to his cheeks and he was starting to look healthy and normal again. But it was all she could do, at the moment, to battle with the resentment she felt against him, and her own guilt at thinking ill of him.

God, the man had been unhappy enough to want to take his own life, and here she was near to hating him because he'd snatched away her last few minutes with Robin. The fact that it'd been the final precious fragment of time they'd share for eleven months was bad enough . . . but the possibility that something had gone wrong, and that was it for good, for all time, forever, she couldn't bear to think about.

Even thinking about it made her groan with pain and, as tears filled her eyes, she just gave in and slumped slowly forwards, across the sleeping man, weeping.

The sobs wrenched at her. It felt as if someone was pulling at her soul and mangling it up. The idea of never seeing, or even sensing, Robin again was agonising. She clutched at the inert body and arms of Edgar for blind consolation.

Moments passed, or maybe hours, but suddenly, as her tears were beginning to subside out of pure weariness, the man beneath her moved, and sighed, and she felt the very lightest touch of fingers on her head, slowly stroking.

'Oh, you're awake,' she said awkwardly, straightening up, unable to look at the rousing Edgar, not quite knowing how to greet him. 'Are you all right?' She fussed with a blanket, tweaking it a bit further up his chest. 'Er, would you like a hot drink or something?'

'Lois?'

The voice was soft and strained, as if speaking was still an almost insurmountable effort, but the single word seemed to twinkle like a silvery bell, ringing beautifully through her consciousness. There was deep exhaustion there, but also – familiarity?

Slowly, fearfully, she turned and looked down into Edgar's waking face . . .

And saw a miracle.

Yes, it was the face of her taciturn fellow holidaymaker, who'd barely spoken to her . . . and yet it wasn't him. A subtle metamorphosis seemed to be under way, perceptible perhaps only to someone who knew what to look for, but the features of Edgar were beginning to change into those of her beloved Robin.

The exhausted eyes were still a little dull and weary, but, already, they were no longer the nondescript hazel they had been.

The left one was blue, and the right one was brown.

'Robin?'

Joy, confusion, fear, relief, a jumble of belief and disbelief suddenly rushed through her like a tidal wave.

She flung herself forwards to kiss his strangely mutable physiognomy and threw her arms around him. His body was warm, deliciously warm, and, when his arms came around her, the sensation was so sweetly that of one coming home after a long and dangerous journey that she burst into more tears, sobs of wrenching relief, and could not speak.

They hugged for quite a while, and as Robin – she supposed she must call him that now, despite the lingering resemblance to Edgar – gained strength, he sat up and drew her on to the bed beside him.

Lois simply couldn't stop smiling, despite the strangeness and incomprehensibility of their situation.

'How is this possible?' She touched his new face, trickled her fingers over his hair, which looked less grey now and bore a growing hint of gold. A thought occurred, and she reared back a little, not knowing how to feel about it. Everything was so confused. 'You didn't snatch his body, did you?'

She was half laughing as she spoke, but felt a thrill of fear that was as dark as it was delicious.

'No, Lois, I didn't snatch his body,' replied Robin amiably, 'although I can see why you have to ask the question.'

'I'm sorry . . . I didn't mean it that way.' She searched his face, wondering if she'd hurt his feelings.

'It's all right, it was a fair conclusion.' He took her hands in his big warm ones. 'I didn't snatch Edgar's body. I simply slipped into it when he left it to go elsewhere.'

'Elsewhere?'

'Oh, he's around here somewhere, I think. Not too far . . . But he's not alone now. He's with somebody he loves.'

Lois blinked, and Robin lifted a long finger to wipe away a stray tear from her face.

'And I'm with somebody I love, so now everyone's happy.'

Lois smiled, still filled with wonder. 'So you . . . you're completely Robin in there . . . Not Edgar at all then?'

Robin shrugged, rolled his eyes and seemed suddenly to go inwards somehow. 'There're memories, knowledge, information that are available to me.' He looked at her and smiled. 'Which will no doubt be useful now that I'm going to have to live my life as a human being, don't you think?'

'Best of both worlds then?'

'Most definitely,' he declared roundly, his eyes twinkling now, looking brilliant and far more colourful. Cradling her jaw, he brought her face to his to steal a kiss.

The healthy human warmth in his lips might be new, but the way he kissed her was completely and utterly Robin. She sighed with pleasure beneath his mouth at the sweet familiarity, and low in her belly she felt another sweetness stir.

She wanted to ask him if he could still read her mind, but it seemed his body was certainly interpreting all the signals.

'Shouldn't you be resting?' she purred as he drew her further on to the bed, and moved over her, unfastening the cord of her dressing gown before plucking it open to reveal her bare skin underneath it. She'd not bothered to dress after the hot shower she'd taken to warm herself. 'I mean, you did just drown about an hour ago.'

'Ah, but it seems our dear friend Edgar was in prime physical condition, with superb powers of recuperation,' murmured Robin, beginning to kiss his way down her throat, towards her breasts, in a way that was unmistakeably and utterly and completely 'him'.

'Yes, he's not in bad nick at all,' concurred Lois, running her hands down the firm and muscular form of her lover's torso.

And reaching his loins she got a deliciously welcome surprise . . . Not quite Robin's fantasy dick, but still a magnificent specimen.

'Not bad at all,' she purred, beginning to slowly fondle it.

'And the best bit is . . . I still know how to use it.'

For a while, they touched and caressed, Lois entranced by the warm human feel of Robin's skin and his sex.

Until a thought occurred to her . . .

She looked up at him, gnawing her lip. She was almost certain that he couldn't accurately read her mind any more, but she knew he could sense her emotion, her quandary.

'What is it, my love?' he asked. His expression was kind and far more tolerant of her hesitation at this crucial moment than any of her previous lovers would have been.

'Um, well, you're human now . . . we need . . .'

'Protection?' His eyes twinkled.

'Well, yes. I'm sorry, I mean, I don't . . .'

Robin drew her back into his arms, close and sweet. 'Don't worry, sweet Lois.' His breath was a whisper against her ear, and, as she nuzzled him, she realised that, very faintly, he still smelt of lavender. 'If you don't have condoms, there are plenty of *other* ways to give each other pleasure. I have the imagination of *two* men now, remember?'

'Well, actually,' she began bashfully, 'I was sort of half hoping for a holiday romance when I packed for this trip.' She pursed her lips. 'There are some condoms in the bedside drawer.' She pulled back a little and looked up at him, with a little smirk. 'Although we can still do some of that other stuff first, can't we?'

'With pleasure, my love.' His lips began the process that his hands and his body would soon complete, beginning the journey down her body, tasting lightly and sampling her skin with his tongue. 'With the greatest of pleasure,' he murmured, looking up at her, his odd eyes twinkling as he kissed the gentle curve of her belly.

Epilogue

The sky was bright, the sun was high and the air was warm. It was summer already, a gorgeous June day, when just a week ago it had felt like deepest winter.

Lois squeezed Robin's hand as they strolled contentedly on the beach. They were barefoot in the surf but the rolling water held no fear for them. A short while earlier they'd taken a swim, frolicking happily.

'Look!' Robin gestured elegantly to a large chunk of driftwood a few yards away and, following his eye-line, Lois saw a pair of birds perched together on its highest branch.

They were billing and cooing, preening each other, a perfect picture of mutual devotion and affection. Lois squinted, in the sun, and wondered if her eyes were deceiving her. The two birds looked vaguely familiar, and very much like the gull-like form her Robin had taken before he'd found this new body, lately vacated by the unfortunate Edgar.

'They could be us,' she observed, as the birds continued to canoodle, despite the presence of two humans so close by.

'Not *us*,' replied Robin, turning to her, an odd expression on his broad handsome face. His hair was gold-tipped now, and it shone in the morning sun. 'But perhaps someone we know . . . and the one he longed to be with.'

'Really?'

Lois's astonished exclamation finally disturbed the two lovebirds, and they took to the skies above the bay, whirling and wheeling, their glossy wings seeming to entwine as they soared in an aerial ballet of sheer exuberance.

'Looks like they're making love, doesn't it?' observed Robin, smiling as he watched their play. 'Shall we go back indoors and do the same?'

Lois looked up into his eyes, smiling back at him. The blue one was bluer and the brown one browner now that, more and more, he became the natural resident of his brand-new body.

'I'd love to, Magic Man, I'd really love to!'

Tugging on his big warm hand, she led the way towards the path.

Buddies Don't Bite

1

'Damn! Damn! Damn!'

Teresa Johnson trudged into the cosy, softly lit kitchen and flung her bag across the room, grimacing at the thought of her mobile and her PDA in a thousand bits, but in no mood to really care all that much.

'Idiot!' Avoiding a damage inspection, she headed for the fridge. First things first, she needed wine. Then a think.

Yanking open the big old refrigerator door, she stilled herself, closed her eyes, breathed deeply. Tantrums were pointless. And so was breaking things. Whether that be her wine or milk bottles, or the ones containing Zack's peculiar 'iron shake'.

'Chill out . . . chill out . . .' Reaching in for her Chardonnay, she wondered for the hundredth time what *was* in those dark-brown vacuum-sealed bottles lined up on the middle shelf. She'd opened one once, and it'd made her cringe. The heavy earthy raw-meat smell had been disturbing. Poor old Zack having to drink that mucky stuff for every meal. She didn't envy him his anaemia and food allergies.

Almost overfilling her wine glass, she teetered over to

the refectory table and slumped down in a chair. Her anger was all but gone now and dim disappointment felt like a low pressure front.

'So what's it to be, Teresa?' She took a long slurp of wine. 'To wedding or not to wedding? Is it nobler in the mind to stay at home like a cowardly, boyfriendless reject? Or to take arms against a sea of smug marrieds and lovey-dovey couples and get laughed at because I'm a loser?'

'Talking to oneself is the first sign of madness, my dear, didn't you know that?'

Wine went everywhere, and Teresa's chair rocked on its back legs. She braced for impact with the hard kitchen floor and the thump of pain – then she found herself upright with her heart pounding fit to burst.

'Zack, for Christ's sake, don't sneak up on me like that! I hate it when you creep around and I don't hear you!'

She'd *definitely* felt her chair going over, but now it was four square again, and *she* was on her feet. And there was Zack, her tall, dark and handsome landlord, mopping efficiently at the spilt wine on the table with squares of kitchen roll.

Teresa glanced at the bottle, disorientated. Even allowing for spillage there was plenty left. She wasn't drunk and she wasn't imagining things.

Zack had put in one of his famous appearances right out of thin air.

And now – domesticated yet still manly – he was cleaning up her mess and making her ears burn with guilt. 'Oh, God, Zack, I'm sorry! I know I shouldn't yell. . . it's your house and you're entitled to creep about if you want to.'

'No problem. I'm just sorry I startled you, love.' With his usual deftness and elegance, her landlord made short work of the clean up operation, and in what felt like a split-second, he'd poured her another glass of wine and was nodding for her to sit back down again.

Not for the first time, Teresa decided that it was a criminal waste to live every day with an unusual but desirable man like Zachary Trevelyan – and not be anything more than good house buddies. His narrow elegant face was alight with pleasure, even though he'd just been soundly bellowed at. What normal man would suck up such abuse and still smile?

'Better now?' Before the words were out, he was sitting down opposite her.

'Yes.' She was. It was always better to be looking at Zack than not looking at him. She loved his beautiful calming stillness that was such a contrast to the spookily swift way he sometimes moved. What would be even better was for him to move swiftly in her direction, take her in his arms and kiss her – instead of clearly observing the boundaries of their respective personal spaces.

In the interests of long-term house harmony and cordial landlord/tenant relations, Teresa always squished down hard on the temptation to think of Zack in 'that way'. But it was hellishly difficult when even after six months of friendship and platonic cohabitation he still did the maddest, hottest things to her hormones.

He was far from her usual type.

The accursed Steve and various assorted men who'd preceded him, had all been healthy, tanned, gym-buffed and metrosexual, and Zack was as far from that as it was possible to be.

The word 'Goth' always sprang to mind when she looked at him. Tall and lean and vaguely etiolated, he had all the characteristics of a typical night dweller, which wasn't at all surprising, considering he suffered from photophobia and sun sensitivity on top of his other problems. And yet his pallor captivated her. As did the stylish gauntness that seemed to suggest his bones were just a bit too big for his skin.

The lean sharp lines of his cheekbones and his jaw conferred on him a louche romantic glamour that reminded her of those sexy silent movie stars who dressed as sheikhs and wore eyeliner. Couple that with the kind of dark curly hair that could have looked like a yokel on anybody else, but suggested wild Byronic decadence on him and the most hypnotic blue eyes, the colour of a rare antique perfume bottle.

Teresa surreptitiously clenched her teeth. If exotic Zack had shown even the slightest hint of a whisker of a glimmer of interest in her, there would have been no need to go out with substandard men like Steve anyway.

'Come on, love . . . what's the matter? You can tell your Uncle Zack.'

Slipping into 'therapist' mode, Zack crossed his long lean arms in front of him, and then settled into a perfect waiting tranquillity. Playing up to his own gothic image, he was wearing a loose frilled poet's shirt, half open down the front to show a tasty wedge of his smooth hairless chest.

Teresa stilled too. She'd whirled into the house in a maxi state about a micro drama, and now, after five minutes with Zack, she could barely remember what had been bugging her.

Looking into his clear blue eyes, she felt a low internal thud deep in her body.

This was the man she'd wanted to go to the wedding with, not Steve. It had never really been Steve. He was just a substitute and she almost felt sorry for him, despite the fact he was a rat. She'd only started dating him because Zack, her dearest friend, was off limits.

She'd fancied Zack, despite his peculiarities, ever since the first moment she'd set eyes on him, one night in a local coffee house. Then, as now, he'd offered sympathy – that time over her losing her flat when her previous housemates decided to sell up. They had been total strangers and yet he'd offered her the hospitality of his big rambling house and without thinking twice, or even once, she'd accepted.

Her fingers prickled with the desire to reach out, unwind those strong arms of his, and coax him to rewind them around her. She wanted to kiss his sweet red mouth, push her tongue between his lips, and find out if those large, white teeth of his were really as sharp as they sometimes looked. She wanted to rip his shirt all the way open and kiss his chest – and maybe his neck too. Perhaps she'd nibble him a bit? She often seemed to find herself imagining that. She wanted to peel off those tight black jeans that clung to his lean legs like liquorice – and see if the astonishing bulge she sometimes saw there was as magnificent as it was in her fantasies.

'Teresa?'

Zack's voice sounded shaken somehow, as if he had sensed her thoughts but wasn't sure he liked them.

'It's the wedding. I can't go!'

'But I thought you were looking forward to it?'

'I was . . . I *love* weddings . . .' Her mind filled with flowers, smiling faces and the sheer sentimental joy of romance. 'But I was looking forward to going with someone . . . and not being part of the usual cattle market.' Zack's serious sculpted face bore a strangely wistful expression and she had a feeling he understood her perfectly. 'I was . . . um . . . expecting a hot, sexy, romantic weekend.'

'So what's happened?'

'Steve and I have split up . . . well, technically he dumped me. I think I might have come over a tad soppy over the whole wedding thing and scared him off. So he bailed.' She shuddered, not because of the loss but at what she might have let happen. Encouraged. 'Unfortunately, though, because he's a friend of the groom, he's still going to the wedding . . . with someone else.'

Zack's eyes were steady, thoughtful and heart-breakingly blue. 'Mmm. That's awkward.' He was as still as ever, but she could see him weighing up her options.

Suddenly, tears welled up, but they were nothing to do with Steve or the wedding. They were for something wistful and glorious that she'd never, ever have. A proper romance with pale and beautiful Zack.

'Hey! Hey! Hey!'

In another burst of freakish speed, he was in the chair *beside* her now, his powerful arms wrapped around her. And it felt so good that their unspoken boundaries were suddenly meaningless.

In Zack's cradling hold she was safe and cherished. He held her lightly but like a rock, like Superman to her Lois, he was so strong. In her mind, she flew back to a precious moment a few weeks ago. Another instance when he'd breached his personal space for her. She'd caught a virus that was going around and had nearly passed out. And sweet Zack had swept her up as if she weighed nothing and carried her all the way to bed.

Unfortunately, when he got her there, he'd left her with a hot water bottle, a selection of painkillers and decongestants and a steaming lemon drink – rather than climbing beneath the covers and giving her the sexual healing that she longed for.

But those moments of being swooped up off her feet and

carried as if she weighed nothing at all had been exquisite, despite her congested sinuses and her headache. And being held now was equally sublime.

'You could still go, Teresa.' His hand was cool against her skin where he smoothed her hair away from her face. 'You're stronger than you think. Why not go anyway and show everyone how fabulous you are? Have fun and just be there for Lisa.'

You're so right, she thought. I will go. Why not?

Peering at him, blinking, she smiled a grateful smile, and then opened her mouth to speak – and brought forth insane words she'd never intended to utter.

'I don't suppose *you'd* come with me, would you? I mean . . . not a "date" or anything? More a friend-type thing, really. You wouldn't have to be outside in daylight. The wedding itself and the parties and whatnot are all either indoors or held in the evening.'

Nothing about the way Zack held her altered, but he was staring at the table, his pale profile intense, almost graven. A single jet-black curl dangled against his brow like an inverted question mark.

What have I done? Teresa thought. Now I've spoilt everything by opening my big mouth. But before she opened that big mouth again, knowing it was futile to even attempt to repair the damage, Zack spoke first.

With his customary measured grace, he unwound his arms from around her, pushed back his chair and stood up. Then he clasped his hands together, rubbing the fingers of one hand against the back of the other, studying them fixedly as if he'd never seen them before. Teresa couldn't have been more shocked if he'd run around the room, shouting and breaking things.

'OK . . . why not? I'll go with you. I'll even be your "date", if you want me to.' His rather sultry red mouth curved into a smile.

What?

Teresa's jaw dropped, and the cosy familiar room suddenly seemed almost alien. This was studious Zack who worked from home writing scholarly historical treatises and never, ever went out during the day. This was Zack, who only ever ventured out at dusk, or at night, for long walks around the city streets. That was how she'd met him, in the coffee shop that night, and he'd been there for her then, just as he was now.

But this was different. *This* was amazing. Without thinking, Teresa leapt up, lunged forward – and kissed him.

And promptly forgot about weddings, and weekends, and perfidious weasel boyfriends.

Zack's lips were soft and cool and velvety. Twice as luscious as she'd imagined and a hundred times more provocative. They were quiescent beneath hers at first, almost innocent, and deep in her groin pure lust kicked, and kicked again. There was something uniquely seductive about a man who was untouched, who was shy and pure. One of her deepest and most secret masturbation fantasies was to seduce a young sweet virgin man. It was an impossible dream when most men were sexually active well before they were even supposed to be. But even so, the magical idea of it still burned in her imagination.

And Zack's beautiful motionlessness played right into those dreams. He simply accepted the kiss, but there was thrilling latency to the lush supple contact. The urge to hurl her weight forwards, wrestle him to the kitchen floor and accept the consequences raged through her.

But then, inside, something intangible tipped over.

Arms like steel bands closed tight around her, and his tongue gently pressed between her lips, demanding entrance. She let him in, loving the strange coolness of the moist and mobile pressure.

Her arms came up, hands roving over his hard back beneath his thin cotton shirt. And the touch of that was cool too, like woven cobwebs sliding over marble.

Although she'd lived with this man for months, she very, very rarely touched him. She'd almost forgotten the shock of his cold skin when they'd shaken hands to seal their house-sharing agreement, but now his hurried talk of poor circulation came back to mind.

But there was nothing wrong with his circulation today. Everything about him was active and hungry and full of life. Where before he'd been diffident, he was vibrant and eager now. Where before he seemed to be holding back, now he'd opened wide the gates.

Tugging at each other, they were suddenly on the kitchen floor just as she'd imagined, kissing like maniacs. Zack threw one long lean leg across her, and acquainted Teresa with that star turn of all her erotic daydreams.

This is demented. I'm kissing my landlord and he's got a hard-on, she thought.

Unable to contain herself, Teresa surged against him, rocking shamelessly against Zack's sturdy erection. So much for keeping their distance and observing 'friends only' no-go areas. Her outburst had re-engineered the parameters. There wasn't anywhere that she couldn't venture now.

He had the most glorious backside. Tight and hard and round like a brace of ripe apples. And when she grasped it, he growled in his throat in a most astonishing way. Deep and fierce, like the call of a jungle animal, it bounced off the kitchen walls and filled her ears. If she hadn't had his tongue in her mouth, Teresa would have said, 'What the fuck is going on?'

But their tongues were dancing and she felt like growling too.

Deep in her belly, a famished hunger was gnawing at her. It was a long while since she'd had good sex. A real, hard, long wonderful fuck. She'd held back with Steve, and had been hoping this weekend would be their romantic first time. But now, she thanked every lucky star in heaven that she hadn't succumbed.

She'd never articulated it to herself, but she'd been waiting and saving herself for Zack, sure in the knowledge that her abstinence would be worth it.

Oh, I want you, she cried silently to him, massaging his sensational bottom, and squirreling herself against his cock.

Zack's answer was to growl again, a low feral sound. His lips crushed hers, his tongue thrusting, thrusting, just like the sex act. Where the kiss had been gentle and controlled at first, it was clear off the rails now. His mouth started to rove, moving roughly, messily, thrillingly over her face, along her jaw, as his hips rocked and jerked in that explicit rhythm that met and matched hers.

It was like being a horny teenager all over again, but magnified to the n'th degree. Every part of her was hot. They were rubbing against each other like crazy animals, and Teresa was the one making moaning noises now, unable to contain herself as Zack's hands went all over the place. Her breasts. Her thighs. The cleft of her bottom. He was surveying her physical geography, and he was impatient. His fingers wriggled between their bodies, tugging at her skirt and searching for access to her sex.

And all the while he was kissing, licking, tasting – and nibbling.

Nibbling? More than that – as his mouth reached her throat, she suddenly yelped and jerked beneath him.

Dear God, that is so hot! He's biting my neck!

It was pure sex. Shocking and primal. Painful but in a way that made her hips lurch against him of their own accord, seeking the touch of his fingertips where they pressed against her panties.

Am I flying? Teresa thought. This is weird.

She wriggled and parted her legs, not sure where the pleasure was, only knowing that it was like melting, dissolving, expiring – coming?

And then . . .

The rail-backed kitchen chair was hard beneath her thighs, and the glass cool in her hand. Her heart was thudding and there was a silvery hum ringing in her ears. But despite this strange physical phenomenon and an accompanying sense of dislocation, she felt calm, almost serene. Apart from a vague prickle of curiosity. She'd been panicking and fretting about something, but it was OK now. Zack had come up with a solution, hadn't he?

Looking up, she was surprised to see him standing by the sink. His mouth was uncharacteristically tense, his lips tightly pursed and his eyes looked huge and very dark. She felt a jolt of worry. Had her silly invitation distressed him?

'Are you OK, Zack? You're not sickening for something, are you? You don't *have* to come to the wedding, you know. It's wonderful of you to offer and God knows I appreciate it. But I'm a big girl. I think I'll be OK.'

There was a long pause. Zack's eyes seemed to skitter a bit, and he pressed his knuckle against his lips, as if pondering.

Teresa wondered what was the matter with Zach. He was not usually like this.

As she watched, Zack gave one long fluttering, almost slow-motion blink, squared his shoulders and lowered his hand to rest it on the forearm he had wrapped around him, reacquiring his stillness.

'I'd like to go. I need to get out more.' He gave her a cautious smile, his white teeth glinting. 'It'll be a change for me . . . all this studying and researching. I need to kick over the traces and have some fun.'

'Um, yes, I suppose so.'

But later, when he'd returned to his books, his research and his computer, Teresa was left wondering about Zack's sudden decision. Wondering about that, and a few other things.

Like, why were her lips so tender, as if she'd been kissed to within an inch of her life?

And what the hell was that bright-red mark on her neck?

2

'Bloody fool! Bloody, bloody fool!'

Zachary Trevelyan fought the hysterical urge to laugh like a lunatic.

Of course, he was a bloody fool – he was a fool for *blood*. With an effort, he managed to control his mania but the irony still made him smile.

For decades he'd coped and adapted and made a semblance of a life for himself, without ever really fitting in. But ever since he'd seen a pretty brown-haired girl in a local street on a warm spring night, then followed her into a coffee house, it was no longer the placid existence he'd carefully nurtured.

And tonight he'd made it a hundred times more complicated. He might have gently tampered with Teresa's perceptions, but it was only a matter of time before she cottoned on to the anomalies. And he couldn't blank out his own memories of that kiss – or the natural and unnatural responses of his body.

In the sanctum of his workroom, he reached into the small beer fridge he kept there. It had never actually contained beer, although he did drink ale now and again. Instead the shelves were stacked with a row of small vacuum-sealed bottles. After flipping the top off one, he flung himself into his big leather wing-chair and took a long quenching drink.

His eyes fluttered closed as the rich familiar taste filled his mouth. The dangerous coppery flavour that defined him.

His roaring hunger calmed immediately. Heart, veins, cells, they all glowed and returned to equilibrium again. The acute stiffness in his penis transformed from pain into a potential source of pleasure. Taking another long drink from his bottle, he laid the fingers of his free hand across his groin.

That had been a close, close call in the kitchen. Flicking his tongue over his lips, he captured a drop of the red fluid there, and then, still lightly cupping his genitals, he passed it slowly over the biting edges of his upper teeth.

They were altered again, just as they'd been ten minutes ago. Kissing Teresa, he'd felt his fangs descend as the crimson madness of desire, so long and so carefully avoided, had gripped him like a stranglehold.

What the hell had possessed him? He'd been at risk of revealing himself since the very day she'd moved in, and he still couldn't work out what had possessed him to ask her. But still he'd done it, wildly embracing the threat to his hard won peace of mind.

Oh, but the taste of her. The touch of her. She was everything he'd dreamt of, everything that had driven him time and again to red fits of frenzied masturbation. And all it had taken was the welling up of sympathy – his for her and hers for him – to tip him past the point of no return.

Zack remembered the first time he'd set eyes on Teresa.

Like any man, he'd first noticed her shiny teak-coloured hair, and her slender yet shapely figure as she'd strolled along, looking in shop windows. But then he'd watched, fascinated by an inner beauty, as she'd knelt down to talk to one of the homeless who sometimes bedded down for the night in the larger doorways. She'd stayed a while, actually talking to the man rather than just flinging the odd coin into his tin and scuttling away. Her face had been warm and animated and she'd stroked the mangy dog tied up to the man's pack. Then, eventually, she'd straightened up, and left, turning back to wave – but not before slipping what looked like a couple of banknotes into his hand, with an encouraging squeeze.

Later, in the coffee house, he'd been compelled to approach her, and expecting wariness and suspicion, he'd been greeted by a sweet open smile and an easy invitation to share her table. She'd welcomed him, a pale and probably rather odd looking total stranger, and generously engaged him in conversation.

Sympathy again. Sympathy, from beauty, for an outcast? Was that it? Was that what had made her the one to change his long cultivated habits?

You're a good woman, Teresa, and you're kind. But would you still have sympathy for me, if you knew what I am?

Would you give yourself as freely as you were about to if you knew that your hypochondriac housemate was really a bloodsucking fiend?

'It's a bit hot in here . . . OK if I wind down the window?'

Not only was it warm in Zack's beautiful classic Mercedes, it was also getting difficult to sit still. Breathing in the scents of polished leather and Zack himself was making her crazy. She loved his old-fashioned floral cologne, but in a confined space it was acting like a drug. She kept drifting into a dreamy erotic fantasy.

Clenching her fingers on her bag with one hand, and a fold of her skirt with the other, she fought the pounding urge to slyly touch herself.

'Of course . . . sorry. I always forget that other people are warmer-blooded than I am.' Zack's eyes were intent on the road. If she didn't know better, Teresa would have said that he was avoiding looking at her. Maybe he was having wayward urges of his own?

But that was nonsense. Zack was always the perfect, controlled gentleman. Alas.

Reaching for the window winder, Teresa frowned. There was *something* up with Zack tonight. He was different. Odd. Not his usual still calm self at all. And his beautiful rosy mouth was twisted as if he were smiling at a particularly bitter joke. Teresa eyed his perfect profile, and suddenly, as if he sensed her puzzlement, he turned briefly towards her with a warmer, less ambiguous, smile.

A second later, he was all attention to the road again and it was Teresa's turn to purse her lips, frustrated.

If you're not interested that way, Zack, why have you made yourself look so sexy?

She'd never seen Zack look all grown up and groomed this way before. Instead of his usual dark jeans, and floppy shirts that looked as if they'd come out of a dressing up bag, he was wearing a proper suit and smart shirt for a change. They were both dark midnight blue, and looked stunning with his pale skin and black hair. The look was restrained and semi-formal, and made a naturally dramatic man look even more dramatic. He'd slicked back his wild curly hair too, and that only added to the effect of sombre gothic elegance.

A quip about Count Dracula rose to her lips but, before it could get there, her head swam strangely. Pressing a knuckle to her mouth, she held in another gasp, all the time grappling with the impression that she was floating upwards in the car as if it were a space capsule.

Frames from a movie flashed before her eyes. And she was the star, seeing it from the inside.

Zack was kissing her, touching her, and holding her against his rampant body. His mouth was at her throat. Pain spiked there, but it was a sweet pain that induced pleasure between her legs. And as the stinging ebbed, that pleasure grew, and Zack lifted his face to look at her.

His eyes weren't periwinkle blue any more, but a wild and violent red – crimson to match the blood on his gleaming lips.

'Are you all right, love?'

No, I'm all wrong.

That hadn't been just a passing erotic fancy about Zack as a vampire. It had felt like a memory, not a fantasy. She could feel it in her sex.

She could feel it in her *neck*.

Her fingertips flew to the place where there had been a red mark. She'd dismissed it as a nervous blotch, but what if it'd been something else? And what if that slightly funny turn in the kitchen yesterday hadn't been due to her just being hungry?

Get a grip, Teresa, she reprimanded herself. Zack is your friend, and your house buddy, and you fancy him, that's all. There are no such things as vampires and you haven't even kissed him, so how could he have given you a love-bite?

'Teresa? Are you all right?'

His soft voice shocked her back into the real world of car journeys and impending weddings.

'I'm fine, thanks . . . just woolgathering. Car trips get me that way.'

She glanced sideways again, and their glances clashed. Zack's blue eyes looked cautious and wary in a way she'd never seen before.

'We can stop for a while, if you like? There's a service area coming up soon.'

He was trying to be kind, and the offer was tempting. The sudden change of atmosphere in the car – from dreamy sensuality to palpable tension – was uncomfortable. But they'd soon reach their destination anyway, and then they could both retreat to their separate rooms . . . and their own space again.

'No. Thanks. Let's push on, shall we?'

'OK. Good idea.' With a smooth change of gear, he put his foot down.

Teresa sucked in her breath again, and stole another sideways look. Zack seemed calm and unruffled again, totally focused on the road. If he'd sensed her inner madness he wasn't showing it.

Turning to the window, and the darkness outside, Teresa squashed down her crazy notions – and thought of nothingness.

3

'You're kidding me . . . there's only one bedroom? When I rang, you said there'd be two.'

'I'm very sorry, Miss Johnson. I'm afraid there's been an error. The hotel's full for the wedding, and there's only one room in your name.'

Teresa hardly heard the rest of the spiel about folding beds and extra bedding *and* a refund. Her attention was locked on Zack and the stormy expression in his eyes. She'd never, ever seen him look this troubled, and it didn't surprise her when he took her by the arm and led her away from the reception desk.

'Look . . . I don't think it's such a good idea that we share a room. Why don't I leave you here and return again tomorrow night, in time for the wedding. It'll be dusk again then . . . and, if I leave the car in the garage, I needn't be out in daylight when I set off.'

For the first time ever since they'd met, Teresa felt annoyed with him. What on earth was the problem? They were friends. Surely even if they weren't a couple they could manage to rub along together somehow in the same room for a couple of nights? For such an intelligent and normally equable man, he was being ridiculous.

'Don't be silly. We can manage. It's not a problem.' Suddenly, though, it did seem like a problem. Zack was as still and unmoving as ever, yet he was surrounded by a strange aura of energy. Anger? Apprehension? Something else entirely? Totally unnerved, she said the first thing that came into her head. 'I won't leap all over you, if that's what you're worried about. It'll be strictly platonic'

Fingers like the prongs of an iron trap tightened on

her arm. 'It's not you I'm worried about, Teresa.' His voice was low, intense and unfamiliar. He released her arm, and automatically she rubbed it. 'This just isn't a good idea.'

'Why not? You're obviously not actually attracted to me or you'd love the idea of sharing a room!'

'You are wrong there, Teresa . . . so very wrong.'

Zack pursed his lips, and looked as if he were about to elaborate, but from behind them the reception clerk asked, 'Shall I call housekeeping about the extra bedding, Miss Johnson?'

Well? Teresa didn't articulate the word, but Zack seemed to hear it. He closed his eyes for a moment, as if he were weighing up a thousand what-ifs in the space of a split second, then opened them again and nodded infinitesimally.

Her mind whirling, Teresa turned away from him and returned to the desk.

Up in the room, they stared at each other across their heap of luggage.

Teresa attempted a smile and, for a moment, Zack's face was inscrutable – a beautiful, blank, unwritten page.

Was he going to explain? Tell her what he'd meant, down there in the lobby?

'Zack, what did you mean downstairs . . . about me being wrong?'

He looked away, towards the bed, and then his eyes nicked instantly away from it, as if it were the sun and the sight of it burnt him.

'You are wrong. I *am* attracted to you but it's just not a good idea for me to follow up on it.'

For a moment, Teresa wanted to cavort around the room and shout, You do like me. I knew you did. I just knew.

'But *why* isn't it a good idea? You must have realised that I'm attracted to you too.' The urge to dance turned into a strong compulsion to shake him for his obtuseness.

'It's not something I can easily explain, Teresa.' There was wistfulness in his voice. She sensed some huge obstacle standing between them. It was hurting him, and it made her want to hug him, not for sex, just to comfort. 'Please trust me . . .' His shoulders lifted in a heavy, resigned shrug. 'But I still want to be friends . . . more than anything. If you can accept that?'

There was such yearning in his blue eyes that Teresa just melted.

'Yes, of course.' Still confused, but feeling better, she smiled. 'We're good, Zack, but don't ever try to tell me that it's us women who are the contrary ones. OK?'

Zack smiled back at her and the tension between them lifted.

'OK. And don't worry . . . I'm fine on the couch.' He shrugged in the general direction of a rather inadequate-looking settee. 'It looks perfectly comfortable.'

Teresa frowned. That was nonsense. The couch was a fussy, reproduction item, a triumph of style over practicality.

The bed, on the other hand, was deep, and well sprung and inviting – and it was more or less time to get into it. Zack's photophobia had meant that they'd had to wait until dusk to set off and now it was past eleven. There was nothing Teresa wanted more than to just crawl under that duvet and sleep. She didn't want to think about what amounted to their first ever argument. She just wanted to fall asleep, knowing that he really did care for her in his own weird way.

Then Zack shrugged out of his jacket and draped it over a chair back, and the sight of his lean body in that fine dark shirt woke her up again. All her good resolutions about boundaries and being 'just friends' melted like Scotch mist.

'But . . . um . . . what about your bad circulation? Won't you be cold just with blankets?' She glanced at the undesirable sofa. 'I could manage on the couch. I'm shorter. I'll fit better.'

Zack's whole demeanour seemed to lighten and he gave her an eloquently masculine look.

'No way.' He shook his dark head. 'I'm an old-fashioned man, Teresa. A lady's comfort must always come first.'

I'll bet it does. The thought was involuntary. As was the image of Zack, kneeling between her outstretched thighs as she sat on that very sofa, his long red tongue licking, licking, licking.

The entire surface of her skin seemed to tremble. She felt out of control, yet suddenly energised. On impulse, she strode across the room, squeezed his hard muscular arm and kissed his cool cheek. 'Thanks, Zack. You're a very sweet man. I don't deserve you.' Right in his personal space, she felt bold and crazy. She sensed danger, but she hungered for the taste of it.

When she pulled back, Zack was staring at her, his eyes wide and strange. He had his full sensual lower lip snagged in his upper teeth, and in the low light they seemed to glint like polished porcelain, sharp and deadly.

Almost dazzled, Teresa felt giddiness whirl her feet out from under her, and without knowing quite how, she found herself sitting on the edge of the bed.

'Wha–'

'Come on, Teresa, you need rest. It's late. Why don't you slip into bed and get some sleep?' Zack's voice was matter of fact. He was sitting a decorous distance away from her, inches and inches of clear space between their bodies.

'Er . . . um . . . yes, I suppose you're right.'

The soft thick duvet was tempting. These funny turns she kept having were worrying, and Zack was right, she'd be better off getting some rest.

She glanced from the bed to the bathroom. The prospect of getting ready for bed made her feel more tired than ever.

Zack seemed to read her mind. 'I think I'll go for a stroll in the grounds. Give you chance to get settled in.'

'But we've only just got here. And it's nearly midnight.'

'You know me and my nocturnal rambles. And I need to stretch my legs after the drive.'

Teresa's heart sank.

She should have let him go home and stay in his comfort zone. When this stupid wedding was over, it might be best if she looked for her own place again. This situation of liking each other but not being able to do anything about it was bound to become intolerable eventually.

Unexpectedly, a strong arm came around her shoulders.

'It's just a walk, Teresa. We're fine.' The arm squeezed, the pressure reassuring, but also unnerving. There was so much leashed power in that lean and elegant body, and he was still wound up like steel wire no matter what he said. 'I'm just giving you space to do your girl things.'

Emotion rolled over Teresa like a wave. This was all a mess but, even now, Zack was being wonderful.

'Thanks.' She flashed him a grateful smile as he released her and rose to his feet.

'I'll just put my bottles away, then I'll leave you to it.'

Ah, the mysterious 'iron shake'. Something picked at Teresa's tired mind as she watched Zack unpack several bottles from a cool-pack and stow them in the mini-bar fridge. One of these days she was going to have to ask him what was in that peculiar unappetising drink.

'I want you to be fast asleep when I get back,' said Zack firmly a few moments later. Teresa looked longingly at him, clutching a pair of eggshell-blue satin pyjamas from her case. He looked more relaxed now that he was about to escape the room, and his expression was almost brotherly. At least it seemed to be.

'OK, you're the boss of this dormitory.' She pinned on what she thought was a light-hearted, just-buddies smile.

But Zack was already out of the door and gone.

The night was beautiful, and the sky full of moon.

As Zack sped across the great park of Hindlesham Manor, he was aware that anyone watching him from the house would wonder if they were seeing things.

Things like a human-seeming figure devouring the yards at inhuman speed.

He was angry with himself. Not only had he muddied the situation between them by admitting his feelings, he'd given in to temptation and put Teresa at risk. And all he could think about now was her lovely body, clad in those blue pyjamas.

In bed.

Waiting for him.

Could he control himself around her for much longer? His cool heart soared at the thought of touching her, caressing her – entering her. Giving her pleasure while she was entirely conscious and her mind was unclouded by his psychic tricks. Making love to her, while she knew exactly what he was.

Would her natural sympathy allow her to see past his fangs and reddened eyes? Would the attraction he knew she felt towards him be enough?

Vampires had always had a bad press. Misinformation had extinguished the extended lives of many of his kind who didn't deserve their demise. As with humanity, there were a thousand different flavours of vampires. They were as different from each other as normal people were, each one's nature predicated by the life he or she had led before being turned, and the circumstances of how that process had occurred.

An evil murderous bastard was still an evil murderous bastard as a vampire – only more so. Likewise, a weak-willed person might also take the easy path and bite the neck out of man, woman or child in order to feed.

But a decent man would find a way to *avoid* harming others after his turning.

His own situation was unusual.

In 1932, as a novice in a Benedictine monastery, he'd fallen prey to a band of hungry vampires of questionable ethics who'd broken in and attacked the brothers. A beautiful female had sensed the diffidence of his faith, and zeroed in on him. Barely ten minutes later he'd lost that faith, and his human life forever, but unfortunately not his virginity. Swooping away, she'd laughed and taunted him, leaving him shattered, terrified, confused – and yet still aroused.

In the aftermath, he'd waited for the inevitable revulsion of his community, and received the surprise of his young, but altered, life. His brothers had been modern, forward-thinking twentieth-century monks and, far from casting him out or turning a Vatican vampire hunter on him, they'd helped him.

A new cynicism suggested that their kindness towards a bloodsucker in their midst wasn't entirely altruistic. His family was immensely wealthy, with old, old money, and the community wasn't about to pass up such patronage in times when other houses were closing. But, Christian charity or no, they'd made it possible for him to adjust and it seemed that the Church had been secretly handling cases like his for centuries.

And so here I am, Zack thought, a virgin vampire, who's in love for the first time in his long ridiculous life.

Hindlesham Manor was possessed of a large, traditional box hedge maze, and as Zack entered its perimeter, his enhanced senses savoured the delicious dewy air. Cool scents of wood sap, pine and moss were balsamic and intoxicating. They assaulted him like nocturnal elixirs, provoking and stirring.

But not as much as Teresa stirred him.

The journey had been agony, requiring a constant intense focus on the act of driving. Her perfume was delicate and floral, a beautiful expression of her natural sweetness and purity. Yes, he knew that she'd slept with men, but deep in her heart he detected a central innocence that no man had breached – an untouched and pristine state that mirrored his own.

But it was more than an artificial odour that had plagued him.

The fresh green smells of the night faded and were replaced with warmer richer human aromas. The lush musky scent of Teresa's body that had kept his penis stiff and his fangs right on the point of descent for mile after mile.

Haunting female sweat. Sex musk, from between her legs. And her blood, just beneath the surface of her smooth heated skin. It had called to him constantly, and it called to him still, demanding more self-control than he'd ever had to exert in all his years.

Plunging on between the tall hedges, he had no fear of losing his way. A natural sense of direction was one of his special gifts. The way was cool and dark, but it didn't chill his passions. He was erect again and he touched himself lightly as he walked, his mind flying back to the hotel room and the sight of Teresa in that huge tempting bed, her body twisting in sleep, her soft brown hair tousled endearingly.

Perhaps the jacket of her pyjamas might come unfastened as she tossed and turned, revealing her rounded breasts to his unholy gaze. With his psi abilities, it would be easy to touch her and pleasure her without her even waking. The remnants of his religious morality, never quite shaken off, abhorred such thievery, but when the blood fever in him was rampant, it would be hard to resist.

Teresa was exquisite, the crystallised embodiment of the perfect dream woman he'd wanted all these years. The woman he'd wanted even while he was an imperfect novice, struggling with his faith, before his change.

The only consolation was that she would *enjoy* the sensual dreams that he induced.

Connecting with his surroundings again, he found himself at the centre of the maze. He stepped into an open area, a spacious oval ringed by benches where explorers could sit and get their breath back, while they tried to work out how to get out again.

Zack didn't sit. Instead he walked across the central turf to the deep ornamental pond that shimmered like a dark eye reflecting the moon.

Staring into the water, he laughed softly, his lust muted by the perennial amusement of another shattered vampire myth.

In the black water, he saw his own face, and his chest and shoulders, clad in his dark shirt.

He was distinctly visible, although not quite as clearly as Teresa would have been if she had been standing beside him. His image was impressionistic, far less substantial than that of a normal person, expressing the remnants of his humanity. On the continuum of vampirism, he was at the 'light' end, complete with spirit, soul and conscience – and it was these that created his reflection in the water. A black-hearted villain probably wouldn't see a thing.

And yet dark passions surged inside him. His sleeping lust was red and violent, roused by Teresa, and whipped to boiling point by their enforced proximity. It had been insanity to come on this trip, but he'd done it all the same. He was still human in some senses, and subject to the wayward foibles of human nature. And a human need for love that compelled him to grasp at the fleeting chance for intimacy, both emotional and physical.

With Teresa safe in her bed, perhaps a quarter of a mile away, Zack surrendered to the chaos of his senses.

His fangs descended – a rush of sensation in itself. And as the truth of his condition was revealed he rhythmically cupped and caressed his genitals, fantasising that his own large hand was her smaller daintier one. His chilly skin seemed to burn with an icy fire and become painfully hyper-sensitive. His clothes irritated every nerve-end.

Ignoring the possibility of other insomniac explorers, he slid off his clothing, undressing far faster than any human could have.

Within seconds he was naked in the moonlight, but still his pale skin tingled. He moaned, knowing that only the gentle caressing touch of Teresa's hands could soothe him. Only her hands could both rouse and give ease to the fury of desire. His own hands, running over his limbs, his torso and his belly, only seemed to aggravate his need.

Yet he couldn't stop. He stroked his body, fingertips tracking over his dense musculature, imagining it was *her* fingers that were moving, sliding and tantalising. His cock was aching and heavy, standing out from his body now, a bar of darker flesh in the blue-white light of the moon, a strangely human phenomenon taking over the body of an other than human male.

At last, he took himself in hand, growling at the impact of his own touch, baring his fangs and tipping back his head, eyes closed.

'Teresa!' His voice was a low rumble of feeling as he began to stroke and pump his flesh. He knew it was not her hand, but in a state of passionate fugue, his own touch was the next best thing. His mind was able to trick him, and he seemed to see her beside him, and hear her breathing and smell her myriad delicious scents.

She was touching him, fondling him, loving him, making him moan with delight, his thighs flexing as he pushed and pushed into the delicious enclosure of warm, skilled fingers. He wrapped his free hand around his torso, but in his imagination, he was clasping her to him, even as she clasped and caressed his cock.

The sensations built and spiralled, the intensity mounting. His sharp fangs pricked at his own lips as he fought to contain his vampire roar of pleasure. He tasted his own blood, the flavour sweet but inert. It was no substitute for fresh warm, living blood, but the fact that it had once had life goaded and lifted him to the point of no return.

'Teresa,' he shouted again, no longer able to contain himself as his penis leapt and his spine felt as if it were melting in a white flame of climax.

Chilly semen jetted from between his fingers, creating a silvery arc that glittered momentarily in the light of the moon. And as it hit the dark surface of the pond, Zack groaned and swayed, his spent body crumpling as he collapsed and curled up on the damp turf, stunned and sobbing with release and renewed longing.

4

It was so hot. Longing for cool, and not sure whether she was awake or asleep, Teresa kicked off the covers.

Her eyelids felt heavy and it was an effort to open them. Blinking, she surveyed the unfamiliar room.

Yes, right. She was at Hindlesham Manor and she was sharing this room with Zack. Who was currently nowhere to be seen.

He likes me. I like him. But we can't do anything about it for some reason.

Groaning, she turned over again. Knowing what the deal was only made her want him more. When something was forbidden, it automatically became the most desirable thing in the entire world. Sod's Law.

Closing her eyes, she pictured his lean male body and wished that he hadn't shot away for a walk in the middle of the night. Even if they couldn't make love, it would have been comforting to sense his sleeping presence across the room.

She imagined his return. And that he'd changed his mind. She imagined him gazing at her, his beautiful blue eyes on fire with lust. He'd lick his lips and his sharp white teeth would glint.

Why on earth am I always thinking about his teeth? Teresa wondered.

Her hand flew to her neck. She seemed to feel the sharp prick of him nipping her there.

Squirming against the sheets, she touched the place where she imagined him biting her, and with her other hand she massaged between her legs through her pyjamas.

A low moan echoed through the room, and Teresa's eyes flew open again.

It wasn't her!

Across at the window, but looking into the room rather than out of it, stood Zack.

She opened her mouth to speak to him, but he made a shushing gesture with one forefinger across his lips. A fraction of a second later, he was beside her, and she felt too mesmerised to wonder how he could move so quickly and so soundlessly. The bed dipped as he sat down beside her.

Heavy inertia flooded her limbs. She couldn't move or speak, yet her senses were acute and the entire surface of her skin felt electrified, receptive, and tingling with an almost sentient longing to be touched. Her hand was still between her thighs, pressing against her sex, her clit. With her other hand she was still touching her own neck.

Zack just stared at her, as if the effort of speeding across the room had drained him and he was resting, restoring himself, feeding on the sight of her touching herself.

His hair was awry, his curls wild and beautiful. They appeared to float as he tipped his head on one side, even now hesitating. To Teresa's horror, he began to edge away.

No . . . No, I shouldn't do this, she seemed to hear him say.

But, as he made to rise and leave, Teresa willed him to hear her silent command.

Stay!

Moving closer again, Zack smiled almost shyly, and

the teeth she'd been so fixated upon glinted whitely in the moonlight filtering in through the fine gauze curtains. She wanted to sit up, reach out and run a fingertip over their sharp biting surfaces and test their keen edge. In her imagination, blood welled from the pad of her forefinger – and, like fate, Zack lunged forwards, grasped her hands away from her body and pinned them in one of his, above her head.

Then he kissed her while his other hand searched and found her breast.

Oh yes . . . Oh hell yes . . .

There was an exquisite roughness about both the kiss and the caress. A fugitive lack of finesse that excited her senses even more. The way Zack's cool tongue probed, and his long fingers squeezed and fondled her only heightened her impression that these explorations were fresh and new to him. She mewled beneath his lips, her virgin lover fantasy surging up and taking flight.

Her response electrified him. Still kissing hard, and massaging her breast, he threw one long leg across her and angled his hips to rub his crotch against her thigh through her silky pyjama bottoms. He was hard as iron, cool and unyielding as he rocked his hips and circled his erection against her flesh.

Teresa began to wriggle in his hold, wanting to press more of herself against as much of Zack as she could reach. She could feel the chilly nature of his body through her pyjamas and the shirt and trousers he wore, but the near contact set flames of lust surging.

He was unusual. He was special. He was like no man she'd ever been with or wanted to be with before. Being kissed and touched and rubbed up against like this was driving her to madness.

'Zack, please . . .' she finally managed to gasp when he

allowed her mouth a moment of freedom and turned away, pressing his face into the pillow as if he were hiding it. 'Please let me free. I want to touch you.' She twisted towards him, trying to kiss him again, nuzzling his face. 'Let me look at you. I want to kiss you . . . Please, Zack.'

'No!'

The word was extraordinarily loud and shocking. As if a lion had roared in her ear, Teresa shrank back, fearful yet more impossibly turned on than ever.

Zack released her hands, but with that strange, unnatural turn of speed of his, he was over her again, half lying on her before she could draw breath. With one long, cool hand he covered her eyes.

'Close your eyes.'

Teresa obeyed him instantly and without question. A part of herself – floating high above the proceedings – was outraged at such submissiveness, but the woman who lay beneath Zack accepted dreamily and complied.

Even when he took away his hand, her leaden eyelids didn't lift. She felt him move off her, but she couldn't follow. It was as if she were pinned to the bed by some force she didn't understand. Even her arms, free now, lay inert at her sides.

Moments seemed to stretch out like elastic as she lay there, and she could feel his cool gaze coasting over her satin-clad limbs. Obediently blind, she still seemed to see his dark head tilt again, in slow contemplation.

But then there was a sudden, sharp, tearing sound, totally unexpected. In the shock of it, the spell on her eyes was broken and they fluttered open. She saw a flash of movement, then all went dark again, and she felt smooth cotton being tied around her head in a makeshift blindfold. The cloth smelt deliciously of Zack's floral cologne.

What had he done, ripped a piece of a fine expensive shirt, just to cover her eyes?

He obviously had, and the action induced a rush of new excitement. There seemed to be no knowing what to expect next. One minute Zack was insisting they be just friends. The next, he was an innocent, tentative lover. And the next, he was dominant enough to play erotic blindfold games. Being with him was a switchback ride, like a sleigh on the Cresta run – her body was a well of pure adrenaline.

Now the effort of keeping her eyes closed was gone, another sensual gate opened wide. The tingling electric field across her skin ramped up sharply. The weight of her silky pyjamas against her breasts seemed to oppress her, and she inched herself restlessly about on the bed as if her body was reacting and fizzing like a volatile chemical.

Perfectly instinctive, Zack began to unfasten her pyjama top. He slipped each button from its hole, but didn't open the panels, moving all the way down to the hem with her body still covered. Then, and only then, did he pluck apart the leaves of satin and expose her. Warm night air sluiced deliciously across her skin.

'Touch your breasts. Show me what you do.'

The words were soft but they made Teresa shudder with desire. Swallowing hard, she drew in a great breath and tilted her head back against the pillow. Her face was hot beneath the blindfold. She'd never displayed herself this way, never performed for a man. She'd always wanted to, but somehow a fugitive spirit had stolen the desire away from her at the critical moment, whispering subversively that the man just wasn't worth the effort.

But now, in the face of strange, mysterious Zack, it was she who seemed to be the unworthy one.

Her face flamed brighter as she took her nipple between her thumb and forefinger and rolled it this way and that, enjoying the twist and tug of it, and the way she always managed to feel the sensation between her legs, as if a ghostly hand was shadowing hers, tweaking her clitoris in the same rhythm. Tonight, the phenomenon was more intense than it had ever been, and instinctively her free hand flew to her groin, so convinced was she that Zack had slid his fingers between her legs and begun to play with her.

But there was no hand down there but her own, and as she wriggled her bottom against the mattress, she clasped her sex and gripped it hard.

Zack uttered a low murmur of approval. She squeezed harder, making the breath catch in her throat.

The clock on the mantelpiece tick, tick, ticked as she handled herself and outside, in the park somewhere, an animal howled. Sticky juice began to trickle down into the cleft of her bottom, oozing from her as sensation gathered and massed.

'Stop a moment. I can't see . . .'

A cold hand prised her fingers away from her crotch, and then slid down her pyjama bottoms, leaving them bunched at her knees. Teresa groaned anew, imagining her exposure, and how rude and wanton she must look with her nightclothes opened and pushed apart to reveal her breasts and crotch to her cool eager watcher.

'Continue . . .'

His voice was still low, but there was a faint ragged edge to it. Teresa longed to see his face, and the desire and excitement painted on it. Again, she had that gut feeling that despite the odds against it, Zack wasn't all that experienced. And this situation was as new and exotic to him as it was to her.

Tentatively, she touched her belly. She didn't know what to do. Masturbation certainly wasn't new to her. She did it quite a bit. But in the dark, on this magic night, all her experience was stripped away from her. She felt new and innocent, just as she sensed Zack was. They were like two enchanted teenagers experimenting.

His hand took hers, guided it towards her cleft. Her heart turned over in her chest – he was trembling.

Oh, bless you, you beautiful man . . .

Then he withdrew his hand again, and let it rest on her thigh, cool and light.

Parting the lips of her sex, she slid in her fingertips, astonished by the swimming abundance of the slippery liquid there. She was wetter than she'd ever been. So ready for something. For anything. She sought out her clitoris, and gasped at the contact. She'd never felt so hyper-sensitive either.

Pinching the tip of her breast, and circling one fingertip around her clit, she suddenly laughed, thinking of the old children's co-ordination game of rubbing your stomach and patting your head at the same time. It was quite an art, fondling herself this way, but she was excelling. The way her sex fluttered and leapt betrayed skill.

In a world of darkness she seemed to see Zack again, his face intense, almost intimidating. He looked nothing like the kind composed Zack who'd given her a home and his company and friendship. His expression was fierce, hungry, wildly feral. His eyes glittered with an unearthly light, and his mouth curved strangely.

His unfamiliarity frightened her, but there was no way to escape it. It was in her mind so closing her eyes, behind her mask, made no difference. There was only one thing to do – go on with her task.

She fingered her clit. She massaged her nipple. The sensation of gathering, deep in her belly, became an ever-tightening knot. She couldn't keep her bottom still on the bed, and in her mind's eye, Zack devoured her lascivious wriggling. His fingertips curved like talons into the tender skin of her thigh.

'Oh . . . oh . . . oh . . .' she burbled. And, between her legs, her sex rippled like a mirror, preparing to fling her over the edge into pleasure.

A hand joined hers in her cleft, one big male finger pushing inside her, sweetening the sensations, making them perfect.

Teresa shouted, her hips bucking, her core clenching and clenching on the cool unyielding intrusion that curved inside her.

Climaxing, climaxing furiously, she wrenched at the blindfold. She had to see him. See his face and his eyes.

But when she did – in the midst of orgasm – her con-sciousness slid sharply sideways and veered away from her.

Zack's eyes were red, and his beautiful mouth framed pointed fangs.

5

The rattle of crockery woke her.

'Hey, sleepy-head . . . Ready for breakfast?'

Her eyes fluttered open.

The heavy net curtains were still drawn but the room was light. It was daytime – with a dullish-looking sky, but perfectly normal.

And Zack, in a soft dark-blue casual shirt and jeans, looked perfectly normal too.

Teresa fought the urge to shrink back against the pillows. Her mind's eye overlaid Zack's pale but fresh-faced appearance with the terrifying modifications from her dream.

Surreptitiously, she fished around under the covers and found her pyjama jacket chastely buttoned and her trousers right where they should be. Even so, the sensations of the night were still vivid.

She'd been blindfolded, but somehow still able to see. And she'd blushed with furious embarrassment on exposing herself to Zack, and masturbating at his command.

But, oh, that hadn't been the most extreme thing.

Those last seconds; Zack's eyes red and burning – and his teeth.

Oh dear God, his teeth! Her vampire fantasies had invaded her dream now, and with bared fangs, Zack had been hell bent on biting her!

'Are you OK?'

Clear blue eyes regarded her with concern. White, even, but perfectly un-pointed teeth glinted in a smile.

He was holding a tray, set for breakfast for one, tempting and indulgent with eggs and bacon, toast and jam, and fragrant coffee.

Am I OK? Teresa wondered.

The juxtaposition between dream and reality still made her head feel vaguely woozy, and right at the edge of perception, she detected just the edge of a slight, peculiar hum. Tinnitus, possibly? She'd have to get that checked out when they got back.

'I'm fine . . . thanks, Zack,' she lied, but, even as she spoke, the sumptuous aroma of a full English breakfast was setting the world and her thoughts straight again. 'It's just that I had a *really* weird dream . . . I think it's sleeping in a strange bed though.' The silvery hum had disappeared, and she smiled back at him, and sat up straight. 'But I'm all right now. And this lot smells heavenly!' She patted her lap and Zack set the tray carefully in place on its folding legs.

'You're spoiling me! This is fab,' she mumbled a moment or two later through a mouthful of sublime savoury bacon. 'I haven't had breakfast in bed for years.'

'We'll have to rectify that when we get home. You need a decent breakfast at least once a week. A piece of toast and a mouthful of coffee as you run out of the door just isn't enough. You need more than that to see you through the day.'

Teresa's heart turned over. He was so thoughtful. But she suspected they both knew it wouldn't happen. There was no going back to their harmonious state of house buddies now. The thought of that cut like a knife, but there was no reason to spoil the next couple of days by dwelling on it. She returned her attention to mopping up egg yolk with fried bread.

And yet, as she munched and sighed with pleasure, she found herself watching Zack where he sat in an armchair, calmly sipping his breakfast while he read the paper.

What is that stuff?

When something looked like blood and smelt like blood, did that mean it actually was blood?

No, vampires are fiction. Dracula and Buffy aren't real. They're just stories.

He doesn't go out in sunlight, but he claims that because of his allergies.

Stop it.

He appeared to be in his mid- to late-twenties, but who was to say that was how old he really was. She hadn't known him long enough to tell.

Stop it.

But weren't vampires possessed of unnatural speed and strength?

Teresa's fork clattered on the plate, and Zack looked up from his paper. 'Something wrong with the bacon?'

'No, it's scrummy, thanks.' She applied herself to the plate again, even though her throat was suddenly too tight to eat.

Zack could move like lightning and lift her as if she weighed nothing.

No, don't be silly. You don't believe in ghosts, spoon-bending or Ouija boards . . . why on earth should you suddenly start believing in vampires?

And yet still she pondered. Scoping him surreptitiously over the rim of her coffee cup as he turned another page of his paper, he looked just like a normal man to her. He was handsome as the devil and had rather pale skin, but there was nothing more sinister.

Mirrors! That was it! Had she ever actually seen Zack reflected in a mirror?

She sipped her coffee and wracked her brain.

No, she couldn't ever remember seeing Zack's reflection. But what did that mean? She'd never *looked* for it.

And she wasn't going to start looking now, she decided, carefully avoiding looking in the direction of the dressing table.

*

By eleven thirty, vampires were the last thing on Teresa's mind.

Ahead of them was a lunch, preceded by cocktails for guests who'd arrived early, as they had. And all her so-called friends would be there, the ones who'd been so solicitous

– and slyly gloating – when Steve had dumped her. And everyone would have a significant other in tow.

It would have been a pure nightmare if it hadn't been for Zack.

When she emerged from the bathroom, fluffing at her hair and hoping her little silk two-piece wouldn't make her bottom look too big, she found him sitting on the bed, waiting for her.

If anything, he looked even more fabulous than ever.

She wasn't sure how many suits he had in his suit carrier, but this one was dark blue, lightweight and pure fluid elegance, just like him. His shirt was blue silk too, a couple of shades lighter, and he was frowning over a pair of toning ties.

Teresa's heart lurched. Why did life have to be so complicated? If Zack didn't have these mysterious issues of his, she could be straddling him on the bed right now, gorgeous outfit and vampire fantasies notwithstanding.

'You might not need a tie. I think it's quite informal.'

Zack whipped around, ties still fluttering from his fingers.

'Are you sure?' His head tipped to one side, light glinting on his dark curly hair, now immaculately groomed again. 'I don't want to stand out by being too casual.'

You'll always stand out because you're gorgeous, she couldn't stop herself thinking.

Teresa curved her fingers against her skirt to stop herself grabbing him. 'That's a beautiful suit . . . you look terrific.'

'And so do you.'

Suddenly, he was in front of her, looking down into her eyes. He lifted a hand, gently smoothing her hair where it flicked around her face. Teresa almost groaned at the effort of not turning and pressing her lips against his palm.

'Thanks . . .' She drew a quick breath, almost a gasp. His sweet cologne made her feel as if she was going to faint. 'Shall we get down there? I think it's probably started.'

She darted away for her bag and their key card, knowing that, if she stayed close to him, she'd do something stupid.

The perfect gentleman, Zack escorted her down the stairs, his hand lightly on her arm as they nodded and said 'hello' to fellow guests. In the busy reception area, a gilt-edged board, studded with plastic letters announced that the wedding cocktail party was in the Walcott Room. People shaking umbrellas indicated it was raining outside, which made things easier for Zack as the party would stay inside.

Vampire's luck? she thought, then gritted her teeth, squishing the idea.

The Walcott Room was large and airy, decorated in a sub rococo style with a lot more gilt, and ornate antique furniture lovingly polished. Brilliant light glittered from a magnificent chandelier. She was just about to gather up her nerves and lead the way in, when Zack's fingers tightened on her arm and he drew her quickly to one side.

'How do you want to play this?' he said, *sotto voce*. 'I'll do whatever you want –' his blue eyes twinkled '– but it'd be fun if we could give them something to speculate about, eh?'

I don't know what you are but you could just be an angel! Teresa thought.

The urge to hug and kiss him for real, never mind as an act, bubbled up again like one of the ornamental fountains outside, but she held it in check and just grinned. 'Yeah, why not?'

At least for a little while, she'd have a bona fide excuse to touch him and hang on to him.

The room's grand beauty faded into the background at the sight of the mass of assembled guests. They all seemed to swivel round to watch the arrival of Teresa, the recently dumped.

A strong arm slid around her waist, and she felt a soft kiss like thistledown settle on her hair. Obviously, Zack was going for the 'new lovers, can't keep their hands off one another' gambit. My, how the gloaters would be taken aback at how quickly she appeared to be back in the saddle.

'Look, there's the bride-to-be.' Teresa pointed to Lisa, between the clumps of chattering, drinking well-wishers. The bride's smile was already looking pretty set and strained as she kept glancing around to make sure everything was going all right. 'Let's go and say "hello".'

'Right ho.' Zack's voice dropped to a whisper. 'And don't worry . . . it'll all be fine. I'm right beside you.'

Doubt drained out of her like water through a sieve. Teresa smiled up into his face, her heart light and overflowing.

He might not actually *be* her boyfriend but, for the moment, he was the next best thing. He was a rock, and he looked utterly magnificent. And she could already see that most of the women in the room were openly ogling him.

Go on, drool, you lot, Teresa couldn't help thinking. He's mine! Well . . . sort of . . .

Even the bride seemed impressed. As they approached, Lisa eyed Zack with a degree of interest that set her frazzled fiancé frowning.

'Hi, Teresa! I'm so glad you could make it. Isn't this place fab?'

It was obvious Lisa was fit to bursting with curiosity about Zack. The minute she released Teresa from their hug, her eyes skittered immediately to the tall dark presence at her side.

'Lisa . . . Tom . . . This is Zachary Trevelyan,' she announced proudly, 'Zack, this is Lisa and Tom, the bride and groom . . . obviously.'

The greetings went smoothly, but both Lisa's and Tom's eyebrows shot up when they shook Zack's hand. Looking down at his fingers, he shrugged and smiled. 'It's a circulation thing.'

Lisa and Tom just smiled, but Teresa's brain whirled back into its former groove. That was another thing. Wasn't cold skin another vampire characteristic?

Leave it. Just stop thinking about it.

'So . . . you and Teresa? Have you . . . er . . . are you. . .'

Lisa's questions petered out, and Teresa's brain went blank again. That was the big problem with play-acting.

'Together?' Zack's voice was soft, almost sultry, and his arm slid back around her waist. Teresa stole a glance at his wickedly smiling face, and for a fraction of second, she half imagined that he winked. But just like so often with him, it was done so quickly that she couldn't be sure she'd seen it.

'Um . . . yes . . .' Lisa obviously hadn't been expecting such a straight answer. 'I know you're Teresa's landlord but I didn't realise you were a couple. Well, I thought . . .' Teresa followed her friend's tracking scan of the busy room, bracing herself for the sight of Steve.

'What better way to get to know one another than by living together.' It was as if Zack was gently explaining the ways of the world to someone very young and naive.

'I've been biding my time . . . waiting until Teresa was free of commitments –' he paused delicately '– and for the moment when it would be honourable to ask her to be my lover.'

'Er . . . yes . . . right. That's great.'

Teresa hid a smile. Lisa couldn't seem to hide the fact she was desperately smitten despite the presence of her soon-to-be husband beside her.

I don't blame you, Lise, she thought.

Far more smitten, Teresa gasped inside when Zack pressed a light, but meaningful, kiss against her cheek.

'Shall we circulate, my dear? Other guests are waiting to meet the happy couple.'

They made way for members of Tom's family, and Teresa felt as if she was floating as they wove across the room, took a couple of drinks and found themselves a corner.

'Everything all right?'

Zack's eyes were twinkling. He was having fun.

Teresa twinkled back at him. It *was* fun being the envy of all her female friends. Especially the ones who'd expected a fine opportunity to pity her.

Here she was with the most handsome, intriguing man in the room, whose presence beside her made her turn to jelly with longing. And on top of that there were all the exquisite little shows of affection – the kisses, the touches on the arm, the light guiding contact of his hand on her waist. They were part of a deception, of course, but that didn't diminish the pleasure.

Sipping her champagne, she watched Zack scanning the room, his keen eyes darting from person to person and from couple to couple as if he was an anthropologist studying a brand new tribe for a paper. Maybe it *was* something like that? She knew he wrote historical studies and treatises. Perhaps he was turning his hand to fiction, or pop psychology, and he was doing a little people watching?

Whatever it was, she had the oddest feeling that a gathering like this was entirely new to him.

'Have you been to many weddings?'

Zack swivelled round and smiled. 'No, this is my first wedding, would you believe?' He put his lips to his glass of mineral water and took the minutest sip. It was the only thing she'd ever seen him ingest so far, apart from his health shakes.

'Really?'

Unease crawled up and down Teresa's spine, and thoughts, conclusions and too many bizarre coincidences jostled and brayed at her. Focusing on the room, and its festive normality, she attempted to silence them.

'What do you think of it all then?'

'Fascinating. It's supposed to celebrate the welfare and happiness of the bride and groom, but, underneath, it's a hotbed of rivalry and envy and one-upmanship . . . it's like a Roman arena full of designer lions.'

'I've never looked at it that way.'

And she hadn't. But Zack's beautiful blue eyes were clear and acute. He wasn't accusing anybody of anything, just enlightening her with his deadly accurate observations.

Until today, Teresa had seen weddings as sexy and positive and fun.

But now, seen through his sharp focus, the undercurrents were obvious. People were catching other people's eyes, people who weren't their own partner. Women were coveting other women's dresses, jewellery and men. Men were blatantly perving available girls and non-available girls with equal lustfulness.

'Actually it's more like Sodom and Gomorrah, isn't it?' she whispered as they dumped their glasses on a side table. Zack smiled like a conspirator as he snaked his strong arm around her waist again.

'But at least we're together –' he pulled her closer, the pressure of his fingertips like electricity through the thin stuff of her top '– and we can guard each other against the prowling hyenas.'

But who's going to guard me from you? Teresa couldn't help thinking.

At that moment, she turned around and saw Steve across the room, apparently devouring his new girlfriend whole in front of an audience.

'Is that him?'

Zack's hold tightened, and strength poured through the contact between their bodies. Her vague doubts about Zack forgotten, Teresa leaned in, and the effect increased. Steve and his trollop looked ridiculous and she was invulnerable.

'Yes, I'm afraid so . . . although I'm hard pressed to know what I saw in him now.'

Beside Zack's lean grace and refined gothic style, Steve was a clod. And fat too! With new clear eyes, Teresa noted that he had a rather angry shaving rash.

'Shall we say hello?' Zack's fingertips caressed her waist, the gentle pressure both sensual and confidence-building. With him at her side, she could do anything.

'Why not? I'm bound to run into him at this gig sometime, so let's get it over with sooner rather than later.'

'That's my girl!' Zack's mouth brushed her hair in another fleeting kiss and just like before her feet felt as if they were lifting off the carpet. This was only a charade they were playing for an audience, but the perquisites were blissful.

Steve and his rather voluptuously enhanced lady friend were still playing tonsil hockey, so it required a discreet but pointed cough from Zack to get their attention.

'Hi, Steve, how are you?' Teresa smiled brightly as the two disentangled themselves. 'Smashing do this, isn't it?'

The girl – Suzy, Teresa remembered – looked astonished, as if she couldn't believe her eyes. A dumped woman confronting her ex? How could that happen?

Steve, on the other hand, seemed about to collapse or have apoplexy or both at once. His eyes widened, not just with surprise, but with astonishingly unfeigned lust as his eyes cruised up and down Teresa's figure.

Take a good look, buster. It's all for him now, not you.

With Zack's hand on her waist, she could understand what the proverbial million dollars felt like.

Steve's mouth dropped open, but no words emerged. His eyes continued to skitter from her breasts to her legs to her face and round and round again until he suddenly seemed to notice that she wasn't unaccompanied. And as he tilted his head up to meet the eyes of a very tall man, the expression on his face made Teresa want to giggle.

I never noticed you were so short, Stevie-boy.

'Pleased to meet you . . . I'm Zachary Trevelyan.' Zack's voice was firm and no-nonsense, while Steve still couldn't seem to locate his own tongue.

Teresa had a hard time containing herself as she watched the handshakes.

Like the rest of the female guests, Suzy seemed bewitched by Zack, but also distinctly annoyed now that her own specimen of manhood was clearly substandard. She shook off Steve's grip and favoured Zack with a pouting smile as she proffered her hand.

'Ooh, cold hands, warm heart.' She batted her mascara-clad lashes at him.

'Something like that.' Zack's response was a finessed

combination of exquisite politeness and a complete lack of reaction.

Steve winced. There was no other word for it. Zack didn't appear to be exerting very much pressure as he gripped the other man's hand, and his smile was amiable. But Steve's face went bright pink and, as Zack released him, he visibly fought the urge not to wiggle his squished fingers.

'You're the landlord, aren't you?' Steve's tone was belligerent and Teresa hid her smile. Her ex was faced with a taller, fitter, altogether far superior male, and she sensed he was seriously regretting his decision to dump her.

'Yes, he's that as well.' Beaming, she slid her arm around Zack's waist just as his arm went around her shoulder.

Steve's eyebrows lowered in a scowl when Zack's cool lips momentarily caressed the side of her face.

'Shall we get another drink, love?' Zack's words against her skin sounded exactly like a sinfully obscene suggestion that Steve and his babe weren't supposed to have heard.

Teresa turned to look up at him, loving the wicked glint in his glorious blue eyes. He was clearly enjoying baiting her ex just as much as she was.

'Or would you prefer to get out of here?' He licked his lips ever so slightly, his black lashes lowering lasciviously.

Oh, hell, yes!

It was just a game, but suddenly it felt real. Zack's dark head tilted, as if he was monitoring her every thought and for a moment, he frowned infinitesimally. Then he winked like a demon, his pale beautiful face all aglow.

'Better circulate just a bit more, for politeness' sake –' she paused, giving him a devouring look that was worthy of Suzy '– and then I'm all yours . . . would you like that?'

Zack laughed, his eyes on hers, and then swivelled towards the nonplussed couple beside them. 'We'll probably see you later. Nice meeting you both.'

Then his strong arm deftly turned Teresa and he began to guide her away through the throng.

They found a corner, and some more drinks, said 'hello' to more people. But, as the moments passed, Teresa found it impossible to focus on the party.

Would you prefer to get out of here? The words tolled in her head.

It was all an act, but she *did* want to sneak away to do what Steve and Suzy gloweringly suspected. And what various other couples, drifting away, were clearly planning on.

Plenty of time for a long lazy session in bed before the wedding at 9 p.m.

In the heady miasma of high-end women's perfumes and expensive aftershaves, Zack's delicious cologne sang like a clear clean note. It was playing havoc with her. Her body tingled in the places he'd touched so decorously, and down between her legs a needy pulse was steadily throbbing.

Wedding lust. Mating rituals. The whole atmosphere was ripe with pheromones and sex.

She turned to Zack and found him staring at her, his eyes dark and strange-looking. His expression was an irrational blend of intense desire – the mirror of hers – and what could only be described as apprehension.

What have you got to be afraid of?

What have I got to be afraid of?

'Look . . . I mean . . . do you *really* want to get out of here?'

The words floated in the air as if they suddenly had a life of their own. It wasn't at all what she'd meant to say, but it was too late to call it back. She swallowed, feeling hot blood rush into her face and neck. 'Damn it, I've embarrassed you, haven't I? Forget I said it.'

She couldn't look him in the eye, but Zack lifted her face to his with one finger under her chin. His expression was more troubled than ever, complex and sexy, and slightly wild.

'No! I want it too –' his voice was odd too. Gruff and deep, yet it seemed to ring. Several people looked around, frowning curiously in their direction '– but as they say in those soaps . . . it's complicated. More complicated than you can possibly believe.'

Staring down at her, his eyes were hot and confused. He pursed his lips and then seemed to run his tongue over his teeth, again and again, as if examining them somehow.

Checking for fangs, Zack?

Her unspoken words seemed to electrify him. He took her firmly by the arm and hustled her from the room and into a small adjacent lounge that was conveniently deserted.

Pushing the door shut behind him, he backed up against it and hauled her into his arms.

His mouth came down on hers, hard and sweet and demanding, just as it had been in her fantasies. The sharp contrast between her warm lips and his cooler ones made her tremble with an excitement that was beyond sex. It was a strange stimulus she was at a loss to understand.

Zack's tongue was cool too. Cool and bold and greedy and undisciplined. There was a rough unpractised quality about the kiss that made her blood sing and her knees go weak as jelly.

Throwing her arms around him, she pitched herself into the embrace, sucking on his sweet chilly tongue and pressing her belly against his, blatantly enticing him. The pressure was intense, and raw, and she couldn't get enough of him. It was as if her body was trying to climb inside his and be closer than his skin.

A moment ago, Zack had expressed doubts, but now they were forgotten. He pressed his pelvis back at her, circling the hard knot of his erection against her softness, growling in his throat as she reciprocated, rocking and pushing against his cock.

I knew you wanted me. I just knew it.

Her exultation was silent, but she could tell Zack had read it. He dug a hand into her hair, angling her head as his lips left hers and began to travel across her cheek, and down the line of her jaw and neck.

The touch of him and the taste of him were exquisite. His breath was almost scented, and it lingered on her lips where she ran her tongue over them. Her mouth felt bruised even though the kiss had only lasted a few moments.

Zack's lips were like thistledown on her skin, the contact magically light and circumspect as he explored her. She sensed that elusive reticence in him again, an impression of caution and lack of experience. Moments ago he'd been a wild man, but now he was holding back.

Sliding her hands under his jacket, she slid them down his back until they reached his firm male buttocks. Then, cupping the delicious muscular rounds she gripped him and pulled him against her belly.

He growled again. Deeper this time. The sound seemed to bounce around the small room as if it were a cathedral, like a feral utterance coming from another dimension. It was the weirdest thing, but it only made her surge against him. And then utter a groan herself as his mouth opened against her throat.

She felt the questing touch of his tongue, licking, searching – and then the contact of his teeth, sharp and hard, against her skin. The sensation made her sex clench involuntarily. Though his mouth was cold, it was the hottest, most exciting moment of lust.

'Please . . . please . . .' she heard herself implore, tilting back her head to give him better access to her neck.

She pressed her groin against him, to ease the ache and reinforce her invitation.

And then she felt it.

Tiny, sharp and keen, his teeth broke the skin of her neck in a little bite. It was pain, but it made her hips lurch, rocking harder and seeking closer contact. Her entire body was burning and silently screaming to be naked against him.

'No!'

Zack's cry was deafening. Teresa swayed, with her back against the door as she clutched and scrabbled at it in order to stay on her feet.

Across the room – impossibly – Zack was standing as if staring at a tall glass-fronted bookshelf full of leather-bound volumes. His dark-clad back was a wall of raw tension and, at his sides, his pale hands were two clenched fists.

He was here. And now he's there. What happened?

He was kissing me. Now he can't look at me. What have I done?

'What's the matter, Zack? What is it? Did I come on too strong?' She started towards him, but he stilled her with a chopping gesture, as if he'd seen her. The air between them seemed to hum. Like an external expression of that strange interior phenomenon she'd attributed to some inner ear problem. 'I'm sorry . . . I don't usually behave like a trollop . . . I thought you wanted me.'

'I do,' he said, his voice low, tormented, 'I want you more than you can possibly understand and in ways . . . ways that you won't understand.'

There was pain in his words, agony in his taut body. Teresa felt a great surge of compassion that somehow melded with her desire.

'Try me, Zack. I'm here for you in any way you need me. I'm crazy about you. Surely you realise that?'

He let out a noise like a sob, as if the news were exactly what he wanted to hear, but painful too.

'I – I'm crazy about you too, Teresa. Really. But this can't possibly work. I thought it might, but I was wrong. So wrong –' his tense shoulders lifted, and then subsided '– I couldn't have *been* more wrong.'

'But why?'

Watching him closely, achingly, Teresa suddenly braced herself – half dreading, but now almost *knowing* what she'd see when Zack turned to face her. Every breath of air whooshed out of her body, and she began to sway.

Then, as if time itself were mutable and malfunctioning, Zack spun slowly towards her.

His eyes were red, and his canine teeth were sharp white fangs.

6

Someone was gently tapping her cheek, and a dear familiar voice was speaking softly but persuasively in her ear.

'Teresa, my love, are you all right? Come on . . . snap out of it. Please talk to me.'

Teresa's eyes fluttered open, and the first thing she saw was Zack's face, pale, handsome and worried. He was kneeling in front of her, and she was slumped in one of the large damask-covered armchairs that were arrayed around the small room.

She had absolutely no idea how she'd got there.

Zack took a glass of water from the low table beside her chair, and offered it to her.

Teresa sipped, feeing numb and weird but with her hackles on the rise, aware of something, she knew not what, barrelling towards her.

'Oh, God! Oh, God! Oh, God!'

It all returned to her.

The glass started to tip, but Zack caught it faster than the eye could see and set it back on the table.

Unable to look him in the face, Teresa stared at the glass, then at his hand, long and smooth, still holding it.

'You *are* one, aren't you?' Her heart thudded, fast and hard. Her mind felt like a wild pony, cantering about, trying desperately to avoid the truth. 'A vampire? They're real, aren't they? And I've been living with one for six months!'

An overload circuit tripped somehow and, without thinking, she whipped out her hand and fetched Zack a ringing slap across the face. He could have deflected it without effort, but he stayed still.

There was no red mark on his cheek where the blow had struck.

'I'm sorry.'

His apology came before hers. She hadn't really intended to hit him, it'd just happened. A reflex.

'I wanted to tell you, Teresa. Time and time again. But I didn't think you'd believe me. And if you did believe me, I was afraid it'd make you run for the hills – and leave me.'

His whole face was full of remorse. Full of humanity. No hint of pointy teeth or ruddy eyes.

Teresa dragged in a shuddering breath, totally at a loss. This was the most momentous discovery of her life. A critical turning point. She needed advice. She needed someone to turn to. Someone to tell about this completely unbelievable thing.

But the only person she longed to tell was the man staring worriedly into her face.

Laughter bubbled up in her throat. How could anyone, ever, manage to get themselves into a situation as ridiculous as this? She'd finally found the perfect man – a decent man, who she wanted as a friend as well as a lover, and who was spine-meltingly gorgeous into the bargain – and he was a vampire!

Hysterical laughter broke free, took a hold of her, and got out of control. Her body shook and tears of manic merriment trickled down her face. Zack's strong arms slid around her and she could feel his chest heaving with laughter too.

Several chaotic moments followed. They rocked together, bonded in a bizarre glee, until the door to the little sitting room opened and someone popped their head in.

'Whoops, sorry!' They were gone again before either Teresa or Zack could stop, but the spell of their mad fit was finally broken.

She stood up, forcing Zack to rise gracefully to his feet too.

'Well, as they say in every romantic film or drama I've ever seen, we need to talk, don't we?' He smiled down at her, his beautiful mouth quirking.

'That's putting it mildly, dark prince.' She reached for his cool hand. 'Shall we retire to our chamber?'

Zack shrugged eloquently. 'I think we'd better.'

In the lift, Teresa noticed something she hadn't seen the last time they'd ridden up.

'Hey! I can see you . . . sort of . . . I thought you weren't supposed to have a reflection?' She pointed to a small courtesy mirror at the back of the lift. In it was Zack's image, faint and shadowy, but definitely visible.

'Don't believe everything you see in movies or read in books.' In the glass, Zack's beautifully curved mouth was hazily reflected. 'There are degrees of vampirism, and as many different kinds of us as there are normal people.'

'I didn't know that.'

'Yes. And I suppose you'd say I'm at the more human end of the spectrum.'

She thought of his kindness towards her, and the way she always felt cared for and protected by him. His attitude had been help, not harm, from day one.

Or at least it had seemed that way.

'So you're not planning to . . . to drain me dry and either kill me or make me into a vampire too, then?' She tried to speak lightly, but her voice wavered.

Emotion played across Zack's face, complex and haunting, and she felt guilty for betraying her lack of trust.

But – but he was a vampire. A *vampire*. Human end of the spectrum or otherwise.

'I would never intentionally do any of those things . . .' He bit his lip, and Teresa thought of all the times she'd naively noted how white and shiny and sharp his teeth looked. No wonder they were sharp, didn't he bite necks with them?

She put her hand on his arm. He felt so strong, so normal – and so human. But still she trembled.

'What do you mean by "intentionally", Zack?'

The lift door sprang open, to reveal a couple who Teresa vaguely recognised, waiting outside. She smiled briefly at them and then led the way towards the room. It would be easier to talk there, but her heart still thudded. How foolhardy was it to lock herself behind closed doors with a vampire?

'So, "intentionally", Zack,' she repeated once they were alone.

Instead of answering, he walked towards the mini fridge. He took out a whisky miniature for her and poured it into a glass, then a flask of his 'iron shake'.

'I'm so stupid . . . I didn't even work out that was blood!' She grimaced as she took a sip of her own drink and she sat down on the bed. She'd never been a whisky drinker, but these were desperate times. Clutching her glass, she stared long and hard at Zack's throat as he took a swallow of his own 'drink'. Dark, terrifying thoughts began to circle.

'Please, for God's sake, tell me that's *animal* blood!' The whole universe seemed to hinge on his answer. Was she just feet away from a mass murderer?

Zack frowned. 'It is . . . and you did, actually . . .' He put aside his flask, as if he'd lost his appetite. 'Work out that it was blood, that is.'

Layers of shock piled on one another. Teresa drank more whisky, not tasting it.

Slowly, he shook his head, lingering across the room from her as if he daren't approach.

'What do you mean, Zack?'

'This is so complicated . . . so hard to put into words. What's happened to me, the way I am – and the stupid, selfish things I've done.' He studied his long narrow hands for a moment, running the pad of his thumb across a nail, then suddenly made a strange elegant gesture, a kind of pass.

Accompanied by that elusive, silvery humming in her

ears, images, impressions, sensations all flooded in. Blanked out memories and exquisite, unearthly pleasure.

'You bastard!'

Teresa flew across the room as if she was the one with vampire powers. Fired by confusion and fury, she thumped and beat at Zack's chest and shoulders. It was like belabouring a statue made of granite. He didn't lift his arms to protect himself. He just took it.

'I'm sorry,' he whispered when the energy had gone out of her, and she stomped back across the room, retrieved her glass and sloshed down more whisky.

'How could you?'

Deflated, Teresa slumped, and let her jumbled emotions settle.

She felt bemused, still angry, slightly betrayed, and bizarrely, as before, she suddenly wanted to laugh.

She'd just beat up a supernatural being who could probably snap her neck in a heartbeat – and she'd got away with it. Eat your heart out, Buffy.

'So why the mind-games?' Across the room, Zack was standing just as she'd left him, but he winced visibly at her words.

'Because, if I'd let you see the truth, you wouldn't have stayed in my house.' He seemed to have regained his beautiful stillness. Something Teresa realised now stemmed in part from the fact he didn't breathe and his chest never moved. 'And if I'd let you remember me touching you, you'd have remembered the biting too.'

His gaunt face was tormented and whiter than usual, if that were possible. Self-recrimination made his eyes darkly haunted.

Teresa put down her glass again, and held out her hand

to him as her muddled feelings dropped into place like the tumblers of a lock. She was afraid of his strangeness, and the fact that he was fiction and magic made real. But he was still Zack, and she still wanted him – and loved him.

Despite everything he'd just admitted, he was a troubled soul and she wanted to hold him and comfort him and soothe him. For all his supernatural potency and his sly mind-warping powers, he was still that lost innocent boy she'd always dreamed of. Still the beautiful virgin she'd longed to initiate.

How she knew this, she hadn't the faintest idea. Maybe it was vampire telepathy, working in reverse?

'Come here.' She slid her free hand across the bedspread. 'You're obviously able to control yourself.'

Zack's eyes were troubled, but unexpectedly he complied, striding across the room and sitting down beside her.

'I'm not so sure of that,' he said, as she reached for his cool hand.

He looked away for a moment, then squared his shoulders and turned to face her again. He took her hand, turned it over and then folded it into his. The process was almost a transformation, the drawing upon an inner strength and dignity to face a crisis. Something he must have done before, many times, to survive.

'The thing is –' his fingers traced her palm '– for my kind, lust and bloodlust are two sides of the same coin. One triggers the other. I don't want to harm anybody. I don't want to damage anybody. So to avoid one, I have to avoid both.'

'But you've been experimenting, haven't you? With me.'

For a being that didn't need to breathe, Zack sighed heavily and looked towards the ceiling.

'I'm not sorry.' When he looked at her again, his smile was a chiaroscuro of emotion. She saw remorse, and genuine penitence, but also the slow impish beginnings of seduction, like a naughty but very grown-up boy beginning to flex his sexual powers, 'You're beautiful . . . and I adore you. I wanted to give you pleasure.' He paused and heaved another faux vampire sigh. 'But it's not safe. I might not be able to hold back another time.'

'How do you know unless you try?'

Teresa's heart was thudding fit to burst. This was the most dangerous thing she'd ever done – but she'd never wanted anything more intensely in her life.

Zack's eyes glittered, brilliant with those conflicting emotions. But Teresa knew she was winning. The fine line of red around his blue irises told her so. 'Teresa, this isn't a game. I could easily kill you.' He ran his tongue around his lips, then over the edges of his teeth – checking. 'And I'm . . . well . . . not experienced. It'll be like handing a learner driver the keys of a Lamborghini.'

'But you're not going to learn anything – least of all how to master your darker urges – if you don't try, are you?'

Are you sure? he seemed to ask silently. His eyes were changing, changing, even as she watched him, and his white fangs were already sharp points of danger.

'Don't worry . . . if you get out of hand, I'll just knee you in the groin,' Teresa answered, 'that's usually guaranteed to stop *any* man . . . alive *or* dead, hopefully.'

Tired of bargaining and coaxing, she released Zack's hand and slid her own up his arm and around the back of his head, drawing him to her. As their lips met, his suppressed growl rang in her brain.

With his tongue in her mouth, he tipped her backwards

onto the bed, pushing her effortlessly across its width and moving over her.

The taste of his mouth was astonishing – both exotic and familiar – and the brush of his extended canines set her nerves shivering with a delicious sense of peril. She felt it tingling in every part of her body, not only against the tender inner skin of her lip. She pressed her tongue back against his, daring to flick swiftly at the sharp points.

As she tasted the tiniest drop of blood, her sex clenched and Zack growled, his hips rocking.

Still kissing, they tugged at their clothes, the tangling and fumbling only adding to the thrill of struggle. Shoes clomped onto the floor, and cotton, silk and high-quality suiting all went flying into heaps, willy-nilly. As the pieces came off, they paused to press skin to skin, and it wasn't only Zack who made unearthly sounds of hunger.

Naked on the bed, he was an object of pure beauty. His skin was milky pale but had an exquisitely dense sheen like polished marble. Muscles in fine long slabs adorned his arms, his torso and his thighs.

His cock was astonishing. Large, jutting, fiercely hard, it reared up from his body, silky and seeping and rosy pink.

'I thought your sort didn't have circulation . . . how does this come about?' She ran her fingertips along it, making him hiss and clench his jaw. A tiny trickle of his own blood stained his lip as he bit down.

'It's not circulation – just hydraulics.' His voice was low and ragged. 'I don't know how it works but right now I'm just glad it does!'

Tipping her back on the bed, he started to explore, his cool fingertips travelling over her body in sweeps that were both hungry and tentative. Again, she got a strong impression that he was in brand new territory, that he was a novice – but one whose powers of instinct and empathy were phenomenal. Maybe it was something to do with what he was? And he could read her feelings and her thoughts? Whatever it was, his touch was perfect without any need for coaching.

Teresa trembled as his mouth began to move on her. Studiously avoiding her neck, he kissed first the line of her jaw, and then darted straight to the curve of her breast, his cool tongue flicking out and tasting her skin. The short, scurrying licks flickered around her nipple, but didn't settle on it. Round and round he went, skirting the sensitive areola but not closing on it.

You teasing devil. Teresa slithered against the quilt, unable to keep her hips still. Every part of her wanted him. She groaned out loud, gripping his strong shoulders, her nails digging into his astonishingly hard muscles.

And then he sucked, hard, on the tip of her breast, his lips pulling, his tongue circling like a rude little serpent.

'Oh God!' she gasped, her molten core rippling as his mouth moved instinctively. She pushed her hips against him, her sex blindly seeking his. Her hands roved over his magnificent back, his flanks and his bottom.

Her body seemed to shout with hunger as his lips parted and she felt the prickle of his fang-tips against the crown of her breast.

Bite me. Please bite me, her mind screamed.

It was madness, sex and yet not sex. Grabbing at him, Teresa's mind grabbed at something indefinable, other, far greater than the fleeing confluence of their bodies. A sense of yearning flooded through her, the longing for a communion that was immense and monumental, beyond time itself.

Zack jerked back.

'No!' he gasped. 'I can't . . . I shouldn't . . .' He shook his head, his dark curls tossing. 'I don't care if I live a thousand years and *never* have a woman!'

The concept she'd been reaching for, dissolved like mist, and despite her desire, Teresa reached up to touch Zack's dear face, frowning as she processed his words.

'Zack, love, what do you mean? What do you mean "never have a woman"?'

How could that be? He was beautiful, exotic, and virile – with hypnotic powers into the bargain – how could he not have had scores of lovers in an unnaturally long life? She'd relished her 'virgin male' fantasies. But surely that was all they were – fantasies.

Sitting up, he turned away from her, his white back a wall of tension.

'It means just what you think it means.' He lifted his hands, smoothed them over his hair, gripping the thick, shiny curls at the back of his neck. Letting his hands fall again, he turned back towards her. 'I've never been with a woman. I've never dared.'

Teresa sat up too, reaching for him. Despite the high sharp thrill of his admission, it was sympathy she felt most strongly. What kind of torment must his long life as a vampire be? He had a soul. He was a good man. And his principles had prevented him from ever putting a woman at risk. Even if the woman *wanted* that risk.

I love you. The thought popped into her head.

So impossible, but she felt it, and knew that the emotion had been with her a long time – probably as long as she'd known him. And all the time her heart had secretly recognised his sacrifice.

But she was still curious.

'What about *before*? Wasn't there anybody then?' But when *was* before? 'How long have you been a vampire?'

Zack seemed to relax. He flashed her a wry, boyish smile.

'I was turned back in the 1930s, so that would mean that I've been what I've been for seventy years, although I've tried not to keep count.'

'But they had girls in the 1930s, didn't they?' Teresa smiled back at him, 'I mean . . . well, you look about twenty-five. Surely at that age you had girlfriends? What the hell happened to you?'

The thought of Zack with other women gave her a bit of a stab, even though they were most likely dead by now.

'I was a novice in a Benedictine monastery, Teresa. Pure as the driven snow, you might say.' He laughed, a shrug lifting his finely formed shoulders.

'Crikey!'

'Crikey indeed,' he intoned, still smiling, 'although after I became a vampire my religious faith took quite a knock.'

Teresa made a decision. It was perilous and foolhardy, but there was no way she was going to let this glorious man deny himself any longer.

And she wanted him more than ever. A thousandfold.

'You've got to trust yourself, Zack. You're a good man, despite the fangs.' She inclined herself towards him and kissed the corner of his mouth. His fangs had retracted a little but she could still feel their points as she pressed her lips against his. 'And I believe you can control yourself.' She kissed the other corner of his mouth, flicking her tongue between his lips, seeking out the sharp badge of his condition. 'I'll help . . .'

His arms came around her, cool-skinned, yet warm in intent. He was shaking, and she imagined tears like jewels trickling down his beautiful face. A moment later she felt the moisture against her cheek.

They kissed again. Slowly at first, yet growing wilder and wilder with every second. Teresa felt free and confident and full of desire, stirred to elation by this miracle of a man, who was her dearest fantasy, and yet so very, very, very much more.

And Zack relaxed at last. She could feel him smiling as he kissed her, his lips curving against her skin, even as his fangs slid against it.

'If I start to bite, don't forget that knee in the groin.' He was laughing as she slid her sex up and down the muscular length of his thigh, loving the friction as she curled her fingers around his chilly but magnificent cock.

'I've thought of that.'

And she had. It was perfect. Rising up over him, she pushed him down onto his back against the covers. He looked like some kind of crooked angel with his dark curls against the crisp white cotton pillowcase.

'I just want you to lie back and think of Transylvania!' She swirled the tip of her finger around the head of his penis, and watched him snarl silently, his upper lip curling to reveal the strange beauty of his fully extended fangs. They were awesome, but she wasn't going to allow him to make a mistake with them.

How long would a man who'd been waiting seventy years for sex be able to last, she wondered. Especially one who had vampire fire burning in his blood?

Still touching his penis, she lowered her lips towards it. Forming an 'O' she guided him safely in.

So cool. So hard. So sweet and clean, not at all like any man she'd ever sucked.

'Oh, God, Teresa!'

Zack's voice was plaintive. Full of wonder. She imagined him masturbating, perhaps frequently, but if he'd never been with a woman this would be a revelation. She let her tongue dance, exploring his sumptuously flared shape, while out of the corner of her eye, she watched him writhe and tear at the bedclothes, his face contorted and his eyes crimson red.

She tasted him slowly, carefully, her exploration circumspect. No harsh suction. No bobbing up and down. Just delicate strokes of her tongue, while her fingers gently played his shaft and balls.

His enraptured cries became more feral. He growled. He snarled. He ripped the sheets, his hips bucking wildly as he thrust himself into her mouth, making a mockery of her carefully measured pleasuring.

'I want you! I must have you!' His voice was ferocious now. He was all primal magic and otherness. Teresa felt fear, the kind that exhilarates and hurls the spirits skywards. She was a mountain climber challenged by Everest, a hang-glider about to freebase off a sheer precipice. Wracked with savage terror, her blood surged with a wild anticipation and sheer joy in the embrace of no going back.

Hauling herself upright, she looked down on Zack's magnificent cock, pale and shining with his own juice and her saliva. Deep inside her, she felt her womb leap and cry to him. Could he make her pregnant? She doubted it. And as a virgin, he was free from disease, surely?

It was his fangs that were the danger to her. But with them, she'd take her chances. She had no choice.

Throwing a leg over Zack's lean hips, she positioned herself over him, his tip at her entrance. Then as he bucked up again, she bore down, taking him in.

7

It was heaven. Paradise. Perfection. More than he'd ever imagined, and he'd had a long time to imagine it.

First her sweet mouth, now her beautiful warm body. The sensation of being enclosed and caressed was exquisite and chaotic. As intense pleasure surged, the call for blood raged in his mind and his veins. He looked up at Teresa, drinking in every glorious facet of her gentle curves and her gleaming rosy skin, seeing her sweet face all haloed in shimmering red.

I must resist, I must resist, Zack repeated to himself.

The battle of his senses was titanic. The knowledge of what his fangs could do to her clashed again and again with raw ravening hunger. A lust for blood such as he'd never experienced before, even in his earliest and most untutored struggles.

And yet the conflict prolonged the pleasure. The primal skirmish between man and vampire kept him from simply thrusting like a maniac, coming and ejaculating almost immediately. Fighting his own urges gave him an edge, just enough so that he could think of Teresa's pleasure.

Reaching out, he clasped her hips, holding her tight and rocking her on the fulcrum of his penis. He knew he was big and hard, and he filled her and caressed her with that hardness. Her eyes and her mouth were wild with sensation and her throat was flushed. As she moaned, and rocked in time to his movements, he felt her channel ripple and embrace him with its heat.

'Oh, God! Oh, God!' he roared, naming the deity he was no longer sure he believed in, 'I can't . . . I . . .'

And yet still she pleasured him, flexing and clenching the

very quick of her sumptuous body around him. His head was spinning, a red vortex of raving desire. Wanting her to share something, some human essence of this sublime sensation, he slid his fingers between her legs, finding the apex of her sex, almost where their bodies were melded. He knew his touch was clumsy and untutored, but her response was a sweet whimper of pleasure, and she pressed her hand over his as if to affirm his efforts.

Then he felt it. Her body reaching the pinnacle. Fast, hard contractions around his flesh. Her fingers gouging into the back of his hand, and his thigh where she was supporting herself.

'Zack! Oh, God, Zack!' she shouted, her triumphant shout as unnaturally loud as his own blood cry.

Beyond control, he reared up, grasping her to him as the red fire of bloodlust boiled in his loins and in his soul. At the last moment, he tried to turn away his head, but she wouldn't let him. Still climaxing, she buried her hands in his curls and brought his face to the curve of her neck, pressing his mouth against the soft damp skin of her neck.

'Do it, Zack!' she commanded him, her voice ringing like a queen's, compelling him to do her will, 'Do it, Zack . . . take my blood. It's what I want.'

Unable to defy her, he bit down softly, and drank her sweetness.

Her human blood was warm with life as his cock jerked inside her and his cold seed spilt and spilt and spilt.

'I now pronounce you man and wife. You may kiss the bride.'

Don't look at him. Don't look at him.

It was useless. Teresa could no sooner not look at Zack than she could stop breathing.

I'm going crazy, she thought.

Zack's idea of formalwear was a gorgeous black Edwardian evening suit, complete with high collar and elaborately tied cravat. She knew now that he could never have worn such a suit when it was actually in fashion, but she loved his quirky fondness for vintage style.

Everybody cheered and clapped as Lisa and Tom kissed enthusiastically, but like herself, Zack appeared vaguely distracted. When he met her eyes, his expression was complex. Part triumph, part confusion, part guilt, part lust – all mixed up with a sweet warmth and tenderness.

She wished he would listen to her when she told him he had no reason to feel guilty.

She'd been the one who'd pushed him into biting her.

His eyes widened as if he'd read her thoughts, and unable to stop herself, Teresa flicked back to those breathtaking moments.

It'd been like falling and flying both at once. There had been pleasure in her belly like a boiling, swirling whirlpool that she also felt in every cell and atom of her body.

She'd never come like that in her life before, and she knew it was because Zack had been feeding at the same time.

The little pinpricks itched suddenly, and Zack's eyes narrowed as she adjusted the silk scarf she'd slung around her neck to hide the evidence. He'd taken barely a few mouthfuls, but it was the act, not the volume that was significant.

The ceremony over, murmuring and jostling guests began to move away from the rows of seats set out in front of the little rose bower where Lisa and Peter had taken their vows. Next on the agenda was the reception, and the groaning tables of delicious buffet food and inordinate amounts of booze behind the open bar were calling.

Dusk had fallen, and there was a tiny bit of descending sun on the horizon, but the weak rays didn't seem to bother Zack too much.

'It'd have to be full daytime sunlight for me to crisp,' he'd told her as they'd made their way outdoors. 'Other than that, I'm fine.'

Teresa circulated through the noisy hectic reception in a dream. Everyone was having a fine old time, ribald jokes were being told, and people were drinking, eating, laughing and flirting. But to her it all seemed at a great distance. Her only reality was the tall elegant man at her side.

From time to time, she caught other women eyeing him, their blatant envy of her written on their faces.

Oh, yes, he is a stud, she silently taunted them. And he's gorgeous. But you don't know the half of it, and if I tried to tell you, you'd think I'd lost my marbles.

Sipping from a glass of wine, she wrinkled her nose because it had no flavour. She supposed that normal human pleasures lost their impact when you were in love with a supernatural being, and you'd just been to bed with him.

Dancing began on the specially laid floor. Teresa watched people jigging and gyrating, and women doing various kinds of sexy wiggle in order to snare themselves a man for the night. At one time she would have enjoyed strutting her stuff too, regardless of whether she was hoping to find a nice man or not. But tonight she felt weary and detached from reality. It was if someone had photoshopped the wedding party into a blur.

'Are you all right?'

Turning from the dancing throng to Zack felt like leaving the shadows behind to embrace the sweet light of the moon.

'You look tired.' His fine broad brow was puckered with

concern, but all Teresa wanted to do was reach out and touch the single loose curl that dangled across it, having escaped from his scrupulously groomed coiffeur.

Trying to think straight, and not get sidetracked by kiss curls and eyes that turned red, Teresa gave him an encouraging smile.

'I'm fine, Zack, really.'

Liar.

'I'm perfectly OK.' She dropped her voice. 'You haven't harmed me. In fact, I feel wonderful.' She touched his arm, thrilled all over again by the feel of hard muscle and unnatural strength beneath her fingers. 'It's just that I'd far rather be alone with you than amongst this crowd.'

Zack frowned again.

'Don't do that.' She reached up and smoothed her fingers across his brow as if to erase the frown. His skin was cool, but the contact prickled like electricity. 'What we shared was wonderful. And I want to do it again. As soon as possible.'

Biting his lip, Zack looked heavenwards, a picture of confusion. There was the slightest bit of extra pointing on his canines, and she could feel desire pouring off him like discreet magnetic waves.

He took her by the shoulders, and looked deep into her eyes, his own already ringed with red.

'And do you think I don't want that too?' His voice was raw. 'I waited for three-quarters of a century for what happened between us, Teresa, and it exceeded even my wildest imaginings.' His long fingers tightened around her shoulders, and the little pain of it was scary yet delicious. 'And next time . . . next time I know will be even better.' His crystal-blue eyes had a red halo. 'But I'm not sure I'll be able to control myself.'

'Right on, mate! I know what you mean! She's a cracker!' slurred a drunken wedding guest as he passed them, swaying and bleary-eyed.

Zack's eyes flared crimson and he glared at the man ferociously. The very air seemed to vibrate with a silent roar of fury.

'Sorry. I'm really sorry,' apologised the chastened guest in a tiny voice, before scuttling away, white as a sheet and terrified.

'See what I mean?' Zack's eyes were normal again even though his voice was still softly fierce. 'Around you, I can't contain myself – I thought I could, but it's a thousand times more difficult than I expected.' He closed his eyes for a moment, thick black eyelashes like two silken fans sweeping down. 'I . . . I love you, Teresa . . . and I don't want to hurt you. I can't bear the thought of what I might do.'

Teresa swayed, and almost before she could register what had happened, Zack's arm was around her waist, holding her up.

'You're *not* all right at all, are you?'

'I'm fine, I tell you,' she shot back, her voice sharper than she'd intended. She couldn't think straight. Her head was spinning and her heart was flying up, like a bird.

He loves me.

She stared around. The wedding seemed to recede away from them – become unreal. New dreams flooded in, swirling and blending with her wild erotic fantasies of vampire sex. She saw herself and Zack, walking hand in hand through a beautiful night, silent in contentment and companionship. For all eternity.

'Come on, let's get away. It's great . . . but we need time to ourselves,' she gasped.

Zack looked doubtful, alarmed, almost angry. And Teresa knew it wasn't anything to do with breaches of social or wedding etiquette. 'Don't worry . . . nobody will miss us. We're not the bride and groom.'

I wish we were. I'd give anything to be the Bride of Dracula.

'What's so funny?' Zack asked as they sped away from the wedding party. Teresa realised she must have laughed aloud. As they left the marquee, shadows were falling like a cloak across the garden.

'Nothing. Just silly thoughts.'

They were silly – but also deadly serious.

To *be* Zack's bride, she'd have no choice but to die.

Driven by some vague, dark compulsion, Zack headed for the maze again, drawing Teresa along at his side.

This is madness, he thought. We should have stayed with the wedding . . . You'd be safe there, my love. I couldn't feed on you with an audience of hundreds.

And yet a part of him knew that he had it in him to do just that.

Now that he'd tasted the bliss of lovemaking and the beautiful alchemical blend of blood and sublime sexual pleasure, he knew that the comfortable arrangement that he and Teresa had shared until now would never be the same again. He couldn't go back now, but perhaps *she* could, if he could persuade her to leave his house and the danger he presented.

And in the meantime, somehow, he had to maintain control. He had to think. Reason. Explain to Teresa what had to be.

The tall fragrant hedges of the maze loomed around them as they entered. The night scents were cool and fresh, intoxicatingly sweet. But nowhere near as dizzying as the delicious odour of Teresa's perfume, and the delicate but piercing aroma of her sex.

'I hope we don't get lost.' She looked up at him as they walked, her face glowing in the light of the newly emerged moon. 'Or can you fly and see above the hedges and find a way out again?'

Zack shook his head, amused despite everything.

'Yet another myth from stories and movies.' He squeezed her fingers, almost wanting to moan aloud at how much the simple contact roused him. His fangs were already dangerously lengthened, just from holding hands. 'I can't fly and I can't turn into things. You'd be surprised how very normal most vampires are.'

'No bats? Wolves? Green mist?'

'Fortunately, no.'

She shrugged, and the slight, subtle lift of her breasts made a jolt like liquid silver speed through his veins. Everything she did, everything she said, and everything about the way she looked only made him more aroused. He was just about to draw her to a halt, and insist they return to the marquee when they turned a corner and found the centre of the maze. The stone benches sat in a silent, accusing circle around the dark pool where he'd spent his passion last night.

Teresa gasped.

'This is so beautiful! What a magical place!'

She drew him forwards, and then looked down into the near black water.

'I love it that I can see you,' she breathed, and then turned to smile at him.

Zack stared down too, looking not at his own faint reflection, but at the clear image of Teresa, her bare shoulders gleaming in the moonlight, beautifully revealed by her elegant dress with its narrow straps. As he watched, she pulled off the silk scarf that had been wound around her neck. Her throat was white and smooth, apart from the twin crimson punctures of his bite.

Lust, both for blood, and in the form of simple human desire, raged through him like a tidal wave. His penis stiffened like iron, and his fangs descended fully.

He had to get out of here. He couldn't resist. He had to be in her – and he had to feed.

Teresa watched the magical change. Crimson gleamed in Zack's eyes and the points of his sharp white teeth glinted in the moonlight. A frightening yet delicious feeling of weakness and yearning enveloped her. It was coming from him she knew, but she guessed it was a subconscious rather than conscious emanation.

It didn't matter which though, her body still sang with need and longing. Her skin tingled, especially around her bite marks, and between her legs her sex melted and grew liquid with raw desire. Moving without effort or conscious volition, she pressed herself against the length of Zack's body, tugging at his collar and then laying her lips against his cool throat as if that might compel him to reciprocate.

She could feel his great strength, and how he was using it to fight her and put her from him, but her own surge of strength and power was almost equal to him. Sighing, she wound her arms around him, opening her mouth on his neck, licking and tasting the delicious flavour of his skin.

'Teresa, no!' he groaned, but there was resignation in his low voice, and a pleasure that was impossible to hide. All these months with her he'd held back, and all the decades before, when he'd kept himself apart and out of temptation's way. They were like a great mass of dammed up emotion bursting forth, a force of nature that could no longer be turned or diverted.

His arms tightened around her, and as she threw her own arms around his neck, he cupped her buttocks, lifting her and moving her against the knot of his erection. She felt her feet leave the grass beneath her as he held her effortlessly, crushed against the length of his body.

'We mustn't, Teresa, we mustn't –'

It was a last-ditch attempt.

'Oh yes, we must,' she purred, wriggling and rocking sinuously against him.

For a moment, all around was a blur of motion, and then Teresa found herself lying on her back, on the grass. Zack was lying half over her, a hand moving seductively over her breast while he supported himself on the elbow of his other arm. Somewhere in the transition his jacket and his elaborate tie had disappeared, and his white silk shirt was hanging open, baring his chest.

Teresa laughed. She was naked on the turf.

'So . . . you've changed your mind,' she murmured, lifting her knee, sliding it against him, her hips twisting, coaxing.

'Yes,' he said roughly, his hand sliding from her breast to her belly, fingers flexing, the middle one tracking down towards her cleft. 'But no biting . . . absolutely no biting! I swear it!'

But his eyes were red and his fangs were long. Teresa shuddered, revelling against all reason in the power of her lover's most basic instincts.

And then he touched her, and as she moaned with longing, he howled, primal exultation ringing and rebounding in the intimate space enclosed by the high hedges.

Only his caress existed, only his long cool body, only his scent. All rhyme and reason and the world of the normal and the sane, cautious and prudent was forgotten. She groaned for the vampire's kiss, and the possession of his body. Somehow he was already naked and moving over her, his heavy penis searching, searching, and searching for its perfect sheath.

Teresa tilted her hips, inviting him and facilitating his thrust. Her hands grabbed at him, clawing at his back and cupping his backside, encouraging him, goading him on, her nails digging in, breaking his skin.

When he pushed inside her, her head went light and she wailed and sighed and thrashed as if she too were in thrall to the lust for blood. Her hips lifted, pushed, thrusting back at him. She wanted him to be inside her, really inside her – inside every nerve and cell and blood vessel. She wanted to be with him, and *be* him, right down to the tiniest denominator of what made them, and she wanted to be inside of him too.

They slid and rocked together, limbs working, bodies pressing and slapping against each other in a natural instinctive dance of the flesh. Great waves of delicious sensation swept through Teresa's belly, her legs, her arms, her fingers and toes. Even her hair seemed to be tingling with delight and almost standing on end.

But she knew there was more, and even in the midst of such a cyclone of pleasure, she recognised again the greater and more life-changing lure. Embracing its ultimate call, she arched her neck and offered her throat, her fingers digging deep into Zack's black curls to draw him to her.

He roared again, a huge sound resonant with joy and triumph, but also a fatalistic 'no' of horror and resistance. But it was too late, those basic instincts were in control.

The pain, when it came was immense. This was no little nip, and the drawing of a few mouthfuls of blood. This was the real thing.

Hard, unforgiving teeth plunged through her skin, probing for and then finding the rich pulsing vessels they sought. Hot blood began to flow, sweet and abundant. Teresa moaned again as her pleasure spiralled and became unrecognisable. Perhaps the pain was pleasure? Or the pleasure was pain? She couldn't tell. She only knew the exquisite joy of feeding and being fed on by her love.

On and on it went, her sex rippling and clenching and contracting around Zack in time to the steady pulsing surge of blood from her throat. The sensations were sublime, and she was aware, somewhere in the centre of them, that Zack was ejaculating inside her, and yet he stayed hard, his cock unflagging, solid and cool.

She began to float, as if weightless, insubstantial. She was drifting on a sea of warm primitive feelings, cosseted and buoyed up by love, suspended in a drifting crimson cloud. The pleasure seemed to melt and change, become ever more languorous, drowsier and less substantial. There was no effort in the union now, just ease, and gliding, flowing sweetness . . .

From a great distance, she seemed to hear an agonised voice, crying, 'No! Oh no!' but it could have been merely her imagination.

Is this a dream? How strange it is. Am I awake or asleep?

Still drifting, Teresa became vaguely aware of motion,

things happening around her and to her. It was disorientating, but she wasn't scared. Zack was with her. Zack was taking care of her.

With very little help from her, he was helping her back into her clothes, while she just stared around, dimly registering her surroundings and even her own body. She could smell blood, rich and tantalising. Staring at her own fingers, she found traces of red on the tips and around the nails, and it being the most natural thing to do, while Zack was searching for her shoes, she popped each finger into her mouth, one by one, and licked off the life-giving fluid. It tasted just as appetising as it smelled.

And then she was being carried along, her arms around his strong neck, her face buried against his scented skin, against his unbuttoned collar.

'I'm so tired,' she murmured, nuzzling, 'I could sleep for a month . . .'

'It's OK,' her beloved whispered, 'you'll soon be back in bed.'

Teresa wanted to say how nice that sounded, but before she could frame the words, she was already fast asleep.

8

It seemed to Teresa that it was many, many weeks before she finally woke up from that dream.

She recalled the carrying to bed, the putting to bed, and then the next morning and conversations with Zack as the two of them packed up their belongings and then drove back to town.

How easy and tranquil it had seemed, chatting to her friend – her buddy – about this and that, and making plans, some vague, some definite, for the weeks and months to come. The only thing that bothered her was the return of her tinnitus now and again. She'd resolved to see a doctor sooner or later.

What an excellent idea it seemed to begin to look for a new flat of her own while Zack was away, visiting his old friends at the Priory of St Benedict in North Yorkshire on retreat. Yes, it really was time she stopped presuming on the generosity of this kind man. She had some savings – in fact her bank account was unexpectedly healthy – and it would be fun to decorate a place exactly to her own taste. And with her out of his hair, Zack could get on with his research and his writing, and they could always pop around and see each other when she was settled, couldn't they?

She was sad to see Zack leave for Yorkshire, and she'd shed a few secret tears. But ever the thoughtful one, he'd arranged for his cleaning lady come housekeeper to put in a few extra hours in his absence, so Teresa would have some company around the place while she was looking for that flat.

Everything was planned, organised and trundling along smoothly. At least it seemed that way at first.

But then the changes began. Or perhaps it was just that she started to notice changes that had already occurred – and her memory began to sharpen.

And that wasn't the only thing that got sharp.

She began to wake in the night from hot red dreams about Zack. Wild erotic flights that left her aroused and yearning and voraciously hungry. But when she opened the fridge, there was nothing in it she fancied.

One night, she dove into the freezer and found some icy packages of Zack's iron shake – the ones he kept for emergency when fresh supplies were delayed for one reason or another. Inexplicably, her mouth began to water, and the shape of it felt strange and unfamiliar.

Defrosting the hard frozen red pillows, Teresa absently ran her tongue over the edges of her upper teeth – then squeaked out loud when she got the shock of her life.

Then suddenly she saw an image of his hand, fingers crooked, moving strangely.

But there was no need for a magician's pass now. The delicious odour of blood brought everything back. Everything he'd blanked out in his misguided attempt to 'save' her.

She smiled.

In the small hours of the morning, Zack let himself into the still, dark house. His housekeeper never stayed overnight, so it should be empty – but the back of his neck prickled when he sensed a vague presence.

Teresa!

She shouldn't be here. He'd deliberately stayed out of contact for the six weeks he'd been away, hoping it would be easier for both of them that way. It was difficult trying to blur the mind of someone as sharply intelligent as his beloved, and if they were separated, the dangerous memories would fade to nothingness.

But she was here. He could tell, but even if he hadn't been a vampire he would have been able to detect her. That was what a never-dying love could do for you.

Jumbled feelings roiled in his heart.

He felt pure joy that Teresa had stayed in his house – and red anger with her for resisting his influence and putting herself in danger.

Racing up the stairs, he felt almost alive. He could swear

his heart was pounding in anticipation, and the blood was surging through his veins. It was an illusion, but despite his confusion, it was exhilarating.

The door to Teresa's room almost broke on its hinges, but the emptiness of her room made him want to howl. Had he been wrong? Was it just the memory of her presence he'd been sensing?

He smelt the air.

The essence of her was strong in the room. Maybe that was it? Her glorious perfume and the lingering sensual odour of her body made him catch the breath he no longer needed. He felt both unmanned and also wildly, insanely aroused at the same time.

Stomping away down the corridor, he sought his own room, still absorbing the scents of Teresa as he went.

In his own bedroom the lights were out, but he could still clearly see that there was a hump beneath his quilt, and tousled teak-brown hair poking out onto his pillow. In the blink of an eye, he was ripping back the covers.

Teresa peered up at him, rubbing her face sleepily. He knew it was feigned – he could sense her sharp mind rising to meet his.

'What the hell are you doing here?'

'I thought you'd be pleased to see me, Zack.'

Her delicate nightgown slipped from her shoulder as she sat up, baring her neck and shoulders, now perfectly smooth and unblemished again. Zack suppressed a groan as his cock went rigid and his fangs instantly lengthened.

He shook his head, more confused than ever.

He wanted her. He felt pure joy because she was still here and in his bed – but the danger, the danger. Last time, they'd gone so close to the edge that he'd feared they'd crossed the line.

'I am . . . but I thought we'd agreed that you were getting a place of your own?' The words came out muffled. He had his knuckle pressed to his face, hoping to mask the state of his canines. There was still a chance to get out of this gracefully, without hurting her. There was still a chance to set her free, so she could live and not be cursed by the condition that defined him.

Teresa laughed – a pure twinkle of sound.

'You don't have to hide. I know what you are. I woke up from the spell you put on me.'

Zack dropped his hand from his mouth and glared at her.

'All the more reason for you not to be here. You know how dangerous I am to you.'

'I don't care.'

Her head came up, her chin lifting. She looked different somehow, he realised, more beautiful than ever if that were possible. Her skin was pale and creamy and her lips were rosy. There was a gleam in her eyes, dark and knowledgeable.

'Well, you should! You can't stay around me. You're not safe.' His fingers tingled with the need to touch her, especially when she came up on her knees in the bed, reaching for him, her face sultry and challenging. Unable to stop himself, he grabbed her by the shoulders, gently shaking her. 'You have to leave, Teresa. Please, for my sake! I couldn't bear it if I harmed you . . . if I changed you.'

'Too late, my love.'

The words were quiet, but they seemed to land in the centre of the room like a great stone.

'No!'

Zack's words weren't quiet. His great shout seemed to bounce off the furniture.

Teresa was smiling at him, the beautiful colour of her

eyes ringed with crimson. Her neat white teeth were made uneven by delicately pointed canines.

'But you didn't feed from me.'

He cradled her jaw, running his thumb lightly over the points of her fangs. They were rudimentary, only slightly pointed, not true vampire teeth.

Yet.

'I tasted a little of your blood on my fingertips. From where I scratched your back.'

Zack quickly wracked his memory, sifting through all the lore he'd studied when he'd first been changed himself. If she'd only taken a few drops, she could still revert. She could still be normal and live a human life. If she got away from him now, and took no more blood.

'Please, Teresa, you've got to go. If you stay around me the compulsion will only grow. . . and I won't be able to resist you.'

'Whose compulsion? Mine or yours?'

'Does it matter? Please, my love, just go!'

But her eyes were clear, despite the crimson. He sensed her intelligence. Her will. Her full knowledge of what lay ahead. And her desire for it.

Most of all, he read love in her expression.

'I can't go, Zack.' Her arms slid around him. 'I love you. I need to be with you.'

A sudden last urge to free her welled up.

'What if I don't love you?' he demanded, trying without success to shake her off him. But she was already far stronger than she'd been before, and she laughed softly, pressing her face, and her body, against him.

'You might be a vampire, Zack, but you're a poor liar.' She pulled open his shirt, kissing his skin. 'And I've already got . . . well . . . powers.'

She kissed him again, her tongue stroking against his collar bone.

'It's no use telling me you don't love me because I know you *do*!'

Oh, but you feel so good!

Teresa smiled against Zack's cool skin as she waited for him to admit what she knew was true. He didn't speak, but his arms closed around her. The sense of being enclosed, and of being cherished made her feel like swooning. It was an old-fashioned word, one she'd never have used before she met him, but it was the only one that fitted.

'I do love you.' His voice was low and clear, but she could tell that the confession cost him. 'I love you . . . and I want to be with you forever.' His arms tightened, and he tilted his head back, as if looking to heaven for knowledge.

'So what's the problem, Zack?' She rubbed her face against his cold-as-marble skin, loving its smooth silky texture, loving the fact that it would never go slack, or sag, or grow sallow with age. Loving the simple joy of the contact.

His hand settled over her hair, gently stroking.

'But forever means just that, my love. Forever. And ever.' A deep shudder passed through him. 'And if you choose it, you'll never walk in the sunshine again. And in a few years, your friends, your family . . . well, even if they wonder why they never see you much in the daytime again, they'll certainly start to notice that you're not ageing.'

He put her from him, looking into her eyes. Teresa saw that his eyes were reddened, and with her already-sharpened senses, she could taste his desire. Despite the stress of the moment, he couldn't stop himself wanting her.

'*You* are my friend, Zack. I love you and I want you, but you're my buddy too. You *always* will be.' She reached out, took his face in hers, made him look at her. 'My parents are dead . . . my sister and I aren't close. And I'll deal with everything else when the time comes.'

'Are you sure?' His eyes were crimson now, burning – happy.

'Completely! Now come on, finish the job. I want to be like you, not just half and half.'

'With pleasure . . . with pleasure, my love,' murmured Zack, his voice gruff with emotion as his arm swept around her again and with his free hand he cradled her face.

Tenderly, he kissed her, his soft lips sweeping over her mouth, then her jaw and on down her neck to the tenderest, most vulnerable spot. She felt his tongue caressing her skin, over the vein, as if soothing the place in readiness.

And then – ah, the pain of the bite! Sharp, blade-like fangs plunged in and immediately the blood began to flow and with it the pleasure. He was supporting her in his arms, his hold on her almost chaste, but it felt to her as if he were caressing and stimulating every nerve-end in her body, most of all her sex.

The sensation was sweet, mind-bending and exquisite, like tumbling and soaring at the same time. She felt both weak and strong, and the very quick of her body was shimmering and rippling with an intense sublime glow. As he drew on her powerfully, she spiralled to a peak, crying out and coming.

As she floated, still in that impossible state of ecstasy, he lifted his mouth from her neck and kissed her on the lips. She tasted her own blood like a sacrament – and hunger surged in her to drink from a different source.

Still supporting her, Zack leaned back, ripped open his shirt and, in the classic romantic vampire's gesture, he drew a nail across his chest, over his heart.

Dark-red blood oozed from the little wound, the ultimate temptation.

And the final step.

After this there would be no going back, no further chance to retain her humanity.

But as she looked up into her lover's red eyes, she embraced her choice.

Inclining forwards, she began to drink – and to change as Zack cried out in his own ecstasy.

Afterwards, they made long, slow, simple human love. Sliding and rocking against each other they kissed gently and stroked each other in leisurely exploration. There was no biting or exchange of blood, just pure sensual pleasure, sublimely heightened by supernatural senses.

Eventually, Zack lifted himself free of her, lay back against the pillows, and pulled her to him again. Teresa smiled. He no longer felt cold to her. Their body temperatures had equalized.

'So we don't bite each other any more then?' she observed, touching her fingertip to his chest where the little cut that she'd fed on was already as good as healed. 'Presumably I can't feed on you and you can't feed on me.'

'Oh we can, but only for mutual pleasure.' Zack's fingers slid down her back teasingly, and to her delight, Teresa felt lust begin to stir again. Before tonight, she would have been too exhausted to go again so soon after such a prolonged dance of love. But now she had strength and energy to spare and she could feel that Zack was ready again just as soon as she was.

'Ooh, I like the sound of that.' Her sex rippled spontaneously at the thought of Zack at her neck again.

'But for nutrition purposes, I'm afraid we're confined to animal blood from now on. Not quite as tasty, but still perfectly acceptable.'

'Don't worry, I've tried it. It's not bad.' She kissed his chest.

'I'm glad of that,' observed Zack wryly, his voice teasing, then immediately, she sensed him become more serious. She no longer had to look at his face to perceive his emotions, she simply *knew* them. 'It's a huge transition, my love. Your life has changed utterly now. Everything's different.' He paused, his strong arms tightening around her. 'But I'm here – I'll always be here. And I'll do everything I can to make things easier for you.'

And he would. She knew that. She had no doubts.

There was an adventure ahead, a different life and an unimaginably long one.

But as they began to make love again, her still heart glowed with perfect happiness.

Zack was her best friend as well as her lover – and everything was possible with him at her side.

Forever.